THE FAULT

Also by Kitty Sewell

Ice Trap
Bloodprint
Cloud Fever

THE FAULT

Kitty Sewell

HONNO MODERN FICTION

First published in 2019 by Honno Press, 'Ailsa Craig', Heol y Cawl,
Dinas Powys, Vale of Glamorgan, Wales, CF64 4AH
1 2 3 4 5 6 7 8 9 10
Copyright: Kitty Sewell © 2019

A catalogue record for this book is available from the British Library.
Published with the financial support of the Welsh Books Council.

ISBN 978-1-909983-99-1 (paperback)
ISBN 978-1-912905-00-3 (ebook)

Cover design: Graham Preston
Cover image: Jukkis/Shutterstock Inc.
Text design: Elaine Sharples
Printed in Great Britain by 4edge

For Ellis,
another "rock"

Acknowledgements

Thank you to Tito Vallejo who provided me with a private tour of the vast tunnel system of Gibraltar, including the fascinating out-of-bounds MOD areas.

Raymond Bellido for taking me 'pot-holing' into the Lower St. Michael's caves in the bowels of The Rock – an unforgettable experience.

David Carr for the excursion through 'The Jungle'.

Civil engineer Stuart Dunn for checking the technical credibility of my story.

Tony Watkins, who told me all about the scuba diving paradise of Gibraltar.

Big thanks – and sorry – to the unsuspecting estate agent who I duped into showing me 'the apartment'.

My gratitude to Dr. Diane Sloma, a long-time resident and expert on all things Gibraltarian.

Most of all, thank you Tim Turner for your support and generosity, and for introducing me to everyone I needed to know in Gibraltar, and to Honno Press for believing in *The Fault*.

Prologue

Holding tightly to his hand she allowed herself to be led into the darkness. The floor was littered with debris that crunched under her sandals. Every few steps she turned her head and saw the sunlit opening through which they had entered become smaller and smaller.

'Don't keep looking back,' he said to her. 'You want your eyes to adapt.'

'Damn it, I don't want to adapt. Switch on my torch, will you? I can't see a thing in here.'

He fiddled with her head set and a strong beam of light shot out from her forehead. She swung her head from side to side and laughed, pointing the beam in all directions. It had a magical quality, this ability to light up any space with a toss of her head.

'Watch out,' she yelled. 'I've got power-vision.' Her cry was sucked down the tunnel; silence abruptly restored.

Step by step, moment by moment she became aware that they were heading straight into a mountain, down a duct compressed by millions of tons of rock. Daylight was now a mere luminous dot in the distance behind them, but she reminded herself that one could still turn around and walk back out. At any moment she could change her mind and get out.

She clung to his arm, yet felt vaguely angry. Men talked her into things, that was her everlasting problem. She was crap at saying no.

The tunnel seemed totally straight for a good twenty

minutes of walking, then turned forty-five degrees to the left. She glanced behind her and the pinprick of daylight was no more. Solid rock enclosed them. They moved on, past openings and passages as black and endless as gateways to the underworld.

At an arched six-way intersection, he took a right into a much narrower tunnel and though she resisted, he pulled her firmly along. They hunched their shoulders and ducked to protect their heads from jutting rock edges.

'Oh, God, I think that's enough now.' A small rivulet of sweat ran down the small of her back. She shivered and tried to steady her voice. 'Let's turn back.'

'I said I would show you something amazing.'

She was no chicken; at least she refused to show it. Confronting one's fear – that was her personal motto.

They turned left into a hole in the wall and descended a long set of circular stairs hacked out of the stone. Down and down they went. She felt almost relieved. With some luck, he'd have her out of this mountain and into open air at sea level, maybe right into Casemates Square. She'd seen strange vaults and openings all over the town: all seemed to lead into the Rock.

The stairs ended and they were in another tunnel.

'Enough now,' she said through gritted teeth. 'I'm not exactly enjoying this.'

'This one was dug out during the siege in 1713. Further down there are even older tunnels. They say one of them runs under the strait all the way to Morocco. Can you believe it?' He was trying to be chatty but his voice was flat and muted in the narrow space. She didn't want any more damned history, but even so, preferred him talking.

It seemed to her they'd roamed the tunnels for well over an hour, but time could be warped by the lack of indicators. She rarely wore her watch so how could she tell? Maybe it had grown dark outside, maybe it was night. She opened her mouth to ask him, but changed her mind.

She remembered how a guy she'd dated had recounted a pot-holing expedition in France. The group had carried a spool of white string. One end had been tied to a rock at the entrance of the cave and they'd unravelled the spool as they descended along crevasses, crawled on their stomachs through passages and abseiled down chasms, so that it would guide them back out. He'd felt as if his whole existence had been hanging by a thread – ha, ha – but the possibility of losing the white string and getting trapped in the bowels of the Earth had convinced him never to go caving again as long as he lived.

She pulled at his sleeve. 'How the hell can you remember which way to go?'

'I know these tunnels like the back of my hand.'

'Really?'

'Yes, really.'

'And to get back out?'

'You've asked me that already.'

He seemed preoccupied and was no longer in the mood for reassuring her. Another droplet of moisture ran down her back, yet her skin felt cold and there was a lump in her throat. She swallowed quickly several times, but the lump persisted.

'You said it'd take an hour,' she whispered.

'Yes, well, it will if you actually walked. You're so slow I might as well carry you.'

'Lay off! I'm not slow.'

'Come on then.'

He grabbed her wrist again and she stumbled along

behind him. They were almost running but it seemed somehow effortless.

'Aren't we going downhill?'

'No.'

'It feels like it. God, I hate this.'

He was quiet for a long while. Too quiet. Then he spoke into the silence. 'You know I love you, don't you?'

She stopped short and yanked her wrist from his grasp. The words seemed so out of place down here, so untimely. She glared at him. 'Now what the fuck's *that* all about?'

'I know you know it, but I just wanted to say it out loud. It's important.'

A rush of rage came over her, but instinctively she tried to subdue it. He'd tricked her. Not just to come with him on this hideous venture but in some other obscure, more sinister way, and now she was stuck with him, totally dependent on him. The thought of it was unbearable. She couldn't stand it for another second.

'You know what? I don't know why the hell I let myself get talked into this. Take me out of here. Right now!'

'Not yet,' he said calmly.

'Well, I'm getting out, with or without you,' she cried.

'No, you're not.'

She hesitated for a second then turned her back to him and began sprinting in the direction they'd come.

'Don't be stupid,' he called after her. 'You'll get lost.'

'Go to hell.'

'Watch what you say to me! If you leave, you're on your own.' He raised his voice and shouted, 'It won't feel nice.'

She ignored him and dashed up the narrow tunnel. If anything conquered her fear, it was anger. When she was really livid (or drunk – preferably both) she was scared of nothing. Her memory was pretty good and pure adrenaline would carry her out of this place. The junctions and turnings they'd taken were still quite fresh in her mind; there were only about three or four, maybe five. If she ran, in no time she'd be out of here.

In fact, as soon as she got back to the apartment she'd pack a bag, grab her passport and money and get the hell out of Gibraltar. She should have done it weeks ago before everything started going wrong.

Within minutes her energy had fizzled out. Her legs were trembling as she ran and she was breathing so hard it hurt. He'd lied; the tunnel was definitely now sloping quite steeply uphill, reminding her of dreams in which you run and run to get away from evil but your body is sluggish and your feet feel like lead. She stopped to catch her breath, her heart drumming wildly against her chest. The tunnel veered to the left in a vaguely circular fashion, something she'd not noticed on the way down. Visibility was a mere twenty metres or so. Or was it the torch? The beam of light seemed to be fading. She stood motionless for a minute, trying to capture sound – any sound. Behind her she saw no distant glow from his torch beam. It seemed he'd not followed her. She was alone.

At an intersection of tunnels she stopped again to take her bearings. To her left, rolls of barbed wire were stacked almost to the ceiling. She'd not seen those on the way down. She turned her head this way and that. With a dull pain in her gut she realised she had no idea from which tunnel they'd come. She ran forward and snagged her jeans on barbs, tearing the fabric. Frantically she tried to disentangle herself and scored the back of her hand. She didn't want to look at the injury but she could smell blood. It occurred to her that perhaps someone else could smell it too. She had no idea what or who lived down here. *No, don't do this,* she said to herself. *Don't lose it.*

But wild panic took hold of her. *'Hey,'* she screamed. *'Please. Where are you?'*

She screamed some more, even though the ghostly echoes of her voice fuelled her terror. She understood now what being truly alone meant. It was no less terrifying than the prospect of death.

An eternity passed before he appeared out of nowhere, but seeing him brought no relief. He looked so strange she hardly recognised him. All her strength ebbed out of her and she sank to her knees. 'I... didn't mean it, okay?'

'Say you're sorry.'

Her teeth clattered so uncontrollably it was hard to form words. 'I'm sorry. I'm really, really sorry.'

'Come on, girl,' he said, coming forward and lifting her into his arms. 'Shhh, come on. Let's forget it.'

She buried her face in his neck. 'I got so scared.'

'Not of me, surely?'

When she didn't answer, he held her closer. He smelled of something. She knew the smell from somewhere but couldn't place it. It stung in her nostrils.

'Be sensible now. I need you to be a little bit brave,' he said in a soft monotone. 'There is absolutely nothing dangerous down here. There are no rats, no snakes, no ghosts or murderers or rapists. There're so many tunnels and so many openings in the Rock, there's always air flowing freely. There's even food and water.'

Her breath caught. 'Food and water?'

He held her at arm's length and peered into her face. His eyes shone with excitement. 'Yes, food and water to last for years. Seven years, more or less exactly. This is what I want to show you. A secret chamber.' He pointed downwards, towards the depths. 'Someone has made a home deep in here. A real home.'

She swallowed repeatedly and shook her head. 'No. I don't want to see it. I'm not interested.'

'We've come this far. We're not going back without seeing it.'

Her fear transmuted a thousand times. So many scenarios traded places in her mind, one more terrifying than the next. Why had she not suspected something like this?

'Please,' she begged, pushing away from him. 'Please don't make me go down there.'

'Just trust me,' he said. 'I am doing this out of love.'

She fought with all the strength she possessed, but he held her easily by one shoulder. A balled-up towel appeared in his other hand. Don't breathe, she thought, don't...

Through a fog of distorted images she remembered where that smell came from...clothes...plastic bags...the dry-cleaners.

London

Sebastian Luna stood at the head of the conference table, his hands held slightly outwards from his body, palms up. To one or two of the delegates, a picture of Jesus Christ had already come to mind. He'd been speaking for more than an hour without pause, fluently, assuredly, his gaze intense yet floating benevolently from face to face.

A long silence ensued and everyone's eyes and ears were tuned to him, waiting for some dramatic summing up.

'Out of the sea, I create land,' he concluded, tilting his face up towards the ceiling. 'You can already see my work from outer space. It's the closest thing to being God.'

The men and women around the table stared at him in stunned silence, some amused, some unnerved, most of them bowled over by his audacity. Someone tittered. Sebastian Luna looked only slightly embarrassed and his face split into a boyish grin. There was a collective sigh of relief and everyone joined him in laughter. They glanced at each other as they guffawed. He was just kidding, of course he was, yet wasn't that exactly what he was proposing? They all knew that it had never been done before. So, if Luna were not God, to accomplish it he would have to be in cahoots with Him.

As the laughter died down Luna leaned forward and put both hands on the table.

'Any questions? Please, tear me to shreds.'

Friendly and open as the invitation sounded, an awkward silence grew as though each felt too intimidated to challenge this smooth-talking powerhouse with some trivia. Instead, they studied him covertly. While on the short side, his physique had the muscular compactness of a boxer. His face was broad; handsome in a workaday kind of way. With his unruly black hair and dark eyes, he did not look wholly English but his skin was whiter than white, as if it had never known sunlight.

'Thank you, Sebastian, you've clearly covered your material to everyone's satisfaction,' said Henry Saunders, standing up. 'You're the last of our three contenders but – shall we say – not the least. As you well know by now, I – for one – am frankly stunned by your proposal. Our engineering team has scrutinised your plans and the model, and it is – what can I say – *groundbreaking* stuff.' Everyone laughed anew at the pun.

'If you'd like to step outside, Miss Norton has this mean cappuccino machine in her office. She'll look after you.'

When the door had closed on Sebastian Luna, a silence hung in the boardroom. The thirteen men and women around the table flicked questioning glances at each other. They'd already discussed Luna's submission for weeks; their people had tested and re-tested the concept, calculated the costs, conferred with the powers that be in Gibraltar. They could certainly choose to go with a conventional land reclamation, and they probably would have, had Sebastian Luna's mesmerising presentation not painted his concept right onto their eyeballs.

Bethan Williams opened a capacious handbag and rifled in it for her inhaler. Ian Shearer leaned across the table to grab the pitcher and pour himself a glass of water, drinking it down.

'He's a bit peculiar,' Fred Weston reflected. 'But if he can do what he claims, just imagine where this could take us in the international arena.'

James Downing, the oldest member on the board, was shaking his head. His pained, incredulous expression spoke for itself.

Saunders noted it and spoke up. 'All right, all right. So Mr. Luna is a bit eccentric and he works strictly freelance, but you've got to admit his proposal is remarkable, and not just remarkable, it's *faultless.*'

'He's a mouthy punk with delusions of grandeur,' Downing protested. 'How old is he anyway?'

'Just turned thirty-six. No offence, James, but did you look at this guy's CV? He's already picked up two awards for the Starfish Development in Dubai, and that article I sent you... he designed the concrete-encased polyfoam islands using plastic waste, long before plastic waste got a bad name. They're churning them out in China as we speak. Personally, I believe Sebastian Luna is a bit of a prodigy. With this project under his belt he could well be the leading light of the civil engineering world.'

A reddish bloom spread over James Downing's sallow cheeks. He picked up the glossy brochure that had been hastily put together for the meeting and tossed it towards the centre of the table. 'It'll cost upward of four million to do the environmental, marine and engineering studies. There are a whole host of other considerations – not least political – quite apart from the fact that I don't think you can build such a structure.'

Saunders sighed with thinly disguised forbearance. 'Look, we know Gibraltar have had several tenders for something to replace the failed Eastside project, and I've gauged that they're gung-ho to see something truly unique. So the outline planning could be had within a month or two. The latest land reclamation in progress on the Rock has surpassed a billion already, and they've run into all sorts of trouble. If

Luna is right, we could do this for a fraction of the cost.' He touched his laptop and an image filled the wall behind him. Someone drew breath. The towering rock that was Gibraltar never failed to stir. 'The actual site looks straight out over the Med, with the Spanish coast on one side and the Moroccan on the other. So far nobody has considered developing there.' Saunders directed the pointer to the precipitous south-east side of the crag. 'Here the cliff plunges straight into the sea. People have never looked at this bit of the coast: the cliff is simply too sheer for any kind of conventional land reclamation. It's also dotted with caves at water level, but Luna has come up with strategies to have them incorporated in a way which will creatively enhance the development.' He rubbed his hands together. 'Sir Anthony loves the concept. If we at SeaChange International – together with the Goodbard Group as architects of this glittering new development…' Saunders let his gaze sweep around the table. 'We'll be fruitfully employed for the next few years. And no doubt beyond.'

'Christ!' exclaimed Downing. 'Luna isn't the only one around here who thinks he's God.'

Saunders narrowed his eyes but didn't acknowledge the insult. 'The Spaniards are making a lot of noise, claiming the seabed belongs to Spain. But what our good Mr. Luna proposes won't touch the seabed.' Saunders paused and lowered his voice. '*A titanic tide-proof cantilevered shelf*…it's so fucking brilliant it takes your breath away.'

His words hovered over the massive table for a full minute, until Bethan Williams tapped her water glass loudly with a pen.

'I'm being politically incorrect here, but Mr. Luna seems a bit big for his boots, for someone so young. We know what he's accomplished, but what do we know of his personal situation?'

Saunders looked at some notes in the pile before him. 'His criminal record check and sickness record are in order, clean bill of health apart from occasional crippling migraines. I had a word with Ian Smith who worked closely with him in Dubai. Outside of his obsession with changing the face of the earth, it seems he's a bit of a loner. A workaholic and an insomniac, according to Smith. Met an American diving instructor in Dubai with whom he co-habited. Apparently, she's got to be part of the package.' Saunders lowered his voice a little. 'Off the record, I was told he had a lot to juggle during his postgraduate studies and early career. The parents were divorced and the mother dumped a much younger sister on him, so our man had a lot on throughout his time at Imperial College. Smith reckons the girl is a bit of a tearaway. She came for a holiday in Dubai and Luna was pretty frantic about her, apparently.'

'Aww, well,' said Bethan Williams softly, 'sounds human enough.'

'He's already got a connection with Gibraltar, a forefather on his mother's side fought in the battle of Trafalgar and was buried in Gibraltar. His father, though a British citizen, was born in Seville, and Sebastian's a fluent Spanish speaker. That might just be very helpful in Gib. Some of the bigwigs are of Spanish ancestry, and who knows what Gib's future is in relation to Spain.'

'I like him,' Bethan Williams declared.

'A *shelf*!' growled James Downing. 'What next?'

'I don't know about you people, but I think we need this man and his brainchild on board,' said Saunders, pointedly ignoring his ageing nemesis. 'Are we really going to hand him over to our competitors?'

After a brief silence he looked around at his colleagues. 'So…are we ready to take a vote?'

Sebastian was in his element when talking to any gathering – conference, symposium or seminar – it was small talk he struggled with. While he sat and waited for the meeting to conclude, he kept quiet so as not to attract Miss Norton's attention. He simply wouldn't know what to say to her and felt bad about it. She had neither youth not beauty to trade on, but he was always alert to that quality of decency and kindness in people who otherwise seemed unremarkable, and yearned to connect to it in some way. Miss Norton's mean cappuccino machine had ground, clicked, pumped, gurgled and fizzed out a frothy concoction that had been cooling in his hands for the last twenty minutes. The doctor had told him – in a long list of measures to combat insomnia – that coffee was a total no-no. Sebastian leaned forward and quietly put the cup on the coffee table in front of him.

'Can I get you something else?' said Miss Norton, poking her head out from behind her computer screen.

'Oh, no. Thank you. This is lovely.'

'Can I get you a magazine or something?'

'Oh, no, thanks. I'm too nervous to read.' He didn't know why he'd said it, because he wasn't a bit nervous. Jittery yes, but high as a kite.

She nodded. 'Trust me, I know exactly what it feels like. Not so long ago I was sitting in your chair, up against three other PAs, and they were all a whole lot younger and prettier than me.'

He smiled at her. 'Good on Mr. Saunders. He knew what he was doing.'

She blushed slightly. 'Maturity and experience still have their place, thank God.' She hesitated. 'But you, Mr. Luna, have nothing to worry about. I read all about you on the internet. The world is your oyster, as they say.'

'Call me Sebastian, please.' He indicated the boardroom

with a toss of the head. 'I only lied about one thing. I'm not a team player, I'll have everything my own way.' She peered at him, clearly suppressing a smile. 'Don't take any notice of what I say,' he said, biting his lip. 'Modesty isn't my strong point.'

'No,' she said with emphasis. 'You should believe in yourself. Us Brits are far too reticent. We'd get nowhere in America with our misplaced modesty.'

'You think so? Eva, my fiancée, would argue that point. She's always on at me to pipe down and not be so cocksure of myself. She is the font of all wisdom.' On impulse he jumped up and drew from his back pocket a slightly concave photo. 'This is her,' he said, dashing over to Miss Norton's desk.

'Ah,' she said, peering at the well-worn image. 'Gorgeous girl.'

She was right, Eva had not at all the look of a wise woman. Embarrassed, he slipped the photo back into his pocket and retreated to his chair.

Another ten minutes passed before Miss Norton's phone chimed.

'Yes, Mr. Saunders. I'll tell him.' She nodded to Sebastian. 'You go on back in there, young man, and be a good team player.'

Sebastian stood up, brushed some flecks off his jacket, bowed to Miss Norton and opened the door. Once inside the boardroom, he paused and looked at the men and women around the table. The lovely lady with the soft Welsh accent smiled broadly at him. Trust a woman to give the game away.

I am the creator, he whispered to himself.

The Rock Hotel, Gibraltar

Sebastian lay sprawled on the bed, naked, sweating copiously and absolutely still. Eva's black T-shirt covered his whole face. He couldn't tolerate any light whatsoever, and yellow industrial-issue earplugs kept out almost all noise. Eva had left him to ride it out alone, having hung the 'do not disturb' sign on the door knob.

Gradually he began to take notice of the faint odour of sweat on the T-shirt mingled with the scent of her favourite body lotion. This awakening of his senses was the first sign of relief, yet he would not allow himself any concrete thoughts. If he began thinking, work would seep in, structures would want to intrude behind his closed eyes and the pain could come crashing back like a lorry load of bricks. He focused on the faint nuances of womanly aromas, and moment by moment he began to return to himself.

He pulled away the T-shirt and took a deep breath. Gingerly he unplugged one ear and bunched the pillow around his head. Through the pillow he could still hear a clash of sounds. Two cleaning ladies in the next room produced a steady stream of giggly chatter, interrupted only by the shifting of heavy furniture and an occasional burst of a vacuum cleaner. Gulls squawked gleefully as they swooped past the balcony doors. He could have sworn they did this on purpose. Gulls were smart, they teased dogs, he'd seen it himself. Worst was the intermittent screech of those damned kamikaze mopeds that every teenager in

Gibraltar had his or her arse glued to. But the noises no longer seemed like hammer blows to his head, a reliable sign of recovery. For a moment he drifted off.

An insistent noise jerked him out of his slumber. It came from a phone somewhere across the room. Annoyed, he dragged himself out of bed.

'Yes!'

'Mr. Luna?'

'Speaking!'

'Good morning. I'm Stephen Stagnetto, the rental agent.'

'Oh, yes, hello. My fiancée has gone across the frontier this morning. I'll tell her you called.'

'Ah, but Mr. Luna, just a moment of your time. Nothing I have shown Ms. Eriksson so far seems to suit and I fear I'm in danger of losing you to some other agent.'

'I'm sorry, but…'

'The reason I'm calling this morning,' Mr. Stagnetto cut in, 'is because I've just been appointed to administer something that might just interest you, something quite special that no-one else will have on their books.'

Sebastian frowned. He knew a sales pitch when he heard one, or perhaps this was the sort of man who thought dealing with the little woman was a waste of time. 'My fiancée and my sister are the people you want to rent it to, Mr. Stagnetto. I'll tell…'

'Mr. Luna,' the man interjected again. 'I'm told you insist on something with space and character. Now this would definitely meet the criteria. The building was constructed in the 1700s as a retreat for Irish nuns. The apartment is huge, near enough three hundred square metres. Apparently, it was also the visiting Bishops' sanctuary.'

Sebastian hesitated. He and Eva had looked at a few 'luxury' apartments in sterile new developments, but all that white and floor-to-ceiling glass didn't fool him. In this tiny colony where space was finite, all new builds were cramped.

'I don't drive,' he said, irritated with himself for confessing it so readily. 'Where is it?'

'As it happens, the upper town is best accessed on foot. I've not actually inspected the apartment yet but I'm just on my way up there now. Providing it's in habitable condition, I'll send someone up to give it a clean and then perhaps you and the ladies would like to view it tomorrow?'

Sebastian looked at his watch. His head had returned to him intact, and he could use some movement. 'I've got a free afternoon for once. Why don't I just come with you?'

Mr. Stagnetto laughed. 'Well now! Man of action. But really, I just need to make sure it's fit for showing. The property has been empty for some time. How about nine tomorrow morning?'

'That'll be "the ladies", then,' Sebastian answered briskly. 'I'm going to be tied up all week.'

He could hear the man's hesitation across the ether. 'Right, well, why ever not? You'll have to take it as you find it. Can you come to my office within half an hour? It's right across from the cathedral.'

Mimi

Mimi drew her knees up and – adjusting her iPad on her lap – re-read the dialogue.

'Am I adopted?' she asked her mother.
Her mother's eyes shifted to the left. 'Of course you're not, Christiana. Whatever made you think such a thing?'
'You don't like me. You never give me a cuddle.'
'You know I don't like cuddling.'
'Yes, you do. You cuddle Rufus.'
'Well, he's not naughty, is he?'
'Yes, he is. He poos on the lawn and chews the cushions…'
'Oh, for heaven's sake. He's a dog.'

Mimi stopped and considered the name: Rufus. It was ridiculous, just the sort of clichéd name her mother would choose for a dog. As for Christiana: well chosen. Pretentious, just like her own name, Imogen.

A shadow moved somewhere outside her iPad and she looked up. She'd seen a few apes wandering nonchalantly along the balcony railings, mainly mothers with babies clamped to their backs or hanging from their underbellies, but this fucker could win prizes. He was huge and, without so much as a by-your-leave, pressed his nose against the glass door. She stared back at him, as much transfixed by him as he was by her. There was something vaguely sexual about his stance, the provocative way his gaze slowly moved down her body and back to her face. She shuddered.

The phone rang. She reached for it without taking her eyes off the animal.

'Imogen's room.'

'Hey Mimi,' said her brother in that annoying put-on cheerful voice he'd adopted to try and jolly her along. 'How's the writing going?'

'You know what I'm looking at? This massive ape on my balcony. It's just sitting there, staring me out.'

'Whatever you do, don't open the door or feed it or anything.'

'What're you like?'

'Look, I'd like your input. I'm going to see an apartment... sounds different to what we've seen so far and...'

'*My* input?' What about *her*?'

'Eva's out.' He softened his voice even more. 'Sweetheart, come on, it'll be fun. I'm tired of living out of a suitcase.'

She studied the ape. The eye contact did not waver and a smear of slobber streaked the glass. How was she supposed to go out and smoke? The apes even nicked the ashtrays off the tables.

'Yeah, okay,' she said with a sigh.

'Great! See you in reception in five.'

She set down her tablet and got out of bed. So much for her disciplined writing schedule. Sebastian pretended to take her ambition seriously, but kept asking if she would like to enrol in the local college for September. Or perhaps get some work experience. He was so bloody transparent. Perhaps he just wanted her out during the day so he could have wild sex with his new woman.

But no-one was going to tell her how to live her life. She'd been gritting her teeth in Surrey, waitressing at Burger King, waiting for Sebastian to say she could join him in Gibraltar. Now was *her* time. She was going to climb out of her mind-pit and reinvent herself, leaving the past in her novel.

Sebastian

Mr. Stagnetto led the way. They walked down Main Street, and at Bishop Rapallos Ramp they turned away from the throng of shoppers and beer drinkers heading up through a warren of narrow streets and pedestrian alleys.

The facade of tacky commerce and hedonism which gave Gibraltar its unfortunate reputation instantly evaporated as they left Main Street. It was like passing through a time-warp and entering a fortified Medieval city. They climbed stepped passageways and ducked through tapering corridors between oddly constructed buildings. Quaint dereliction and neglected elegance jostled for space in the tightly packed Upper Town. Walls were crumbling and vegetation had taken hold in every crack and fissure. Clothes lines and electrical wires hung willy-nilly.

'Would I be expected to climb this mountain every day?' said Mimi, panting in the heat.

'You could get a scooter, Miss Luna,' said the rental agent. 'All kids here have one.'

The property was up a dead-end passage called DiMoretti's Ramp. The buildings on either side of the passage were precipitously high and seemed to lean into each other, so that a mere strip of sunlight illuminated the tiled walkway below. It looked as if the whole quarter had been long abandoned, though between two shuttered windows hung a line of frayed underwear, like prayer flags worn ragged by the wind.

The ramp narrowed further and ended abruptly at a door.

Within was a long arched vestibule and a cavernous stairwell. The walls and stairs were lined waist high with patterned indigo tiles that had fallen away in patches, and high on a wall hung a wooden carving of Jesus on the Cross. The floor was so worn it had a groove in the flagstones that led to the stairs.

'Wow,' said Mimi, staring up into the vast turret of the stairwell.

'It's a historic building,' said Mr. Stagnetto, pointing to a stone plaque with 1754 carved into it. 'As you can see, we don't look after our heritage as well as we should.'

The flopping of Mimi's sandals echoed in the empty space as they climbed the steps. She poked Sebastian in the side and whispered, 'mindblowing'. He patted her shoulder and whispered back, 'Hold your horses. Let's just wait and see.'

'*Carlo Montegriffo*,' read Mr. Stagnetto from a name plate. 'Oh, yes. I know this man. But wrong apartment. Ours has got to be on the top floor.'

They trudged up two more turns of steps. On the top floor were two doors, one of them open to a large roof terrace from which sunlight flooded in. Mimi and Sebastian walked straight out and drew breath. Together they looked out over a higgledy-piggledy roofscape that formed a chaotic foreground to the spectacular view. Below them lay the old part of town; beyond it, the new luxury developments on reclaimed land, and the harbour, teeming with tankers, cruise ships and ferries.

'*Mrs. Esther Cohen*,' Mr. Stagnetto called out. 'We're in the right place!'

Sebastian left Mimi patting a black cat that had appeared out of nowhere. With interest, he watched the rental agent fumbling with one key after another until at last he found one that fit and the door swung open.

'Well, now,' he said, pulling out a crumpled kerchief to

mop his brow, 'what treasure will we find?' adding, 'I did warn you.'

'No worries,' Sebastian said. 'You did.'

'Mrs. Cohen passed away recently and left the property to her nephew. He forewarned me that the apartment probably hasn't been updated for decades. He's not set foot in Gibraltar for years himself and is not planning to, so if you're interested in a long lease we can surely come to some arrangement on the rent. A free hand to adapt it to your needs. Within reason, of course.'

Sebastian smiled. 'What are we waiting for?'

They stepped into a wide corridor towards the interior, lined waist high with the same patterned tiling as the stairwell. Mimi caught up with them and trailed a hand along the cold tiles.

'*Grandeur*,' she said, true to her habit of testing out words.

The high ceiling in the inner hall was festooned with intricate plasterwork – now crumbling – cherubs missing wings and roses with broken petals. There was a stillness – a sense of lifelessness – as though every particle of dust had settled a long time ago and no movement had been made, no word uttered in these rooms since. Sebastian felt his steps creating an almost visible turbulence of molecules.

Stagnetto led them straight through a wide corridor into the living room. The expanse of it lay in darkness, the walls a dull mud colour and crammed like an auction warehouse with antique furniture. At the far wall were four tall, arched windows. Sebastian stepped up and parted the heavy velvet curtains. He smiled when he saw that it faced the Rock, although the sharply rising incline didn't let much light in. The tower of the ancient Moorish castle loomed to the left under the highest peak.

Studying this vertical bit of wild nature, Sebastian saw nothing that betrayed the mystery within, the secret spaces hidden in its interior. He knew that the Rock of Gibraltar was honeycombed by nearly fifty kilometres of manmade tunnels, most of them burrowed by thousands of soldiers during World War Two. But there were others, hundreds of years old. It was a structural engineer's dream, the layering of passages and spaces within this megalith of solid rock. Also, there were one-hundred-and-sixty natural caves, some with subterranean lakes. As soon as he had a moment, he'd apply to the Ministry of Defence to have one of their private tours of the tunnel systems.

'*Sebastian,*' Mimi called from the doorway. 'Get your butt back on the tour here.'

He let the curtain fall and a cloud of dust billowed into the room.

Beds, overstuffed armchairs and enormous oak wardrobes filled the three bedrooms. Two of them were tidy and austere, like show pieces. The biggest room, however, looked like it had recently been lived in. It had a dressing table covered with numerous pots and flasks. Two pearl necklaces hung over the mirror. The double bed had been hastily made and had a burgundy dress draped over it. On the back of a chair hung a pair of old-fashioned women's drawers, a petticoat and a brassiere, as if the occupant had just slipped out of them in order to do her evening ablutions. Sebastian felt uneasy about trespassing on a woman's intimate space. A dead woman, at that.

His attention was drawn to the middle of the floor. Where a dark patch stained the floorboards, a lady's shoe lay, as well as something hairy and dead. Mimi was the first to react, approaching to pick it up by her thumb and forefinger.

'Ah, goody, a dead rat. Can I keep it? If you don't mind, Mr. Stagnetto. I love desiccated bodies.' She dangled it in the air and winked seductively at the rental agent who had not ceased sweating.

What had got into her? One of those devilish moods. Perhaps she was coming out of her glumness and getting over her resentment at finding Eva installed in his life.

'Not funny, Imogen,' said Sebastian, trying to keep a straight face. He patted Stagnetto's arm. 'I think it's a wig.'

'Would you like to see the bathroom?' said Mr. Stagnetto.

'How far is it?' said Mimi, draping the wig on a bedpost.

The bathroom, too, was like a ballroom, floor and walls tiled in white. A tiny frosted window threw a grey gloom over the fixtures. A Victorian bathtub – big enough for a regatta – dominated the room, and above it, heavy black iron brackets anchored a massive hot water tank to the ceiling. It sizzled audibly, and a red light indicated that the contraption was lit.

'Did you know this water heater is on? Sebastian asked. 'It's boiling.'

'Goodness!' said Mr. Stagnetto, staring at it for a long moment. 'So it is.'

He quickly motioned them into a vast kitchen. Along three walls were vintage hand-built counters laid with beautiful antique tiles. An enormous pine table dominated the centre of the room. Only one chair belonged to it, and on it, one plate and one glass. Some substance on the plate had shrunk and cracked, and the contents of the wine glass had dried to blood-coloured dust. A linen napkin lay neatly folded on the side, graced with one clear impression of red lipstick.

The three of them stared at this tableau for several

seconds and even Mimi was speechless. Taking a few steps forwards to peer at the plate, she gave a tinny laugh and quickly covered her mouth with her hand. Sebastian approached, putting a paternal arm around her shoulders. They studied the leathery remains of a meal.

'Oh, heavens!' Mr. Stagnetto threw his hands in the air. 'I can't apologise enough. I was told the place had been sealed up, but somehow I never imagined... I should have checked before bringing you here. I did warn you, Mr. Luna, but you insisted...'

'How did she die?' Sebastian asked quietly.

'Right, well... I won't lie to you. She choked, I'm afraid. But be assured, it was a while ago. A year perhaps...at least six months.'

'*Macabre*,' murmured Mimi. 'Who found her?'

'I understand it was the downstairs neighbour who raised the alarm. He used to drop in to check on the old dear from time to time.'

'How long?' Mimi wondered. 'I mean, between his visits.'

'*Mimi!*' Sebastian gave her a stern glare.

'Well, think about it,' she went on. 'It's pretty obvious what's happened here. A piece of that very meal got stuck in her throat. She managed to run into the bedroom where she tore off her wig. Or perhaps the wig fell off when they carted her out of there. I just wondered how long it took for the neighbour to come and visit.' She lowered her voice. 'Shit, it would make a great subject for a short story.'

Sebastian's hand tightened on her shoulder. 'C'mon. Cut it out!'

'No, no. This is all my fault,' cried Mr. Stagnetto. 'I should have trusted my instincts and not brought you here. This apartment is not... I shouldn't have...' With his short chubby arms he tried to herd them back towards the hallway but Mimi stood her ground.

'It's perfect,' she declared. 'We'll have the place, won't we, Sebastian?'

'Mimi, don't get ahead of yourself.' He turned to the agent. 'My fiancée will have to see it. I'm not sure the girls will see eye-to-eye on this.'

Mr. Stagnetto's face was florid, but he chuckled. 'Of course, of course. I understand. Miss Luna can obviously see the potential here. With the right little touches, this place could be quite impressive. Fit for a king.'

'*Majestic, capacious, imposing,*' Mimi whispered.

Sebastian tried to look unconvinced but the truth was, he agreed. Dilapidated though it was, the apartment had space to house an entire army, and the cool darkness of the building appealed to him – too much light intensified his insomnia. Besides, the particular 'spirit' of this apartment moved something in him. Within his very bones stirred a memory of wellbeing and security. Of course! It was the same dark rooms, the echo off the indigo tiles and the high ceilings, the smell of old furniture of his grandfather's house. In his childhood he'd spent many a month in Seville with Papito, until his parents divorced, his studies took precedence and he became Mimi's designated babysitter.

But would Eva like this sombre atmosphere? He hoped that the extensive terrace might win her over. He could get someone to rig up some sort of awning and buy a barbecue, some potted plants and garden furniture; perhaps that way she could be swayed.

While Mimi had another dash around the rooms, Sebastian took Mr. Stagnetto aside in the hallway. 'If my fiancée wants to see the apartment, could you make sure all traces of Mrs Cohen have been removed? In fact,' he lowered his voice further, 'I'd appreciate it if you didn't refer to it. I think it's best to just forget whatever it was that happened here. There is no reason why *we* should know about it.'

'Quite, quite,' said Mr. Stagnetto. 'In fact, there is absolutely no need for me to be present. Come by the office tomorrow afternoon and pick up the keys and you can show Miss Eriksson around yourself. I'll send someone over this afternoon to clean and remove any evidence of the...tragedy.'

Eva

She'd left Sebastian to his migraine and walked through Gibraltar, crossed the airport runway and the frontier, flashing her passport at the Spanish border guards. Ten paces further and she was in the Spanish town of La Linea, and knew immediately she'd entered another country; it had a totally different feel to it.

The shop was easy to find; Movistar was a popular cellphone network provider. She waited patiently in the line-up. The girl behind the desk was taking an inordinately long time, dealing in passable English with a handsome young German. Eva couldn't believe the sheer leisureliness of the transaction, but nobody else in the queue seemed particularly bothered. This was Spain after all, with its famous cliché: *mañana*.

Finally it was her turn and she opted for a cheap model with a pay-as-you-go contract.

'Are you sure it will have coverage in Gibraltar?'

'Yes!' The girl sighed with a slight roll of the eyes. 'I said this already.'

'From Spain, and outside Spain, with this Spanish number?'

'Movistar don't like this, but Gib is too near, so what can we do?' The girl launched a long scarlet fingernail towards the glass frontage of the shop. 'There, look! There is your English Rock.'

Everyone in the line-up turned in unison to look behind them, including Eva. Yes, there it was, the megalith of

Gibraltar penetrating the sky, so near you could almost touch it… a tiny British colony and a great big thorn in the Spanish flesh.

'I'm not English,' Eva said quietly. 'I just live there.'

'If you live on the Rock, why you not get Gib phone?'

A couple of people sniggered affirmatively.

'Look… I'll take the damned phone.'

She sat down on a bench on the La Linea seafront promenade and looked at the gadget in her hand. Calling California would eat up a chunk – if not all – of her free minutes, but this first phone call was shamefully overdue. Her hand felt unsteady as she dialled the number from memory, then held her breath while the call raced across the vastness of the Atlantic and the whole landmass of the U.S.A.

'Yeah?'

'Is that you, Linda?'

There was a long pause. She'd forgotten all about the time difference.

'Linda?' Eva repeated. 'It's me!'

'What!' Linda shrieked. 'I can't believe it! Chantelle?'

Eva flinched on hearing the name. It sounded so foreign. 'Yes, well no. Forget Chantelle. I'm back to being plain old Eva. How are you, Linda?'

'My God, girl! *You*! It's been almost a year.'

'Yeah, I'm really sorry. I just didn't dare call anyone back home.'

'Never mind,' Linda said softly. 'I got your message, right after you did it. I was so thrilled for you, but totally terrified. Where are you?'

'It's better I don't tell you. But I'm okay. I'm happy. I'm with someone…'

'Someone?' said Linda, at once suspicious.

'You'd approve, I think. He's amazing, but different.'

Linda wasn't easily convinced. 'Different from what?'

'Very different from Adrian.'

'Oh, baby, I hope you know what you're doing.' Linda paused. She was lighting a cigarette – some things never changed – then inhaled deeply. 'You can tell me anything, you know. You trust me, don't you?'

Eva regretted sounding cagey. Linda was the best friend she'd ever had, her only confidante for nine unbearable years.

'Of course I trust you. I'm in Spain,' she said knowing that this truth was a roundabout lie, and the very logic behind getting a phone in Spain instead of Gibraltar.

'Spain! How romantic,' Linda trilled. 'So who is this mystery man? Spanish?'

'No, English. I met him in Dubai, diving. He's an unusual guy, very smart and…intense.' She laughed. 'Linda, you have every reason to mistrust my judgment, but I think he's the one.'

'Well, you sure as hell deserve it,' Linda said darkly. She'd hated Adrian. In fact, the feeling had been mutual. Adrian had done everything to keep Linda at a distance.

'Do you know anything about *him*?'

'No,' Linda said. 'I saw his brother in a gas station a few months back, but he didn't recognise me. I didn't see the point of saying "hi". He might have mentioned me to Adrian and he'd come looking for me with a cricket bat. He had ways to make you talk, didn't he?'

'Yeah, just as well you didn't.'

'Have you googled him? That might bring something up.'

'A few times, but it's pointless. I'm sure his identity and movements are classified for security reasons.'

'Right, of course. I didn't think of that.'

'I'm putting all bets on the present.'

'That's my girl. Just be sensible.'

'I miss you, Linda. I'm so sorry I've taken this long. Listen, you've got my number now, you can call me if you hear anything you think I should know.'

'Hey, I'm thinking about a holiday. Where in Spain are you?'

Like a small tornado, anxiety stirred within her. She was not ready for it – opening the door to let her past come back in – not in the flesh. 'God, Linda. I've not even asked you how *you*'re doing. How's Michael? You still together?'

'Ah, no. He went back to his wife. The kids, you know. I can't say I blame him. He comes around for a tumble once or twice a month and while he does a good job, why should I put him off?'

Eva chuckled. Linda, practical as always. 'And sales...? Are you still with Century 21?'

'No, I've teamed up with Miles Haynes and opened our own little agency. We're doing great...that's why I feel I can afford a holiday. Haven't had one for nearly a year.'

'Give me a couple of months to get settled,' Eva said hurriedly. 'It's all very new and I've inherited a teenager – a little sister – and I've got to try and form some kind of working relationship with her, which is proving quite a challenge.'

Linda hesitated. 'Okay. I get it. No worries. Maybe in the fall, then. Let's keep in touch.'

'Yeah. Let's keep in touch.'

Linda must have caught the restlessness in her voice. 'All right, baby. You take it easy, you hear?'

'Big hugs, Linda. Thanks again for being such a wonderful friend.'

She surfaced from a dive in a murky sea, awakened by Sebastian's dynamic pacing around the room. The first thing she saw was the open suitcase at the foot of the bed. She had no idea what time it was but she could hear the squawking of thousands of gulls, a sure sign of the Gibraltar morning. Her new partner was an early riser: he was dressed, shaved, his black hair slick from a shower.

She stretched and flung the sheet off her. The air-conditioning unit buzzed gently but it was already hot, the tropical humidity entering the room by God knows what means. It would be good to breathe the night air, but a sign on the balcony door said 'Keep Closed' to stop the apes sneaking in to rummage through guests' possessions.

She opened her eyes fully and saw the cable car whooshing past their balcony on its way up to the Rock. A man stood balanced on top of the cabin, just one hand holding on to the upper frame. For a second or two he looked straight down at her naked body. She could even see the smile on his face.

'Did you see that?' she cried out. 'There was a man riding on the roof of the cable car.'

Sebastian laughed. 'Yeah, I saw him, and he saw *you*, lucky sod. Next thing, all his mates will be doing the rounds, pretending to do maintenance work. Good morning, my love.'

She rose up on one elbow and looked into the half-filled suitcase. 'This is good bye to the legendary Rock Hotel, then?' she said wistfully. 'My last Greta Garbo day. Then I've got to go back to being boring old me.'

'Boring old you,' Sebastian said, laughing, 'was the most exciting thing ever to happen.'

She thought briefly of who she was – who Sebastian thought she was – who she wanted to be. There were no reliable markers. She was an amoeba, a lost chameleon, a free-floating and formless entity looking for a resting place.

'Saunders has been generous but he won't cough up forever,' Sebastian said. He stopped folding shirts and sat down on the bed. 'I hoped you'd want to set up home with me?'

Set up home! The notion caused that whirling of her innards, but she forced a cheeky smile. 'Yeah, what the hell. Bearing in mind I haven't got a domestic bone in my body.'

The idea of leaving all her bygone baggage behind and 'setting up home' with this remarkable man was so seductive. How to tell him? Day by day she'd put it off. It was easy, as he never offered confidences of his own. Sebastian lived utterly in the present and– by example – invited her to do the same. She had thought they shared an itinerant spirit, but this talking about nesting showed a new side to him. Perhaps it had to do with Mimi…the need to give her a solid point of reference.

Sebastian was taking her shoes out of the wardrobe and putting them into a vinyl bag. Eva yawned and let her hands glide down her torso. Her skin was moist with heat. 'Oh, drop that, will you?'

Six months on, his mind was still a mystery to her, but she was good at reading every reaction of his body.

'Let's damage this hotel one last time,' she whispered, and heard a little rip of cloth as he wrenched off his shirt.

*

Eva glared at the pile of boxes and bags arrived from the UK, dumped by the 'man with a van' inside the entrance of the building. He'd made a fuss of having to cart them up DiMoretti's Ramp because there was nowhere to park and though of hulking build, refused to go any further, even though she'd offered him twenty, then thirty, then forty pounds to carry them up to the apartment.

As she stood there wondering what to do, she heard footsteps down the stairs. Pretty though Mimi was, it was hard to locate her attractiveness behind her punk getup, the black eye makeup, the facial rings and studs, the spiky hair and torn fishnet tights. Strange, all that seemed so last century.

'See ya',' she murmured as she passed, heading straight out of the door into the bright sunlight.

'Hey!' Eva called after her. 'Where are you off to?'

Mimi slowed her step and turned. 'Sorry you have this cuckoo in your lovenest, but don't feel you have to be my guardian.'

Eva reflected on this statement for a moment. Acquiring a teenager without warning had not given her time to adjust to those undercurrents of rudeness.

'Me, a guardian? Give me a break.'

'I'll stay out of your way as much as I can, but I come and go as I want, okay?'

'Awesome! But could you help me take some of this stuff up to the apartment? A third of it belongs to you.'

'Leave it there. I'll take it up when I come back.'

'If it's still here,' said Eva. 'Nothing valuable, then?'

'Just gear,' said Mimi. 'My work stuff is already upstairs.'

Mimi was turning to go, but Eva gave interaction one last effort. 'You haven't told me what you're working on. Sebastian says you've got a great way with words.'

'He does, does he?' Mimi stopped and studied a chewed black-painted fingernail, as if considering how to further mutilate it. 'He doesn't demonstrate much confidence in my writing, but I think the problem is he hates any delving into our mutual past.'

Here was an opening and Eva cast around for something neutral to ask, something about their past, some question that didn't compromise Sebastian. 'So that's what you are writing about, your mutual past?'

'I'd rather not talk about it,' Mimi said with finality. Then added, 'Ask your lover, see if you can make *him* talk.'

Eva shrugged in defeat. 'Why don't you just give me a hand?' she said, gesturing at the pile. 'It won't take a minute if there's two of us.'

With a sigh Mimi came back, grabbed two suitcases and began to drag them up the innumerable steps to the apartment. Eva followed with all that was hers, a mistreated suitcase and two plastic carrier bags. On the first floor landing they stopped for breath.

'*Onerous*,' Mimi muttered.

When they bent to grasp their loads again, a door opened and a man stepped out. Both looked at him with a start, having neither seen nor heard a single sound in the building during the two days they'd been there.

The man locked the door with exaggerated care, but then he turned and smiled at them. 'Those look heavy. May I help you carry them up?'

'Thank you, but we can manage.'

'Is there no man to help you do this?' He had a deep melodious voice with the same lilting Spanish inflection of most Gibraltarians she'd met so far.

She held out her hand. 'I'm Eva. We've rented the apartment on top of yours.'

He took her hand and held it in a dry grasp. 'I guessed as much. I'm Carlo Montegriffo. It'll be interesting to have neighbours. I've been alone in the building for a while. I'm used to the place being quiet.'

She wasn't sure how to interpret the remark. 'Don't worry. We don't have television, dogs or kids.'

'Isn't this your daughter?' he said, smiling at Mimi. 'She looks very much like your husband.'

'I'm Imogen,' Mimi said drily, 'Sebastian's sister, though not a child.' She indicated Eva with a gesture, 'And they're not husband and wife.'

Thanks, kid, Eva thought. He really needs to know.

The man raised an eyebrow in obvious amusement, then went on to explain something about the communal water tank on the terrace. Eva wasn't really interested in the water tank, in fact she regretted that she'd been outvoted when it came to this particular apartment. It was huge and dark, with a depressing air.

She studied Carlo while he put forth their obligations as tenants in the building. He was around her own age, forty or so, tall and thin, a bit stooped of posture and wearing an expensive-looking black suit. His eyes were large, dark and expressive, looking into hers with uncanny sincerity. His hairline was edging away from a wide forehead, greying at the temples and spilling over his collar in immaculately moulded waves. An eye-catching silver crucifix hung at his neck. She couldn't decide if he was deeply religious, just eccentric or possibly gay: maybe all three.

'Do you own the building?' she asked.

He hesitated. 'Your apartment is owned by the late Mrs. Cohen's nephew, but the rest of the building is property of the Catholic Church. In times gone by it was a retreat for Irish nuns.'

'That explains it,' she said, throwing a glance around the yawning stairwell.

Mimi pointed to the name plate on his door. 'Are you Spanish?'

'Ah no, I am pure Gibraltarian, but my name is Genoese. Gibraltar has a very big community of Genoese and Maltese descendants that have been here for generations, centuries in fact. You'll find there's lots of Genoese in Yanito.'

'Yanito? Is that a district?' asked Eva.

He smiled forbearingly. 'Yanito is Gibraltar's own creole language, a mix of Spanish and English, with a dash of Genoese, Maltese, Portuguese and Hebrew. You'll have to learn to speak it or you will be forever a *guiri*.'

'*Guiri*?' Mimi asked. 'What's that?'

He thought about it – a tad too long. 'An outsider.'

Mimi gave a small laugh and mumbled, '*Xenophobia*.'

'Well, good luck with changing the face of Gibraltar,' said Carlo.

Eva looked at him, puzzled. Perhaps Sebastian had already met this Montegriffo and told him all about his grand scheme for Gibraltar. When it came to his work, he dropped any vestige of restraint, telling any Tom, Dick and Harry about his world vision.

'We're not here to do that,' she said, hoping to deflect any discussion about the Frontiers Development Project. It had already caused controversy, dividing local people. She guessed Carlo Montegriffo knew all about it and would have some strong opinions on the subject.

Instead he said, 'And you...what will *you* do?'

'Me? Ah, I'm a diving instructor. Apparently Gibraltar is a diver's paradise.'

'Be careful,' he said. 'Many things lurk under the surface of these waters.'

Eva looked at him, waiting for some explanation,

wondering if he was alluding to Sebastian's work rather than to her own.

Mimi was more forthright. 'What exactly do you mean by that?'

'Heavens!' he said, glancing at his watch. 'I'm keeping you ladies here chatting when you're trying to move in.' He grabbed a suitcase in each hand and started up the stairs, two steps at a time.

Mimi

The streets of Gibraltar were teeming. Pushing through the crowd on the square, Mimi saw that the portals of the cathedral were wide open. The interior was jampacked. Even outside, men and women were kneeling on the pavement, praying, their faces turned to the open door.

She'd never seen anything like it – people on their knees right there in the street – but even more surreal was the hundreds of miniature brides: tiny girls in wedding dresses. The Main Street was crammed with doll-like creatures in white frocks, bridal veils, trains and tiaras, their anxious parents trying to make them kneel, or at least stop them from running around and getting dirty. The girls couldn't have been more than nine or ten, and each more elaborately and expensively bedecked than the next. There were boys too, though not as many, dressed like little admirals.

Mimi placed herself with a group of tourists on the fringe of this holy mob and stared, conscious of her disparity. All that white silk and satin made her suddenly feel drab in her black skirt, scuffed combat boots and multiple piercings. Her hand went involuntarily to the gel-hardened spikes of her hair, black as coal and unpleasant to the touch. Her recent heroine was Lisbeth Salander from *The Girl with The Dragon Tattoo*, but knew she lacked the awesome I.Q. and bad-ass attitude, so absolutely no-one would make the connection.

She lit a cigarette and turned to a young woman leaning on the handle of a well-used pram. 'Excuse me. What is this thing? What're they doing?'

The woman shrugged. 'Beats me, I'm not a Catholic. I think this performance is called Corpus Christi.'

Corpus Christi. It had a macabre ring to it. Though it was white and bright, the ceremony seemed dark.

'*Idolatry.*'

The woman smirked. 'Sure, if you say so.'

The ceremony must have ended, as people in stylish clothes began to stream out of the cathedral and gather in groups in the square, talking, laughing, at ease with each other and the world. The little brides lost all decorum and ran about, shouting and playing tag. The air of mysticism had vanished and she felt as if she were gatecrashing a cocktail party.

Walking slowly through the crowd, she saw a man she recognised – their downstairs neighbour, Carlo Montegriffo – talking in a group. She'd assumed he was some kind of sad Jesus-freak loner, but out here in the open he looked totally different. He topped his friends by almost a head and everyone in the group was absorbed by what he was saying. She conceded that the guy had the looks that could pull women, at least older ones.

When she slipped past his back, he turned around as if he'd known she was there all along.

'Hello Imogen.'

'Oh. Hello,'

'I saw you watching the Mass.'

'Yeah.' She shifted her gum to the other cheek. 'It's allowed, I assume?'

He nodded in approval. 'Are you born Catholic?'

'Oh, no. It just looked interesting. Different.'

'Yes, we do give free reign to our worship in a way that can be disconcerting to outsiders.' He had turned away from his group and spoke to her with a relaxed and casual air.

'Ah yes, us *guiris*,' she said. 'I looked up the word. Isn't it derogatory, like "wog" or "Chink" or "Paki"?'

He looked at her for a moment, then laughed. 'You're a sharp young woman. It is not a very flattering expression and I apologise.'

Embarrassment set in. What else was she going to say to him?

'Well, better get home,' she lied. 'Cheers.'

Carlo glanced at his watch. 'I need to get home too. Why don't we walk together?'

She swore to herself but couldn't come up with an excuse. 'Ah… I guess.'

Despite their laughable disparity – a middle-aged guy in a slick suit and a teenaged punk – she found herself surprisingly at ease. Carlo pointed out a couple of landmarks, and chatted amiably as though they'd known each other for ages. He was fitter than she was, walking up the steps and ramps without so much as a hint of sheen on his forehead, while she panted, her lungs like bellows.

'I smoke,' she said in defence. 'And just for the record, I like smoking.'

He laughed softly. 'I remember loving a Lucky Strike when I was your age. My brother and I used to break the filter off. The problem was that no-one could see how cool we were. We had to sneak out on the roof terrace and smoke under cover of darkness.'

'You've got to be at least thirty-eight, forty,' she said, feeling bold.

'Yes,' he admitted ruefully. 'At least.'

'What do you do for a living?'

'I work for the Ministry of Defence. I am also a failed priest and a struggling writer.'

'Cool,' she blurted. 'So am I.'

'Ah no, not another failed priest,' he said laughing.

She laughed too. 'The outfit just didn't look good on me.'

'Well, well.' He looked genuinely interested. She'd got so used to people smirking at the idea of a teenaged writer, she hardly ever owned up to it.

'What are you working on?' he asked.

'I'm writing a novel using my family as a subject. There's fodder there for an entire conference on psychological and relationship dysfunctions and every type of family fuckup under the sun.'

He was chuckling about her confession, but somehow she didn't mind. 'A semi-autographical novel?' he mused. 'I could imagine that has its tricky moments. Especially when your family comes to read it.'

'Yikes!' she cried. 'Over my drawn and quartered body.'

'You'd better publish under a synonym,' he said. 'Imogen Luna stands out.'

Her name rolled easily off his tongue as if he'd said it loads of times.

'What're *you* writing?'

'I write mainly poetry…of a spiritual nature. I've also written two books about Gibraltar's colourful history, and right now,' he hesitated a moment, 'I am writing a book about what I am discovering about the tunnel system in the Rock.'

'I've heard about the tunnels. So what's in them?'

He touched her arm to stop her. 'Honestly, that just slipped out. Please forget it. I'm keeping it tightly under wraps until I am ready to publish.'

'No worries,' she said quickly. 'I feel the same about my stuff.'

42

They continued up the ramp. 'If ever you want,' she said. 'I've been told I am good at checking continuity. It's good practice.'

He looked over at her. 'You know, I could really use an impartial opinion on a couple of my poems.'

'Sure. Though poetry isn't about continuity.'

'You've got that right,' he said approvingly. 'So just your opinion, perhaps. I don't know any other writers to ask.'

'Okay, you're on.'

They walked on in silence for a while. Strangely, she felt taller next to him and realised it was because he treated her like an adult, spoke to her as an equal. What a great feeling that was...just to be heard, your ambition understood and respected.

'Have you got a cat?' she asked. 'A big fat black one?'

'That would be Raven, my partner in crime.'

'Well, he got into our apartment yesterday with the front half of a rat.'

'Ah, yes, he still misses Mrs. Cohen. She used to give him full fat cream by the bowl full. Her passing was a great loss for him,' he said pensively. 'But not for his arteries, of course.'

'Eva doesn't much like uninvited visitors through windows. She gets jumpy.'

'It's the Eucalyptus. He climbs up just about anything. I guess we could try cutting off some of the branches.'

'With a name like that, he'll probably just fly in.'

He turned and studied her for a moment as they walked. 'You're a funny young woman.'

She narrowed her eyes and looked back at him through the black clumps of her mascara, grudgingly pleased that he'd called her a woman, not just once but twice. 'I'm just warning you. Eva might look like an angel, but don't mess with her.'

He laughed. 'Warning logged.'

After a little while she asked, 'So, did you know her?'

'Who?'

'Mrs. Cohen, the lady who died in our apartment.'

'Yes.'

It was such a short answer she resolved to grill him at some future opportunity. When they got to DiMoretti's Ramp, they were walking abreast, but as the ramp narrowed their bodies were gradually brought closer, until her shoulder touched his arm. He was a gentleman and motioned her ahead. As they climbed up the stairwell she became mortified about the length of her skirt. How much could he see from behind?

On the landing he reached out to shake her hand.

'You need to make friends with Raven. That way you can tell him off yourself. He does listen if he respects you.'

'*Preposterousness*,' she said under her breath.

Carlo waggled a forefinger at her. 'You've petted him. He told me.'

She rolled her eyes. 'Kiss and tell. Damned cat! You can't trust anyone these days.'

They looked at each other for a long moment. He had very white teeth when he smiled.

*

Mimi had been writing about Mother Jane before falling asleep, and the text had morphed into dreams. Always reverting to a black-clad little girl, she ran down a tree-lined avenue in an otherwise barren landscape, pursuing a car in which she could see Jane in the back seat. Her mother's immaculate head had not a hair out of place, and she never turned to look at the child running behind the car, forever trying to reach her.

Mimi was out of breath as she struggled towards wakefulness, the lingering cloud of sadness gradually turning to anger. Was it too fucking much to ask that a mother should be a little bit concerned about her child? She'd not heard a dickie-bird from Jane, and she knew she never would. She had probably got Mrs. Carmichael to clear her room of every trace of her residence, then got the decorators in. No expense spared to exorcise her daughter, the Princess of Darkness.

She switched on the light and reached down to pick up her iPad off the floor.

When Marcus opened the door, he found his mother on the doorstep. She was holding Christiana by the hand. Christiana had not grown much in size since he'd last seen her, but her little face had changed and her hair had darkened.

Marcus fell to his knees and gently took her by the shoulders. 'Look at you, sis. Six years old. Did you get my present?'

She stared at him shyly but suddenly grinned in recognition. 'I didn't see you for a long time.'

'I know, sweetie. A whole year. I've been in Japan.'

'Why?'

'I was being a student there, learning lots of great things.' he said and pulled her close. 'Come here, give me a hug.' She didn't resist. Her soft little arms wrapped around his neck. He looked up at Antonia. 'You could have called first.'

She just stood there, her tightened cheeks and botoxed forehead not reaching any definable expression. Her hair was cut into a pixie style and she was slimmer, her new figure draped in an expensive-looking cream suit. Altogether she looked young, untouched by iniquity.

'So how are you, Marcus?'

'I've been good. My ambition has cured me.'

She looked sceptical but said, 'Glad to hear it. How is your dad?'

'Tired. Forgetful.'

'Are you going to invite me in? I need to talk to the two of you.'

'Dad's at the club,' he said, 'but we're happy to have Christiana for the weekend. I'm assuming that's why you've brought her.' He squeezed Christiana's little hand and winked at her.

Antonia shifted on the step, looking anxious and trying to peer past him.

He released Christiana and stood up. 'Did you know I'm doing my PhD at Imperial College London?'

Her eyes softened a little. 'Well done. Make sure you stay... healthy.'

Now he saw the bags and luggage on the walkway below. His eyes widened. 'You're not wanting to move back in, are you?'

She gave a short sharp laugh. 'Good Lord, no. But I'm leaving her with you. Tell dad it's his turn.'

'What do you mean?'

'What I just said.' She paused. 'I'm going to the Bahamas next week, to get married.'

He stared at her. 'I'm assuming it's the Featherington-Haugh bloke.' He saw no denial in her taught expression. 'Well good for you, mother. Coming up in the world. I guess Dad and I can manage for a week or two. I'll ask Auntie Beth if she can pitch in, but you could have forewarned us.' He gestured at the pile behind her. 'A bit of an overkill, don't you think? We do have a washing machine.'

'I'm not coming back for her. Your dad has to do his bit from now on.'

Her words took a while to sink in.

'Wait! You can't just do this,' he blurted. 'Dad's not up to it. He's all over the place, and I'm deep into my work. You left us. She's your responsibility.'

Her expression changed. Anger was just beneath the surface. 'I've done my bit and it was his idea to… keep the baby. I wouldn't have.'

His bewildered stare travelled from Antonia's face to Christiana's. She was looking at her mother, her face crumpling. She was just a little girl, but of course she understood the gist of the rejection.

'You bitch,' he growled at his mother, grabbing Christiana by the hand and pulling her towards him. 'So fuck off. You don't deserve her.'

'Be good,' she said to Christiana, kissing her own forefinger and not quite touching it to the child's cheek. Down on the walkway, she almost stumbled over one of the bags, then hurried away to a taxi idling at the curb.

Mimi tossed aside her iPad and wondered how different this scene would look if Sebastian himself had written it. Had he actually told her, word for word? She remembered it clearly, but she had been only six, so surely she wouldn't have understood all that was said. Did it matter? It was *semi*-autobiographical after all.

She got up, then stubbed her toe hard on a suitcase, swore under her breath and staggered towards the kitchen. It was a starry night and she had no idea what time it was, but a slightly purplish hue was spreading over the sky. There was Sebastian sitting at the table, papers and charts and drawings spread out all around him. Dressed in black shorts and a T-shirt, he hammered away on his laptop, his curly black hair on end. She walked past, touching him on the head.

'Hey, sis,' he said, startled. 'What's up?'

'*I* am, and so are you.'

He glanced at the clock above the cooker. 'But it's five in the morning.'

His eyes had shadows, all the darker against the paleness of his skin. A tide of conflicting feelings surged through her, part affection, part alarm. 'Likewise.' She headed for the kettle. 'Coffee?'

'No thanks. I'm well and truly weaned.'

'How long have you been sitting here?'

'No idea. Hours.'

'Shouldn't you be servicing your new lover?'

Oh, God! Why had she said that? She turned her back to him and stuck the kettle under the tap so he couldn't see her reddening face, but she heard him sigh and his chair scrape back. She braced herself for some reprimand, or worse, some gentle questioning or reassurance. He probably thought she was jealous, which of course she was. She'd hoped her presence would prove the fatal passion-killer, or that the American beauty queen would get fed up with Sebastian and his strange ways.

She felt his hand on her shoulder. 'What's the matter, Mimi?'

'Forget it,' she said to the sink. 'I was just being a bitch.'

He put his arm around her shoulders. 'Give Eva a proper chance, will you?'

'What choice do I have? I'm never going back to Jane's, that's for fucking certain.'

He turned her around and wrapped his arms around her. She wanted to resist but found herself giving in. He didn't hug her very often these days, probably because she'd grown too many thorns.

'I promise –' he said into her hair, 'as long as you act like an adult, don't do drugs, don't run away, don't sleep with weird unsuitable men, and don't try to wreck my romance with Eva – I will never ask you to leave or suggest you go back to Mother's.'

'That's a fucking long list of dont's,' she said, her face in his armpit. 'What about you? Are *you* doing all your should-do's? Like still taking all your tablets, Sebastian?'

'Oh sweetie, how old am I?'

She hated having to do this. 'Just answer me, will you?'

He pulled away and sat down, his eyes on his laptop. 'Yes, of course I'm taking care of it.'

'How much does Eva know?'

'I can't see the point of involving her. I'm perfectly fine and she's got her own problems to deal with.'

'Miss Perfect? What kind of problems?'

He thought for a moment. 'That's *her* business. Some skeletons in the cupboard, just like everyone else. I already told you, neither of us believes in wallowing in the past.'

Mimi considered this for a moment. 'So…I'm the only one around here who knows?'

'Does it *look* as if I'm having problems? I'm hurtling towards the zenith of my career.'

She raised an eyebrow. 'Hurtling?'

Sebastian reached for her hand. Getting up, he stretched and yawned loudly. 'God, I'm stiff. I never get any proper exercise.' He closed his laptop. 'Hey! Let's go for a walk?'

Quietly they got dressed. Sebastian wrote a note for Eva and propped it against the coffeemaker. They put on their shoes in the hallway and left the apartment. A wind had whipped up outside, making the dim light bulb in the stairwell swing on its long wire. They tiptoed down the stairs. When they passed Carlo Montegriffo's door, the man himself stepped out as if he'd been waiting for them.

'Hey, Carlo,' Mimi said, surprised. She'd not seen him since he'd invited her in for a cuppa in order to give her a couple of poems to read. Whatever else he did in his apartment, he was definitely noiseless about it.

'Hey yourself.'

She eyed up his black suit and starched white shirt. 'You going to a funeral?'

'No, Imogen,' he said, fiddling with the keys to his door. 'I'm going to a special dawn Mass.'

'Really? What happens in a dawn Mass?'

'For many of us it's a deeply moving experience. You could attend it sometime and see for yourself.'

She became aware that Sebastian and Carlo had not so much as exchanged a word. 'Bro, have you met our neighbour?' she said awkwardly.

The air had that rubber-band quality – ready to snap – but she wasn't sure exactly who had created the tension.

'Yes, we have introduced ourselves,' said Sebastian tersely. 'My sister is not a Catholic, Mr. Montegriffo.'

'There is no such prerequisite to attend a Mass,' Carlo answered with a serene expression. 'Our God doesn't discriminate.'

'I'd love to witness a dawn Mass. Sounds intriguing,' Mimi said cheerfully.

Sebastian had no religion but engineering, and she could see how Carlo's piety grated on him. She grabbed her brother by the arm and pulled him away. 'Have a good one, Carlo.'

Once they were out in the empty street, Mimi glanced back to see if they were alone.

'Why did you pull a snooty on Carlo? He's quite an interesting guy. You could talk to him, you know. He knows everything about Gibraltar and he writes poetry. He's asked me to look over some of his work.'

'*Jesus*, Mimi! You're not to go into his apartment.'

'I did already. We had chamomile tea in fine bone china cups,' she grimaced. 'Just like at Mother's.'

'Mimi, it's not appropriate. In fact, I forbid it.'

'I was only there for ten minutes and he gave me some of his poems to read. He's an ex-priest, for fuck's sake.'

'Ha, what you don't know about Catholic priests,' said Sebastian with a derisive chuckle. 'I don't like the way he eats you up with his eyes.'

She looked at him in surprise. 'When? Just now?'

He didn't answer right away. 'I saw him following you the other day.'

She frowned. 'You saw him following me?' Where?'

'In town.'

'In town? Where in town?'

'I think it was the road going to the Cruise Liner Terminal,' he said evasively.

Her frown deepened. 'Are you sure it wasn't *you* following me?'

Sebastian avoided her eyes. He knew damned well how she felt about his overbearing protectiveness. Didn't he realise that she'd grown up since they last lived together? She wasn't thirteen.

'I'm not having you police my movements!' she exclaimed.

'Maybe I shouldn't have, but still, it was bloody unnerving.'

'Why don't I believe you?'

Sebastian had that pinched look on his face as he marched ahead, and she regretted that what had started so well had now been fractured. She followed him as he picked his way down the steps and alleys towards the lower town. A small dog yapped at them from an open window and the noise echoed down a passage. The wind picked up a sheet of newsprint which chased them down the steps. In the early morning the dilapidation of Upper Town seemed starker. Walls had conserved the heat of yesterday's sun and a whiff of sewage pervaded the air between the buildings. Everywhere were signs of times gone by: ancient stone ramparts, flagstone steps worn down by centuries of feet, strange passageways leading deep into crumbling buildings, archways, tunnels and enormous wooden gates opened hundreds of years ago and never shut again.

In the lower town there was the stirring of activity. They followed a group of Jewish school children walking purposefully in single file along the impossibly narrow Governor's Street, the girls modest in their head coverings and the boys in ties and skull caps, no doubt on their way to an appointment with some spiritual activity. From the little mosque on the Line Wall came that eerie wailing, the call to prayer. It seemed that dawn summoned believers of every faith. She felt a gnawing emptiness, always yearning for some faith herself but never finding any she could take seriously.

'Why don't we keep walking and I'll show you my development,' said Sebastian, nudging her with his elbow.

She knew she should take a bit of interest, but the site was like a thousand miles away and it would take them at least an hour. 'Okay, okay but for God's sake, don't run.'

The sky was lightening and the gulls were beginning to circle high above the limestone ridges of the Rock. The huge harbour was filled with what looked like toy ships. They walked through an arched gate coming out onto Europa Road and were met by the first rays of sun. Like opening the door to a sauna, the heat welled towards them.

When finally Europa Point came into view Sebastian paused, waiting for her to catch him up.

'Look! Jebel Musa,' he whispered, pointing to a huge black mountain rising out of the mist on the Moroccan coast. 'The Rock's twin.'

'*Stupendous*,' she conceded.

'Did you know that Hercules smashed through the Atlas Mountains to open this strait between the Mediterranean and the Atlantic?' He put one arm around her shoulders and with an extravagant sweep of the other arm, laid claim to the horizon. 'One day I'm going to re-connect Europe with Africa.'

'How the hell do you plan to accomplish that?'

'I'm going to build the bridge.'

'Oh, right!' she pulled herself out of his grasp. 'Here we go.'

His gaze shifted towards the black mountain in the mist. 'Every structural engineer worth his salt must have a bridge to his name. Mine will be monumental, the most beautiful and majestic structure ever built. Luna's Crossing… It'll be the absolute climax of my work.'

'Be careful, Sebastian. Sometimes you give yourself away.'

'There's nothing wrong with having a vision, Imogen,' he countered vehemently. 'You want to become a novelist. Isn't that a grand vision?'

'It's an ambition, not a vision. I don't trust that word,' she said uneasily, 'and neither should you.'

Sebastian marshalled her forward, insisting she ought to see Europa Point, at least to imagine his Luna's Crossing. What she saw was the two oceans, Mediterranean and Atlantic, colliding wildly against each other in a strange and formidable dance.

Eva

They sat on the narrow seats at the stern of the boat, bobbing in the waves off the east side of Gibraltar. Sebastian had his wetsuit on and was ready to gear up. Eva took her time with the preparations. She knew the importance of being absolutely meticulous.

Sebastian indulgently followed her every move with his eyes, but when she separated her hair into three strands and began braiding them together, he reached out to stop her. 'Is it really necessary?' he exclaimed. 'Your hair floating free in the deep is the most beautiful sight a man can behold. Please, don't deprive me of it.'

'Are you kidding me?' She shivered. 'Don't ever forget that coral.'

During those first days in Dubai, Sebastian must have spent a fortune booking her for private dives. She overheard her boss taking his calls, suggesting other instructors, male ones, but Sebastian insisted he would only dive with her. It soon became obvious that he wasn't there just to improve his diving. Sure, he was impressed with her professionalism and skills, but – he would later tell anyone – 'her long fair hair, rippling around her in the water like a cape of seaweed' so mesmerised him, he seemed convinced she was a mermaid.

He overcame his tongue-tied awe of her and suggested dinner. Being quite intrigued by this quietly intense man, she threw out her principles and defied the rules of her employer. During dinner in an out-of-the-way restaurant he talked of nothing but his work. He was nervous, not at all like the smooth-talking playboys that tried to hit on her at the diving centre. His shyness turned into fiery enthusiasm and she was unable to take her eyes off him as she listened, imagining for herself the edifices he built with words for her benefit.

At the end of the four-hour meal he called for a taxi. They waited for it outside the restaurant, sitting on a low wall in the balmy evening.

'I can't bear to take leave of you,' he said, for the first time taking her hand and lightly kissing the tips of her fingers. 'Will you come home with me?'

'Tonight?' she said, surprised at this sudden boldness.

'We don't have to make love. I've never slept with a mermaid, I wouldn't even know where to begin,' he said. 'We could just submerge ourselves in my bath tub, head to foot.'

She burst out laughing. What a weird and wonderful guy! As he looked at her, a feverish glow shone from his dark eyes and she felt herself go weak inside. Just as quickly, fear grabbed at her, not sure about that look. Desire, lust or something darker, how could she know? He looked away to give her space to decide. It was a subtle gesture that said such a lot about him. He expected nothing. He was unfathomable in some ways, but her instinct told her she was safe with this man.

The taxi drew up beside them and they hopped off the wall.

He opened the door for her. 'Where would you like to go?' he said quietly.

That night she became his mermaid and showed him how it worked, though they never got as far as the bath tub.

A few weeks after their first night together, her hair got

tangled up in the salmon-pink peak of a coral reef, thirty metres below the surface of the Arabian Sea. Sebastian reacted instantly, first trying to disentangle her but this just snared her hair more firmly to the barbed surface of the coral. He gestured for her to be calm, and swiftly pulled out his diving knife. The task of cutting her free was difficult – wet hair does not shear easily with a knife – and it was made all the more urgent by her own escalating panic.

The incident had an air of fatalism; for Sebastian, at least. He was convinced that their future together was sealed. They needed each other, they had saved each other. He asked her to marry him that same evening. Of course she said it was too soon, and she didn't really believe in marriage, though she couldn't bring herself to tell him the reason why.

She was still trying to tell him.

It was four in the afternoon and the sun stood high. Sebastian kissed her before pulling on her hood, tucking her braid in. The boat hardly moved. The water was calm despite the violent power below the surface; two seas, heaving, tugging at each other through the narrow gap of the strait. The air quivered with the thunderous noise of a plane taking off. The runway began and ended in the sea, covering the length of the isthmus, the narrow bridge of land that separated Gibraltar from the Spanish mainland. Gibraltar was a tiny, confined peninsula. It had two oceans and a strip of a border with guards requesting passports.

Nowhere to run, nowhere to hide.

With that tightening in the pit of her stomach Eva turned around to look at Jonny Risso. He met her gaze with customary indifference. Jonny owned the boat and he always watched their preparations with beady eyes, the only part of his face that showed awareness. On a day-to-day basis he fished out of Catalan Bay, preferably with paying tourists on deck. Fishing was a fantasy job these days, he'd told them, but he'd inherited the boat from his fisherman father, and a man had to earn a living somehow. Jonny also bragged about a time when he'd made bags of money smuggling duty-free tobacco into Spain. Everyone with a boat had done it, but then the fishermen were outdone by rich kids in high-speed launches – so he'd gone back to ferrying scuba divers and taking tourists out fishing. Money was his great motivator and – should it ever become necessary – for a fee, Jonny would slip her to the mainland, bypassing the border.

The drone of the plane faded away. Just as they were about to fit their masks, Jonny spoke.

'Sorry? What did you say?' Sebastian asked.

'Nobody dives on this side of Gib. I bet you and the missus have found something down there. You'll think of your boatman, won't you? I want my share.'

He made it sound like a joke, but she knew it wasn't. If they hauled anything from the seabed, he'd want his cut. It was the second time he'd taken them to the site, and she suspected he still had no idea what made Sebastian Luna want to dive in that particular spot again and again. The Mediterranean side of Gibraltar had poor pickings for divers. Eva had told Jonny they were exploring an Italian submarine sunk during WWII, but there wasn't much of it to see, really, and Jonny Risso knew it.

'My wife here is a pre-history nerd,' said Sebastian. 'She hopes to find a Neanderthal spearhead or something.'

Jonny rolled his eyes in obvious contempt. Eva had to turn away to hold back a fit of giggles. Pre-history nerd! What a cheek, why *her*? Why not him?

'Come on, missus,' Sebastian said, grinning at her. 'Put on your mask. Time is short and the deep beckons.'

They were in the water, sinking, sinking, hand in hand. Sebastian swam towards the cliff, pulling her along. With excited gestures and boyish eagerness he pointed out the marks – made by members of the geotechnical team only the day before – where giant T-shaped interlocking concrete-and-polymer encased steel brackets would be anchored in twenty-metre deep slots in the rock. She nodded and gave him a thumbs-up, all the while wondering if this wall of rock really could sustain a cantilevered shelf weighing countless thousands of tonnes. She'd heard that some of Sebastian's team members were concerned about the hydrodynamic forces acting on the brackets and if the strain resistance of some of the composite materials had been correctly calculated. Then again, Sebastian's project wasn't her concern, and maybe her foreboding was fed by her own deepest fears.

Yes, she decided, as always this was the root of her anxiety. When everything seemed wonderful and rosy, you were in fact teetering on a pinnacle from which the only way was down.

They descended further, and he showed her his signature carved into the rock-face. The seabed was just visible but the water was murky. Along the submerged cliff were a few large cave openings, some extending above the waterline. Tens of thousands of years ago these had been clear above the surface and apparently home to small groups of Neanderthal people. This was another disrupting factor: archaeology zealots objected to any tampering with the caves, pointing out that Gibraltar – despite its puny size – was one of the richest places on Earth for Neanderthal findings.

Sebastian was taking dozens of photos of strategic places

in the cliff. Eva looked at her watch and began to feel the sting of urgency. Twenty-five minutes to go and she could already feel the pull of the tide. Though the Mediterranean showed no discernible tidal fluctuations, millions of gallons per second were forced back and forth continually through the narrow gap of the strait. It was something that not even her lover could contain. And the tides were deceitful, pulling in different directions at different levels, in some places dragging the diver straight down into the depths.

She touched his arm, pointed to her watch and he nodded. Slowly they swam towards the surface until they saw Jonny's impassive face peering down at them through the water.

*

Roller in hand, she began to paint walls of the kitchen white. Mimi, a silent witness to her efforts, was in the process of mixing a fruit smoothie.

'Okay, okay, d'ya have a spare roller?' Mimi asked with a grimace. 'Is there only one stepladder?'

'Here, have my roller.' Eva fetched the ladder. 'Would you like me to lift your foot onto the first rung?'

Mimi tried unsuccessfully to hide a smile. 'I'm only doing this for one hour, max.'

Eva shrugged and started on the door. She opened a pot and dipped a clean brush into it, then let the creamy pale paint glide over the dark wood. She knew she was committing sacrilege, painting the oak doors a pale eggshell blue, but Mr. Stagnetto had said to do absolutely anything she wanted. After all, the place had not seen a paintbrush for a century, and they'd all get depressed enfolded in this shade of dung.

'Why only an hour?'

'I've got a date.'

'A date? Already? Quick work, buddy.'

No response. She tried again after a while. 'Is he nice?'

'Of course not, he's an absolute troll.' Again, a long pause. 'Carlo has invited me to do a tour of the cathedral.'

'Carlo?' Eva almost dropped her paintbrush. 'The downstairs guy, Carlo Montegriffo?'

'Yes, him!' Mimi asserted. 'Some of us need a bit of mysticism in life, so whatever snide comment you're about to make, don't bother.'

'Hey, don't make assumptions,' Eva said. 'You know nothing about my beliefs, okay?' After a moment she added, 'But it's slightly mysterious why a Catholic bachelor in his forties might want to hang out with a seventeen-year-old girl.'

'The snide comment,' Mimi said, laughing sarcastically. 'Mind like a sewer, just like my bro. You guys think sex comes into *everything*?'

Eva went on with her painting. She had ascertained that if you wanted any kind of conversation with Mimi you had to be thick-skinned. But why give up while there still was a conversation?

'So when did this invitation happen?'

'I saw Raven making a dash across the street. It's a scooter death trap, so I picked him up and brought him home.'

'Okay, so you saved the blackbird killer. And he just invited you, just like that?'

'I guess I've expressed an interest. I actually envy people with a faith. Catholicism has some kind of dramatic appeal. It's cryptic, all those strange rituals and stuff.'

'Yeah sure, but I still have to wonder what he's up to. The age difference...'

Mimi sighed exaggeratedly. 'Don't *you* start... I'm not planning to screw the guy. Not unless I get desperate.'

'Okay okay. Good forward planning.'

Mimi sniggered, and Eva couldn't help chuckling too. She had no experience whatsoever of rough-edged teenagers and had never been allowed to be one herself. At the same time she'd never had to care for anyone vulnerable, and Mimi did seem vulnerable even though perhaps she wasn't. She'd probably blossom into a delightful and responsible adult, and – three months short of eighteen – she might not be around for long.

They painted in silence for a while, then Mimi began humming a Meatloaf track Eva loved. She joined in, and they both began to bellow out the lyrics. They sounded quite good together. Mimi had a great voice, rich and husky.

Eva stood back from the door and studied the result. Sure, oak was a very fine material, but the truth was, the door looked even more elegant in eggshell blue. In fact, it looked absolutely stunning.

'Look at this, Mimi. Tell me I'm right.'

Mimi, who had made good inroads with the walls and the plaster cornices, came down from the ladder and stood beside her. 'Yeah, all right,' she conceded. '*Sophisticated.*'

Eva put a hand on her shoulder. 'Do you think you could be happy here? It's a new beginning for all of us.'

With a visible shudder, Mimi shrunk free of the hand. But seeing Eva so startled, her frown softened. 'Worry about yourself, Eva. You've got good reason to.'

For a moment Eva stared at her, wondering if the girl knew anything about the menace that never stopped breathing ice onto the back of her neck. No, of course not, how could she? 'Why? What do you mean?'

Mimi looked away, then plopped the roller into the paint bucket. 'Look, I've got to go. Religion beckons.'

Eva watched her skulk down the corridor towards her

room. Twenty minutes later she re-appeared in the doorway, dressed slightly less punkily in jeans, and pink instead of black lipgloss.

'I'm going.'

Eva tried not to look surprised at the token courtesy. 'Okay. Have a good cathedral.'

'Bye then,' said Mimi. 'Enjoy your white.'

A great leap forward – she'd said goodbye.

Mimi

'In ancient times a Moorish mosque stood right here.' Carlo tapped his foot on the worn-out tiles. 'Then, when the Spanish conquered Gibraltar in the fifteenth century, it was demolished and a Catholic church built in its place. But make no mistake, this very courtyard here is a true remnant of those Moorish devils.'

'Devils?' Mimi said, raising an eyebrow. 'More racist slurs?'

'Look, the Moors had this place by the neck for over seven hundred years, and they were cruel in the extreme. After one of the last sieges of Gibraltar by the Spanish, the Moorish governor decapitated the Spanish commander and his headless body hung on the walls of Gibraltar for the next twenty-two years.'

'Yeoww!' She grimaced. 'Twenty-two years. That could not have been a pretty sight. Reminds me of Mrs. Cohen.'

Carlo narrowed his eyes. 'You know about Mrs. Cohen's death, do you?'

'Uh-huh,' she nodded. 'She choked to death and you found her…how much later?'

He shook his head. 'It's not really a good subject for discussion during a tour of the cathedral.'

'Fair enough.'

Carlo led her in through the main doors of the imposing building. Mimi had never set foot inside a Catholic church. She took in the solemnity of the place with wide eyes.

'Hey, awesome,' she exclaimed.

To the left was a huge sculpture of Jesus on the cross, his mother and an angel looking up at him. It was horribly realistic, with its painted backdrop of hills and sky. Jesus' bloodied face mesmerised her. His pain was so brutally real.

'No wonder people have felt guilty for two thousand years,' she said.

Carlo smiled and beckoned her into a small niche. He pointed to the long list of names carved into the flag stones. 'Until the nineteenth, century any person who died in Gibraltar had the right to be buried under this floor.'

'Any person?'

'Yes. Hundreds, perhaps thousands of people lie under here.'

She bit her lip. 'All those bodies...stacked on top of each other. Each layer rotting in turn.'

Carlo laughed and touched her cheek. 'Some sinister speculations churn inside that pretty head of yours.'

She flinched slightly at his touch. She hadn't expected it. 'Am I that easy to figure?'

'It's not a criticism. A true writer is always on the lookout for the dark side of existence. That's what the human race ultimately battles with. That's what we need to explore and understand.'

She felt herself relax. 'What are we waiting for? Show me more dark stuff. I need to feed the writer in me.'

'Are you interested in the tunnels? I told you I'm writing a book about them. They're dark enough, as long as you're not claustrophobic.'

'I'm not claustrophobic,' she said, knowing that was not entirely true.

'I'm planning to do a bit of exploration this afternoon. Nothing too dirty or daunting. You are welcome to come if you want.' He glanced at her feet, and if nothing else, she *was* wearing sensible footwear.

Her stomach clenched slightly, but her motto was to experience life to the full, even the daunting stuff. 'Yes of course I'll come.'

Sebastian

Henry Saunders looked weary. He had just flown into Gibraltar on a British Airways flight and come straight to the meeting in a taxi.

'The Levante?' he said, peering at Claudio Fontaneiro, the climatologist Sebastian had engaged whose specific area of expertise was wind-driven surface current analysis.

'*Correct!*' maintained Claudio, 'The Levante is the wind that rises up in the central Mediterranean and blows westward. As this wind begins to funnel into the narrowing gap of Gibraltar strait, it gathers intensity and speed, creating a Venturi effect. Though it is an entirely natural phenomenon, it is a great problem for your works.'

'A great problem? I don't like the sound of that,' said Saunders. 'What does this mean exactly? Put it in layman's terms.'

Sebastian sighed. Why did Claudio have to exaggerate so? He had been determined to sit back and let Claudio do the talking, not wanting to be held responsible for an unforeseen holdup which fell well outside of his own brief. But as usual, he found it impossible to keep his trap shut.

'Henry, Claudio is saying we've got a bit of a challenge. We'd correctly estimated the strength of the tides, but not the Levante's effect on surface currents. Though the brackets are calculated to withstand the hydrodynamic forces, as a precaution we should reduce the impact as much as possible.'

He let Claudio continue to explain the problem in rapid-fire delivery, and Saunders listened with a blank face, clearly not understanding his Portuguese accent. Lars Bengtson, a Swede who spoke a dozen languages, acted as occasional interpreter.

'Can we move on?' Sebastian interrupted, chewing his lip with impatience. 'I've come up with a very elegant solution to the problem.'

Saunders hiked his shoulders in a tense shrug. 'Which is?'

'Simply, we elevate the entire structure by about two and a half metres.'

'Two and a half metres?' Saunders stared at him.

Sebastian was well aware that Saunders was purely a businessman with no engineering background. He had a sharp intelligence and great imagination but the technical minutiae was Chinese to him.

Saunders looked agitated. 'With such an alteration in the design, the cantilevered platform would be projecting from the cliff into thin air. It won't give the impression of being connected to the water. It would look precarious, unsafe. It'll put investors off.'

Sebastian opened his laptop. 'Look at this new image. Try and be open to it, Henry. I think it's exciting. There is no actual change in the load-bearing elements, but visually, it's just amazing. The brackets will barely be visible except from out at sea. What you have is a city projecting straight from the cliff out over the water. Why hide the fact that it's a shelf?' He paused to gauge Saunder's expression. 'I've already consulted with Goodbard and the other members of the design team and tried to work through the various structural options to produce the most cost-effective solution.'

'Shit, Sebastian! You should have consulted me before talking to Goodbard.'

Sebastian ignored the admonition. 'If you think it's too futuristic in appearance, too far out for your investors, I'm working on a design for a system of pontoons that will inflate and deflate automatically with the water levels. It will be an aesthetic feature only, giving the whole development the appearance of sitting on re-claimed land. Large waves will just compress the pontoons and disappear underneath the platform, to dissipate against the cliff.'

'Jesus... This is a whole new plan. How much will it cost? And how do you expect me to account for this to our people back in London?'

Sebastian breathed through a tide of impatience. 'Don't look at *me*, Henry. The climatological concerns aren't my department.' He gestured towards Matthew Davies and Lars Bengtson. 'That's what you've got your engineers for. I'm pioneering a whole new system of building on vertical terrain, and you know as well as I do that there's always going to be an element of the unknown. We've simply got to work with this new data, and I'm showing you the solution.'

Despite the air-conditioned office in the cool dark lower ground floor of Eliott Hotel, the heat of the discussion was getting to everyone. Henry Saunders pulled at his collar and wiped a tissue over his forehead.

'The Levante!' he said with a sneer. 'It must be a Spanish initiative.'

'Yes, damned nuisance,' said Sebastian, laughing. 'They'd come up with any old thing to scupper Gibraltar.'

'Ah, but the Levante is mostly benign,' Claudio Fontaneiro exclaimed, not having understood the joke. 'Sometimes it causes a strange spectacle along the ridge of the Rock. From the town it looks as if the length of the ridge is on fire. Swirling air currents dance wildly along the crest. Perhaps you get to see this phenomenon, Mr. Saunders. It will not disappoint. Am I not right, Sebastian?'

'I need a drink,' said Saunders and steered Sebastian to a table under the huge palm trees in the hotel's court yard.

'Pineapple juice with ice, please,' Sebastian said to the waiter.

'That's not a drink,' Saunders huffed. 'Do me a pint of lager and a single malt.'

Once the drinks were before them, Saunders leaned forward with his elbows on the table.

'Now look here, Luna. I want you to get this right, because,' Saunders paused, looking surreptitiously left and right, 'I've spread the word a bit and we've had several enquiries. A Japanese firm is hounding me, wanting an experimental tsunami-proof development. They mentioned you by name.'

'Of course. I'm their man.'

Saunders smiled a small smile. 'You'll have to formally join our team. That's the condition.'

As Sebastian didn't respond, he continued. 'Could you see yourself doing a stint in Japan?'

'After Gibraltar, you mean?'

'There is no reason we can't get the skids under and get you out of here a bit sooner. I can send over a couple of our high flyers. You can get them up to speed, have them take the tedious stuff off your hands. You could in principle work from Japan and just fly back here every couple of weeks. I mean, you're young, and by God, you've got an inhuman amount of energy.'

Sebastian had a sip of his juice and closed his eyes for a second. Luna's Crossing flashed before his inner eye in all its majesty. He clenched his teeth but felt his resolve slacken. He knew he shouldn't risk his credibility, but his excitement and the tension of the meeting had unarmed him. He thought of Dad and his voice warning him, *loose cannon*, but his mouth opened and he was speaking, his thoughts flowing uncensored into the air.

'I'll think about joining Sea-Change, but listen, Henry. I have a dream... I know it's a bit much to throw at you right now, but you know the various ideas that have been flying around over the last few decades about a bridge?'

Saunders looked at him, squinting against the sunlight. 'What bridge are we talking about?'

'I am talking about *the bridge*.' Sebastian moved forward in his chair. 'The bridge that will join Europe with Africa.'

'I haven't heard anything new. Who's proposing it?'

'As far as I know, all initiatives have been scrapped, for the very reason we were talking about earlier. The surface currents in the strait and the massive pull of the tides would make building support structures near enough impossible.' He paused for effect. 'But *we* could do it.'

While speaking he'd whipped his laptop out of his briefcase. Within less than a minute he was showing Henry Saunders a rolling series of drawings, the concept he'd been playing with since he first set eyes on the Pillars of Hercules. The pinnacle of the Rock, and its Moroccan twin, Jebel Musa, acting as the buttresses for a gigantic suspension bridge.

'Don't freak on me now, Henry,' he said defiantly. 'This idea looks pretty wild, but the principles are the same as any garden-variety suspension bridge.'

Saunders was mute, staring at the screen. Finally he opened his mouth to murmur, 'Incredible.' He shook his head as if to clear it, and choked up a laugh. 'How do you come up with this stuff?'

Sebastian smiled to himself and flicked through a further series of images. 'I'm determined to do away with any supports on the actual seabed itself, but we have two mountains... The bridge would simply be suspended between the peaks. Because of the length of the span, it would clear the water by two hundred meters at its centre. Central cables suspended vertically into the sea would end in steel and fibreglass keels creating enough drag to prevent the span from being affected by high winds. It's a hell of a span but I've done the calculations and *it can be done.*'

Saunders' mouth stayed open and his almost catatonic stare told Sebastian what he already knew. No-one had ever seen anything like it.

'Of course, we'd have to think of some kind of causeway around Gib to bring traffic from the rest of Europe. It will be big, Henry, a monument on a par with the Eiffel Tower, the Pyramids of Giza, or for that matter, the Great Wall of China.'

He tapped the screen with his forefinger. 'Why don't you stay here in Gib for a couple of weeks, Henry? You can see that I've done quite a bit of the ground work, but perhaps bring some of your top guys over, then you can take it back to the board and introduce them to the concept.'

'You've got to be kidding?'

Sebastian frowned. 'No. I'm not kidding. Sure, something on this scale will take a few years to hammer out, even a decade or two, but SeaChange is a big outfit and needs big challenges. The first joining of Africa with Europe. How will the board be able to resist it?

'Stop, Luna. *Just stop,*' Henry Saunders bellowed, holding up both hands as if trying to halt a runaway train. 'Are you barking mad?'

Sebastian stared at him. Did Saunders just call him

barking mad? 'What the hell do you mean? You just called the concept incredible.'

Saunders sank into his chair and rubbed his forehead as though he were trying to eradicate what he'd just seen and heard. After a moment, he looked up to meet Sebastian's insistent gaze.

'Yes, it is *in*credible, just like a bridge to the moon itself... You do scare me sometimes, you know.' He grabbed his whisky glass then put it down again. 'I know you have a brilliant mind, Sebastian, but can't you see how outlandish your proposal is? A bridge like that is unfeasible for so many reasons. I don't need to count them out. You're in Cloud Cuckoo Land, you're decades into the future. No, not decades, centuries.'

Sebastian was speechless. Was he *that* far off the radar? Saunders was staring at him with a deep frown. And there he'd been thinking that Saunders was a man with vision. The vision was all his. He stood alone.

He knew he should have asked Saunders home for dinner, but after their distressing interaction and Saunders' complete rejection of his life's ambition, he simply couldn't face it. Leaving him – with the excuse that he was giving birth to a migraine – to a comfortable room and the rooftop dining at the Eliott, Sebastian quickly walked down Canon Lane, past the quaint eponymous hotel and the cafes frequented by elderly Moroccans, until he emerged into the throng on Main Street. It was a very hot afternoon. He felt stunned by disappointment, and he'd not told a lie. His head was pounding and the beginnings of that telltale nausea washed over him in waves, shooting red stars distorting his vision. 'Barking mad'? Saunders' insult had escaped before he'd been able to restrain it.

To get away from the crowds, the tourists and the street performers, he nipped across the Piazza into Irish Town, a narrow pedestrian thoroughfare lined with pubs. He felt he needed to walk, to physically discharge the strain of the meeting, although he knew he ought to go straight home and lie down in a darkened room. His lovely Eva would plant featherlight kisses on his eyelids, whisper soothing things he didn't have to answer. Mimi was good in a head crisis too, fetching his pills and icepacks.

No sooner had he thought of his sister than he recognised her walking ahead of him. At first – not being entirely certain – he just observed her back. When he saw, or rather heard, the bag she was carrying, he knew for sure it was Mimi. He'd bought it for her on a weekend trip to Oman, an intricate leather creation bedecked with tiny silver bells that chimed as she walked. She was still too slender in body, somewhat short in stature but clearly no longer an adolescent. Her walk seemed more confident, surprisingly womanly. Her hips swayed in the tight black jeans and she held herself erect. Despite the heat, she'd covered her crazy hair with a French beret.

Suddenly something happened which he could not at once assimilate. She walked closer to a tall man who had till now seemed unconnected to her, and said something, making him laugh. Sebastian stared at them in bewilderment.

Was this man someone she knew, or was she trying to pick him up, just like that, off the street? It wouldn't be the first time.

He was at once in his apartment in Dubai, in the grip of desperate anxiety. Mimi had not come back from the gym. The gym in the building closed at 23.30, and now there was no-one left there to open the door or answer the phone. He tried calling her mobile every fifteen minutes, but got no answer. At last there was a message: *I am staying over with friends. See you in the morning. xxx.* What friends? She had just come for a two-week holiday and he'd not yet introduced her to a soul.

It was six in the morning when he heard the apartment door open and quietly click shut. He shot up from the sofa and marched to meet her in the hall before she disappeared into her bedroom.

She looked dishevelled, her eyes hollow with fatigue. All his dread and worry surged up in one unstoppable wave, and he slapped her. Her cheek reddened instantly and she covered it with her hand as though to protect it from further blows.

The act instantly deflated his anger, his own cheeks reddening to match hers.

'I... I am so sorry,' he said, hiding his face in his hands. 'I was just...so worried.'

'You don't own me,' she said coldly, 'and you're not my father.'

'But where have you been? Why didn't you let me know?'

'I did,' she hissed. 'I told you I was with friends. I don't have to account for who they are.'

'You're only a kid,' he shouted back. 'Dubai is a fucking dangerous place for any woman, let alone a teenage girl in skimpy clothes.'

'It's your *girlfriend* you should worry about,' she sneered. 'Men stare at her like hungry dogs.'

'Eva's thirty-eight, not seventeen and she knows how to look after herself, you dingbat.'

He went to her and put his arms around her. She let him, but didn't return the hug.

'I love you, kid. Don't be jealous. You come first, always.'
She didn't answer, but after a moment encircled his back with a limp arm.

'I am so so sorry, sweetheart,' he said, stroking her hair. 'I can't believe I actually hit you. It's unforgivable. Tell me how I can make it up to you.'

'You didn't,' she said, looking up into his face with a frown. 'You didn't hit me.'

Looking at her now, her womanly form next to this tall mature-looking man, he knew he was powerless to shield her from predators. The way she chatted easily to him, she seemed so trusting, so naïve. It soon became obvious that he was not a stranger to her. Mimi laughed at something and punched him lightly on the arm. Sebastian quickened his step, trying to ignore the nausea washing over him in waves.

'Mimi,' he called out, trying to sound cheerful.

She turned, then frowned. 'Hey, Sebastian.'

'Where're you off to?'

The man had slowed and now he too turned. Sebastian glared at him in recognition. 'You?'

'How's it going?' said Carlo Montegriffo. 'Not expanding our territories today then?'

'Working, you mean?' he answered, more aggressively than he'd intended. 'Of course I am. What about you? Aren't *you* employed?'

'I am indeed.'

'Oh, yes? Where?'

Mimi stepped between them to say something, but Carlo stopped her with a slight gesture of his hand. 'With the Ministry of Defence.'

'Are you really?' Sebastian cast an eye over his civilian clothing. 'In what capacity?'

'I have a number of responsibilities, too many to list,' Carlo said with a cool smile. 'Is that so?' Sebastian turned away from him to address Mimi. 'So, what are *you* up to?'

'We've been on a tour of the cathedral.' Mimi said. 'And now Carlo is going to show me one of the MOD tunnels.'

'They're out of bounds to the public,' said Sebastian.

'We're not the public,' Carlo interjected. 'I'm the foremost authority on the Gibraltar tunnel system. It's one of my jobs, giving tours of the military installations. Imogen told me how interested you are in the tunnels. Perhaps you'd like to come along.'

'Really! I *don't* need a chaperone.' Mimi said lightheartedly, giving Sebastian a stern nod, a warning not to humiliate her.

'You're taking my sister in the wrong direction.'

'We're picking up a young friend of mine first,' Carlo said.

'Oh, yes? Who is that?'

'You're embarrassing me,' whispered Mimi, a clear note of anger in her voice.

'Imogen is in perfectly safe hands,' Carlo said calmly, then to Mimi, 'But look, your brother is not comfortable with this excursion. Perhaps we should postpone it.'

Mimi's face clouded over and she stomped her foot on the pavement. 'Stop organising me, the pair of you!'

Her outburst caused an awkward silence. She looked progressively deflated as if she weren't sure with whom to go. She turned to Sebastian. 'Trust me, bro. Just go home. Anyway, you don't look well.'

Multicoloured darts pierced his vision as the migraine gathered strength. It was impossible to deal with this situation when he knew he could be sick without warning. Involuntarily he pressed his hands over his mouth for a second, then mumbled. 'Don't be long, Mimi. I'd rather not have to phone the MOD to go looking for you.'

He turned to walk away. Still, right through the pain, he could not bear to let her go and glanced behind him. The pair of them strolled languidly down the road, chatting as if they'd never had that disturbing confrontation. Mimi turned around and their eyes met. Sebastian read a thousand things in the look she gave him, but perhaps all her glance said, *I'm not the one with a problem.*

Pain stabbed at his left temple and splintered. He stopped and stood still, breathing deeply to compose himself. He'd once projectile vomited in the street and he didn't ever want it to happen again. Once more he looked back and saw his little sister slip down an alley.

Mimi

Carlo led her up a pedestrian-only alley called Tuckey's Lane. Between a betting shop and a dry-cleaners was a door into a long narrow corridor. It took a while for their eyes to adapt to the dark and at the end of the hall they came upon a set of stairs. On the first floor there was another long corridor lit by two striplights. A series of doors had numbers on them. The building seemed to be totally empty of people, but the lingering odours of urinals, sweat and exotic spices made her guess it was a men's rooming house, probably for transient workers.

'Is this where your friend lives?'

'Yes. His name is Mohammed.'

'I see. A Moorish devil?' she said in an attempt to tease him.

'He's my assistant,' said Carlo, not taking the bait.

He knocked on a door marked 6. There were no sounds from inside the room, and suddenly she felt uneasy. She didn't mind being alone with Carlo, but this hostel had an uncomfortably familiar feel. Perhaps because it reminded her of when she ran away at fourteen and spent two weeks living rough in London. She'd lost her virginity in a hostel much like this one. Desperate for a place to sleep she had ended up on a filthy mattress with a boy she hardly knew.

'He's not there,' she said resolutely. 'Shall we go?'

Carlo tried the door handle and the door opened. Hesitating, she let herself be ushered into the room when a sudden panic set in. 'I don't feel comfortable barging in to his place. Doesn't he have a mobile? Can't you just call him?'

'He doesn't have a phone, but he told me he'd be back about now.' Carlo seemed to sense the deeper meaning of her discomfort and put a reassuring hand on her arm. 'I meant it when I told your brother that you are perfectly safe with me.'

She relaxed a little and looked around the room. The place was squalid and stuffy, but it seemed as if the occupant had lived there for some time. The walls had several pictures of terracotta pots and market scenes. Colourful throws covered the single bed, and under it, a piss pot and a very short row of shoes: leather sandals and one pair of yellow Nike trainers. A rickety picnic table was covered with food stuff in plastic bags and cartons.

'Is it okay for us to be here?'

'He wouldn't have us waiting in the corridor,' Carlo said, looking at his watch. 'Let's give him a few minutes.'

She stood awkwardly, looking about the room. It was tidy enough, and the Moroccan decor showed that the occupant had a bit of flair, but the smells and squalor of the building itself pulled at her, as though in a place like this you were hidden within a void, or space warp, removed from yourself even, and anything was possible. Sometimes she had enjoyed the things she'd done in rooms like these. It was afterwards, facing daylight, that the distaste and shame began to seep back into her and the truth of her degradation stared her in the face.

'Don't look so worried,' Carlo said, sitting down on the bed. He patted the bed cover, motioning her to sit. Reading her expression he said, 'Look, I've promised Mohammed that every time I take someone on a private tour of the tunnels, I'll let him come along. He's a good lad, a natural linguist. I'm training him up to be a tour guide, especially with his French. It's the one language we don't cover. You don't mind him coming, do you?'

79

'No, of course not.' She sat down, still feeling like a trespasser.

After a moment of awkward silence, she cast about for something to talk about.

'Hey…we never got to Mrs. Cohen. Remember, in the cathedral you said you'd tell me about her *demise*.'

'Did I?'

'Yeah, you did,' she lied.

'What would you like to know?

She screwed her face up in thought. 'Well, you found her body, right?'

He stood up and walked over to the table with the food stuff. He picked up an apple and scrutinised its surface. After a long pause, he spoke to the wall. 'Apart from the police I've not talked about this to anybody, and I probably shouldn't now.' His face grew older as he seemed overcome by painful recollections. 'I can safely say it was the worst moment of my life.'

'Oh, God,' she groaned, seeing his pain but glad to find a potential talking point. 'Please, tell me about it. See it as therapy.'

He faced her with a wry smile. 'What a ghoulish young woman you are.'

'How long had she been lying there?'

'She'd been dead a couple of weeks.'

'God! The body must have been in some state.' She was riveted.

'Let's just put it this way…it was at the height of summer, late July.'

She gasped and put her hand over her mouth. Maggots writhed in her mind, but she'd asked for it. 'It must've been terrible, the smell and all. What room was she in?'

He shook his head. 'In her bedroom.'

'I thought so. Bloody hell!'

Her fascination made him laugh. He came back and sat beside her. 'I shouldn't really tell you, but I know what would impress you.'

'What?'

'But it must stay between you and me? You have to swear to keep it to yourself.'

'Of course. I swear.'

He patted her hand, as if to warn her of what was coming. 'Her death wasn't an accident.'

She gasped. 'You mean she was murdered?'

'No.' His brow knitted and again he looked pained. 'The choking story was the official version. In Gibraltar we have a code, a respect for the dignity of our people that you outsiders probably don't understand... Mrs. Cohen did not choke to death. She sat down to her last meal and then hung herself from the central beam in her bedroom.'

She stared at him in horror. 'Hung herself?' She shook her head. 'No way! How could she possibly have managed that?'

'There is a large hook there which, as it happened, I'd put there myself. She wanted to suspend a really heavy canopy over her bed, some antique thing that had belonged to her mother.' He paused. 'She pushed the bed aside, got a stepladder and unhooked the canopy somehow.'

Distressed by the memory, he put his face in his hands for a moment. 'I should have suspected something was wrong when I saw the canopy slung over a trestle on the terrace, day after day, getting bleached by the sun. She was so fussy about her antiques. Afterwards I wondered if she'd put it out there for me to realise...'

'Oh Christ!' Mimi blurted, instinctively putting her arm around his hunched shoulders. 'That's how you found her?'

'Actually, it was worse. She'd fallen down by the time I got to her. She was a big woman and,' he closed his eyes as though the image were still in front of him, 'it was the sound of her falling that finally alerted me to the fact that something was amiss. I was in my own bedroom at the time and I literally felt the bulk of her hitting the floor above me.'

'How awful!' Mimi knew her eyes were like saucers, but she couldn't help herself. 'How did her body come away from—'

'*Please*,' he interrupted sharply. 'Don't make me explain it.'

They were quiet for a moment.

'Yes, she was a very unhappy person.' Carlo said finally. He bowed his head and murmured, as if to himself, 'She couldn't believe what she'd done.'

'What do you mean? What had she done?'

He shook his head. 'Look, I've told you far too much already.'

She knew she shouldn't press him further, but ignored it. 'You can trust me.'

Carlo sighed deeply and crossed himself. 'Okay, but remember your promise…'

'Yes, yes,' she said impatiently.

'Three months before she died, Mrs. Cohen won 230,000 euros in the Spanish National Lottery.'

'No! She *did*?'

'I was the only person she told about it.'

'Really?' She studied his face for signs of deception or trickery. It was almost too fantastic a story. But why should she doubt him? People won lotteries every day. She'd watched a documentary on them and how ninety per cent of winners end up unhappier than before, some even committing suicide. 'Why was it only you that she told?'

'We were friends, of sorts. The two of us were the only tenants in the building for nearly eighteen years; fourteen since her husband died. All her relatives had either died or left Gib and she didn't trust people on the whole. She was a devout Jew, though she rarely mixed with her own kind. She hated the way the Jewish community here was becoming divided and radicalised by ultra-orthodox elements imported from the UK. In her Jewishness she was a staunch Gibraltarian…a true Yanito. Like me.'

'Go on,' she urged when he seemed to get lost in thought.

'She wanted to tell someone about her good fortune, so she told the only trustworthy kindred spirit she had.'

'So why should the win make her want to do away with herself? I don't understand.'

'It all went, that's why. Every last penny.'

'On what?' She waited for him to continue, but he was studying his watch, clearly wanting to end the topic of Mrs. Cohen. 'Ok, so let *me* tell *you*,' she insisted. 'You know the guy who owns our apartment, her nephew in America? She gave it to him.'

Carlo shook his head. 'Oh, no. He knew nothing about the lottery win. I kept telling her she should save it for the day she might need care, but she said she was going to spend it, specifically so it didn't end up in *his* pocket. She was quite bitter about him. He never kept in touch and she always said he was too rich for his own good.'

'So how *did* she spend it?'

Carlo just shrugged. She was sure he knew all about it but was feeling uncomfortable with having told so much already. She'd have to use her feminine guile to get it out of him.

'All right then…let me guess… What about some charity?'

Carlo shook his head in a meaningful way. Mrs. Cohen was tight, obviously.

'Clothes, shoes, designer handbags?'

'No, nothing like that.'

'Was she an alcoholic?'

'Absolutely not. She hardly touched a drop. Stop now, Imogen.'

'I bet she blew the lot in the casino. Gambling can lay waste to a fortune in an evening.'

Carlo kept shaking his head, but without conviction.

'I'm right. Aren't I?' she said excitedly.

He rolled his eyes and laughed softly. 'You sharp little woman.'

'Go on!' she urged, pulling at his sleeve. 'Tell me all.'

He stroked his silver crucifix between thumb and forefinger. 'Mrs. Cohen was devout and proper in almost every sense, but she had a secret vice – or more appropriately – an addiction. That's why her apartment was so shabby. Her pension was poured straight onto the blackjack and roulette tables. And she always bought lottery tickets by the bundle. The winnings…it took no more than a couple of months to get rid of them.'

'Did she actually tell you about losing the money?'

'Not at first, but this is a small place and I have my sources. She was a very private person, but eventually she had to confess to me that she'd lost the whole lot.'

'How totally sad,' Mimi said with feeling.

'She was obliged to tell me she was broke. She didn't even have enough for a pint of milk.'

'Oh, Christ. Was that the reason she…?'

'Without doubt,' he said quietly. 'Besides, she'd been diagnosed with early signs of dementia. She was fully aware of what that meant. I kept on at her that the lottery money would pay for a luxury care home, but she was adamant she would never enter any kind of institution.'

'I don't blame her,' Mimi concurred. Sadness overcame her when she remembered how dementia had destroyed Dad. That proud fierce man reduced to terror of being dumped into a care home. Thank God he died first.

'Why did no-one go in and clean up after her Last Supper? Couldn't *you* have done it if you were her only friend?'

'I most certainly would have, but no-one was allowed in. The apartment was sealed up pending the presence or permission of her next of kin. With no suspicion of foul play, there was no real need to investigate, and as I was not family I had no authority to enter.'

They fell silent again. Mimi reflected on Mrs. Cohen's story. It had some kind of sad glamour about it, the idea of a last fling in the casino, the last supper, and the final courageous act. It was brave, violent but also an act of ultimate self-preservation.

She looked over at Carlo who had his mobile out, reading some message. He had held her attention for sure. Winning the lottery was everybody's fantasy. Something a silly teenager with writing ambitions would find riveting.

'I hope this wasn't fiction, Carlo,' she said, peering at him. 'That would be really out of order.'

He frowned at her. 'Honestly Imogen. You must know me better than that.'

He'd said he kept the story confidential out of respect, and perhaps this was true, but she was starting to suspect he had no-one else to confide in. For all his greeting acquaintances in the street, he seemed a total loner. She was an outsider, a *guiri*, and perhaps that made it easier. The other reason that occurred to her – a more sinister reason – was that he wanted to freak her out, or test her in some way.

Living with a suicide could give a kid nightmares. Perhaps he hoped she would go home and blurt the story, and all three of them would pack their bags. No, she did not think this of him. If she was any judge of character, he was just desperate for a confidante, no matter how ill-matched.

Her thoughts were interrupted by the door opening. A short, dark man stood in the doorway, clad in a Moroccan cape. He pushed back the pointy hood that covered his head. He was young, almost as young as she was, and had a downcast expression. He started in surprise at seeing Carlo and Mimi sitting on his bed, then looked mortified as if he'd walked straight into a seduction scene.

'Mohammed,' Carlo said, getting up. 'I want you to meet a friend of mine.'

She stood up and went to shake his hand. 'Hi, I'm Mimi. Sorry we barged in like this.' He mumbled something in return.

'The tunnels, Mohammed,' said Carlo. 'Today is a good day for me. I want to show the pair of you something really interesting.'

Mohammed seemed to shrink further. 'I can't, Mr. Montegriffo. I must work.'

Carlo looked skywards in obvious irritation. 'You're in training with me, remember?'

'I'm cleaning the mosque. It's a proper job, Mr. Montegriffo. Please.'

'You don't want to end up cleaning the mosque when you could be a certified tourist guide. Think of your future.'

'I need an income, Mr. Montegriffo. My rent...'

Mimi shrunk in commiseration with the lad. Besides it didn't seem right to be party to this exchange.

'Well, I can't go,' she said firmly. 'It's too late now. I've got to go home.'

'Imogen, don't *you* pull out as well,' Carlo said with a sigh.

'Can we do it another day?' she suggested. 'Perhaps tomorrow, or when Mohammed has time off his job.' The boy raised his eyes to look back at her in surprise and a little gratitude. He was actually very handsome, with smooth dark skin and fine features.

'Yes, please, Mr. Montegriffo,' he said. 'Any morning, or at the weekend.'

Carlo shook his head resignedly. 'I'm trying to up the stakes for you. You wouldn't stand a chance without my support. Don't blow it, Mohammed.'

'Absolutely not, sir.' Mohammed sounded cringe-makingly servile, but there was a flare in his eye that said something different.

'So don't go looking for moonlighting jobs without my permission.'

Mimi winced, but to interfere in any way would make it worse. She'd already noticed that Carlo had that other side to him, an ultra-conservative attitude bordering on bigotry.

The young man was still standing in the doorway, looking unwelcome in his own home.

'See you guys another day then?' she said and he stepped aside to let her pass.

'Wait, Imogen. Let me walk you home,' she heard Carlo call as she strode purposefully down the stairs.

Once in the throng of Irish Town, she turned to look and was disappointed. Carlo was nowhere to be seen.

*

Good morning Imogen. I am sorry about the botched tunnel tour. Let me know if you want to pursue it, or any other aspect of Gibraltar. Also, I look forward to hearing your thoughts on my poetry. I am happy to read some of your work if you're interested. Have a good day. Carlo.

She re-read the message and kicked off her bed clothes. He'd not given up on her, after all. She felt flattered but felt it best to take a little distance. Anyway, Sebastian clearly didn't approve of the friendship. She texted Carlo back and asked him to let her know if he was taking any other group on a tour.

Later she put the synopsis of her novel and the first chapter in a brown unmarked envelope and tiptoed down to lean it against his door.

For the next few days she worked steadily on her novel. The writing was flowing well, but the more she wrote, the more personal it became. The apartment felt like a tomb. Sebastian was out at the site all the time and Eva did not disturb her. Mrs. Cohen's ghost seemed the only other real occupant. Mimi felt no disquiet or unease about it. She sensed a kind of benign guardian, black-clad, stout and elderly yet featherlight and hovering near the ceiling. The subtle presence was strangely comforting, especially when writing about 'the mother figure' which never proved to be any kind of therapeutic purging. On the contrary, it just brought up one hurtful memory after another.

'Get dressed, sweetie,' said Marcus, laying out her green flower dress, her pink leggings and the ballet slippers she refused to go anywhere without. 'You're invited to McDonald's.'

'I thought we were having my party here,' said Christiana.

'We are, later. Your mum and her husband are coming to take you for lunch.'

'Will you come too?'

'No, just you.'

'I don't want to,' she said. 'Why do I have to?'

Dad tapped on her bedroom door before hobbling in. He was still in his pyjamas and had his slippers on the wrong feet. He looked ever so old, at least a hundred.

'Marcus, take Christiana down to her car,' he said. 'I don't want to see the woman.'

'I don't want to see her either,' said Christiana. 'I'm not going!' She started crying and threw the green flower dress on the floor.

Dad grabbed his hair. It was too long and greasy. 'Please child, just do it for me.' He turned to Marcus. 'Make the child stop bellyaching. I can't cope.'

'I'm not going,' she cried again and kicked off the ballet slippers. 'I'm scared of her.'

Marcus took her by the arms and looked her in the eye. 'Christiana. Your mother sees you only once a year. Maybe she'll give you a nice present. Please put the dress on.'

'I hate her. I don't want to be eight.' Her tummy had begun to hurt. She wasn't lying. She was scared of the woman they called Mother. Mothers were soft and cuddly and laughing, like Helen's mum and Rosie's and Neil's. Mother was tall and skinny and made her feel like a...slug, slimy and pukey. She just didn't like kids. Her husband was nice sometimes, but he had his own kids and preferred them.

The doorbell rang and Marcus ran down to get ahead of Dad. He was embarrassed about Dad's slippers, and not shaving and not changing his pyjamas. Dad always opened the door like that, and he shouted at the postman. Christiana pulled the dress over her head, not caring if it was the right way around. They were a crazy back-to-front family. All the kids in school said so, but nobody knew she had a mum who

pinched her leg and left a mark like a purple pen stain, or
pulled her hair really hard, or scrubbed her skin off with a
washpad meant for pots. Marcus said it was against the law to
hurt children, so she should really be in jail.

To break with the utter silence of the apartment and the
gloomy topic of child abuse, she put away her iPad, grabbed
some supplies and walked to the Rock Hotel. As a former
guest she'd ascertained that the pool terrace was easy to access,
separated from the hotel by Europa Road and surrounded by
the lush botanical gardens. When asked, she nonchalantly
gave her old hotel room number to the pool attendant who
took it for granted that she was a guest.

Sprawled on a lounger, fully clothed, she observed the
holidaymakers. They were mainly middle-aged couples,
come here to see the sights, the apes, to shop and wallow
in the historic atmosphere of the grand old hotel. There
were a few kids having fun in the giant pool. Everybody
seemed so deliriously happy, as if they'd never had a dark
day in their lives. She wished momentarily she was the
sort of girl who could jump in the water and shriek and
splash around. But her gelled hair made that idea
impossible: with her white skinny body, rings in her navel
and a skull tattoo on her hip, she felt utterly alien in that
sunny, happy world.

She played with her mobile for a while and wondered
who she could text. It dawned on her that she had no
friends left. Brittany had become all posh and distant when
she scored a Cambridge student, Andrea had slipped her
black leather skirt into her own holdall while she was
ostensibly helping Mimi to pack: that had been a nasty
surprise (what else had she nicked?) Russell had disappeared
from her radar – crack, she suspected – he could be dead

for all she knew, and Bea had changed beyond recognition since she'd had the baby, totally shunning her old mates. Anyway, they were scarcely diehard friends, all lived far away and none of them had called or texted to ask how she was getting on.

One by one she deleted them from her contact list, severing the ties to her old life.

What the fuck, let's go all the way, she thought bitterly. Before deleting Jane, she texted her a message. *Mother. Rejoice, because I won't inconvenience or embarrass you ever again. Your utterly unlovable waste-of-human-tissue daughter is out of your life. I'm never coming back to England. Good bye.* She pressed 'send' and the uncompromising message swooshed out into the ether.

Contact deleted!

She lay back again, the pool towel rolled up behind her head. The message was sent, too late to take it back. Written by a fucking ten-year-old. She could just see Jane roll her eyes in self-righteous disapproval, just what she would have expected from this errant daughter. But a mother was supposed to love her child no matter what, wasn't she?

The tears won over, misting up her sunglasses. *Shit! Get over it and grow up, you moron!*

She sat up and looked at her mobile. There weren't many numbers in her contact list left to choose from: Sebastian, Eva and Carlo Montegriffo.

She punched out another message: *I'd love a tour. I'll pay with a drink.*

*

Coming home from the pool, she found Eva sitting at the kitchen table sorting through a mountain of stuff.

'I'm trying to empty the last of our boxes,' Eva said and pushed a cardboard box towards her, marked:

MIMI
Private – Sacred – Keep Out

Mimi sat down opposite, ripped off the packing tape and flipped the lids apart. Inside were hundreds of handwritten pages, notes and passages she'd scribbled over the past couple of years for her novel. She'd been so miserable and mixed up, perhaps she shouldn't even read them. Better to go on with a new perspective.

'Is that your manuscript?' asked Eva, looking at the pile of papers.

'Bits of it,' said Mimi, casually sliding the pile towards herself.

'You're lucky to have a talent like that.'

'Who says I have?' she snorted. 'Everyone's supposed to have a story to tell. Telling it is a question of discipline and determination, not talent.'

Eva's mouth smiled but her eyes looked pained.

'What's *your* story?' Mimi asked on impulse.

'A passion for diving,' Eva said quickly. 'Back home I was a paramedic.'

'Right,' Mimi said, gazing at her. 'That's a short story.'

Fabrication, she thought. Stuff in the closet...that's what Sebastian had said. She felt a smidgen of sympathy, and wondered what the attraction of this whole setup was for Eva. She was obviously crazy about Sebastian, but did she understand who she was dealing with? He was not a guy who got close to people. His work was everything. Conversely, for him, Eva must be a great piece of arm candy. He'd have to watch out; she could afford to be choosy. It was just Mimi's luck to have this gorgeous specimen of womanhood witnessing her own pale and spotty face across the breakfast table. There should be a fucking law against it. It wasn't fair.

She rifled through the stack of notes, looking for something worthwhile. Restlessness overcame her, and she gathered them up and dumped them back in the box. 'I think I'll have a shower.'

Eva looked at her in surprise. 'Go for it! There's enough hot water in that tank to float an ocean liner.'

'I know. It's been boiling for near enough a year.'

'A year? What do you mean?'

'Yeah well...ever since the former occupant hung herself.'

She had turned towards the door, but she felt the startled silence against her back, then her own rush of regret. Shit! How had that happened? She'd just merrily told Eva the truth about Mrs. Cohen, breaking both her promise to Carlo and to Sebastian.

'I'm sorry,' she mumbled and rushed from the kitchen with her box.

Eva

An hour after a remorseful Mimi had slunk out of the apartment, Eva was out on the terrace with a carpet beater, taking out a multitude of feelings and frustrations on the heavy velvet curtains from the living room. She'd hung her victims on a trestle which seemed put there for the purpose, and the beating created the most satisfying clouds of dust.

The nerve of it…to think Sebastian and Mimi had had a conversation between them to consider how best to keep her in the dark. What had made Sebastian think she should be protected from the truth? True, a woman dangling by the neck from a hook in the ceiling right above the bed in which she and Sebastian made love, and slept and drank coffee and ate toast in… was gruesome in the extreme, but she didn't like being treated like an emotional cripple.

The insistent ring of her mobile stopped her, arm aloft. She considered the distance to the hall, then remembered that Sebastian was going to call to let her know about his evening schedule. She threw down the carpet beater and ran to answer it.

'Butt out! I'm busy destroying curtains.' Her barbed joke was met with silence. 'Sebastian?' No response. 'Mimi. Is that you?' Stopping to listen, she could hear breathing at the other end. So why didn't whoever speak up? 'Yo… Sebastian? Bad network, this. Try me again.' She gave it another few seconds, listening to the steady breathing. 'I'm hanging up now.'

She rang off and checked 'received calls'. Number withheld.

Three minutes went by. Three minutes was a long time when you were waiting. But the phone remained silent. Number withheld! Perhaps it was just a random nuisance caller, but she had a nagging feeling about the call. There could only be one person in Gibraltar wanting to spook her. Hadn't Mr. Montegriffo hinted at reasons for wanting to remain alone in the building; all that noise they might make, laughing, singing, making love, listening to music and then putting garbage in the wrong place? But he was interested in Mimi, and why would Mimi have given him Eva's number when she had her own mobile phone? Maybe it was Mimi herself, but would she really stoop to such nonsense? Perhaps she'd been phoning to apologise but then lost her nerve.

Eva went back to the terrace and picked up the carpet beater. All her strength went into the flogging and she continued even when a blister began to form on her palm. She'd been so cool for so long – almost unflappable – but the silent phone call had torn a little opening in her defences. Some part of her was always waiting for the call, but she was not going to let the waiting back into her consciousness. She was not going to let it nibble away at the edges of her happiness. She'd severed all ties and she'd started afresh. Perhaps it was her relocation from Dubai to Europe that had inadvertently opened a little window of fear, or perhaps it was the phone call to Linda. If she'd had a choice, she wouldn't live within such restricted borders. *Nowhere to run, nowhere to hide.*

Not again! Don't think it. Don't think it.

An angry ripping noise paused her attack on the curtain. When the dust dissipated she surveyed the long rent in the fabric. That wasn't too hard. One down, only seven to shred.

Sebastian

The taxi driver refused to take his pristine vehicle down the ramp into the works yard. He stood on the road and shouted down for his passenger to come up to the layby. Jorge Azzopardi, their head security man, took his new job seriously: he threw the driver a firm gesture of disapproval; that was no way to talk to the principal engineer.

'Thank you, Jorge, but really, I don't mind walking up,' Sebastian said and nodded appreciatively at the man. 'How are you settling in here?'

'It's a very stimulating appointment, Mr. Luna,' said Azzopardi, 'and a privilege.'

'Call me Sebastian, won't you?'

He marched up the ramp and climbed into the back of the taxi.

'Upper Town, please.'

As they roared off towards the entrance of Dudley Ward tunnel, he craned his neck to look down onto the site. It was a stroke of luck to have secured a large depot in such a strategic place, having formerly been the works yard for the tunnel during the decade it was being restored. The site almost hung over the sea and had great accessibility, via the ramp, directly from the main road. A tower crane had just arrived to allow materials to be lowered onto a hundred-and-fifty square metre barge that had been assembled in Malaga docks and towed to Gib as a secondary floating yard. Materials and equipment were beginning to arrive from various sources around Europe, and so far, everything was going to plan. No other unforeseen problems had arisen and the Gibraltar authorities seemed very enthusiastic about the development. Various international engineering journals had sent people over, and articles about the project and its creator had begun to appear. Several large developers were contacting Sebastian directly with enquiries. At this rate, it wouldn't take long before he could pick and choose his projects, and SeaChange could go to hell.

Whenever he had a quiet moment, for example during journeys home, his mind soon focused down on the ultimate structure, Luna's Crossing. In fact, if its combination of materials and its assembly worked in the way he anticipated, bridges such as his could span mountains around the world and allow a different way of travel.

Slow down, son. Dad's voice was loud and clear. *Who do you think you are?*

'I'll show *you* who I am, Dad. I'm the creator of a new world.'

'Did you say something?' asked the taxi driver, peering at him through the rear-view mirror.

'Just thinking aloud,' Sebastian murmured, biting hard on his lip.

He put his key into the lock then stepped back to look at the door. Something was different about it. It appeared freshly vandalised. In the middle was a small square patch of rough wood as if something had been prised away. Of course, it was the name-plate. Perhaps Eva, or indeed Mr. Stagnetto, had realised the indelicacy of a dead woman's name on the door. Still, it had been badly done...perhaps Eva had planned to strip the whole door and paint it. She was going mad with her paintbrush. He'd have to watch out, or he'd wake up one morning painted white along with everything else.

He stepped into the hallway. It too had been transformed, the former sombreness swept away as though washed clean by a tornado of pure bleach. The cherubs in the ceiling looked down at him, smiling beatifically. A bouquet of snow-white lilies looked glacial against the indigo tiles. The walls were alive with glittering dots from a chandelier made out of hundreds of tiny mirrors. He had no idea that Eva had such flair. But then, how would he? During the months they'd known each other, she'd lived out of a suitcase.

He put his briefcase on a chair and went into the kitchen. Eva could not have heard him come in. She was sitting in her armchair, her hands covering her face. Gently, so as not to startle her, he put his hand on her shoulder. She flinched and looked up. Her face was blotchy and her nose red. She'd been crying, he was sure of it. He'd never seen her cry and he had no idea what to do with a crying woman. In all her distress and vulnerability, she looked angry.

'You told me the owner of this apartment died in hospital,' she said quietly. 'But the truth is she committed suicide in our bedroom.'

He frowned. 'Suicide?'

'Yes, she hung herself. Hung rotting for weeks from a hook in our bedroom. Just what I needed to add to my nightmares.'

'What nightmares, Eva darling?'

She flinched. 'I am talking about what you and your macabre sister have been hiding from me.'

He fell to his knees and put his arms around her. 'I think you've got this wrong. What happened was, the old lady choked on her dinner. At least that's what the Stagnetto fellow had us believe. Why the hell should we upset you unnecessarily with that kind of information? Let's face it, people die…an old place like this has no doubt seen many a death. I mean think of…'

She turned to look him in the eye. 'Didn't you notice that stain on the floorboards near our bed…*her* bed! She'd obviously been dripping rivers of body fluids in the summer heat. I couldn't get rid of the mark no matter how hard I scrubbed and bleached. That's why I painted the floor, I just had a bad feeling about it.' She blew her nose on a strip of household paper. 'I knew there was something sinister about this place. Why didn't I just listen to my instincts?'

So Mimi had let the cat out of the bag, and added a chilling twist of her own. A suicide! She'd promised to keep quiet about Mrs. Cohen's untimely death, but Mimi had her hidden agendas. She had every reason to be jealous and resent her new rival.

'We can move somewhere else if you want,' he said gently, hugging her resisting body as close as she would allow. A sudden alarming thought crossed his mind: the moment she no longer liked this situation, she could just pack up and go. There was nothing to stop her. 'I know you've done a huge job here, but if you don't like it, I'll capitulate and we'll rent an apartment in Ocean Village. Hang the hassle and the cost, we'll just do it. We can get a removals firm to pack us up and move us in a couple of hours.'

Her eyes softened a little. 'Oh, come on. That's plain ridiculous. I'm not that pathetic. But I'm moving bedroom, I'm telling you. Your twisted sister can live with Mrs. Cohen's dangling ghost.'

Maybe that was the reason his twisted sister had leaked the secret: she wanted the room with the ghost. She'd always had a ghoulish streak.

He took her hand and kissed it repeatedly. 'Are you sure?'

'To be totally frank, I don't like Gibraltar.' She said it quickly, forcefully and her eyes shifted away from him. 'As soon as you can possibly finish here, I'd like to be away.'

He was taken aback. So it wasn't just the apartment: it was the whole territory. She'd been so excited about going to live in Europe and she'd been in Gib not much more than a month. She hardly even knew the place.

He studied her for a moment. He couldn't claim to understand women, nor had he ever really tried, yet he had the definite feeling that her distress was a coverup for something else. He hoped with all his heart it wasn't Mimi driving her away. If ever he was faced with a choice, he would have to choose his sister, no matter how passionate his feelings for Eva. He could never abandon Mimi again.

'You know...my love, you should get out and do more diving. You've got an amazing skill and a huge amount of experience. You owe it to Gibraltar. This place ought to be your oyster, really.' Eva's eyes were still averted and she didn't answer. 'What's wrong, my love? What's this about?'

She turned to him with a tired smile. 'You're right. I'm at a loose end here. Of course I should be diving. I need a job, but there's the hassle of getting a work permit. It's an impossible process, and by the time I managed to get one we'd probably be ready to leave.'

He took her chin in his hand and looked into her eyes. 'You know the solution to that, don't you? All you have to do is marry me and you'd be British.'

She sighed. 'Come on! Surely you don't want me to marry you just so I can get a job? That's not good enough a reason and besides, it's illegal. You're the one who's usually such a stickler for correctness.'

She was right, of course, but her words stung. From beneath the love that he felt for her rose that nebulous mist of misgivings. He still could not understand her refusal to marry him, but after the humiliating fiasco at the embassy in Dubai she'd at least pledged to give their love a chance and be, at his insistence, his 'fiancée'. They'd agreed that the move to Gib should be a thick black line across that incident. They could start afresh, in a place new to both. He'd told her there was no need to explain her motives or give account of what had led to them. He'd made these concessions partly in an attempt to hold on to her, but also to justify his own history, his own silence. Even so, he could not deny the feeling that she was not who she said she was, or what she said she was. She'd risen out of the sea, but from where? And why?

Eva

The place was situated between two waterfront restaurants in Ocean Village Marina, behind an opulent casino. It was surrounded by swish apartments and boardwalks with the water lapping under one's feet, yet right next door was the airport runway extending far out into the sea. Despite the occasional roaring of jet engines, it seemed a very pleasant environment from which to conduct business – and from her point of view – was only a ten-minute downhill walk from the apartment.

There was a man behind a rack of wetsuits, on his knees talking affectionately to someone. She peeked over the rack and stood watching him for a moment, smiling at the sight of a grown man making baby noises to the world's ugliest dog. He sensed her presence and stood up, clearly not at all embarrassed. 'He's sixteen,' he said. 'Painful hips.'

'I'm Eva Eriksson. Jonny Risso told me about you. You sometimes charter his boat to do offshore dives.'

'Oh, yes. Jonny Risso. Always has some insult to throw at me.' He reached out to shake her hand. 'And I don't mean you, of course. Brian Lockmarsh.'

She found her hand encased in a warm grip. Brian Lockmarsh was a stocky but handsome man in his late forties with the flushed and freckled complexion that comes from a life spent in windy, sunny, salty conditions. His face was open, topped by a thick pom-pom of brown hair and eyes of a disconcerting blue. Brian noted her glance around his premises.

'People who like my dog get a discount,' he said. 'What can I offer you?'

'A job,' she said simply. 'I'm a PADI qualified open-water scuba instructor and paramedic. I've taught diving for several years, most recently in Dubai.' She reached into her briefcase and pulled out a plastic folder containing all her certificates and a few letters of reference. 'I'm good,' she added.

Brian laughed, but took the folder from her hand. 'I wasn't really looking for anyone.'

'The best things happen when you're not even looking. And you know what? I come free.'

He regarded her with a mixture of appreciation and incredulity. Perhaps he thought she was a madwoman, or else he wasn't used to that sort of directness.

'If I hadn't guessed from your accent, now I *know* you're American!' he said as if it explained everything. 'Though you look Scandinavian, I dare say.'

'Right on both counts, born in California but both my parents have Scandinavian roots,' she replied. 'I can't be bothered with a work permit, and I live on my savings, so just to keep my skills up, I'll work for nothing. If you'll have me.'

'Hold it now, slow down a little,' Brian said, rubbing his chin.

He invited her into his tiny office. It was the only place with chairs. After sitting her down, he leafed through the contents of her folder. 'Impressive!' he said after a moment. 'Actually, I could use a hand occasionally and there is no reason why you shouldn't pocket the gratuities. That's often sizeable sums, as the divers here tend to come off the yachts. We don't get a lot of beginners. It's more a case of guiding experienced divers around the sights. Have you dived around Gibraltar at all?'

'Yes, I dive with my partner quite frequently, but only on the east side. That's why we need Jonny and his boat.'

He raised an eyebrow. 'Not much of interest on the east side, I dare say.'

She shrugged. 'It's got to do with an engineering project Sebastian is involved with. That's our excuse anyway.'

'Engineering project?' Brian looked interested. 'Under water?'

'Yes…that's right.'

'I don't suppose it's to do with the land reclamation project, what are they calling it…? The Frontiers Development Project.'

She sighed imperceptibly. 'That's the one.' She'd read the Gibraltar papers and couldn't fail to notice how polarised opinions were. Brian's attitude would probably settle her job application one way or another.

'Well, I'll be damned,' he said. 'I was so impressed with that thing, I even went to the planning offices to look at the blueprints. Everyone says that's what we need here in Gib – groundbreaking ideas and money to back them – but I can't help wondering about the ecological damage and the destruction of the natural beauty of the cliffs.'

She nodded unhappily. At least here was a guy who looked at both sides of the coin, and was honest to her face with no obvious bias. 'Sebastian is very excited about the project, but it's not him who's forced it on Gibraltar. He was simply hired by the developers.'

'No need to justify his work. We all do what we have to do. I'm not lily white by any means. I don't actually know anyone who is.' He smiled reassuringly and she relaxed and smiled back.

'Well, Eva Eriksson. All these bits of paper look good, but you'll have to show me what you're made of. I'm free tomorrow morning. Why don't I take you into Camp Bay and show you the treasures on our sea bed? Nine o'clock?'

She jumped up, trying not to look too excited. She wanted to throw her arms around Brian Lockmarsh, but instead she shook his hand. 'You won't be disappointed.'

The feeling of pleasure and achievement had had time to subside by the time she got home. Since the silent phone call, her world had shifted slightly on its axis. The ground she walked on had become unstable, tiny noises made her jump. The sun here had been so warm: now it seemed harsh and penetrating, exposing her. She didn't want to even think it, but couldn't help but wonder if the call had anything to do with renewing her contact with Linda. No, no...surely not. Linda was her best friend, as loyal and dependable as any person she'd met in her whole life.

Once inside the apartment, she stood at the bedroom door and looked in. This was not just a room. A person had been hanging there, flies laying eggs in bodily crevices, in the corner of the eyes, in nostrils and earholes, under nails. The sun rising, lighting up the room, the sun setting and many hours of darkness. Mail gathering on the floor by the door as the days and weeks passed, while a woman's body hung from a rope, dissolving into a corpse, then a rotted carcass.

She'd seen a film of a dead rabbit once, at some art exhibition. It just hung on a hook, its putrefaction speeded up so that the flesh was decaying before the spectator's eyes. She'd stood there watching the film several times over, as if there were some mystery to be solved or that she would discover something about death that she'd not understood. But all it revealed was how precarious her own existence was. Death by violence seemed a close possibility. Adrian had injured her seriously more than once, but what was the point of being scared? Death would hit her in one form or another. She'd come away from the gallery feeling oddly liberated. That was when the seed began to grow. She could defy the future Adrian had in mind for her: take destiny in her own hands and escape.

Eva looked at the spot on the floor where the stain had been. She could move into the middle bedroom, it was big enough to accommodate the population of a small village but it had only a tiny window facing the courtyard, or perhaps she could convert the living room into a bedroom. They all lived in the kitchen, after all. Or just take Sebastian up on his offer to move to Ocean Village. It was light and airy and new, and it would be next to Brian Lockmarsh's shop.

She stepped in and opened the wardrobe. Lying flat on the bottom shelf was her sorry excuse for a suitcase. She had bought it in Marseilles, a charity shop bargain at four euros. So many times had she thrown her belongings into it that – especially at the beginning – the act had acquired a comical quality. Just like in movies, the heroine decides she's had enough, she's going to leave him. She is either mad with rage or frightened half to death. Clothes are pulled from hangers and flung willy-nilly into a suitcase. He rushes in and begs her not to go, or he pads in to stop her escape. More often than not, she's prevented from going, ending up in his arms, or on the floor, a corpse.

She decided to move into Mimi's room. It was smaller than the other two, but furthest away from the place of the tragedy. The apartment was quiet, the only sound her bare feet against the floorboards as she walked back and forth between rooms with her stuff. In the middle of her labours, her mobile rang and startled her.

Her hand hovered above the phone as it lay on Mrs. Cohen's bed. It rang ever more insistently and she picked it up.

'Hello,' she said quietly.

Because she'd just been thinking about him, she wondered if she'd conjured up the silent caller, stirred the aura of his anger. She listened to his breath, the slow measured inhalation and exhalation. It was not the sound of a prodded beast, but then again, this beast didn't always roar; preferring stealth and silence.

'If you've got something to say, just say it.'

Moments passed.

She rang off, and stood there looking at the phone. It rang again as if she had been willing it to do so. Number withheld!

'Leave me alone,' she shouted into it, her voice trembling, giving her fear away. 'I am dead and gone...do you hear me!'

Mimi

Mimi came in and closed the front door behind her. After the heat of the streets, she rejoiced in the cool, still air of the apartment. She heard Eva shout something in the bedroom. As she sneaked up to listen, Eva saw her and furtively dropped her mobile into her pocket.

They looked at each other and, despite the recent antagonism between them, Eva's stricken expression moved something in Mimi.

'Who was that?' Mimi asked.

'God knows. Wrong number.'

'Jeez, poor man!' Mimi said with a small laugh. 'Time of the month?'

'What made you think it was a man?'

Conjecture, Mimi thought, or *hypothesis*. No, *certitude*.

Eva was throwing clothes into a suitcase.

'Why are you packing? You're not moving out, are you?'

'No such luck. You and I are trading rooms.' Then she hesitated and turned to look at her. 'You know, your new friend...Montegriffo.'

Here we go, thought Mimi. 'Yeah, what about him?'

'Have you given him my phone number?'

'Why would I do that?'

'He might have wanted to be able to call us for some reason. Like to give us hell about the garbage or music or something.'

'Well, I haven't. He'd knock on the door if there was a problem, wouldn't he?'

Eva shrugged.

Mimi went to the kitchen to make herself a sandwich, then she sat down at the kitchen table to eat it. Every few minutes she saw Eva pass by in the corridor, carrying her and Sebastian's possessions from the master bedroom to the room at the end of the hall, Mimi's room…Mimi's former room.

Mimi grimaced to herself. Telling Eva about Mrs. Cohen's death had been despicable, and she couldn't decide whether it had slipped out accidentally or on purpose. She was quite capable of that type of devious manoeuvre, so it made no difference if she'd done it consciously or not: it had worked. Sebastian had been mad at her, of course, but in the end he promised not to reveal to another soul the true nature of Mrs. Cohen's death.

She put down the half-eaten sandwich and watched Eva through the door, pulling a big cardboard box filled with Sebastian's folders along the floor through the hall.

'Let me help you.'

'Get out of my way,' Eva snapped. 'You got what you wanted.'

'Come on…I'll help you move the double bed. I feel bad, really I do.'

'You feel bad? Who d'you think you're kidding?'

'Honestly, I feel like a real shit.'

Eva let go of the box and stretched her back. 'You can keep Mrs. Cohen's bed, okay? It's all yours – you perverse little creep – stains and all.'

Mimi smiled wryly, glad to collect a proper insult. It was about time Eva stopped being so fucking nice to her.

'Come on, you two lovebirds can't sleep in single beds,' she insisted. 'Listen, I'll take the mattress out onto the terrace and scrub it with detergent. I'll rinse it out with boiling water and it can dry out in the sun. I'll buy you a thick new mattress cover too. Will that compensate for my fuckup?'

A faint smile pulled at the corner of Eva's mouth. 'Really, it's Sebastian I'm mad at. He should have known better than to lie to me, and embroil you in it.'

'Withholding the truth is not the same as lying,' Mimi said. 'Anyway, Sebastian himself never knew about the hanging. I just found that out through my own sources.'

Eva looked uncomfortable, as if she were familiar with the concept of withholding truths.

'What do you care if some old lady died here?' Mimi insisted. 'People die all the time.'

'Something to do with the grotesque way she went, I guess.'

Mimi studied her with a frown. Nah, that explanation didn't ring true at all. Eva looked angelic, but in fact she had to be a gutsy kind of woman, with her deep-sea diving, rescuing injured people and living alone in Dubai. Would she really be freaking out over some dead old lady? It was clearly a coverup for some other anguish. She'd looked edgy for quite a few days. Perhaps things weren't going so well with the fairytale romance and she was thinking of using Mrs. Cohen's dangling body as an excuse to get the hell out of there. Where would she go? Looking back, Eva had never said a word about her family or her past. She never phoned anyone…but recalling Eva's outburst earlier, it was possible that someone was calling *her*. 'Okay, Mimi. Make us a cup of coffee and then you can carry the rest of my stuff over to your old room.'

Mimi rushed to make the coffee and Eva fell back into an armchair she'd hauled from the living room to the kitchen and called her own.

'Your Royal Blondness,' said Mimi, handing Eva a mug of instant. She parked herself at the kitchen table, watching Eva quietly sipping her coffee. Her hair was braided into a French

plait, and her face looked older than when they'd first met…
that fleeting couple of meetings, engineered by Sebastian
during her holiday in Dubai. She wondered what Eva had
been doing when she was eighteen? Surely she'd been a
rebellious teenager, like everyone else.

'So…huh…tell me more about what you got up to, before
you became a Luna affiliate?'

Eva was startled out of her thoughts. 'Me? I was a
paramedic. I told you already.'

'But you must have got a family, like, parents.'

'Yeah, but I don't see them anymore.'

'That sounds weird. Are you hiding something?'

'I wish,' Eva said with a tired laugh. 'I'm not that
interesting.'

'Perhaps you're a terrorist, on the run from the CIA…and
someone is on your tail.' Mimi observed a twitch, ever so
small, at the corner of Eva's eye. 'Did you kill someone?'

'I wish I could have,' Eva said pensively, 'but no such luck.
I just don't really care for my past. Come on, slacker. You're
trying to distract me from the fact that we've got a job to do.'

Mimi shrugged and tossed down the dregs of her coffee.
She followed Eva to the hall. When they bent to pick up the
box between them, she noticed that Eva's hands were
trembling.

Mimi smiled knowingly. *Dissimulation.* Stuff in the closet.

Guilt and regret not withstanding, it didn't take her long to get
used to inhabiting the dead woman's private space. She had a
good snoop around to see if there was anything that the
lovebirds might have missed, but the massive freestanding
wardrobe was empty. The two chests had drawers lined in
newsprint dated 1949 and 1951, held down by historical
thumbtacks. There was nothing but two ancient postcards

addressed to Mr. & Mrs. Sol Cohen, one from Venice and the other from Tel Aviv.

It was surprisingly hard to get used to lying on the bed with that hook in her sightline. Eva was right, how could you avoid seeing Mrs. Cohen hanging there? It was during such a moment – staring at the hook to try and imagine Mrs. Cohen's thoughts and feelings at the definitive moment – that something flashed past the corner of her eye: the tip of a wooden object poking over the top of the wardrobe.

Jumping up, she ran to get the paint-spattered stepladder from the larder. She reached for and pulled down the item. A violin! The bow followed and hit her on the head. She got down and, sitting on the bed, held the instrument reverently in her hands. She turned it over and over. It was well used, very dusty, but in beautiful condition. Examining it carefully, she noted a word scratched on the back with a knife or a needle… *Socorro*. She put the violin on her bed and looked up the word on her Ipad. *Succour, help, relief.* Who would damage an exquisite instrument in that way? That dire call for help had to be Esther's.

So… Esther Cohen and Imogen Luna had more than one thing in common.

Dad had taught her to play, even bought her a baby violin. When Dad died and she had been forcibly shoved in with Jane and Gordon at their mansion, Jane complained that her playing sounded like two tomcats in a scrap and soon confiscated the little instrument. Mimi never saw it again. In any case, by then it had become too small, as well as being water damaged, and reminding her too much of Dad.

She cradled the violin in her arms and felt in it more of Esther Cohen's presence than any other artefact in the whole apartment, including the hook.

Eva

Eva looped her arm through Sebastian's. They were walking on top of the Line Wall that ran along the western side of town. She was stealthily leading him towards the leisure complex housed within the King's Bastion, a centuries old fortification that was set in the middle of the wall. It took some effort to get Sebastian away from his drawing board, and she'd not foreseen how intensely he would get wrapped up in this project. Of course, it followed that the beginning of a new job – and one as important as this one – would have him focusing all his energies on it.

Sebastian, oblivious to her intentions, was enthusing about the construction of the fortification and the brilliant engineering effort that had produced such a structure over two centuries ago. Right now, she couldn't give a damn about the engineering effort; she could really use an effort on his part to have some good, old-fashioned fun. A movie, followed by a few drinks in a nice bar, then dinner, a nightcap somewhere romantic and finally rolling around the (single) bed for hours, making love. Wasn't that what an evening out with one's boyfriend entailed?

'Sebastian,' she interrupted, 'I was going to tell you over a drink, but I can't wait. I did what you suggested. If I live up to expectations tomorrow morning, I might have a job at a diving centre.'

He stopped. 'Hey, sweetheart. Congratulations!'

'Not full time, or salaried or anything, but it's a start.'

In plain view of other pedestrians he grabbed her around

the waist and picked her up off her feet, swinging her around full circle. 'Behold this gorgeous mermaid,' he yelled. 'She's the best diver in the seas.'

'Put me down, Sebastian,' she pleaded, laughing. 'We'll get arrested.' He kissed her loudly full on the lips several times. 'Stop,' she yelled, laughing. 'Anyway, I have to prove myself first.'

He put his arm around her shoulder and they walked on. 'Oh, you'll prove yourself, all right! Now, what shall we do with this glorious evening…would you like me to take you on a tour of the fortresses and batteries along the west side of town and you can tell me about your job on the way?'

'No thank you.'

He glanced at her. 'What do you want to do?'

She rolled her eyes. 'I want to celebrate my appointment with a magnum of champagne, and there is a film I want to see.'

'A film,' he said in confusion. 'But it's sunny!'

'Yes, it tends to be that here. But films are still made and played in movie theatres across the continents, no matter the climate.'

He laughed. 'Is that a fact, smarty-pants?'

She knew he was too restless a man to sit still watching a film, but just once in a while she should be able to have things *her* way. She steered him firmly toward the King's Bastion, feeling the slight physical resistance, as if he were being cajoled into a trap.

After a moment of mooching along in silence, he asked, 'So how are you getting on with Mimi…after the suicide setback?'

'She helped me move our stuff around yesterday. We're talking.'

'Good, good.' He slowed his step further. 'What about?' Do you talk about me?'

She heard a twinge of anxiety in his voice and turned to look at him. 'Is there something you don't want her to tell me? Something you don't want me to know?'

He drew her closer. 'Of course not. I told you, I've never been married or engaged up till now. I was madly in love with a girl when I was eighteen, but she turned out to be a faithless little witch. After that I gave up on women and concentrated on my work. So there is nothing to tell, really.'

'I wasn't necessarily referring to other women.'

He had told her about what he called the pivotal moment of his life – waking up one night at the age of nineteen to a vision. He'd seen his own future, a long and difficult path to become a famous structural engineer, a vocation he'd never even considered before. And he'd told her how difficult it had been to juggle a sky-rocketing career with being responsible for Mimi.

Sebastian interrupted her thoughts. 'Have you figured out what she's doing with the Bible thumper? Has she told you anything?'

'Oh God, no,' she said, distracted, 'but at least she's on the pill.' As soon as she'd said it she cursed herself. She had no business divulging this. There had been no need for Sebastian to know.

He stopped. 'Really? She actually told you that?'

'No, of course not, and don't you go questioning her.'

Sebastian grabbed her arm to retain her. 'So how d'you know about it?'

'I found them accidentally when I was moving us into her old room. I shouldn't have told you. It's none of our business.'

He didn't seem to register the firmness in her voice. 'So she's having sex with someone.'

'Not necessarily. It's probably just a precaution. Girls her age have usually long since lost their virginity, as I'm sure you know. She's being sensible and responsible and you should count your blessings.'

'But *him*?'

'Oh, come on, honey. I think they've only met two or three times.' She gave a little laugh. 'He's probably gay. Gays tend to collect safe girlfriends, too big, too young, too old, or precocious and clever like Mimi. That could explain the attraction.'

'But what the hell does she see in *him*?'

Eva shrugged. 'Safety, maturity. Think about it. She's been brought up by older men.'

The sun was still high in the sky and the heat shimmered above the concrete of the rampart. It did seem crazy to watch a film in this gorgeous weather, but the coolness of the building beckoned to her.

Once they got inside, it had already started, but they went in anyway and sat down in the darkness. On the screen a couple were exchanging wedding vows in front of two witnesses. Eva glanced at her lover. His eyes were on the screen but his mind was clearly elsewhere. His profile showed deep furrows across his forehead, and his full mouth was thinned to a grim line. Her hand found his and she turned back to the screen. The bridegroom leaned forward to kiss the bride with barely disguised passion.

How would Sebastian react if she told him the simple truth about her refusal to marry him?

Only days after the fateful diving incident in Dubai where her hair had become entangled in coral, Sebastian arranged a visit to the British Embassy as a surprise. She had no idea how he'd swung a marriage licence with only her passport, but it was presented to her all ready to sign. According to the registrar, all they needed was to post a notice of the pending marriage at both their embassies, provide blood tests for the U.A.E. authorities and, after three weeks, they could get married in the Anglican church.

She'd been so taken aback that she didn't know how to react. 'How *could* you...without asking me?' she whispered to him, aware that the registrar was waiting. 'It's a huge decision. I'm not ready for it. I told you already.'

Seeing his dismayed reaction, she took him aside and tried to reason with him. 'We've only known each other for a matter of weeks. Why can't we just live together?'

'Because as you well know, in Dubai it's illegal,' he said quietly but forcefully. 'Cohabitation outside of marriage is forbidden. Put yourself in my position, I absolutely can't afford any mistakes or scandals.'

'We know more than one couple living in sin and nobody seems to give a damn.'

The registrar was overhearing their conversation and butted in, 'Sebastian is absolutely correct in his unwillingness to break Sharia Law. He's hired by a high-profile government agency and his face in the business sector is known.' He gave her a stern look. 'The embassy will take no responsibility for the consequences of any charges laid against people breaking the local laws. The consequences can be harsh; brutal, even.'

Sebastian turned her around so that he could look into her eyes. 'You are the person I want to spend the rest of my life with, and that new life can start right here, right now, with your signature.'

She glanced away from his insistent gaze. 'I am so sorry. I'm not ready. It's too soon.'

Sebastian lifted her hand to his lips, then leaned over and whispered in her ear. 'Are you enjoying this?'

'I guess you're not,' she whispered back, realising what a bad choice of movie this was.

'I'd rather go home, crack open that magnum and pretend we've done what that couple just did,' he murmured, taking a strand of her hair and combing it out through his fingers. 'Look at you, with your hair spilling gold. Come on, Queen of the Deep. The bathtub awaits.'

Mimi

They'd arranged a meeting on the Line Wall – next to the old cannons – as the starting point for a tour of the town. She was waiting on a bench in the full sun, since any bit of shade could not be found on the promenade. Looking to spot Carlo, to her surprise she saw Sebastian and Eva walk towards her, arm in arm in intense conversation. She prepared herself for some awkward exchange – what was *she* doing here? – but they continued right past, almost looked through her. She peered down at her getup. God, was she *that* invisible? She had toned down her appearance, wearing regular jeans (with rips and holes but everybody wore those, even housewives) and a black shirt tied at the front showing a little skin but not her be-ringed navel. She'd washed the gel out of her hair and it flopped clean but untidy over her forehead.

'Hello, Imogen.'

She smiled and stood up, and he kissed her on both cheeks, Gib fashion. His suit was a glaring reminder of their age difference. He looked very good though, slim and elegant, but mature. He flinched slightly when he noticed her precious silver safety pin. She'd put it through her eyebrow and connected it by a delicate chain to the ring in her nostril.

'I didn't just stick it in,' she reassured him. 'The holes were there already.'

'Thank God for that,' he exclaimed, clearly casting around for something positive to say. 'You do look truly unique, and underneath it all you're…quite beautiful.'

'Cheers,' she said and plucked the gum from her mouth. She rolled it between her fingers and tossed it into the bin next to the bench. 'I hope I didn't take you away from your work.'

'How could I not take you up on a tour? I'm a guide, after all. Ask me and I'll show you.'

'I'm looking for more stuff to stimulate my descriptive powers.'

'Aha, I know where to take you.'

'Can we start with a drink?'

He didn't answer but led her down the steps, crossing the big carpark and then following the South Bastion wall. Five minutes on, as they were nearing Ragged Staff Gates, he suddenly took her by the elbow and pulled her through a door into a hole in the wall. It was a grotto of sorts, but as her eyes adapted to the dark she saw that they were in a tiny pub. It had no windows, was grimy and squalid and utterly without appeal. It seemed an appropriate place to take someone you were embarrassed to be seen with.

The publican was a surly Scotsman whose enormous gut strained the buttonholes on his shirt to breaking point. By contrast, his wife was skeletal, clearly waging a losing battle with alcohol. Her bony hands trembled as she poured them both a vodka – so much so that she could hardly stop pouring – and she offered them Sprite since there was no tonic.

Not surprising, they were the only customers. Taking her drink off the bar, Mimi looked around at the five Formica tables. Where to sit was a tricky choice, but the blistering draft coming in off the street won over the cool interior, because even for someone who enjoyed a smoke, the stench of urinal and cigarette butts soaked in stale beer was overwhelming.

'This tavern is well on its way towards a change of hands,' Carlo commented bluntly, not bothering to keep his voice down. 'Pity to see it like this; it's been patronised by sailors for centuries.'

They sat down at the table closest to the door and sipped their drinks in silence. Mimi fought with an urge to giggle. Carlo looked so out of place in this setting, perched on the rickety chair. From time to time, he stroked his silver crucifix with one long, well-groomed hand, a habit he seemed unaware of.

'Sorry about this,' he said, gesturing around the hovel. 'I didn't realise...'

'I know why we're here,' she said.

'Because this is a truly historic drinking establishment, hundreds of years old. Perhaps the oldest in Europe.'

'Because here nobody who matters will see us.'

He looked hurt. 'I'm not the least concerned about being seen with you, Imogen. Why should I be? Besides, you're a very attractive young woman –'

'– from outer space,' she added.

'Who says I'm not from outer space? I feel like it often enough,' he replied.

The first sip of the almost-neat vodka had gone to her head and she felt bold. 'When did you last have a girlfriend, Carlo?'

He laughed stiffly. 'What kind of question is that?'

'A straightforward one.' She smiled, enjoying her advantage.

He glanced towards the dark interior of the establishment but the publican and his wife had disappeared through some interior doorway covered by a filthy curtain.

'It's refreshing to be with someone who's so forthright, but your question is very personal.'

'Haven't I given you something very personal to read?'

121

She put her elbows on the table and leaned her chin in her hands. 'Look, I was brought up in a family where nobody communicates, at least not honestly. It's all subterfuge, lies and hidden agendas. Nobody calls a spade a fucking shovel, or asks any questions, for that matter. I'm sick of it.'

'Does that go for your brother too?

She hesitated. 'Sort of. He's got the same background. He loves me a lot but never tells me what's going on.'

Carlo leaned forward. 'What do you think is going on?'

She drew back. Booze made her tongue flap. She absolutely must not blabber to anybody about Sebastian.

Carlo had noticed her withdrawal. 'Okay, let me answer your question,' he said. 'I retired from the priesthood ten years ago because I fell in love with a young woman. I gave up my calling in order to marry her. She wanted us to live together for a year before taking our marriage vows, but I insisted we should do the right thing. In retrospect, I realise she was unsure and needed time. Now that I'm older and wiser, I can't say I blame her.'

'So what happened?'

'We weren't really compatible. She was quite a bit younger and found me too introspective and serious. She called it off in the nick of time.' He looked forlorn. 'I see her around town with two children in tow. It took a while but I think I've risen above it.'

'And that's it? No more women in your life?'

'I have a lot of women acquaintances,' he said, fiddling with his crucifix. 'I try to live a spiritual life and I still believe in chastity.'

'Chastity? That's when you can't have sex, right?'

'Chastity is not punitive, as in "can't do this" or "can't do that". It's empowering because it frees men from the shackles of immorality.'

She shook her head. 'Personally, I don't see the freedom in that. And what's immorality, anyway? I had an argument with Sebastian the other day, about your religion? He told me what you Catholics did to natives in the colonies – in the name of your faith. I even googled it in case he was having me on.'

Carlo frowned. 'I have a feeling your brother would say anything to discredit me.'

'Why would he?' she asked, knowing that it was absolutely true, but perhaps not because of his religion. 'He's not your favourite person either, is he?'

'At least with me it's not personal,' Carlo said coolly. 'But I can't deny that I belong to the faction that is utterly and totally against your brother's project. The destruction of Gibraltar is something that weighs very heavily on me.'

She was perplexed. 'Why destruction?'

'It's all about money, power and prestige, my young friend. Socially and environmentally, your brother's project is a disaster.'

She stared at her hands, embarrassed about her lack of knowledge on the subject. 'Have you told him how you feel about it?'

'Your brother doesn't deign to talk to me, and anyway, as we're neighbours, I'd prefer not to touch on the subject. I tackle it in other ways.'

'What other ways?' She peered at him, suddenly suspicious. 'Where do I come into the equation? You're not hanging out with me to piss him off, are you?'

He looked at her with his large liquid eyes. 'Heavens, Imogen! Of course I'm not.'

His outrage was so genuine, she felt ashamed. Another silence ensued while they sipped their drinks. Her head was spinning a little but that early stage of drunkenness was so powerful. *Inebriated*, she murmured into her glass.

He had hardly touched his, even though he made a show of drinking. She studied him from under the rim of her floppy fringe. He must have been a beautiful guy in his teens and twenties. He still was, in an old kind of way. Too bad the hair was going.

'Let's get back to the chastity thing,' she said. 'Is this a requirement for Catholics, before marriage?'

He reached out and slowly pushed her glass away from her. 'You're not really old enough to drink, are you?'

She reached out and pulled it back. 'Only for three more weeks,' she said.

'Simply put, it's about me respecting and appreciating a woman as a whole person, not as an object.'

'So what do Catholics do with their needs, I wonder?' Mimi said, knowing she was being intrusive.

Carlo burst out laughing. 'Pray and meditate. In my case, I write poetry. You're a writer, I bet it could work on your needs too.'

She liked it when he laughed; he had perfect teeth and it made him look young and relaxed. And she was intrigued about his spiritual life, the prayer and meditation. She would like to learn about it, but there was no way she was buying the chastity thing. It just sounded too unreal.

Her eyes tried to focus on a sign on the bare stone wall, claiming Christopher Columbus had stopped here on his way to the New World, as it had been famous for its special fillet steaks. It was not hard to imagine the rowdy sailors tossing bones onto the sawdust covered floor. 'Is it true?' she said, slurring slightly.

'Yes, I believe it is documented. Gib was a handy stopoff point for those Spanish ships setting off across the Atlantic.'

'Oh, my God, imagine that.'

'Imogen, leave that vile drink and let's get out of here.

Remember, I'm supposed to be your guide to Gib, not get you drunk in seedy pubs. Besides I want to prove to you that I have no problem being seen with you. Let's go to the busiest place in town, the Convent. I might be able to show you the interior. There's a marvellous Dragon tree in the garden which is over five-hundred years old.'

'Oh God, let's not. Just look at me. Nuns wouldn't have me for love nor money.'

He chuckled. 'It not a convent any more, it's the official residence of the Governor of Gibraltar. Franciscan Friars founded it in 1531, and it's well documented that one of the guest bedrooms there is haunted by a Franciscan Nun – the Grey Lady.'

Well, he must have known that a ghost would get her attention. 'Okay, if it is a true story, tell me it while I finish this drink.'

He laced his long fingers around the crucifix. 'She was the daughter of an affluent Spanish family who had married against her father's wishes. When her father found out about her clandestine wedding he put her into the Convent of Santa Clara – then situated in the Main Street – where under the eyes of the Mother Superior she was forced to take her vows and become a nun. But her husband wasn't about to give up on her. He joined the Franciscan Order at the convent. The couple managed the odd encounter in the confessional of the King's Chapel next door where they hatched plans to run away.

'On the night of their escape they made their way to the harbour where the husband had arranged for a boat. However, the alarm had been raised and, in the ensuing chase, the husband fell into the water and drowned. The young woman was arrested. For breaking her vows – as was the punishment for such a sin – she was walled up, alive, in one of the rooms in the convent.'

Mimi stared at him. 'Walled up alive? Well, *that* can't be true.'

'I'm afraid it's absolutely true. You can read all about it in one of my books. I don't know about her ghost wandering around the place, but her death by entombment is documented. Entombment or live burial of nuns who broke their vows of chastity has been practised since the Vestal Virgins in Roman times. The punishment was abolished in 394 AD, but many historical accounts prove that it continued for centuries after that.'

She put her hands over her ears. 'Stop! That's awful! I know I'm creepy and ghoulish, but the idea of that just makes my skin crawl.'

He chuckled. 'And there I was, thinking you were such a bombproof young woman.'

'I am,' she protested.

'I had hoped you'd allow me to show you the tunnels. You're not scared of them, I hope.' He clearly wanted her to show some enthusiasm for his pet interest. 'Mohammed and I are going on Wednesday. The invitation is there if you want to join us.'

'Maybe,' she said, thinking of Sebastian's likely reaction. Of course he didn't need to know. She pushed away her empty glass. 'Let's go visit the Grey Lady.'

Eva

It was like swimming through history. Beneath her, a seabed littered with shipwrecks: ships sunk in storms or blown apart in many hundreds of battles. Wrecks dating back to the Napoleonic times were almost intact. She shivered with awe as she reached out to touch a Phoenician anchor, half buried in the mud. She knew this dive had been intended to show off her diving expertise, but she felt like a child in a toy store. If only it had been Sebastian by her side instead of Brian. Sebastian would just love this.

They swam through modern ships and barges that were derelict and had been sunk deliberately into Camp Bay to form an artificial reef for a conservation project. Two planes, looking as though they dated from World War Two, were parked incongruously on the seabed, out of their element.

As they went further out along Gib's coastline, she saw deep caves and sheer dropoffs, the peaks of the Seven Sisters. All the while, excitement mounted in her. Thank God for this! If she got the job, it would be her salvation. The element of water always floated her demons away. Here she could feel invulnerable.

Towards the end of their dive, Brian took her to where only the most experienced divers should venture – a clear sign that he trusted her ability – Europa Reef. The narrow way between the two oceans had a constant and vast water turnover and was teeming with sea life, including vibrantly coloured fish, a host of rays, sunfish, bass and mullet as well as the more rare dwellers of the deep. Though she was well up on her marine biology, he pointed out the dodgy guys who could pose a danger to divers: the Scorpion fish, the Morays and Conger Eels.

Back up on dry land Brian said nothing at first. Once in the shop she dried off and changed into her clothes in his little toilet, then helped him rinse and hang their gear.

'Well,' she said, bending down to scratch the world's ugliest dog on his scabby head. 'What do you think? Can I be of help?'

'Yep,' he said. 'I can see you're up to speed. Small groups to start.'

Brian reminded her a little of Austin, the man who had discovered in her a talent for diving. As a young woman of twenty, she'd gone wild trying to catch up, doing openly everything that she'd done in secret during her teens. A film of a woman deep-sea diver had inspired her more than anything her God could have asked of her.

After the 'excommunication', after fluttering around the country like a paper tissue in a wind, after working at many mindnumbing jobs to raise some money, she'd done her first dive. She'd met Austin, a veteran diver who'd worked on oil rigs and for the navy, welding steel hulls deep in the most inhospitable and cold waters. They were lovers for a while, then the best of friends. Austin taught her everything she knew about diving, and after he died, she went through the rigours of formal training as he'd made her promise to do. A few years on, her qualifications paved the way to becoming a paramedic specialising in rescue at sea. The future looked bright, the future looked rosy. She met Adrian and the future looked solid and safe.

Sebastian

A muted applause welcomed him on stage. He looked out over an ocean of faces – the men and women of Gibraltar who had come to listen to his presentation – and he felt high in mind and spirit, soaring above them with boundless enthusiasm and goodwill.

The old Inces Hall Theatre was full to maximum seating capacity. Everyone in Gib now knew about the Frontiers Development Project and wanted to know more. Disappointingly, the Governor and Chief Minister had – through their offices – turned down the invitation, but before going on stage he'd been told by the organiser that both the Minister of Housing and the Minister of Enterprise, Development and Technology were in attendance. A considerable portion of the audience belonged to the Gibraltar Environmental Safety Group. He hoped they'd take on board his passionate commitment to environmental concerns and understand his plans for a new future, a new world. He would convince his guests that his project would impart a huge boost to investment, tourism, and commerce, which in turn would enhance and enrich Gibraltar in carefully projected but also unforeseen ways. He'd rehearsed his talk in front of Eva a dozen times and was confident he would make everything sound simple and painless, environmentally safe and politically shrewd.

It started well. Using every visual aid at his disposal he kept switching his delivery between English and Spanish. Almost everyone in Gib, even those of British birth, was

Spanish speaking – certainly Yanito speaking – and his fluency impressed them, made him one of them. If Saunders had seen him now, he'd have to eat his words: "barking mad"! One day he'd bitterly regret expressing such doubts about his lead engineer.

Half way through the presentation he spotted their neighbour, Carlo Montegriffo. He was sitting near the front, in the company of several influential persons Sebastian had been introduced to. Montegriffo gave him a curt nod.

Now, during the closing applause, they held each other's gaze for a moment. There was something unnerving about the man's impassive expression. His lack of enthusiasm was obvious as his arms were folded firmly across his chest.

'Let's have some questions,' Sebastian invited. He was aware of the strong 'no-more-concrete brigade' in Gibraltar, part of the reactionary old guard that wanted no new developments, or any change, for that matter. He hoped they weren't going to give him flack, but if they did, he was ready for them.

What happened next came as a cold shower.

Montegriffo stood up and said, 'I'm afraid your development is being put on hold.'

Sebastian forced a smile. 'Perhaps you've not listened attentively. We've got every approval to go ahead and construction is already underway.' He looked around for some other raised hand to take Montegriffo off his case. He sensed that entering into a public debate with him would leave the audience with a different impression of the evening.

'In the meantime,' said Montegriffo, 'Gibraltar Museum's own people have done some research. We've contacted Princeton University, which has a special interest in the

Neanderthal history of the Rock and we've been granted a month's suspension of any project relating to that particular stretch of coastline, so that a team of archaeologists can perform some preliminary investigations of some recent unusual findings.' He looked behind him at the audience and waved some papers in the air. 'I've just picked up the paperwork, signed by the Governor and the Chief minister.

'Hallelujah,' intoned someone at the back.

'What unusual findings?' Sebastian's voice twanged through the loudspeakers, making it sound slightly hysterical.

Montegriffo spoke in an even voice and with definite authority. 'That's for the archaeologists to divulge. All I can say is, it looks important and highly sensitive.'

'I think you might be mistaken. There is no reason why construction would be put on hold for something like that. Anyway, I'd be the first to hear of it.'

'In that case I regret to be the one to inform you.' He waved his papers again. 'In effect as of Monday.'

He walked out in a daze. Eva was waiting in the foyer where drinks were being served at a makeshift bar.

He looked at her in that rose-coloured mini skirt, the plain white blouse, the flat but elegant sandals, and wondered what this stunning creature was doing *with him*. Her hair cascaded down her body like a golden waterfall and her long swimmer's legs were smooth and brown. Never had she looked so beautiful in her simplicity. He glanced around and hoped that others would see the real live mermaid standing there amongst men, and notice that she was his. Anything to boost him after his shattered triumph.

'Was it very bad? Did I lose them?'

'No,' she said flinging her arms around his neck. 'You

were brilliant.' Just as quickly, she disengaged him. 'Shouldn't you be talking to your guests?'

'No. Let's get the hell out of here.'

'How do you feel about the holdup?'

'Mightily pissed off, but it's not my money on the line. Saunders will go apeshit.'

People were streaming out and Sebastian looked around him. 'I see Mimi isn't with you. She decided not to come?'

'She had a date.'

'Really?' he said with a mixture of disappointment and relief. 'At least it's not with Carlo Montegriffo.'

'He just left,' Eva pointed out, 'but he stopped to say "hello" to me, as if nothing –'

'He did, did he, the self-righteous bastard?'

'He's not exactly evil, but he could have told you, either before or after the presentation. That manoeuvre in there was a bit underhand.'

'Underhand?' Sebastian barked. 'He did his damned best to humiliate me.'

'You've got to be prepared for some opposition, honey. Some people have genuine concerns.' She took his arm and steered him out of the gates and into the street.

'Yeah, yeah…a few diehards who think the Rock of Gibraltar is unique and timeless. They're so fucking entrenched in their beliefs, they'd risk exposing Gibraltar to those intangible vultures: opportunists of the tax system, like online gambling companies. When what they really need is revolutionary developments which can put their poxy little peninsula on the world map.'

Eva gave his arm a shake. 'Oh, *please*, let's not go there again. Can we just try and enjoy the evening! I thought you did quite well in there. I can see you have support.'

At once he was sorry to have spoiled Eva's joy in the

evening. She was so supportive, so tolerant. She deserved more than he gave her.

'Look, there's Mike and Trevor,' she said. 'Why don't we ask if they want to have a drink with us somewhere?'

'Oh, God!' Sebastian said with a grimace. 'Let's not.'

'You never want to socialise with your colleagues,' she said. 'Why *is* that?'

He cast about for the right answer. 'Because I've got you and Mimi. I've got no time left over for anyone else.'

'You'll like Brian, my boss,' she said. 'He says that about his dog. He'd understand someone as weird as you.' She laughed merrily and planted a kiss on his cheek. 'And I mean that in the nicest possible way.'

They walked arm in arm towards Casemates Square. The atmosphere in the streets was festive, the town heaving with revellers, tourists and locals alike. It was the middle of June and the busy season had begun. Luxury cruise ships swelled the crowds daily, flights increased and the tax-free booze and cigarettes brought visitors over the border from Spain in droves.

Sebastian felt a telltale tension behind his eyes but determined not to spoil the rest of their evening. His presentation had, after all, not been a disaster. Hadn't he determined, just before it, that he was on top of the world?

Since cutting down on his medication, his confidence had soared and his social skills seemed so much more fluent. On his last appointment at the Harley Street clinic, his doctor, Liam Matthews had advised him to stay on the pills. Matthews had been his dad's doctor and was getting on for retirement and perhaps not as clued up as he should be. But understanding Sebastian's potential, he'd bailed him out more than once. A reference here, a signature there, a few creatively modified medical reports. In some ways, it was Matthews' doing that he was here at all.

133

'You won't like this, honey.' Eva said softly. 'I should tell you Mimi's date was with Montegriffo. They were meeting up for a drink. Just in case we run into them, please don't make a scene.'

He stopped. 'You've got to be kidding! Are you telling me that asshole went straight from humiliating me to seduce my teenage sister?'

'You're making too much of it, Sebastian. What I've seen of Mimi, she's quite capable of holding her own. You can't shield her from life. For all you know it's just a friendship.'

'It's that bloody mother of mine. If she'd only showed Mimi a smidgen of love, she'd be safe and sound in the heart of Surrey.'

'Maybe, but it rarely works that way, honey. She is almost eighteen. I had long left home when I was that age.'

He stood there, rooted to the ground beneath him.

'Are you with me?' Eva said, nudging him in the side with her elbow.

'I am with you all right, till death do us part.' He put his arm around her shoulder. He had to be cool. He knew his future depended on it. 'Let me take you to Gauchos, my love. They apparently do the best steak outside of Argentina.'

Mimi

They sat at under a parasol at one of the bars in Casemates Square.

'I don't think I've seen you smoke a cigarette,' said Carlo. 'You said you liked smoking.'

'I am trying to quit.'

'Good girl. I'm all for trying everything life has to offer, but once you've tried smoking you can leave that particular habit to the lowlife.'

She sniggered. 'Lowlife? One of the many undesirables on your list?'

He leaned forward. 'I'm afraid your brother is not very happy with me.'

'What did you do?' she asked, frowning.

'I showed him up in front of the audience tonight. I think I pricked his balloon, somewhat.'

Oh, God. She hadn't even been there to support Sebastian. She'd not had the stomach to witness his performance, knowing precisely how inflated his ego would be after having worked himself up into a frenzy.

'What did you do exactly?'

'I just told him that the Frontiers Development is on hold for a month as of Monday. He had no idea.'

'And you did this, why? To humiliate him in front of everyone?'

Carlo's hands clenched around the arm-rests of his chair. 'I could not be witness to the absolute drivel he was spouting.' His voice rose a little. 'Does he honestly believe that his monstrous creation is going to improve Gibraltar?'

'Yes, he does.'

Looking at her, Carlo must have read her dismay. His eyes shifted from hard to gentle, and he smiled sadly. 'If you want, I'll apologise to him. Poor you, in the middle of this. You are being very diplomatic and levelheaded, stuck between two crazy guys.'

'I will always take my brother's side, Carlo. He's just doing his job. If he's out to lunch about the benefit to Gibraltar, it's not for me to question. I don't understand the ins and outs of this business anyway.'

They sank into silence and drank their beer, their eyes held by a street performer, a wizard sitting crosslegged high on a pole. He was utterly immobile, his eyes closed but his face showing a shadow of pain. *Self-immolation,* she mouthed, not sure if it was.

'I've gone through all the scenes you left for me to read,' Carlo said softly. He took out the brown envelope she'd left him from his jacket's inside pocket. 'Sorry it took so long. I kept starting and then feeling like I was peeping into something that wasn't for my eyes and ears.'

She took the envelope from him and sat up expectantly. 'Never mind. What did you think?'

He reached over and touched her hand. 'I can't say I loved it, because I found it disturbing. But the writing is excellent, stark, unsentimental, very proficient. I've made some notes in the margins, in case you want to know. Some things to clarify, some to shorten perhaps, some asking for more detail.'

She was thrilled with his review. It wasn't a story anyone would love, exactly, but it was about real life and it had moved him. On impulse she half stood and planted a kiss on his cheek. He closed his eyes and touched the kiss, putting his hand over his cheek as if to stop it fading in the air.

All at once she got worried that she'd shown him a scene in her narrative which could compromise Sebastian. She had no trouble baring her own past to Carlo, but after what he'd just done to her brother during his presentation, why should he be privy to any of Sebastian's troubles?

When Carlo's mobile rang, she slipped out a few pages and scanned them quickly.

They sat in the taxi, but Christiana refused to open the door. Marcus made no move either, his face hidden in his hands. The driver played with his mobile and waited patiently. He was Polish or something, his licence showed his photo and the unpronounceable name. Having seen the house, he probably thought it worth waiting, a big tip in mind.

Her heart felt like a stone, but she was not going to cry. She was angry, too, and sad beyond belief. It was only three weeks since Dad's funeral, three weeks to pack, three weeks to cry, three weeks to say goodbye to Helena, Rosie and Neil, three weeks to find a home for the cat. She'd helped Marcus sort out Dad's clothes, books and other stuff. That was the worst part. That big man with his huge trousers, his worn-down slippers and threadbare Panama hat. Each item went into plastic bags, for refuse or for the cancer charity. With each item, Dad was dying again, over and over.

'Why can't I just come with you? I can go to school in Japan. There's got to be schools there.'

He reached for her hand. 'Listen, sis. We've been through all this probably a dozen times. You know I can't look after you. I've got a huge project starting and if I keep my nose clean, probably another one in Dubai right after.'

'What?' she wailed. 'You didn't tell me that. Where the fuck is Dubai?'

He sighed. 'You know these breaks are vital for my career.'

'Your fucking career,' she sneered. 'Get a nanny then. Surely they have nannies in Japan, or a governess, like Jane Eyre. You can pay someone to keep me shackled.'

The whole conversation was like a broken record; even she was fed up with it. She could puke just thinking about the days and hours they'd argued and cried, both Marcus and her. Crying, then shouting, then promising, then crying and shouting again.

'You're only thirteen, sis. Tokyo is a bad place to have you running amok.'

'I don't believe you, you just don't want me,' she said and yanked her hand from his.

He turned suddenly and looked her fiercely in the eye. 'Okay, listen, I shouldn't really, but I'll give you the real reason – the main reason – but I don't want you to talk about it to anyone. Mother and Gordon know, but no-one else.' He paused and took a breath. 'I'm simply not allowed to take you with me. Dr. Matthews has helped me far beyond the call of duty, but when it came to letting me be your sole guardian, he said no. He would not sign anything, in fact, he said he would make my past known to social services.'

'But why?' she said, understanding but rejecting the reason.

'You know very well why. Maybe Dad had his hand in it, from when he knew he was getting ill. Or maybe Dr. Matthews just refuses to be responsible for me taking you away. He said you would be better off with your mother and he's not far-off right.'

'Mother doesn't want me,' she cried. 'And I hate her.'

'Listen, sweetheart. I'll come back often, or I'll send for you every holiday I get.'

They'd come to the end of the line. Every argument had been exhausted. She turned her head and looked out. The Featherington-Haugh mansion loomed like a huge grey box. It wasn't Downton Abbey, but she had never set foot in a house that big.

'Let's go,' she said and patted Marcus on the hand. He was dabbing at his eyes with a tissue. 'I'll make the best of it,' she said to make him feel better. 'But please don't abandon me forever. Promise to send for me.'

As if he knew the stage they were at, the driver got out and started unloading the suitcases. Marcus and Christiana looked at each other: no more words were needed.

'I love you, sis,' he said anyway, in case she'd not read it on his face.

Mimi blanched as she read, but the vital information had been left out. She'd alluded to it, *make his past known to the social services. You know very well why.*

She looked at Carlo who had finished his call. He smiled at her, his face giving nothing away.

'Can I get you another beer?' he said.

Eva

She began to badger him first thing in the morning about coming along to the beach. It was Saturday, for heaven's sake, but no, some design problem on Luna's Crossing was consuming him and it had to be solved. Sebastian seemed increasingly fixated, taking advantage, while Frontiers was on hold, to work on his private obsession. She tried her hardest to convince him that Luna's Crossing could wait...he had not even begun his present project, let alone securing the UK and Moroccan governments' agreement to fund the world's most spectacular bridge. Even Mimi gave him a stern look and said something that Eva did not pick up. He'd hesitated for a moment, but in the end he couldn't be swayed.

She didn't doubt her lover's talent, capability and energy, but he seemed engrossed to the point of neurosis. She'd never before been associated with a creative genius, so it was difficult to know what to expect. Sometimes she wondered if it was her duty as his partner to try and slow him down, provoke some kind of reality check. He could certainly do with spending a little bit more time with her, and with Mimi in particular.

She glanced over at Mimi. The girl was not much company either. She was lying on the sand on a large black towel in the black bikini Eva had bought her (after having ascertained that she didn't own a swimsuit) with her eyes behind black sunshades. Her cellphone was in her hand and she was tapping her foot to some music. There was no telling what was going on in her head. She was too thin, her skin was translucent, whiter than white and smooth as a baby's. The skull tattoo looked cruel and incongruous on the jutting hipbone. It seemed too childlike a body to be ravished by a man with a receding hairline.

She put the thought out of her mind and looked around, observing other families laying out blankets, erecting parasols and unpacking huge picnic baskets with coolers full of wine and beer. They were revelling in simple pleasures, being close, chatting animatedly, soaking up the sun and watching the kids play. The beach was rapidly filling up, people claiming spaces within spaces so that sunworshippers were practically laid out head to toe, like the proverbial sardines. There were few sandy beaches in Gibraltar, and she regretted not having gone to the Eastern Beach which stretched several hundred metres along the east side of the isthmus. It was undoubtedly less claustrophobic and she could have used the opportunity to check if it was possible to swim out and around the barrier into Spain, but Mimi had insisted on Catalan Bay. Mimi was quite taken with its fishing village flavour and the fuck-you attitude of the Genoese descendants who lived there. She was right: one could easily imagine being in Italy.

It was getting on for midday and she took out her factor 50 sunblock and began to cover herself in the waxy substance, wondering if she should poke Mimi and force her to do the same. The stuff was all over her hands when her cellphone rang. She rubbed her hands on her towel before rummaging ineffectively in her bag for the phone.

She didn't make it, and peering, at the screen against the harsh sunlight, she saw that the number had been withheld.

'Why didn't you answer your phone?' said the lifeless Mimi.

'I didn't find it in time.'

141

Mimi moved her sunglasses up and frowned at her. 'So phone back. It's got to have been Sebastian. He's probably feeling guilty. He could be in a taxi in his oversized swimming shorts coming to look for us.'

'The signal is so intermittent here,' Eva lied. 'I'll just go for a little walk and see if I can pick it up on the road.'

Mimi snorted. 'Over there? The Rock's in the way.'

'I'll give it a try,' Eva said and stood up. She pulled her sundress over her head and slipped on her rubber sandals.

'Get me a gin and tonic, will you?' Mimi said.

'At lunch time? What're you like?'

'Be a devil! Get yourself one too.' She rolled onto her side and raised herself on an elbow, pointing to the little beach bar no more than ten paces from where they lay. 'See? People keep coming out of there with large plastic glasses.'

'Maybe. See you in a moment.'

The village of Catalan Bay was only a few houses deep, spread between the road and the beach and cowering under the looming precipice of the Rock. Eva ran up to the road on shaky legs and sat down on the railing. She took out her phone and dialled California.

'Linda?'

'What the hell…is that *you*, Chanta— *Eva?*'

'I'm sorry. I know it must be the middle of the night.'

'Are you okay?' Linda wheezed and the scramble for a cigarette was unmistakeable.

'I know I can trust you absolutely, Linda, but could you have mentioned my phone call to anyone, anyone who knows Adrian? Could you have passed my number inadvertently to someone or written it down somewhere…? I know it's a totally ridiculous idea…of course you haven't, but…'

'Eva, Eva…whooa, stop,' Linda cried down the phone.

'What's going on? Why would I do a thing like that? I've even tried to forget ever knowing you so I wouldn't accidentally as much as mention your name.'

Eva's shoulders sagged as she realised how crass the insinuation was: an insult to Linda's intelligence and loyalty. As if her best friend would recklessly give away her whereabouts or her phone number. 'Oh, God, Linda. I know I sound hysterical. Please forget what I just said. I know you're discretion personified.'

'What's brought this on?' Linda asked, taking a long drag on her cigarette.

'Silent phone calls. Ever since I got this damned cell phone, just after I got in contact with you, some man is calling my number then breathing down the phone. I just can't think who'd want to freak me out like that...except of course Adrian. It'd be just up his street. He used to enjoy unnerving me with his eerie mind games, remember?'

Linda was wheezing and coughing down the phone, sounding as though she were a mere few metres away and not in California. 'Listen!' she said. 'If I'm the only person who knows where you are, then it can't be him. Anyway, knowing Adrian, he wouldn't bother to goof about on the phone. If he knew where you were, he'd just come after you, wouldn't he?'

'Just because he's discovered my number doesn't mean he can find me. It's a pay-as-you-go phone and Spain is quite a big country.'

'He's *not* discovered your number. It's got to be some guy stalking you over there. I mean, honestly Eva, you're not exactly hard on the eye.'

Eva felt the goosebumps puckering her arms even though the temperature was well up in the thirties.

'Perhaps. Hopefully, that's the explanation.'

Another bout of wet cough. 'Goddarn, sweetie pie, you practically gave me a heart attack, waking me up at this hour.'

'Please don't be mad at me,' Eva pleaded.

'I'm not, I'm not,' Linda reassured her. 'Trust me. You're safe. I'd never betray you.'

'Oh, Linda, I miss you. I could sure use a friend right now.' She realised how true this was. She was madly in love with an amazing guy, so why had she not told him about the phone calls, why did she feel so alone with it, so removed from who she tried to represent...so *fake*? As though she were living someone else's life and soon she'd be exposed for who she was, and sent back to where she belonged.

'I'm always here,' said Linda soothingly. 'I'm always at the end of the phone. Just call me whenever. I don't care if you wake me up. Just ignore my cursing and coughing, okay sweetie pie?'

'Okay, buddy. I better go. My new little sister is waiting for a great big gin and tonic.'

'Love you, kiddo.'

'Same here, Linda. And quit smoking, ya' hear.'

She stood for a while in the shade of the Rock, looking out over Catalan Bay. She peered across the water. Wasn't that Jonny Risso's boat bobbing in the distance? Probably just wishful thinking. With a surge of dread running through her, she felt an impulse to just swim out. There, curving eastward, was Spain, the golden beaches of the Spanish costas. She was a strong swimmer, she'd make it easily if the tides were right.

At the same time she hated her own fear and knew that, to be truly free, she ought to be considering a trip back to California and a confrontation with Adrian. She'd so hoped and prayed he'd meet someone new and forget about her, but even that left her a bad taste in her mouth; how could she possibly wish him on some other unsuspecting woman? She was a coward, and it was easier to cover her ears, eyes and mouth, and live life in the present. It was easier to forget, or if she couldn't forget, just keep running...

She wandered down to the little bar and the throng of sun-worshipping Yanitos waiting to be served. She jostled with all that bronzed flesh, determined to put the silent breather out of her mind and enter the pervading spirit of carefree hedonism.

Finally a topless young barman with an amazing head of hair and a stunning smile (why wasn't Mimi attracted to someone like him?) came to her rescue and she ordered two extra-large gin and tonics with plenty of ice.

Sebastian

He sat in the kitchen in just his boxer shorts, a large fan directed onto his face. The papers on the table fluttered wildly and he kept moving cups and glasses around to hold them down.

Mimi and Eva were spending the day at the beach. He'd seen them off, blown them kisses down the stairs. Their earnest imploring to join them made him feel both deeply loved and incredibly sad. For a moment he'd been torn with indecision. Part of him longed for a family getaway, time for the three of them to have a bit of fun and relaxation together. There was so much he'd needed to engage with Mimi about, (a serious conversation about her relationship with Montegriffo was long overdue) and the sheer pleasure of watching Eva's graceful form in a bikini, see her laughing and carefree...she'd looked heartachingly disappointed when he forced himself to say no. He had so much work to do, so many ideas to be harnessed, committed to paper. He couldn't afford to let them run out in the sand, literally.

In addition, he had made a commitment to write an article on Sustainable Development of Critical Infrastructure for the Arab Association for Bridge and Structural Engineering. Normally he would write such a paper with his eyes closed, but he kept stopping and starting, wondering if he was giving too much away. The multihazard-resistant bridge supports of flexible concrete-filled steel tubes was one of his designs that had been adopted without his personal involvement, and he'd grown wary of his ideas being plagiarised.

He picked up and scrutinised a page covered in his spidery black scribbles and doodles. His brain was tired and he couldn't quite recall what he'd meant by them. He was working too hard, sleeping too little, and this lapse of memory had happened more than once in the last few days. It worried him. How was it possible that he could see something with such brilliant clarity and, only hours later, have forgotten the actual basis of the idea?

What was worse, some sketches showing the structure of Luna's Crossing's keels had gone missing. He'd looked high and low for them, their disappearance a total mystery. It was almost a case of wondering if someone could have stolen them, but he knew that was just plain stupid. No-one but Eva and Mimi knew he was working on an important private project, a concept so innovative it would leave the world agape.

He knew he'd have to wait, perhaps years. His name must have a chance to grow, his work become famous, not just within the engineering world but among ordinary people: city councils, governments and heads of nations. Then he could propose the un-proposable. Let's face it, just half a century ago the Channel Tunnel had seemed a totally screwball concept.

The day passed quickly, too quickly. He'd forgotten to eat and was suddenly very hungry. He heard the girls come home from the beach, chatting. Mimi, who'd been so aloof since the move, was giggling uncontrollably. If he didn't know better, he'd almost think they'd been out drinking. It was lovely to hear them get on. Mimi seemed to be softening towards Eva; these days he often heard them talking in the kitchen, and a trip to the beach together was bound to improve their relationship. It was probably just as well he'd stayed behind. Nothing would make his life more perfect than if his two ladies grew to be close friends.

He knew that cutting down on his tablets had its side effects. He was lying in that narrow bed beside a beautiful woman but he was uncomfortably awake and wishing the hours to pass. So many concerns traded places in his mind. When his legs became jittery and his heart fluttered in his chest, he turned to watch Eva's sleeping face. Even though something wasn't right with her – and that something made him very uneasy – the sight and smell of her still calmed him.

At dawn he began to hear movements in the apartment below. What was the guy doing at five o'clock in the bloody morning? He tried to rationalise that there was nothing sinister about a man who went to dawn Mass or got up early to write poetry, or some other sissy pursuit. It was his unhealthy interest in Mimi that didn't tally, or perhaps it did just that. A paedophile in sheep's clothing, or priest's cassock. He stifled a laugh, even though the thought made him queasy.

Suddenly he realised that Eva had gone. The light had changed, and he could see he'd overslept. His watch said ten past ten. Flying out of bed he pulled on a pair of shorts and stumbled to the kitchen. The kitchen window was open and Montegriffo's black cat was up on the kitchen counter, looking right at home. He waved his arms and shouted wildly at it. Leisurely it hopped down and out of the window onto a branch of the Eucalyptus.

Eva appeared at the door. 'What's the matter, honey?'

'The damned cat again.'

'It brought us half a bird this morning. That means he likes us.' She went up to give Sebastian a kiss, her cool lips like silk on his. He felt a sudden rush of desire, and was about to grab her around the waist and press his hardness against her when she moved away.

She put the kettle on. 'I've got my first assignment in a couple of hours,' she said.

'Hey! Good for you, baby. Make sure you tie up your hair. I don't want to lose you to some smarmy rich boy.'

'It's three women, actually – Italian – wanting to dive through the interior of the *S.S. Excellent*. It's an easy start. Beautiful though; it sank in 1888.' She sliced some bread and began to anoint it with Marmite, topping it with peanut butter. 'Here, get this down you. I can see you've lost weight.'

He took the slice from her and sat down to eat it. He wasn't really hungry; he hardly ever was these days.

Eva was hovering by his side.

'What's up, sweetie?' he said, putting out an arm and drawing her onto his lap. 'You nervous about the dive?'

'I need to tell you something,' she hesitated.

'Go on.'

'It's about a man back home.'

He stiffened. Here it was, something he'd always suspected but didn't really want to know.

'You still love him?' he asked, then biting his lip knowing he should let her do the talking. 'Is that why you don't want to marry me?'

'Don't make wild assumptions,' she said with a small laugh. 'It's you I love.'

'So what do you want to say about him?' He'd felt this presence, the man hovering in her past. Someone she could not let go of.

She moved on his lap to face him. 'We've not talked about this, we've not talked about *anything*, and we need to. *I need to*.'

'Okay,' he said cautiously.

Eva looked away. 'When I lived with him, he told me if I ever left him, he'd come looking for me and kill me.'

He peered into her face, wanting to read between the words. What did this mean? People kill for love, he'd heard this, read this. But it was also a figure of speech, surely.

'But you're here now, with me. I assume he's back there.' He paused. 'Is he?'

'I hope so,' she said, 'but listen; I've had some silent phone calls. I'm scared of him, Sebastian. He might have figured out where I am.'

'How could he have worked that out?' he said, trying to sound neutral. 'You're about the most elusive and secretive woman I've ever known. He can't know where you are if you haven't kept in touch with him.'

'Don't be naïve, Sebastian. There are ways. Especially if you're a federal agent. He's evil: he made my life a living hell for years.'

He looked her in the eye. 'For years... You must have really loved him to stay with him for years. If he was that bad, why didn't you just leave him?'

Eva jumped off his lap, her face reddening. 'Not you too!' she cried. 'It's a damned cliché: *why didn't you just leave him?*' She aped his question with bitterness. 'Everybody comes out with the same inane comments. When you've been bullied and stomped on, threatened, intimidated, beaten and humiliated, you lose the person you are. You become weak and scared. I'm sure you've heard of women who stay a lifetime with abusive husbands. *Why don't they just leave?* Because they're scared to death, that's why, and more often have nowhere to turn. No-one helps you, no-one wants to get involved just in case they themselves become subjects of his threats and abuse.'

He felt almost cowed by her tirade. 'Oh, sweetie, I'm sorry. I just don't understand it.'

She shook her head. 'Of course you don't. You live in a bubble. This guy is an FBI agent. What chance have I got against someone in his position? It was always his word against mine.'

'Come here,' he said, reaching for her and drawing her back into his arms. He smoothed her hair, trying to calm her. 'Let's talk no more about this arsehole. If he comes anywhere near you, he's got me to contend with.'

'Yes, but what...'

'Shhh,' he said and put a finger on her soft lips. 'I'll protect you. With my life.'

He felt exhausted by that strained interaction and hoped she'd come back excited about the dive and not wanting to pick up where they'd left off. He looked forward to hearing her account of it, no doubt peppered with witty asides about her customers. But her keen sense of humour seemed to have wilted lately. Maybe that was down to the man who wanted to find her. The man who was still in her life.

He got up from the table and stretched. He needed to get dressed and ready for the taxi to take him to the site. Eva had claimed the wardrobe when they traded bedrooms with Mimi; his clothes had been relegated to the hall closet. He took out some clean shorts and a shirt.

Hesitating a moment, he went back into the room, moving towards her wardrobe, and put his hand around the ceramic door knob. The door was jammed, having been warped and distorted with age, and the wood squeaked loudly when he pulled it open.

Carefully he handled the clothes on the hangers. There weren't many garments and few had pockets. He passed his hands amongst the modest piles of T-shirts, tops and jeans. A shoebox held her underwear, the only items of clothing that revealed a splash of extravagance. He picked up a pair of lace knickers and pressed them to his face.

The wardrobe had a bottom shelf and he pulled out her suitcase, placing it on the floor. He let his hand slide through the side pockets. He opened the clasps and pushed back the lid. The inside was lined with a silky material in blue and yellow stripes. The cloth was so old and worn it was coming apart at the seams. He could see she'd made an attempt to hold it together, having stitched it roughly with blue cotton. With the flat of his hand he patted the sides. He stopped and nodded: it was definitely still there, behind the lining.

He'd discovered an object there on her very first day in Gib, when he'd been helping her put her things away at the Rock Hotel. She'd whipped the suitcase from his hands but not before he'd spotted the stitching and felt the foreign body slide sideways behind the lining.

Now he got his nail scissors and carefully unpicked another seam, then eased out the slim volume. It was an American passport. He opened it and saw it wasn't the one he knew, belonging to his fiancée Eva Eriksson.

But it was Eva's face in the photo. The name under it, however, was Chantelle Hepping. He read the name over and over, scrutinising the image. *Chantelle Hepping*? Who the hell *was* she?

Mimi

She hesitated on the first landing, then checked her phone. It was only nine in the morning, but Carlo had probably left for work already. Just standing there was lame, so the moment decided itself. She lifted a knuckle and tapped on the door.

She heard sounds behind it but it took a while to open. Carlo, dressed in a bathrobe, looked ill at ease when he saw it was her. She wondered whether the chastity story was a great big fib, and he'd had a woman staying the night.

'Sorry,' she said, shrinking slightly. 'I'm off for a walk up the Rock and just wondered if you'd be free to continue our tour of the place.' She gestured at his bathrobe. 'No worries, another time, maybe.'

Carlo looked at her brand-new trainers. 'Don't venture up there on your own, Imogen...'

'Why not?'

'It's not advisable for a young woman alone. I'd be happy to take you some other day.'

'I'll be fine,' she shrugged. 'You can't get lost up there, now, can you?'

'Believe it or not, it's easy to get lost if you go off the road.'

She smiled. 'I'm a big girl, and I've got a phone.'

'I would love to accompany you, but I've got a commitment this morning.'

'Like I said, no worries.'

Sebastian

He was working at the kitchen table while Eva was peeling veggies at the sink. She'd been very quiet the last few days since telling him about the man who wanted her dead, and he knew he should encourage her to talk about it.

'Are you okay?' he said.

'Why do you ask?'

'Any more of those phone calls?'

'If I said yes, what would you do?' she asked.

He thought carefully about his answer. 'Next time, let *me* talk to him.'

There was a movement at the window and he dashed over to shoo the black cat from the tree. There had been enough offerings of parts of birds, rats and mice in the kitchen, his work space. He couldn't abide it: it was worse than the image of Mrs. Cohen hanging from a beam. He leaned out of the window and clapped his hands loudly, while the cat moved leisurely through the branches, turning occasionally to give him an insolent stare.

The sound of girlish laughter wafted up the patio. Perhaps it was the Moroccan family that had moved into the next house on the ramp, but no, their apartment couldn't have windows to the patio.

Again he heard the laughter.

'Where is Mimi?' he asked.

Eva looked up. 'She said she was going for a walk up the Rock. She's on a mission to get fit and quit smoking.'

There it was again.

'Come here,' he said to Eva whilst leaning further out of the window. 'Isn't that Mimi laughing?'

Eva leaned out too, but the laugh had stopped. 'I can't hear a thing,' she said.

He sat stock still on the window ledge. Eva went back to the sink, turned the tap on and began rinsing the vegetables.

'Shhhh,' he said, putting up a hand. 'That's Mimi, alright.'

He jumped down from the window. 'She is down in Montegriffo's apartment. Bloody hell! I'm not happy about this.'

He marched towards the bedroom to put a T-shirt on.

'Sebastian, where are you going? Don't make a scene. Talk to her when she comes back.'

He knocked on the door. It seemed to take ages before Montegriffo came to open it. He looked dishevelled and was wearing a black bathrobe.

'You caught me in the shower,' he said with a faint rebuking smile, though there was nothing wet about him. Sebastian glanced at his feet. They were bare but had left no marks of damp on the tiles of his hallway. 'What can I do for you?'

'Is my sister here?'

Their eyes met. 'Your sister?'

'Yes, that's what I said. My sister. Imogen...is she here?'

'No,' said Carlo, but he spread his feet and crossed his arms in a defiant pose, as though intent on blocking the way. Sebastian craned his neck and tried to look past the man into the apartment. All he could see was the hallway, a replica of his own.

'*Mimi!*' he shouted on impulse. 'Are you in there?'

Carlo kept looking at him but did not budge. Sebastian felt

a cold rush across his neck and shoulders, now almost certain that his little sister was ensconced in this predator's lair, probably in his very bed. Mimi was no virgin, he knew that only too well, she'd probably had more sexual partners than he'd had himself, but the thought of her in the hands of this arrogant bastard alarmed and enraged him in equal measures.

'Move aside,' he growled, taking a step forward. 'I want to see for myself.'

'Out of the question.'

Sebastian knew he ought to stay calm. He took a deep breath, reminding himself that aggression was the least effective way of achieving what you wanted. He took a step back and held up his hands in surrender. 'Tell you what. Just let me talk to her, okay. Then I'll go.' He waited a few seconds and saw the other man vacillating. 'Go on, call her. I just want to see she's all right...'

'You can't just come barging in, being rude and accusatory,' Carlo said calmly. 'Please *leave*!'

Sebastian shook his head. 'Come on, man. Be reasonable. Put yourself in my shoes.'

Carlo put his hand on the door to close it. For some reason the gesture struck panic in Sebastian, the thought of being shut out, not being able to rescue Mimi, being powerless to intervene. He barged forward, hands held out in front. The door flew open and the solid bulk of him, the sheer strength of his will, sent Carlo stumbling backwards into his hallway. Carlo managed to keep his balance and effectively blocked his sides with his arms.

'Out of my way, damn it,' Sebastian snarled.

'Get out!'

'Not without my sister.'

'She's not here, but if she wanted to be, that would be her prerogative. Now get out of here. You're trespassing.'

He did not believe it. Mimi was in the guy's bed or he would not have answered the door in a bathrobe so late in the morning. He'd already noticed that Montegriffo was a very early riser. An unwholesome picture flashed through his head. It almost made him reel with nausea, and he felt an overwhelming urge to murder the arsehole. 'You dirty bastard. Bring her out here *this minute.*'

Carlo was still blocking the way with his arms spread wide. 'Get out or I'm calling the police.'

Would he? Did he actually believe he had a right to her? Sebastian looked at him, then arched his brows and sneered. 'You think the police would take your side in this? You think they'd approve of some creepy middle-aged bachelor having his way with a vulnerable teenager?'

'You've got some imagination.'

'Yeah? Prove it. Let me come in and see her.'

Carlo regarded him thoughtfully for a moment. 'I get the feeling you have a problem with your *own* feelings towards your sister, Mr. Luna. It doesn't seem entirely natural to me that you...'

Sebastian went for him, this time with a fist. The first blow glanced Carlo's shoulder as he'd moved swiftly to avoid it. The next one hit him square on the left cheekbone, just below the eye. He staggered backwards and crumpled to the floor.

A few seconds passed. Carlo lay there, knocked out cold. Sebastian stared at him in surprise but didn't for a moment believe he'd done the man any real damage. He'd been a good boxer in his school years but surely the punch had not been one that would injure a grown man. Injured or not, Montegriffo would hardly let him get away with it. This over-dramatised fainting act was good for a charge of grievous bodily harm.

He jumped over the prone body and ran into the apartment. The layout was identical to their own, though the decor made it feel entirely different. His footsteps fairly echoed as he hurried from room to room. He was not at all looking forward to the scenario he would encounter, how he would deal with Mimi, what he would say, and how she would react in turn – especially when she discovered what he'd done to her lover.

But the dreaded confrontation did not materialise. There was no-one in the living room…nor in the bedrooms. Two of them were entirely empty except for some cardboard boxes, and the third and largest had a wardrobe, a desk and a single bed. The bed was unmade; the sheets and pillows in disarray. He recoiled at the sight, but still bent to look underneath it. He checked the wardrobe then went quickly to inspect the kitchen and bathroom, but Mimi was absent.

He stopped in the inner hallway to reflect on the situation. There wasn't a sound from Montegriffo, and he heard no movement whatsoever from anywhere else in the apartment. He raised his head to take his bearings and noted that the walls were an oppressive dark green, an odd choice of colour no matter how cheerless the occupant. What little there was of furnishings was sparse and dated, though not antique. Bare lightbulbs hung from dated wiring and some of the windows were covered with some stick-on textured plastic, the type poor people used in bathrooms instead of net curtains. Within the line of his vision a gecko darted across the wall, confirming his impression that no warm-blooded creature would voluntarily set foot in this eerie environment. Perhaps the black tomcat was a special type of cat, cold blooded. What the hell was his sister doing? Where the hell was she? The whole situation was grotesque. He couldn't believe he'd been reduced to this.

Looking around again, he retraced his steps, now searching for other hiding places. She could easily have slipped into a cupboard or hidden behind the living-room sofa. She had every reason to do so, because by now he was livid.

Minutes later he was forced to give up. He saw no sign of her: not her shoes, clothes nor bag. Unless there was a trapdoor, some hidden space, or like the cat she'd climbed out of the window and shimmied down the Eucalyptus, he'd been wrong. He'd have to eat humble pie and apologise to Montegriffo. Perhaps he'd be forced to call him a taxi and take him to see his doctor. As he walked towards the outer hallway he began to see how stupidly he'd acted, how serious a charge Montegriffo could lay against him. What a fool he'd been, and how cunning the bastard he was dealing with. Now he could hardly come and repeat the performance, Montegriffo had seen to that. His access to Mimi would be guaranteed.

Montegriffo was still on the floor, just as Sebastian had left him. He resisted the urge to poke the man in the side with the tip of his shoe, but instead gave his arm a little shake. There was not a flicker of response. He bent down to study his face. It was pale and the eyes were partially open. There was a bluish swelling where his fist had caught the cheekbone, in fact, the marks of three of his knuckles were clearly visible. There was no movement in his chest. Oh, God, he looked like a corpse.

Sebastian knelt down to put his cheek near the half open mouth and waited to feel that faint exhalation of air, but none came. Impossible! Carefully he turned the head to check for an injury to the skull, but there was no sign of a wound, no gash or indentation, no blood. Perhaps he was epileptic or had some neurological condition that would cause him to pass out. Or worse, perhaps the blow had triggered a stroke, or the stress of the assault, a heart attack.

He tried to feel for a pulse, first in the wrist then in the neck, quietly gagging while he pressed his finger deep into the cool flesh. There was nothing.

Jesus!

He knew what he had to do. Grabbing the head in both hands, he tilted it backwards to open the airway. He pinched the thin nose between his fingers, then placed his mouth over the dead man's and blew forcefully into his lungs. Next, he placed his hands on the sternum and used his entire weight to pump the chest in an attempt to re-start the heart. Minutes went by as he alternated between pumping and blowing, yet all the while he knew it was pointless. He could see the man was dead, stone dead.

Sebastian let go of the lifeless body and jumped back, the gravity of the situation slamming into him like a door in a strong wind. He was breathless and trembling, a sense of unreality threatening to overwhelm him. Could this really have happened? Was he really the cause of it?

He heard a noise from below and looked towards the door. It was still wide open and he ran to close it. His mind was reeling as he dashed to find a telephone so he could phone for an ambulance. He found the phone in the kitchen and sat down on a chair to think through what he would say when questioned by the ambulance men, the doctors and police.

Whichever way he turned it, this death would have far-reaching consequences, the enormity of which was beginning to descend on him. Even if Montegriffo had suffered a heart attack, which was the most likely explanation for his death, Sebastian's action had been the immediate cause of it. He'd have to confess to their altercation, to having punched Carlo. With that very obvious mark on his face, there was no point in denying it. He had effectively killed the man. If it did not amount to murder, what *did* it amount to? Manslaughter? There had been provocation, of sorts, but hardly deserving a brutal blow to the face. The physical aggression had been all his. And for what? He'd thought his young sister was in the apartment, in the process of being seduced by this reclusive and seemingly ascetic and sober man, a devout Catholic, a former priest and a pillar of the community. Attacking a man like him, on an assumption that turned out to be false, would make him seem like a thug or a crazy man, or both.

No, no, *no*. He had to remain in a rational and coherent frame of mind and convince the authorities that it had been an unfortunate accident. He'd been rightfully worried about his troubled and fragile sister. Montegriffo had taunted him, provoked him, led him to believe that she was in his bed in order to create the very scene that transpired, in order to humiliate Sebastian into surrender and acceptance. It had been the most insidious manner of provocation, and he'd known exactly what he was doing. But the police would not believe any of that – why should they? They may have some understanding of how a brother would be protective of a younger sister, but as far as the law was concerned, Montegriffo had done nothing wrong, neither legally nor morally. He was – he *had been* – an innocent man, viciously attacked for no reason within the sanctity of his own home.

He let the phone drop onto the table and put his head in his hands. A groan of sheer terror escaped him. Where would it end? Whatever his punishment in law, he was certain to lose the project. Probably lose his loved ones. If he was lucky enough to escape incarceration, he'd have to leave Gibraltar, he'd be dismissed from SeaChange, his entire career would be in jeopardy. No, not in jeopardy – it would be over. *It was over*. They would quickly discover the falsification of his medical reports. Who would place their millions of pounds, euros or dollars in the hands of a person with such a record, such a reputation? No matter how brilliant a mind, a man who appears out of control and dangerous cannot be trusted.

Another groan rose from his insides and ripped through him. A man was dead, but his own existence hung in equal balance. Barred from fulfilling his life's work, he could not live. By killing Montegriffo, he'd killed himself. It was as simple as that.

A few minutes passed as he considered his options. There weren't many. In fact, there was only one, and it would make him doubly guilty. He stood up and went back into the hall. Bending down he hooked his arms under the dead man's armpits and began to drag him along the floor into the bedroom. His strength seemed to have returned to him fully and with no effort he hauled the body onto the bed. In the process, the black robe fell open and ended on the floor. Sebastian kicked it aside and tried to arrange the body with its long limbs into a natural looking pose. The skin was deathly white and devoid of hair, except... The sight of the purplish genitals, bloated and grotesque, emerging from a tangle of excess pubic growth made him gag anew. He knew he should keep Mimi out of the equation, but he couldn't help himself. Whatever did she see in this...?

Something above the headboard swam into his vision. He looked up at the wall with a start and saw it was a carving of Jesus on the Cross, almost identical to the one that hung downstairs in the entrance. He peered at it for a second and noted how eerily similar Montegriffo looked in death to the crucified Christ. His large doe eyes half closed and his black wavy hair spilling over the pillow, the crucifix on a chain around his neck, his feet long and white and crossed quite naturally one over the other.

Quickly he tidied up the bed and pulled the covers over the corpse, and lastly closed his eyes. Were it not for the mark under the eye, he looked almost serene. On a sudden inspiration he looked around for a book. The only one in evidence lay open on the desk. He picked it up and examined the cover. *Unlocking the Poet Within.* A thought made him stiffen with a mixture of surprise and dread. Was it possible that Mimi was the muse for this poetic ambition? He'd made the worst possible assumption about Montegriffo as a predator grooming a young girl for his own vile needs, but could he have fallen in love with Mimi and harboured genuine affection for her? Sebastian quickly dismissed the idea as sentimental. It made no difference, a man his age had no business with such a young woman. He placed the opened book face down on the corpse's chest and lifted the right hand to rest on it. He stood back to examine the result. All he could see was the truth: *foul play.*

He hung the black robe on a hook behind the door, then proceeded to the kitchen where he grabbed a tea towel from the draining board. He covered the hot tap with it and turned the tap on. Having wet the towel, he proceeded to rub off every mark he might have made with his hands, on the telephone, the edge of the table, the chair, the door handles, door jambs, working his way towards the front door. Carefully he opened it and glanced outside. The stairwell was dark and quiet and he slipped out, gently closing the door and wiping the handle as he went.

Mimi

A lump of grey fog was concentrated over the city. It was that damned Levante that Sebastian was always grumbling about, the cloud formed by moisture piling up against the Rock. Beyond it the sky was blue and sunrays danced on the two seas.

She ambled southward through town, towards the edge of the cloud where the air was clear. That's where all the nice houses were. Not surprising.

An enormous cruise ship had docked in the harbour that morning – she'd seen it from the kitchen where she'd been feeding her breakfast to Raven. It disgorged its vast cargo of human flesh, pouring like liquid fat into town. She'd seen this routine a dozen times by now. Once on the High street, the mass would fragment into thousands of smaller units – round globules dressed in gaudy colours – and these would shoot in and out of shops as though Gibraltar were the only place on earth that sold cameras, laptops, watches, gold and designer sunglasses.

Taxi-loads of them passed her as she walked, on their way to the Upper Rock for the ubiquitous tour of Jew's Gate, St. Michael's Cave, and the Apes' Den.

Coming around the corner from Queens Hotel was the Cable Car Base Station. She dug in her bag. No, she only had seven quid and something, not enough to be hoisted up through the air to the top of the Rock. *Impecuniousness,* she swore to herself. She was broke, and she hated having to keep asking Sebastian for money. She'd have to find a part-time job, didn't all struggling writers? It would help to be eighteen, and that was soon.

She trudged up the hill past Rock Hotel. Further up, she passed a derelict building with a large sign on top: CASINO. Mimi stopped to stare at it. Glittering opulence, long abandoned. She wondered who'd been the last customer to leave when they closed their doors for the last time. Mrs. Cohen, maybe. After she'd gambled away all of her 230,000 euros, the owner had seen an opportunity to cut his losses. No, the place had been deserted for a lot longer than a year, even though Sebastian always said that even with the most formidable structures, nature began taking over the moment man turned his back.

Just as she decided to continue up the road, she saw an opening in the vertical cliff bordering the carpark, and was drawn towards it. It was the entrance into the interior of the Rock, one of the dozens around town. A gate of metal bars held a large padlock, keeping people like her from wandering where they didn't belong. Just a few metres in, it was as black as the entrance to hell. She shivered, not sure if it was the current of cool air that flowed uninterrupted from its interior, or something that came from within herself. Did she really want to get to know these black tunnels? No, that was one tour she could do without.

She turned away quickly and followed the road up the hill. There were just a few more houses and then nature took over. Slowly she climbed upwards in the blazing sunlight until she came upon a little gatehouse with a barrier.

'Are you a resident, miss?' said the guard through a little window.

'I've seen all those foreign tourists head up here,' she said, feeling defensive. 'Just because I'm on foot doesn't mean you can hassle me.'

'I'm not hassling you,' said the bemused guard. 'I'm asking if you are a visitor or a resident?'

She thought about her status for a moment. 'I'm a *guiri* living in town.'

'Let's call you a resident then. No charge.'

'Cheers,' she blurted, embarrassed by her rudeness. 'Which way to the apes?'

'Just follow the road around to the left and keep going. There'll be a sign to the Ape's Den, and there's another clan up at the summit. There are a number of newborns around the place, so just don't get too close. Apes have been known to bite.'

'It's OK. I know one personally. He's expecting me.'

The guard laughed. She gave him a little smile and was on her way.

She ambled for another half hour along the hillside on the single track road. It had doubled back on itself and ran parallel to the ridge. She was high above the town, surrounded by lush vegetation and wild olive trees. She'd written off Gib as being all concrete and construction, but she'd been wrong. There were mysterious footpaths and stone steps everywhere, leading into the dense underbrush. The pinnacle looked awesome even from this height. Sebastian had told her that Neanderthal man had come here from Africa some 100,000 years ago, and this rock was their first and last settlement in Europe. Traces of them had been found in the caves on the east side. The place had magic, and humans through the ages had been drawn to it.

Glancing back, she saw a man walking some hundred metres behind her. He sauntered along, his face bent towards the ground as though in deep thought. So she was not the only pedestrian here. Despite the taxis and minibuses that passed at regular intervals she felt a bit vulnerable. She didn't like walking in lonely places with some random man walking behind her.

She spotted a path which looked like a burrow up through the dense shrubbery. Glancing over her shoulder she saw the man had stopped but was looking out across Spain. On impulse she jumped across the ditch and scurried up the path. Breathless she crouched in the vegetation to see if he'd noticed where she'd disappeared to. After some minutes she saw him pass below her, continuing his easy amble up the road. She breathed out the air she'd been holding in her lungs. By the looks of him, this guy was no menace at all. In fact, he seemed quite slight himself. She could probably eat him for breakfast.

Even so, she decided not to re-join the road. There was no real way to get lost on the Rock, because most vantage points were high up and you could see exactly where you were. After walking for some twenty minutes she realised that the path narrowed to a ledge. It had turned left on itself and she was heading counter-clockwise around the Rock towards the east side, where Sebastian's project was to be built. That side was just a sheer gargantuan cliff. But surely the path must lead somewhere, it even had proper steps cut into stone.

In fact the path was increasingly just steps, a stone staircase climbing upwards alongside an increasingly vertical cliff face. Intermittently there were ropes to hold on to, as though whoever had made the path recognised how treacherous it was. In the distance below her she saw the tip of the mosque's minarets on Europa Point. She rounded a corner and could no longer see land. Now she was looking straight out over the Mediterranean sea. Dozens of tankers and container ships were anchored in the waters; from this height they looked as tiny and pitiful as walnut shells. She felt herself going dizzy with vertigo. Should she turn back? The path was plain dangerous, climbing ever higher, snaking back and forth along the cliff face.

Yet the longer she climbed the more daunted she was by the prospect of the return. An hour must have gone by, and going back would mean a plunge down the steps with only a rope to keep her safe. She passed a couple of lookout buildings perched on ledges, and a large cave in which modern humans had left signs of their presence. She smiled wryly; who'd have thought piles of used toilet paper could give one a sense of hope and comfort?

The sun was beating down on her head, making her feel faint. She was thirsty as hell and pretty hungry too. Surely, if she kept going she'd get to the ridge of the Rock and could descend on the other side, right down to town. Looking up, she saw the huge cliff looming above her. No person could surely go all the way up there... but the path went on, and out of sheer dread of having to retrace her steps, so did she.

Turning another bend in the narrow steps, she came upon three apes resting on the path in the shade of a shrub. She stopped dead. They looked harmless in their torpor but after a moment they rose from their lethargy and moved towards her. She knew the apes were rarely dangerous, but they had no fear of humans and would steal anything from you if they thought you had food. Two of them sat down again to stare at her but the third – a much larger one – slowly approached. Instinctively she started to back away.

'There, there,' she whispered. 'Don't look at me like that. We had a date, didn't we?'

The ape came ever closer and suddenly bared its teeth.

Her heart started hammering in her chest and her mouth had gone dry. At the same time her teeth clenched in anger. They ought to do away with the fucking animals if they could freak a person out like this. This was worse than meeting a pack of snarling pit bulls. She would rather die than turn her back on the nasty looking creature, and anyway, she knew she'd gone too far to retrace her steps. Neither was there a way they could pass each other without touching. Perhaps she would be forced to defend herself. Oh God, not that! She took a sudden step forward and screamed, 'Back away, you bastard. Fuck off. Now. You dirty piece of shit. Go away!'

Her rant had no effect on the ape; in fact he moved towards her, his lips curling right back over a set of long spiky teeth. Perhaps there was a female with a baby in the vicinity, the ones the guard in the gate house had mentioned. Hadn't he said they bite? Again she backed off, fearful of losing her footing yet terrified of taking her eyes off the creature.

The other two apes were getting agitated. One of them let out a long otherworldly shriek. It echoed eerily as though it came from the very bowels of hell, the worst sound she'd ever heard. Three full-grown apes could surely kill a person. Those teeth were twice the length of a pit bull's. She reckoned that apes must be so quick and agile they could hurl themselves at you and sink their teeth into your throat. Maybe that was what they wanted…to take secret revenge on the tourists that tormented them. What better place to attack a lone, small, defenceless woman than out here on a wild cliff?

The biggest ape still maintained a menacing stance, immobile with its lips curled back. Mimi was trembling, her throat dry as paper. Her panic had frozen her. Running was not an option; she'd tumble down the cliffside if she tried. Besides, nothing could induce her to turn her back on the apes.

The path was littered with loose stones, and slowly she bent down and picked one up. Raising it in her hand had no effect on the animal. It felt now like a fight to the death. She hurled the stone towards the ape with all her strength, but missed him by inches. A surge of adrenaline made her grasp at more stones, and with unaccountable power she flung one rock after another at the snarling ape. A rock hit him in the side of the head and he jumped up into the air. She took it as an imminent attack and screamed at the top of her lungs. The echoing shriek made all three apes turn and disappear along a narrow ledge into a clump of sparse shrubbery.

Just as quickly, the energy drained away from her body and she sank to her knees. After a moment she looked up, scanning the cliff face before her to check if she was truly alone. Her eyes fixed on the shape of a man some fifty yards above her. He held a rock in each hand. He raised one fist and seemed poised to hurl a rock at her.

'No, please don't,' she shouted putting her hands up in front of her face.

He dropped both rocks at once and called down to her. 'Don't move. I'm coming down.'

She lowered her hands slowly and stared at him. She sensed it was the man she'd seen along the road. The sun shone in her eyes and she could not quite discern his features.

'No need,' she shouted back in a trembling voice. 'I don't need help.'

Nevertheless, he bounded down the path swift as a mountain goat, and in five minutes was down to her level. Her fear transmuted into puzzlement.

He smiled. 'Mr. Montegriffo introduced us, remember?'

It was Mohammed, the lad in the rooming house.

'How the hell did *you* happen to be here?'

'I was just out for a walk and I heard screaming. So I came...'

She knew no-one in Gib, so how come, in the middle of nowhere, she'd come across someone she'd already met? 'Well, thanks. That was quite scary, actually.'

'Yeah, the apes on this side get very little bother from people. They must have felt threatened or something. I doubt they'd have hurt you, though.'

He had a strong French accent but his English seemed good.

'How can you be so sure that those apes weren't about to go for my throat? I read in the paper that a Spanish family was attacked few weeks ago.'

'I heard about that, but I bet the kids were pestering them in some way. Apes usually don't attack people for no reason.'

Her knees still felt weak, and her hands trembled, but she didn't want him to see how scared she was. He reached into a voluminous pocket on his trousers and pulled out a small bottle of mineral water. He held it out to her. Gratefully she uncapped it and swigged down several mouthfuls before realising what she was doing. 'Sorry. Here...I didn't mean to gulp it down like that.'

'It's OK,' he said waving away the bottle. 'I'm not thirsty. You have it.'

She glanced at him as she poured the rest down her gullet.

Wiping her mouth with the back of her arm, she asked, 'Where does this lead path to?'

'It gets you right up to the top, near O'Hara's Battery.

You're on the Mediterranean Steps, part of the nature reserve, but you rarely get people walking here.' He looked down the plunging cliff below them. 'You can see why, can't you?'

The sense of menace assailed her again. One shove and she could be hurtling down a thousand feet. But why would he want to do that? Why had he followed her here anyway? And how had he got up ahead, without passing her on the steps?

'Well, I'm heading on,' she said abruptly. 'Thanks for... your good intentions.'

He was too quick to react. 'I'll go with you if you don't mind.'

'No really, you carry on. You do what you came here to do.'

She wondered what he'd come here to do, exactly. Just meet her, or worse? The coincidence was too unlikely.

She took a step towards him. 'Why were you here just at this moment, huh? Don't you think it is a bit of a fluke?' He shook his head vehemently but was lost for words. 'Don't think up any bullshit,' she said, her voice raised. 'You've got no reason to follow me. It's a bit creepy, don't you think?'

'No, no. To be honest, it was Mr. Montegriffo...he wanted me to make sure you were safe.'

'Carlo?' The bottle dropped out of her hand and went bouncing down the steps. They both turned to follow its trajectory towards the sea until it disappeared from view. Then they looked up and their eyes met.

'See, he was right,' said Mohammed softly. 'You might well have needed my help.'

'When did he ask you to do that?' She shook her head in consternation. 'I'm not sure I like this.'

'I'm sorry,' said Mohammed.

'How did he get hold of you so quickly?'

Mohammed rubbed his eye, pretending he had something in it. He was not a sophisticated kind of spy: you could read him like a book. 'He bought me a phone.'

'Did he offer to pay you for spying on me?'

'Oh, no... I owe him, I mean, I do things for him.'

'Doesn't sound very healthy to me,' she said, vowing to take this up with Carlo. It showed some nerve to have her followed, but then again, he'd said she could get herself into trouble. 'Come on then,' she said sourly. 'Do your job. Get me out of here.'

'This way,' he said and led the way upwards.

The cliff still looked utterly vertical. How the hell were they supposed to get up there? One of her socks had slid right down and bunched at her toes and her trainer had rubbed her heel raw. She was too proud to stop and put it right, but Mohammed sensed her discomfort and reached for her hand. She took it gratefully and was surprised at his strength. He pulled her upwards and she let herself be dragged along.

Within twenty minutes they'd reached the ridge. She was panting with exertion as she took the last steps up, then stopped and stared at her surroundings. The sides of the Rock dropped away steeply. It was like standing on the knife-edge of the world's highest mountain. For a moment she was swept up by exhilaration and threw her arms out to physically capture the beauty. Sweat was pouring off her and her T-shirt stuck to her back. She peeled it back and let the air in. The wind whipped over the crest, cooling her. Mohammed stole a glance, ever so discreet. He couldn't possibly have meant her harm. He was so innocent – cute, too, she decided: cute as a button.

'This is the highest point,' he said.

'My god,' she said pointing at the battery. 'That must be the mother of all guns.'

'I guess it was, back then. It could shoot a missile across the water right into my country.'

'No kidding? Morocco, right?'

'Yes,' he said, looking across the strait. 'Home is far away…too far.'

'I'm sorry,' she said, 'but isn't there a direct ferry? It can't be more than a couple of hours.'

'There's far, and there's far,' he murmured. 'Perhaps it's hard for you to understand.'

They began the long walk down the western slope into town. She now found his presence quite companionable, but questions still circled around her thoughts. What the hell did this weird intervention mean? She was grudgingly grateful that Carlo had sent someone along who might possibly have saved her arse from being mauled by a bunch of irate apes, but did she need this cradle of protection? All in one day she'd quit smoking, tackled a vertical mountain and fought off wild animals with (almost) bare hands.

It took them a good hour to get down from the heights, walking side by side on the road, not saying much. After the confrontations they'd had, first with the apes and then with each other, both had retreated into a default reserve. Even so, she kept glancing at the boy at her side. He had those fine Berber features she'd seen in *National Geographic*. A slim straight nose and slightly pointed chin, glossy black hair that curled haphazardly on the nape of his brown neck. She fought an urge to touch those curls with the tips of her fingers.

The Angry Friar opposite the Convent was bustling with tourists. Rows of long tables brought unrelated drinkers together, and a drunken conviviality extended over the whole plaza. As they walked past on their way to Upper Town, Mimi peered into the dark empty interior of the pub.

'I've got enough money for two pints,' she said.

'I don't drink alcohol,' Mohammed said.

'A coke, then?'

'I think Mr. Montegriffo wouldn't like us...socialising,' he said. 'But thank you. Perhaps some other time.'

'Do you obey Carlo in everything? What's wrong with you and me having a drink? He doesn't own either of us, you know.'

'He sort of owns *me*,' Mohammed said with surprising bitterness.

'What does that mean?'

'Well, I work for him, don't I?'

'That's it?'

His hands were strong and mature with square nails. They moved constantly, clenching and unclenching, with an obvious yearning to express suppressed feeling.

'Imogen, maybe you should be a bit careful. Mr. Montegriffo is a generous man, but he's also demanding. Don't let him do you any favours.'

She fixed him with a sharp look. 'How do you mean?'

Mohammed literally squirmed in embarrassment. 'He's a powerful man.'

'Powerful in what way?'

'Influential, you know, in the Catholic Church, in the town. It's difficult to say no to him.'

She frowned. 'For *you*, perhaps'.

He paused for a moment, then murmured. 'Between you and me, I'm not legal. Mr. Montegriffo is trying to sort it out for me.'

To be illegal sounded quite exciting in theory, but she

was sure it wasn't. And how grim to be beholden to someone, be forced to do his bidding and then be grovelling in gratitude as well. 'I see other Moroccans live here and work quite openly,' she said.

'Yes, they have jobs and work permits. I'm hoping to get there one day. I need to send money to my parents. They're very poor.'

Mimi was humbled into silence. She took material comfort for granted and, thinking of it now, she'd seldom had to worry about the welfare of others.

Eva

The dawn light seeped in under the door. The fan made a gentle buzzing and the soft air caressed her naked skin. Sleepily, she turned her head to look at her lover, wondering if she could make love to him without properly waking him up. He was lying on his back, his eyes wide open. She traced his chest with a finger, waiting for him to turn to her, but he didn't seem to be aware of her scrutiny. At once she felt cold. There was something unnatural about the way he lay there like a corpse.

She'd noticed that he'd been unusually preoccupied for the last couple of days, but had stopped probing as he seemed unable to articulate any specific worry or concern. This inwardness was a side to his character she'd not yet experienced. Was it her; was she lacking in some way? Was it her confession of the other day? She knew that he'd never lasted very long in relationships: perhaps this cooling was a pattern in his life. He'd fall madly in love, ride high on the feeling for a few months and then, as familiarity set in, begin to lose interest. The thought made her heart ache, surely…surely…he wasn't that fickle. Surely he'd not been lying when he'd told her she was the only woman he'd ever truly loved. Surely he couldn't hold against her that there had been other men in her life.

Gently she put her hand on his cheek. 'Sebastian.'

She felt colder still when she saw no response. Suddenly he flinched and turned to her.

'Where were you?' she said, her voice breathless.

'At work,' he said and smiled. It was not his usual unbridled smile and he didn't move to embrace her.

'Are you worried about something?'

'Am I worried about something?' he repeated slowly. For a moment she thought he was about to speak. His mouth opened, then closed. He chewed his lip and rubbed his forehead with the tips of his fingers.

'Tell me, please? Let's talk.'

'What about? I've got nothing to say right now.'

'You never told me what happened the day before yesterday.'

His brow furrowed. 'The day before yesterday?'

She sighed. 'Yes, when you stormed down to confront Montegriffo. In fact, I don't think you've said a word to either me or Mimi since.'

'*Nothing* happened.'

'So what did you guys talk about? I mean, after you realised Mimi wasn't there? Did you have it out about his stunt in Inces Hall?'

'No, that's water under the bridge.'

'So, is it the works holdup? Please,' she pleaded, 'tell me what is bothering you.'

'Only I can deal with it.' He got out of bed and pulled on his shorts. 'I better get to it.'

Even when he was short of words, his love had always enveloped her like a warm cloud. She had come to take it for granted and felt acutely the chill of his withdrawal.

Sebastian

There was a notable absence of diggers, bulldozers, cement lorries, deliveries, assemblies or production; no hard-hatted specialists scurrying around the works site trying to be effective. Sebastian wandered aimlessly around the perimeter, kicking his feet in the dirt. Equipment and materials were stashed high and covered the storage yard. He stopped to stare at the components of a fifty-ton double-leg gantry crane which would need, somehow, to be assembled, mounted and affixed on a precarious ledge above the development site. He wasn't genned up on the mechanics of this particular crane, but he could see that the main hoist did not have the correct capacity, an inexcusable delivery blunder which could take weeks to put right. The other tower crane stood motionless, like a giant mechanical giraffe frozen in time. It was, in due course, to be re-assembled on the barge. The barge itself was to be attached to the cliff by an articulated arm. However, when it had been connected and put to the test, the arm proved inadequate to the task. The subaquatic drill was still in house-sized crates, cluttering up the limited space. The giant steel and concrete brackets were also arriving by sea in dribs and drabs, having been manufactured on mainland Spain without the poor bastards knowing they were meant for that much-disputed Rock they thought they owned, or should own.

In any event, the team of Princeton archaeologists and their damned study was the main cause for the delays in the commencement of the structural framework. They'd swung a further postponement from the Gibraltar government to make way for more indepth studies of the cave findings. Saunders had come over personally to attempt to convince the department that they could start construction of Phase One without encroaching on the site of the excavations, but no, there was some hold-up that no-one could quite explain to their satisfaction. The board members of SeaChange were apparently extremely unhappy. In addition to the vast sum already issued to the government of Gibraltar, just the equipment in the yard was a good fifteen million pounds, not to mention the cost of the geological and environmental studies.

He tried to maintain his interest in these problems, but it was the horror in Montegriffo's apartment that occupied his every waking moment. He imagined this was how it felt to be given news of a terminal illness. First shock, then denial. You pretend it can't be true, you wake up and think it was just a dream, a nightmare. Everything seems as normal, like night follows day. Then you remember that something has happened to knock your life from its safe and predictable perch down into an abyss of madness.

A sudden gust of wind whipped up the dust around him. He felt the grit on his teeth, and wondered what the hell he was doing there. As he headed towards the prefab office block, Jorge Azzopardi saluted him.

'Ready to pack it in, Mr. Luna? Not much happening today, huh?'

'Be so kind as to get me a taxi, would you, Jorge?'

Azzopardi did as he was bidden and together they walked up to the gate in silence. While waiting for the car to arrive, Sebastian observed the burly Gibraltarian. He'd long stopped trying to get Azzopardi to call him by his first name. It still felt wrong, Jorge was surely twenty years his senior. They'd stood there almost every day waiting for the taxi, chatting amiably, and it was the first time he'd taken proper notice of the man's features. He had hands like shovels and his nose was flattened like a boxer's, obviously a man who'd been in a fight or two...but hardly a killer. The irony!

'Any word yet, Mr. Luna? *The Chronicle* has gone quiet about it. Everybody's asking.'

He liked the guy – salt-of-the-earth sprang to mind – but resented having to explain, even justify, every glitch and snag of what should really be a straightforward project. He reiterated his standard answer with a resigned shrug. 'It could be a week. It could be a month. It could be six months. It could be six years.'

Azzopardi chuckled convivially. 'Should I take a holiday?'

Sebastian gestured around the site with a sweep of his hand. 'Careful, now. You don't want to make yourself dispensable. Let's face it, anyone wanting to get their hands on this equipment would have some difficulty removing it.'

Azzopardi's face fell. 'I was just joking, Mr. Luna. Obviously it's not theft that you need worry about. It's malicious vandalism.'

'Really? You think so?'

The man moved from one foot to the other, and clasped his hands behind his back. 'Not everyone thinks this project is going to improve Gibraltar.'

'I'm aware of that,' Sebastian said, then peered at him with a frown. 'Are you referring to anyone specifically?'

Azzopardi grimaced. 'I read that several groups are campaigning. The International Environmental Investigation Agency...'

'No, I mean locally.'

'Ah... Well, the Marina Trust, for example. They have some clout. There is the Spanish element, it's a historical thing but they are still bona-fide Gibraltarians with a voice. And then, of course, the Church. As far as they're concerned, everything in Gib should be approved, and preferably owned, by the Catholic Church. Now I'm as good a Catholic as any, but I don't think there's…'

Sebastian's attention faltered. His thoughts snapped right back, like a tightened rubber band, to Montegriffo. Being a zealous Catholic and a staunch reactionary, Montegriffo was without doubt a powerful adversary, but of course, *he was dead.* There was still time to call the police, say *he'd had an altercation with his neighbour and was worried. He'd knocked on his door a couple of times to try and settle their differences but the man didn't answer the door.* No…he knew he couldn't carry it off with a straight face.

Azzopardi's voice swam back into his awareness. 'No worries, Mr. Luna. The place is safe with me and the boys here, and we're all totally behind this project. It's the biggest thing ever to hit Gib. You are highly regarded here, you know…by some.'

Sebastian patted him on the shoulder. If the guy only knew how misplaced was his respect. 'It's just a case of a short delay. No worries, my man. The place will be buzzing in no time.'

He sat back in the taxi and sighed deeply. None of the frustrations and wranglings of the project – or what people thought of it – had any significance in the face of what he'd done. Since that fateful day (how long was it: a week? Two?), his obsession with his work had receded, to be replaced by the terrifying knowledge that when Carlo Montegriffo was discovered dead in his apartment, his own world might collapse. An investigation into the death would surely lead back to himself. The more he'd thought about it, the more he realised his idiocy in thinking the police would be fooled by the serene scene in Montegriffo's bedroom, *Unlocking the Poet Within* resting on his sunken chest. Christ! The guy had Sebastian's knuckles imprinted on his face. Could knuckle prints be identified? He'd read somewhere that the slap-mark of an open hand can betray many characteristics of the hand itself and thus its owner. And then there were the fingerprints around the apartment that he surely had missed cleaning off. Both his own and, no doubt, Mimi's. A clever investigator would put two and two together. Perhaps Mimi would be the suspect, or at least implicated. That must simply never happen! He'd have to confess.

Who might have seen him enter and exit Montegriffo's apartment, who might have overheard their confrontation, if not the fatal one, the previous encounter they'd had in Irish Town? Eva had seen him go downstairs to confront Carlo, Eva had asked questions; she suspected something was wrong. Eva was his love and his partner, but would she lie on his behalf? She – and probably others – knew of the 'friendship' between Mimi and the ex-priest. No self-respecting man would allow his sister to be seduced by a man old enough to be her father. The trail would lead back to the outraged brother, and with forensic science as it was he would surely be convicted of murder. Not first degree perhaps, since it was hardly premeditated...though how could anyone ascertain that? Montegriffo was a respected resident, and Sebastian a controversial outsider who invited misgivings and conflict. Just 'assisting the police with their inquiries' would draw such attention and animosity that he would have to leave Gibraltar if ever he was free to go. He would lose the project, and his reputation in the engineering world would be permanently damaged. But what worried him more was how Eva and Mimi would take this bombshell. Mimi would never forgive him for killing her boyfriend, and Eva would hardly want to stick around with a man capable of such violent outbursts, seeing that she'd gone to such lengths to get away from one. She would leave him, and love would disappear from his life as quickly as it had entered it.

All through the last week he'd lain awake beside her in that single bed. How could he make love to her with the graphic scene in the apartment beneath them etched on his inner eye? Come to think of it, she herself seemed distant, worried; almost as though she'd guessed his crime. Her body jerked in sleep and her long legs kicked viciously. Hour after long hour, while they lay there spoon fashion, his eyes had been open and he went over his movements again and again. Consumed by anxiety and exhaustion, he was sure Eva would soon read *murder* on his face. She kept asking if he was okay and commenting on how loose his shorts had become around his waist. He wondered why he didn't just tell her everything. Wasn't that what trusting, loving partners did? If she'd have married him when he proposed to her in Dubai, perhaps he'd be more likely to open his heart to her. If they were man and wife, she'd stand by him through anything, but her rejection had put a small wedge in his trust. Anyway, he'd long ago given up confiding in people. Dad had laughed at his childhood upsets and blamed his creative imagination, even accusing him of making things up, of out-and-out lying. Having grown so used to being guarded and secretive about his inner self, it had become a habit difficult to break.

The driver could not take him further than the Garrison Library. A car had broken down in the middle of the Town Range so he got out to walk the rest of the way. The sun was shining relentlessly and the heat amongst the old buildings was stifling. As he walked up Library Steps his head pulsated with an irregular echoing sound, deafening, like bells in a church tower. He tasted blood on his lip.

Walking through the passage towards his own building he slowed his steps. He stopped and stood in front of the entrance, rooted to the pavement. Something within him absolutely rejected the walk up those stairs, past the door behind which his victim lay decomposing in the summer heat. He realised that he could not face living one more day, spending one more sleepless night, with the rotting corpse a mere couple of metres below.

Checking his watch, it said 6.05. He turned abruptly and fairly jogged down the passageways, ramps and steps onto Main Street. He walked quickly through the throng of visitors, ducking between shoppers, street performers and young mothers with pushchairs. The rental agency was in the main square almost directly opposite the cathedral. He found it open still and dashed in to see Mr. Stagnetto at the front desk, briefcase in hand, apparently on his way home.

'Thank God I caught you,' Sebastian said.

'Mr. Luna!' the man exclaimed with insincere delight. Visits from existing tenants could only mean complaints. 'Everything all right with the accommodation, I trust?'

'Actually…that's why I've come. All's well but there is a problem I can't fathom, much as I have investigated.'

Stagnetto glanced at his watch. 'Yes? What's wrong?'

'It's a smell.' He felt like an idiot and a fraud, but this was the only strategy he could think of. 'I think I've ascertained that it comes from the apartment below. I've knocked on the door a number of times but it seems the occupant is away, I assume he might have gone on holiday or something.'

'A smell?' Mr. Stagnetto looked weary. 'What kind of smell?'

'I think it might be the large cat belonging to the occupant. It might inadvertently have been shut inside and…you know…perished.'

'Good God! What a thought! It's Carlo Montegriffo, isn't it?' Stagnetto rubbed his chin. 'Well, I guess I could come by tomorrow, but really, if he's away somewhere, I'm afraid I don't quite know what I could do about it. He's no client of ours.'

'But *we* are your clients, Mr. Stagnetto, and something must be done, *today* preferably. It's a health hazard and the smell is intolerable.' Sebastian hoped he sounded convincing enough.

'Quite! Perhaps someone in the cathedral offices will have the key to his apartment. I'll pop across the road and ask.'

'I'll be at home…expecting you,' Sebastian said.

On his way back, forcing himself past Montegriffo's door, he flicked the letterbox open and stuck his nose in. He was almost relieved to find that the odour of death was definitely there, though still not overpowering. Then again, the corpse was far inside the apartment, the building was cool enough, shaded by others, and Montegriffo's place was insulated from the heat of the sun by the floor above.

Sebastian mounted the stairs and let himself into his own apartment. Neither Eva nor Mimi was at home, thank God. He searched around for the black cat, on the roof terrace, in the Eucalyptus, in the stairwell and then outside in the passageway. It would not do to have the damned kitty show up when Stagnetto arrived. That might just make him turn around and leave. But what the hell would he do with the thing if he caught it, that is, if it allowed itself to be caught?

But the problem of the cat's disposal did not present itself. The wretched animal was nowhere to be seen.

He waited for the rental agent, pacing back and forth across the kitchen. Stagnetto would have obtained a key and hopefully felt justified in using it. They'd go down together and knock on the door. The smell was sure to assail them when they got into the apartment, and they'd find the body. They'd call the police and the medical/legal process would be set in motion and in due course determine his future and his fate. At least the wait would be over.

He'd heard nothing, he'd seen nothing. His relationship with Carlo Montegriffo was 'cordial' although he was not very happy with him entertaining his sister; then again his sister was almost legally an adult and Mr. Montegriffo was a decent enough sort. Too bad really, poor man. He'd had a definite pallor to him and was very thin. He'd seen the man bent over once in the stairwell, trying to catch his breath and looking like death itself. No – for Christ's sake, he mustn't overdo it.

No matter how much he rehearsed his patter, nothing sounded natural. But then again, there was nothing natural about discovering a dead neighbour. There was every reason to appear unsettled by it all; it was no small thing.

He opened the door and almost jumped back with alarm. The rental agent was accompanied by a policeman, a regular English bobby, traditional helmet and all. Sebastian realised his face must have been a picture of guilt but he quickly recovered his composure.

'This is PC Malcolm Garcia,' said Mr. Stagnetto. 'Try as I might, nobody seems to have a key for Mr. Montegriffo's apartment, so I thought it was wise to bring a...eh, a second opinion on the legality of acting on this. We can't just go breaking down doors, now, can we?' He laughed uneasily and glanced at the bobby. 'Anyway, I don't think it'll be necessary. We stopped outside Mr. Montegriffo's door, and to be perfectly frank, neither of us could get a whiff of the smell you're complaining about.'

They made their way down the stairs. Stagnetto rang the bell insistently then banged on the door with the flat of his hand. Not a sound from the interior. The policeman bent down on one knee and peered through the flap. He sniffed audibly, then he stood. He was an exceptionally tall man in his midthirties and looked like he didn't suffer fools gladly. He peered down at Sebastian as though trying to ascertain if the complainant was one of those neurotic fusspots he was loath to deal with.

'Mr. Luna, as far as I'm concerned, there is no smell of putrefaction whatsoever. I cannot see a just cause for entering the premises.'

Sebastian felt his nerves begin to give way. He'd come this far, they'd have to conclude the business. He could take no more waiting. 'I'm telling you, Constable Garcia. My fiancée, my sister and I... we all have been disturbed by it. The smell is far worse in the central patio. It must surely be coming from one of the bedrooms. You can see that Mr. Montegriffo is not here, and he's not been here for at least a week. I'm telling you, he's got a very large cat...' His voice had risen and he saw Stagnetto and Garcia exchange glances.

'Let's wait a day or two,' Garcia began.

'No!' Sebastian insisted. 'We can't take any more of this.'

He suddenly thought of a card he could pull that might just sway them to act. 'Listen. My fiancée is extremely distressed about what happened to Mrs. Cohen in our apartment.' He glared meaningfully at Stagnetto. 'You see the connection, don't you? I expressly asked you to get rid of all the evidence because I didn't want her to find out, but you left the greasy stain on the floor where Mrs. Cohen's remains had decomposed…God knows for how long. The truth came out and since then she's been suffering anxiety and nightmares. Just last week we had to move out of the bedroom, she couldn't stand another night in there.' He gestured to the door. 'Now Mr. Montegriffo is missing and there is a distinct odour of decay coming from his apartment. I'm afraid I don't think my fiancée can live here under these conditions…' He knew he should stop there, before he went too far.

Stagnetto looked suitably perturbed by this turn. He took the bobby by the arm and moved him aside a little. '*Venga*, Malcolm. *Abrimos la puerta*. I'll fix the lock at my own expense. Montegriffo *lo entenderá*. He's a reasonable man.'

The policeman still did not look convinced, but after a brief hesitation pulled out a metal card and a small tool from his pocket and with his back to them began fiddling with the lock. 'Damn,' he said under his breath. 'It's a ten-bolt security job. It's no good.'

'Let *me*,' said Sebastian, and before either man could react, he'd aimed a kick at the door with such force that the wood of the door frame splintered with a deafening crack. The door slammed open and bounced hard against the hall wall, ricocheting back and hitting him on the toe.

The two men stared at him, open mouthed. Sebastian stared at the door, wondering where on earth he'd got the power to kick a door frame out of a wall.

'That was a bad idea,' said PC Garcia, not without a tinge of admiration.

'That'll cost to put right,' said Stagnetto, pulling a large handkerchief from his pocket to wipe sweat off his brow.

The deed was done and Sebastian, both his head and heart pounding, hung back in the hallway as Garcia and Stagnetto went in. He heard the two men talking in rapid Yanito as they wandered around the apartment, but there were no sudden silences or exclamations of surprise, shock or disgust.

'*Nothing*,' said Garcia through clenched teeth as they came back out. 'No cats, rats, birds or other beings, alive or dead, anywhere in this apartment. Perhaps there is garbage left in the inside patio, Mr. Luna, or a dead rat in the floorboards of your own apartment.' He indicated the wreckage of the door with an indignant gesture. 'You'll have to settle up with your rental agency regarding the damage caused here. And you'd better try and explain this to Mr. Montegriffo. Luckily for you he is a very decent person.'

Sebastian was so shocked by the outcome of the search he could only nod. Where had the body disappeared to? What had happened to it? The man was dead, he'd been stone dead when he lay on his bed. Stagnetto was talking to him, but he couldn't grasp what he said. They were looking at him and he knew he was expected to respond in some way.

'I'll pay for the damage. Do you know any good carpenter? I'm...I feel...very stupid,' was all he could manage.

'You get yourself a chair, Luna, and guard this door until I get back with my maintenance man,' said Stagnetto. 'It'll be a while. We'll have to try and get the materials to replace the door frame, and a temporary lock as we can't put the old lock back without the key. With some luck perhaps the actual door can be salvaged.' He looked at his watch. 'Most likely we won't be able to get what we need tonight, so we'll have to bolt some sheets of ply to the opening somehow.

Let's just hope Mr. Montegriffo is away another day. He'd have a hell of a shock coming home to his front door demolished and his apartment bolted shut.'

Just as they were leaving, Mimi came walking up the stairs with the black cat in her arms. She stopped to take in what she was seeing, her mouth half open and a frown forming under her fringe. She recognised Stagnetto and nodded, then stared at the ruined door and the debris and wood fragments on the floor.

'It's all right,' Stagnetto said to her, his voice gentle. 'I can see that the cat is okay, and you'll be glad to hear that there was nothing else *untoward* in Mr. Montegriffo's apartment. Whatever the smell…there is certainly none coming from in there.'

'What smell?' said Mimi, innocent as a child

Eva

She arrived home from the dive to find Sebastian sitting on the steps of the first-floor landing. He was resting his forehead on his knees, a strangely passive posture for a man who was usually so dynamic. He looked like a little boy lost and she hurried up to him. Then her eye took in a definite change in the landscape. Carlo Montegriffo's front door was not where it should be and the door frame was in splinters.

'My God, has there been a burglary?' she asked, staring at the wreckage.

Sebastian lifted his head and looked at her. 'I'm just keeping guard until a carpenter arrives,' he said evasively.

'Hey, that's good of you.'

'Please, my love, can you get me a glass of water,' he said, reaching for her hand. 'And give me a kiss before you go.'

She was puzzled but intuitively she knew that it was best not to ask too many questions, sensing that Sebastian was the culprit. No doubt the broken door had something to do with Mimi's visits there, though when Sebastian had been down last week ranting at Carlo, it turned out Mimi hadn't been there after all.

In the days that followed, Sebastian seemed to come back to himself, in fact, for a few days he was almost inappropriately elated. Her partner was more complex a person than she'd realised, and it pained her to realise how little she understood him. What mattered most was that the intimacy and warmth between them had been restored, which made her own ghosts retreat for a while. The renewed strength of their love made her feel safe. While Sebastian's powerful aura surrounded her, surely nothing could touch her.

*

One breezy afternoon she came home to find the apartment empty. She kicked off her shoes and got a glass of wine from the fridge. She grabbed the book she was reading and, with her drink, made her way towards the terrace. True to his word, Sebastian had brought home a catalogue, and together they'd ordered a fine-looking rattan sofa and a triangular sail which she'd fastened to the poles for the clothesline, providing hours of afternoon shade. Her phone rang just as she was about to sit down. Assuming it was Sebastian, she went to look for it. She should have known better. Sebastian rarely called before he was ready to come home, and five o'clock was far too early.

With her heart beating, drum-like, in her chest she listened to the silent breather for a full minute, trying to think of a strategy. It had been a lifesaving idea to go across the border for a phone with a Spanish number. Spain was a big country. Obviously she was au fait with the directive: always cut a nuisance caller off. But she didn't have the courage to dismiss *this* caller.

'What do you want from me?' she said at last. 'At least tell me that.'

Still the silence, the breathing, not heavy but in some way impatient, exasperated even, willing her to speak.

'Montegriffo... Is that you? Is this really necessary?'

She knew it wasn't him, but just saying his name reassured her. Who knew, perhaps it *was* him...or some other person in Gibraltar that was so against the Frontiers

193

Development Project that he'd go to any length to get its perpetrator off the Rock.

As she listened to the breathing man – for the sound and depth was definitely that of a man – she saw herself packing her suitcase; no not a suitcase, a bag. She saw herself on a ferry to Morocco, or handing Jonny Risso a wad of Gibraltar Pounds as he dropped her off somewhere along the Costa del Sol where she could get lost amongst millions of foreigners and find passage to some other remote corner of the world.

She sank down into a chair in the hallway and massaged her forehead with thumb and forefinger, keeping the breather company in his silence. He just went on breathing, as though willing her to say more. That was what he wanted: a reaction – any reaction. But she was tired of running.

'Adrian,' she said finally. 'I know it's you?'

The breather stopped, only for a second, but he stopped. *So it was him.*

'Yeah,' he said in a low raspy whisper. 'Chantelle.'

She rang off, dropping the phone to the floor where it clattered along the floor tiles. A wail escaped from her throat and she clamped her hands over her mouth. She'd get rid of the phone, she'd go away for a few weeks... perhaps if they moved to some little village across the border. No, it was never going to work. Never! He was shrewder, more determined than she gave him credit for.

He'd find her. It was only a matter of time.

Sebastian

He lay back on the bed trying to have a rest. Gradually cutting down on his medication had alleviated the worst of his migraines, so it made sense to try and reduce it further. Despite the stress he'd been under since the altercation with Montegriffo, and then the bizarre disappearance of the body, the phase-down of his medication seemed to have had no adverse effects whatsoever. It was a clear sign that he no longer needed it.

The mystery of Montegriffo wouldn't leave him alone, however. Since there'd been no visit from the police, no interview conducted or arrest made, it probably meant that the body had been discovered by a cleaner, or a colleague, or a fellow Catholic, and removed from the premises, then deemed to have died from natural causes. But surely everyone in town – Stagnetto and PC Garcia included – would have known about his death and informed him? Yet what possible other explanation could there be? Part of him felt high on the fact that he might not end up in prison, removed from the women he loved and his career ruined for all time, but he now understood just what that ridiculous word 'closure' meant. He wanted closure, he *needed* closure.

He closed his eyes and tried the visualisation exercise he'd been taught in hospital, imagining himself on a beach, lying in the sand, listening to the waves wash over small round pebbles. Palm trees shaded him, a breeze wafted the air and he was supposed to become suffused with bliss. The problem with that was that he disliked sand, couldn't stand bright sun light and hated being idle. Lying on a beach was a form of torture. That psychologist had read him all wrong. What made him feel good was power and control. He was a creator and initiator, proactive and in charge. Getting joy and relaxation out of a passive stance to life was for the weak and timid.

His thoughts went back to the small world within the apartment. He was so happy that Eva seemed to have forgiven him his bizarre behaviour, he couldn't keep his hands off her. At the same time he was painfully aware of how this display must make Mimi feel, believing she had been dumped by her boyfriend without so much as a word of explanation. In some perverse way, he was happy to have been the instrument of her deliverance. Poor Mimi. From her very beginning she'd been denied the love she deserved. Jane gave birth to her, but as with him, there was not a morsel of love for her to chew on. Only Dad had been crazy about her, but the insidious spectre of Alzheimer's had soon begun to show and he'd found it hard to cope with a lively and precocious daughter.

Sebastian thought back to the first time he'd laid eyes on his little sister. He had just been released from a year-long spell in hospital, age nineteen. He'd come out of there a grown man, a *new* man, full of energy, enthusiasm and focus.

Dad signed him out. During the drive home Sebastian had a lot to say, and talked nonstop about his new vision. He'd had a dream only a few weeks earlier where he'd become the world's leading structural engineer. He knew the dream was prophetic, and from this day onwards he was going to focus on its realisation.

Dad glanced at him. 'Prophetic?'

'Don't worry Dad. I said *vision*, not *illusion*.'

After a short silence, Dad said, 'We have a surprise for you when we get home.'

'Oh, no,' Sebastian said, laughing. 'What is it? A dog?'

Dad laughed too. 'No, not exactly.'

'A gerbil, then? A parrot? Last time it was the tarantula, very appropriate!'

'Getting hot,' Dad said, still with a laugh, but one that sounded more like Santa's hollow 'Ho Ho Ho'.

Sebastian looked him over. Dad had aged. He wasn't a big man but had always had a presence, with his bushy grey hair and the moustache he liked waxing into bizarre styles. He seemed to have lost pride in his appearance somewhat. The moustache looked like a small lifeless creature draped over his mouth and his belly obscured his belt with the shirt half hanging out.

'I'm mighty glad you've decided to focus on engineering. Papito would have been so proud and happy you're following his footsteps,' Dad said, 'But son, you've got to look after yourself. Dr. Matthews has moved mountains for you. You must go and see him to thank him.'

'Yeah, yeah…' He felt like a ten-year-old. He'd had enough of being emotionally frail and treated like an invalid. He didn't need Dr. Matthews to move mountains. He was going to fucking move them himself.

Despite his protestations, Dad helped him with his bag. Jane waited for him in the living room, though she didn't get up to greet him.

'Hello, Mother.'

'Welcome home, Sebastian.'

She'd not come once to see him in hospital, but then he'd not expected her. She looked good, as usual, but tired.

Suddenly he noticed that beside her on the sofa was a baby. He stared at the little thing, sleeping soundly on a blanket, its long eyelashes casting shadows over the rosy cheeks.

'Whose baby is that?' he asked, mystified.

'Ours,' said Jane.

'Yours? Are you serious? Yours and Dad's?'

She looked affronted. 'I said so.'

'I thought you'd be too old to have kids.'

'I'm forty-three, Sebastian. You call that old?'

'No, of course not, but...why did you want to?' he said, turning to Dad who had come in behind him. He couldn't believe that the old man had it in him. Jane had never allowed him to touch her – as far as anyone could remember – but who knew what went on behind closed bedroom doors? 'You're a bit past childrearing, both of you, aren't you? Dad, you're over sixty.'

'Who cares?' said Dad, bounding up to the sofa, arms already outstretched.

'Don't touch her,' Jane hissed. 'For Christ's sake, don't wake her up.'

'What's her name?'

'Imogen,' said Dad, sitting there gazing down at the little one, a picture of a besotted father.

'I can't believe you didn't tell me.'

Dad didn't even look up when he spoke. 'We felt it would be too stressful for you. You were quite unwell, remember?'

'A sister! Bloody hell!' Sebastian groaned. 'Don't ask me to babysit, okay? I've got to get my head down if I'm ever going to be an engineer.' He sat down on the sofa and looked at the baby. You couldn't deny that she was cute. Imogen...it was too grownup a name for such a little thing. Mimi, he thought. Hi, Mimi.

'We'll manage,' said Dad, throwing Jane a warning glance.

'I wouldn't have had her, but your wonderful father insisted we keep her,' said Jane sarcastically. 'She wasn't planned, that's for certain. All of us have to pull our weight. You too, Sebastian. You *must* help. I'm not doing this alone.'

Sebastian looked at his parents, an incongruous pair from the start, Jane marrying for money and status, Dad for youth and beauty. There had been no love between them then (she'd said so herself), and even less now. It was astonishing that they were still together, especially her with him. The whole thing felt wrong. Dad shouldn't have exerted his own will, not on something as colossal as this. He saw suddenly how the future might look. He was the one with the youth and the energy.

Mimi

'Off to paint the town black?' Eva asked as she was leaving the apartment.

It was irritating to have to justify her movements; even so it was kind of comforting that Eva actually cared where she went.

'I'm just going out for some air,' she said and pulled the door shut.

She went downstairs and knocked on Carlo's door, as she had every day for eight days. She had a good excuse, she wanted to give back some of his poems with her annotations. There was no answer to her knock and she had to accept the obvious, Carlo was avoiding her. She was almost sure that Sebastian had engineered this somehow. On the other hand, Carlo didn't seem like a guy who'd be easily intimidated, and she could not overlook that he'd cared enough to have her followed.

Standing there like a lovesick dog, she wondered if she was falling for him. Some counsellor Jane and Gordon had forced her to see had explained her taste for older guys: she was searching for the idealised version of her dead Dad, the protector and provider. Nah, bullshit! She just found in Carlo a kindred spirit, an intelligent and interesting man who could help her become a writer. That was it. Surely!

The building was normally so quiet, but from the passage came the echoing sounds of children laughing. Another Moroccan family had moved into one of the apartments on the ramp. A cockroach scurried past and disappeared into a crack in the wall. How stupid of her to think Carlo would be interested in her and her pathetic novel for more than a few minutes.

Walking through the entrance to Ocean Village, she passed a group of people pointing towards the harbour and talking excitedly. Craning her neck in the same direction, she saw a huge cruise ship standing in port, rising high above the buildings of the docks. She overheard someone say it was the *Allure of the Seas*, the world's largest cruise liner. Drawn by the idea of the world's largest anything, she diverged towards Waterport Road and the Cruise Liner Terminal. There she stopped to gawp at the massive floating city before her.

Hordes of passengers were streaming through the terminal and getting into taxis and minibuses, while teams of dock workers were loading crates of stuff onto cranes which were hoisted into gaping openings on the side of the ship. She stood there watching the loading for a while. Enormous boxes of vegetables were delivered to kitchens, slings of netting filled with potatoes, lettuce and cabbages, enough to feed an entire city. The workers were all big muscle-bound guys, effortlessly tossing the loads as though they were beach balls. Only one of them stood out as almost weedy in comparison, but what he lacked in muscle he made up for in sheer speed. Smiling, she observed his frenetic pace until she noticed his footwear: bright yellow trainers. She'd seen trainers just like those before...under a bed somewhere?

When they'd finished loading the hoist, they moved away for a break and a couple of them lit cigarettes. The little guy with the yellow trainers turned around.

'Hey!' she called and waved. 'Mohammed!'

He peered into the distance and then bounded up to her. 'Hello, Imogen.'

'Call me Mimi, for God's sake,' she said laughing and kissed him on the cheek. 'I see this surveillance lark has gone all wonky. Here am I, checking on you, when you should be checking on me.'

'Please don't tell Mr. Montegriffo you saw me here.'

'Hey! It's a job. That's brilliant, isn't it?'

'I'm just filling in for one of my countrymen. He pulled a muscle in his back. His boss said I could do it for two weeks, no more… so please don't tell.

'Of course I won't. Where is he, anyway? I've not seen him for days.'

Mohammed looked down at his feet. 'I don't know. I've not seen him for a week myself. I think he's gone underground.'

She squinted at him. 'Is that 'underground' or under ground?'

He clearly understood the difference and smiled his lovely shy smile. 'It could be either,' he said. 'Mr. Montegriffo loves his tunnels. As you know.'

They stood there a moment longer and then one of the men shouted for Mohammed. He reached into his voluminous pocket and took out a can of coke. 'Would you like a drink?'

She laughed. 'Ask me some other time.'

Sebastian

Finally! The site was bustling with activity and noise. Engineers, project managers, site foremen, machine operators, divers, and a multitude of other specialists had all piled back on the job after almost a month laying fallow. Everybody was busy with some task or other. Sebastian was in his office, trying to coordinate their efforts and direct operations. The planners' go-ahead had galvanised him. He felt fit and proactive; his headache had vanished and he was down to his last bottle of tablets, after which he would make an attempt to cope without. The last few weeks seemed like a bad dream from which he'd now suddenly awoken. Apart from the fact that the waistband on his trousers was loose and Eva had noticed small tufts of white hair at his temples, it was as though nothing had happened at all.

The noise was deafening but he felt his mobile vibrating in his pocket.

'Hey, Luna,' Saunders booming voice was upbeat as always. 'Some guys from the *Canadian Journal of Civil Engineering* are flying over to do a piece on the Frontiers Project. They should be there on Monday.'

They chatted for a while about the good news of the project's go-ahead, and Saunders ended the conversation with, 'Listen now. You're our lead engineer – don't get me wrong – but when you meet with the Canadians, I expect you to stick to the subject.'

Sebastian frowned at the warning, thinly cloaked as a piece of advice. 'Exactly what do you mean by that?'

'What I mean is, don't talk about any other future projects, or yourself in relation to any other project, real or imagined.'

'Henry, I have *never* been told what to say or not to say in an interview.'

'Well, I'm the managing director for SeaChange – your employer – and I am telling you what this article should be all about. Keep to the brief.'

He was stunned by the sheer impertinence of it. It was like being pulled up in front of a schoolteacher and told his presentation was unsatisfactory. He grudgingly agreed and they said a mutually curt good bye.

No sooner had he rung off when the phone went again. It seemed all he ever did was act as his own P.A. As though he had time to talk on the damned mobile!

'Mr. Luna?' A solicitous female voice.

'Speaking.'

'I'm calling from the offices of the Ministry of Defence.'

Sebastian's heart skipped unpleasantly. 'Ah…why…what can I do for you?'

'I'm sorry we've taken so long in getting back to you.'

He frowned and pressed the phone closer to his ear. 'What about?'

'You applied to have a tour of the tunnels… I think it was at the beginning of last month.'

'I did?'

'Well, your name is down on the list. In fact I think it might have been one of our guides, Mr. Montegriffo, who put your name down. Now, we don't usually offer private tours during the summer months, but – well – you are obviously doing something pretty amazing for Gibraltar, and being a structural engineer and all, why shouldn't there be an exception to the rule?'

'*Montegriffo?*' Sebastian blurted. 'Is Mr. Montegriffo about?'

'No, I'm sorry. I think Mr. Montegriffo is away. There aren't very many guides available right now, but Mr. Jose Molina can take you on Sunday morning at ten, if that suits you… He's an amateur historian, very knowledgeable, in fact he's the one who saw your name on the list. A big fan of the Frontiers Project. I have to warn you, he'll want to grill you about it.' She laughed. 'Perhaps a tour for a tour!'

Sebastian laughed too, almost hysterically.

'A tour for a tour? I should be able to arrange that. So Sunday…yes, brilliant. It's my one day off. Where do I meet Mr. Molina?'

'You can leave your vehicle in the carpark of the old Casino on Europa Road. He'll meet you there.'

'Can I get to the starting point of the tour on foot from the upper town?'

'I suppose you can meet him at the tunnel entrance if it's more convenient. It's on the upper end of the disused thoroughfare just below the Devil's Gap Battery. It's been closed to traffic for some years due to rock fall, and I'm afraid you have to climb around the gates. Strictly speaking it's out of bounds, but it's not difficult.' She laughed coquettishly. 'I've done this tour myself so I know. There are three tunnel openings along the road, and you want the middle one.'

He sat down in his chair and thought about the commitment he'd just made. He was interested in the tunnels, all right, but he could not, for the life of him, remember having mentioned it to Montegriffo. Perhaps the man had taken it upon himself to put him on this list, or Eva or Mimi had asked him to, as a surprise. What a horrible quirk of fate: the man having done him a good turn prior to being bashed to death by Sebastian himself. He had no choice but to honour it.

*

He woke up in pitch darkness, then he remembered why. Eva had bought him some eyeshades at a pharmacy. He peeled the shades off and everything seemed different. He felt awake and alive down to the very molecules of his being. Every detail of the room looked clear and sharp, even in the twilight.

He looked over and studied his sleeping companion. Eva's back was turned to him, her hair flowing like liquid honey over the pillows. Moving a strand of it carefully aside, he studied the scar that ran inside her hairline from the side of her ear, almost circling the back of her neck. It was faded and white, but the stitch-marks were still visible. He leaned over and softly grazed the scar with his lips. He wondered why he'd never asked her about it, what had caused such a strange wound, as though someone had tried to scalp her. Some things were better not known. Perhaps he'd been all wrong about her and she was fallible and brittle and damaged? He couldn't bear to find out.

He lifted the sheet a little to look down at her body. She had the legs of a woman, not the fishtail of a mermaid.

'Don't tell me who you are, Chantelle.' he whispered.

She trembled a little in her sleep and flung an arm out, uncovering herself to the waist. Her breasts shone in the darkness, whiter than white. He put his lips to the whiteness and felt a sudden ache in his groin, then reached down to feel the mother of all erections. Oh, God. Not again! Carefully he lifted her hand and placed it there. She groaned a little, half with interest, half in protest. Her hand closed around him and he moved slowly against it. She rolled onto her back, still in a twilight zone but clearly willing. He mounted her and was grateful for her compliance, because nothing could have stopped him. Nothing! It didn't last long. He twitched convulsively as he came.

For a while he lay still on top of her, catching his breath. 'Sorry,' he whispered.

'You're like the fly,' she murmured sleepily.

'Who?'

'*The Fly*! Don't you remember? The movie with Jeff Goldblum. It's a classic.'

He raised himself on his elbow and looked down on her. 'Yeah, I remember it. I watched it with Mimi years ago, and I was more scared than she was. He turns into a freak, a nutter with bug eyes and his fingernails ooze slime and drop off.'

She ruffled his hair and chuckled. 'I was thinking more of his sex drive. When he comes out of the teleportation pod and he suddenly has this unbelievable sexual potency and when his girlfriend can't take this frantic action anymore, he goes out and finds a prostitute.'

'I'm not like that, surely?' he protested. 'Anyway, the film wasn't about that. The theme was about how not to meddle with nature. How you can't try to step in and be God...'

She let out a meaningful little laugh. 'Who's talking!'

He put his lips on hers to silence her.

'Yeah, but you know what I mean,' she insisted, turning on her side and tipping him off her. She pushed a wisp of his hair out of his eyes. 'Suddenly you're horny *all the time*. What's that all about?'

'I don't know why, and sorry, that was a pretty crude show.' He traced her eyelid with a finger. She looked sad. 'I feel like a real shit,' he said. 'Don't trade me in, will you?'

She didn't answer and he thought about what she'd said. It was true; he *was* rampantly horny. His erections in the last few days had taken him by surprise. Suddenly he remembered. *Of course!* It wasn't the first time! He'd not made the connection. It was simply the result – and benefit – of coming off the medication.

'I fancy you, woman, that's why. I'm helpless around you,' he said hurriedly, and kissed her again, but she drew back and studied his mouth.

'And what's this chewing on your lip all the time? Look at you. You've got a great big lesion there.'

'No, I haven't,' he said indignantly. 'That's always been there.'

Again, they were without words, just asking questions with their eyes. He knew it was a moment in which he could have asked her about the passport and told her about his past illness, perhaps even about what he'd done to Montegriffo. But something stopped him. He trusted Eva with his life, but whoever Chantelle was, how could he know what *she* might do with this information? What did he know about *her*? The name was on his tongue, but the opportunity for frankness was lost when the radio came alive, declaring it was morning.

'Will you take me away from here soon?' Eva said. 'I want to go and live somewhere far away, in the middle of nowhere. And without a phone.'

'This *is* far away, my love,' he said with a chuckle. 'How about Japan…in about a year?'

'Must it be that long? I feel…hemmed in here.'

Her words filled him with dread but he tried his best not to show it. Was she going to leave him? Could she disappear out of his life in the same way she'd come into it? He put his arm around her and drew her head onto his shoulder.

'Hang in there. You love your job, don't you? And Brian is a nice guy, isn't he? Easy going and treats you with respect. And I adore every cell in your body. What more could you want? Tell me, and I will provide.'

She laughed, taking her time to answer. 'Okay, get me away from here…for a day at least…this Sunday. I could use a day off the Rock.'

'Of course I will,' he said, relieved.

'What about Mimi?' she said. 'I think we should try and get her to come along too. She's in a very morose mood. I have a feeling Montegriffo has made himself scarce in order to shake her off. What did you *really* say to him?'

'Yes, let's all go,' he said quickly, 'the three of us. Why don't we go to Tarifa and take the day ferry over to Tangiers?'

'Brilliant!' Eva pulled herself closer into him. 'I so look forward to it.'

Carlo Montegriffo! The fucking tunnels! Sebastian let out a fearsome groan. He rolled her over, raised himself above her and looked her in the eyes. 'I am so so sorry, Eva, I've just remembered I have a commitment. I've accepted an offer of a private tour of the tunnels. But listen, I know what! Perhaps you'd like to come. You and Mimi both!'

Eva was quiet for a long time. 'Perhaps I'll go diving.'

'Come with me, my love.'

'No, you go. Water is my element, not rock.'

*

He gave himself half an hour to reach the tunnel, and the instructions proved to be precise. Where Upper Town ended, wilderness began. Hidden within the foliage were all manner of ancient building works, from crumbling military lookouts to gun casements and lime kiln chimneys. The path was rarely used and in bad order – no wonder, as it led to a road which was barred. He hauled himself around the side of a grilled gate – hanging perilously over the steep hillside – and in the effort, snagging his shirt on the wires. There were more than three tunnel openings but some of them had been bricked up. The one he was looking for was sizeable and had a proper sheet metal double door.

He stood at the tunnel entrance, waiting for what seemed like ages. Mr. Molina was late. At 10.15 his irritation began to rise. He sat down on a ledge next to the tunnel. Small stones tumbled down from the rock-face above at regular intervals. The heat was building steadily and already his shirt clung to his torso. He was wearing his seldom-used hiking boots, not knowing what sort of ground he'd be treading within the tunnels. Now they felt like a couple of torture devices, oppressive, heavy and very hot.

'Well, good morning, Sebastian.'

Sebastian swung around and looked up against the sun. The voice was unmistakable, deep and self-assured. He leapt up, not sure whether to flee, to fight or just faint.

'Surprise, right? You didn't expect to see *me* here.'

Eva

She dreamed of Remus. One moment he was a puppy and he was tearing an oven glove to bits, growling and snarling as though it were a rat he'd caught. When she'd tried to take it off him, he stood his ground and growled at her...she'd laughed – it was a great game – and Adrian had laughed too. The nipper was only two months old and already knew his own mind. She loved that dog like a child. In the next moment Remus was a large dog, tied to a stake at the far end of the yard and whimpering pitifully. She looked at him through the kitchen window. His ribs seemed as though they were on the outside of his chest. His head was too large and his hipbones stood out like door knobs. She was only allowed to give him water. Why did Remus have to suffer so, when it was she who'd tried to run away? She obeyed, but she couldn't bear his death being so slow.

She tried to wake up. The sheets stuck to her damp body and she felt nauseous. That image would never leave her – some things you simply could not erase from your mind. She could never have a dog again, ever. She heard the morning screech of gulls and she knew she was in Gibraltar. Then a door closed. That must have been Sebastian leaving for his tunnel tour.

*

'Tell me something about yourself?' said Brian.

The waiter sidled up to them and she was relieved at the

211

interruption. Brian ordered coffee, fresh orange juice and croissants.

'They bake them on the premises,' he confided, 'but only on Sundays. You'll see, that's why everyone is here and not next door.'

They were sitting at a table on the uttermost end of a pier called Basser's Landing. It was one of the three piers in Ocean Village, housing several eateries. A yacht had just motored in to its mooring beside them and water sloshed against the footings. They had an hour to kill before preparing for two customers who had called to book a spur-of-the-moment dive. She'd tried to tell Brian he should take the day off as she was available and was quite happy to handle the couple, but Brian had wanted to come as he'd nothing better to do.

The coffee was delicious and she savoured it slowly, enjoying the elegance of the place and feeling like a hypocrite. Ocean Village reminded her of Dubai, the wealth of its residents ostentatiously on display. Dozens of mega-yachts jostled for space at the moorings around the village. The enormous casino sat on its own island and – behind it – the impressive *Sunborn* super-yacht, a ship made into a permanent 5-star hotel. High-rise apartment blocks in blue glass, fabulous pools and garden areas surrounded the leisure development.

She recalled Sebastian's contempt for the place, saying it was poorly planned and executed. She would have enjoyed living in one of those apartments. Instead she had to trudge up through the cramped and shabby Upper Town. Ultimately, that's where she belonged, hidden among common folk who took little interest in each other's background...yet, someone was interested – someone was looking for her, calling to her.

'You sure found yourself a very good location here,' she said. 'Smart move.'

'Yeah, but the rent and the rates are crippling… Did you just change the subject? Come on, don't make me do all the talking.'

She'd only known him for a couple of weeks yet it would be so easy to unburden herself on him, spew it all out: the phone calls, her fear, Adrian.

Brian had mentioned a divorce, and his ex-wife taking their eight-year-old daughter to a new setup in Los Angeles with the British courts' full approval. Eva was in sympathy with his predicament, and impressed that he'd not held her American citizenship against her.

'Nothing much interesting to say about my person. As you gleaned from my diplomas, I'm a certified paramedic. I was teaching diving in Dubai when I met Sebastian.'

'So you decided to give up your freedom and follow a mere man?' Brian probed with a smile.

She laughed. 'Yes, I fell in love. He swept me off my feet completely. We're like chalk and cheese, but as they say, opposites attract. He's very special, a very unusual person.'

So special she would not consider confiding in him? Why was she sitting here chatting with Brian when she rarely did so with Sebastian, the love of her life? It seemed Sebastian couldn't cope with her being damaged goods, he seemed to have forgotten about the sinister phone calls. He certainly had reverted to his exalted view of her as the perfect specimen of womanhood.

Brian was peering quizzically at her. 'Are you happy?'

'Sebastian has me on a bit of a pedestal,' she confessed. 'It can be hard work to stay up there. I feel as if I'm going to fall off sometimes. Sooner or later I probably will, and then the question is if he'll love me as I really am.'

She stopped, wondering what the hell she was saying. Her private thoughts were fluttering out of her mouth like demented butterflies. She went on hurriedly, 'To answer your question, yes, I'm happy. There are no shackles in this relationship. Sebastian needs to be at liberty to pursue his career, and conversely he lets me get on with my life. That's what I love about him.'

Brian looked puzzled as though he wondered where intimacy fitted into all this freedom. Perhaps her face didn't match her words. 'And your parents, siblings?'

'I'm an only child,' she said, looking out over the water towards that distant land. 'My parents are – or were – Jehovah's Witnesses.'

'Aren't you in touch?'

'No, I was cast out, excommunicated.'

Brian leaned forward, a frown on his face. 'What on earth for?'

'I was a rebel, I refused to conform. I had a liaison with a Catholic boy, I was caught drinking, smoking dope. It all led to being shunned by the community, shown the door.'

Brian looked shocked. 'Goodness, girl. That's harsh.'

'Don't worry. That's nearly twenty years ago.' Then she added. 'I had a ball to begin with – free as a bird and thought I was going to conquer the world – but sooner or later that early brainwashing comes back to haunt you. Deep down you're defective, isolated…worthless.'

They were silenced by the roar of a Monarch Airbus preparing for takeoff, then watched as the plane soared off over the bay. She wondered if Sebastian had asked about her family, she couldn't remember ever talking to him about that murky pit of her youth.

'I can't think of anyone less defective,' said Brian. 'But self-esteem is a funny thing. It often has no connection with reality.'

He was right, and right now, they were getting too connected to her reality for comfort. 'Don't ask me any more questions, Brian. I've re-invented myself and my past is dead, as far as I'm concerned.'

'I wish I could do the same,' he said with a despondent sigh. 'It doesn't work when you have a child. I can't stop thinking about her.'

'I bet.' She shook her head in empathy. 'I hope I never have to discover what that feels like.'

'So what's the special and unusual boyfriend doing with *his* Sunday?'

She gave him a wry look. 'He's swung a private tour of the lower tunnel system. He'll be hours. All day, probably, if it's up to him.'

'Let's have another coffee,' said Brian and waved at the waitress. 'And another heart-attack inducing croissant. On Sundays, anything goes.'

Sebastian

Sebastian was speechless, hardly able to catch his breath. He'd never seen a ghost; he had never believed in them. His heart was beating so fast that for a moment he thought that he was having some kind of seizure. After a long moment, he managed to nod.

'Apologies on behalf of Jose Molina,' said Carlo Montegriffo pleasantly. 'His wife was rushed to the hospital in premature labour early this morning. She gave birth to a healthy boy only a couple of hours ago. So Molina called me to fill in for him. You don't mind, do you?'

Sebastian stared at him, searching his face for some clue to the mystery of his standing there before him in the flesh.

'You don't look happy.' Montegriffo's eyes narrowed a bit. 'I can assure you I'm every bit as informed about the tunnels as Molina, actually, quite a bit more so.'

'Where were...you?' Sebastian stammered at last.

'Me?' Montegriffo pointed to his own chest in puzzlement.

'Have you...have you been ill?'

'Heavens, no! What makes you think that?'

'You've...you've not been at home.'

Montegriffo's face broke into a repentant grimace. 'Of course...but please tell Imogen I've revised the work she edited for me. Her input was ever so helpful. She's got a sharp eye.'

Sebastian could not stop himself staring at the man come alive. 'Where you on holiday?'

'Not exactly. I've got a little place in Both Worlds where I go when I need a bit of peace and quiet. You know it, don't you? The little community near where you're hoping to build your so-called Frontiers Development Project.'

Despite the mayhem in his mind, Sebastian registered Montegriffo's provocation but was too unnerved to react to it.

'You see,' Montegriffo leaned towards him as though to whisper a confidence, 'I'm actually working hard on a book of my own.'

'A book?'

'Yes, about the tunnel system itself. I'm almost there.'

Sebastian flinched. 'The tunnel system, Mr. Montegriffo?'

'Call me Carlo, will you? Apart from writing about the history of Gibraltar, my scribblings are mainly of a spiritual nature, a way to express my deep personal awareness of the Divine Spirit. I'm not a little proud to say that two of my poetry collections have been published by Catholic World Publishers.'

Montegriffo peered at him. 'Are you all right, Sebastian? Look...what are we doing standing here in the sun? Let's get into the tunnels. The temperature down there is a perfect twenty-two degrees. It never changes.'

Sebastian flinched, taking a step backwards. The very idea of going into that alien space with Montegriffo seemed inconceivable. How could he go into that dark interior with a man he thought he had killed? Perhaps this was a plan to take revenge on him in some way... In fact, the ways to inflict harm on a person in the bowels of the Rock seemed infinitely varied and sinister. What could he say to get out of it? Perhaps the only way was to bring up the dreadful incident. He needed to know what had really happened between them in that hallway. But what to say? The sheer sense of unreality he felt about this encounter made his thoughts fuzzy, and he found it difficult to formulate his words. He thought frantically about how to broach the subject.

Montegriffo was looking at him with a puzzled expression. He seemed oblivious to Sebastian's confusion. Perhaps it was better not to bring it up at all? No, he simply had to try and find out what had really occurred that terrible afternoon, and Montegriffo's own perception of it. He had to keep him talking while they were still outside.

'Listen, Mont— Carlo. Let's not ignore what happened last time we met. I'm sure you agree that it was bloody unpleasant. I was very upset and I think I lost my temper.'

Montegriffo frowned. 'Well, yes, you did. But why bring it up again? I thought we dealt with it at the time.'

Sebastian felt increasingly bewildered. How far should he press this? Was it possible that Montegriffo had had a lapse of memory after the blow? Maybe he himself had had a blow to the head, been concussed and delirious and imagined the whole thing?

'But...I want to apologise for any...pain or...harm...I might have caused.'

'You already did!'

'I did?'

'*Oh*...you mean the door.' Carlo put the tips of his long fingers together as though to think of some appropriate reprimand. 'I admit I was shocked and surprised to come home and find a brand new front door to my apartment. I liked my old door, it had history, but apparently it was damaged beyond repair. A bit of unnecessary vandalism, I dare say.'

His demeanour had changed and he looked peeved,

waving his hand dismissively. 'No need to go into it, I know I've been reimbursed. Stagnetto explained it all to me. You'd been under a lot of stress and you have a thing about smelly cats. Raven doesn't like coming to Both Worlds so I always leave a window open for him and plenty of food and water. Raven happens to be totally tomcat, and why shouldn't he be true to his nature? I think you should just accept it. He's been in the building a lot longer than you, and he'll still be there after you've moved on.'

Sebastian couldn't think of an answer to this absurd declaration. Everything about this encounter had unhinged him and he didn't want to be there. He was thinking of how best to get out of the tour, what excuse he could give that would not cause offence. In the meantime Carlo got a key from his pocket and unlocked a padlock on the doors to the tunnel.

'I'm sorry, I don't feel well,' Sebastian said. 'I don't think I can do this.'

Carlo turned to look him over. 'For heaven's sake, man, you look pale as a ghost. It's the heat. Come on, you'd better step into the shade or you'll get heatstroke. It's cool in here.'

Against his will, he allowed Carlo to lead him into the entrance of the tunnel. Carlo was right; the darkness and constant flow of cool air from the interior instantly made him feel better. A single light bulb hung from the roof near the entrance, dimly illuminating it, but the sunlight cast their shadows along the floor.

As he stood there peering into the alien space, he saw another shadow join theirs. He spun around. A figure stood in the opening of the tunnel, clad in a dark robe. The person was short, and against the intense light it was impossible to see if it was a man or a woman. Sebastian squinted and saw that the robe was a Berber *djellaba,* such as those worn mainly by men, with the distinguishing pointy hood pulled low over his face. The weather was too hot for the *djellaba,* yet Sebastian remembered seeing men in the Saharan desert wearing them in forty-degree heat.

'You're late,' Carlo said. 'We were about to leave without you.'

'Who is this?' Sebastian said, his voice cracking slightly.

'Mohammed,' was Carlo's curt reply, as though the man who had joined them were worthy of no explanation whatsoever.

The man acknowledged the one-sided introduction with a reserved bow.

'So…why's Mohammed here?'

Carlo pulled out three torches from his rucksack. 'You're getting this complimentary tour courtesy of the MOD. You can't expect it to be exclusively for you.'

'No, of course not.' He could hardly argue with this rebuke.

'We're running a bit late,' said Carlo and swiftly locked the door from the inside.

'Wait,' Sebastian exclaimed.

'All right, Sebastian? Feeling better?'

'Well… yes, but I think I'll…'

'Don't worry,' Carlo interrupted, smiling knowingly in the dim light. 'Lots of people feel that initial sense of dread, even panic. It usually passes. We can always turn back if you can't cope.'

The patronising comment grated, and Sebastian's pride won over. Once he'd made the decision he looked ahead into the darkness and felt an inexorable draw towards the interior. Carlo gave them each a torch and told Mohammed to leave his *djellaba* by the door.

Sebastian followed the two men towards the interior. Walking in Mohammed's footsteps he wondered who the man was. He was short and slight, and something about his walk made Sebastian guess that he was quite young. So far he'd not really seen his face or heard his voice.

There was little chance to look around, having to tread carefully as they went. Sebastian kept his eyes on Mohammed's yellow trainers in front of him. The tunnel was wide and high, with a flat floor which at some stage must have been tarmacked or concreted but now was strewn with rubble, rocks and grit. Were it cleared, there would be room enough for a vehicle to drive through it, even a military truck.

As though he'd read his thoughts, Carlo said, 'This is part of the World War Two tunnel system. Follow me.'

They passed over several intersections, all wide and high, fit for driving through. Large rooms opened to the sides at regular intervals, and Carlo explained the use of some of them. 'Troops were stationed in here, working on the excavations. They were accommodated in comfortable Nissen huts, some forty men to a hut. These had windows and every amenity to imitate life on 'the outside'. The men didn't see daylight for weeks on end.'

One huge chamber had been a hospital. Carlo stopped and switched on some dim lights to let Sebastian look around. The open ward was vast in size. Sebastian was keen to have a good poke around and he left the two men sitting on a stone ledge in murmured conversation.

He'd been riddled with doubts and mistrust, especially after the shock of finding Montegriffo alive, but as soon as he was alone, all these feelings dissipated. Something about these underground rooms calmed him: the temperature, the darkness, the lack of sound. It had a womb-like feel, safe and solid, a shelter from the sensory bombardment of life under the sky. He felt strangely comfortable, as though he belonged to some species that had evolved underground.

Taking his time, he walked the perimeter of the chamber, noting the operating theatres and store rooms. His imagination took wider and wider sweeps of fantastic engineering feats: whole cities – countries, even – evolving under a world that had lost its ozone protection and grown too dangerous, too polluted or overpopulated. At the same time, he felt like a kid playing house in a cave.

When he returned, Carlo and Mohammed were still in intense discussion. He had an uneasy feeling that they were arguing about him, even plotting something. Approaching them quietly, Mohammed sensed his presence and went quiet. He saw now that Mohammed was a mere teenager. He had a pleasant smile and an air of innocence. He certainly didn't look like someone who'd drag an unsuspecting person down into some cave and inflict unspeakable tortures on him. But you could never be sure of a man's capacity for violence, or what went on in his head. And he could not get over the feeling that there was something very odd about Montegriffo. Everything he said was pleasant and reasonable on the outside, but had a compelling and sinister undertone. If he'd had some sort of power over Mimi, he might well wield similar influence over Mohammed.

Sebastian waited for Carlo to stop talking, but the feeling that this expedition was ill-fated intensified in him.

'You know, it's none of my business what you two are discussing, but it seems that you have other things on your mind and this is not the right time for you to conduct this tour.'

'Please be patient,' said Carlo. 'We're in dire need of a French-speaking guide and I'm trying to train Mohammed, but he has a lot to learn.'

'So I'm right, my presence is more of a nuisance,'

Sebastian insisted. 'I don't mind in the least. In fact I would prefer to get Mr. Molina to take me some other time. If you don't mind, I'll find my way out. I've got a good sense of direction.'

Carlo stood up abruptly. It was obvious that his vanity had been pricked. 'You're *not* a nuisance,' he insisted. 'Molina will be indisposed for some time and it will be at least October before we reinstate the tours.'

Sebastian vacillated, torn between his unease and his reluctance to give up on this fascinating warren of passages. 'Well, whatever it is you're telling Mohammed, perhaps you could share it with me? I'm very interested in everything to do with the tunnels.'

'Of course. I appreciate your interest. Believe me, this is just the start.' Carlo hesitated a fraction of a moment. 'I'll tell you what. I've got the time. Why don't I show you something that was only recently discovered?'

'What's that?'

'Have you heard of Operation Tracer?'

'No.'

Carlo shone his torch down a side passage. 'The place I'm going to show you is strictly out of bounds. Are you prepared for a long hike?'

'Where is this? How long are we talking about?'

'Two, three hours; perhaps more.' Carlo peered at Sebastian with a gleam in his eye. 'Eva is not expecting you home for Sunday lunch, is she, because your mobile won't work in here?'

He disliked Carlo's referring to Eva with such familiarity, but his curiosity about this out-of-bounds area had been stirred. 'What's Operation Tracer? What's it got to do with the tunnels?'

'Operation Tracer was a top-secret British spying mission

that was only to be implemented if Hitler captured Gibraltar.' Carlo had begun walking, Sebastian and Mohammed followed on his heels.

'It's a hidden chamber that has taken on an almost mythical status. The chamber was meant to be the location for the spying mission and was well documented, but almost everyone connected with this project has died. Nobody knew where the chamber was and it was even rumoured that it was a hoax to attract tourism.'

'Are you saying *you* found this chamber?'

'No,' Carlo admitted reluctantly. 'The Gibraltar Caving Group found it by pure accident in 1997. They were in here sniffing around and felt an unusual gust of wind in a tunnel. So they began searching the walls, looking for the source of the airstream. They found a small fissure in a wall which led them to begin to excavate. They soon broke through to a thick brick wall, which in turn led into what turned out to be a series of chambers. These had never been used and had remained totally sealed and hidden for over fifty years.'

Sebastian needed no more encouragement. If this story was true, he sure as hell wanted to see these chambers. 'So they'd sealed the chambers to hide *what* from the Germans? Equipment? Arms? Documents?'

'Not equipment or documents...*people*. If Hitler had invaded, six men were to be sealed inside the chambers and left with supplies to last them upward of seven years. The volunteers were two doctors, three signalmen and their leader. They would run this as an observation post with two 12 x 6-inch slits to the outside of the cliff, one looking due east out over the Mediterranean and the other west over the Strait of Gibraltar and the harbour. The team would then wire back all military and shipping movements to the British Admiralty.'

Mohammed, who was walking at the rear, spoke up for the first time. 'Seven years? Were they to stay there all that time…sealed up?' Sebastian noted how good his English was, but the strong French accent pointed to him being either Algerian or Moroccan.

'That's right,' said Carlo. 'Before they volunteered they were told there would be no way out and anyone who died within the chamber would have to be embalmed and cemented into the walls. Only if Germany was defeated would they be released. If Germany took power over the Rock, these men would have to live out their lives entombed in the chamber. They would live as long as their supplies lasted. They had a sizeable water tank with a constant flow, probably water filtering through from some catchment higher up.'

'But why did they have to die?' asked Mohammed with a note of anguish in his voice. 'They could have come out and just been made prisoners of war.'

'No, this observation post was never to be revealed to the Germans. These heroic men volunteered to be entombed and pledged to die in the chamber if necessary. Anyway, they were to be sealed in such a way that they wouldn't be able to dig their way out. The mission was top secret, as similar secret lookout posts were being prepared throughout the world in the event of future wars.'

'What a terrible fate,' said Mohammed quietly.

'Indeed! They took great care in choosing the men who could endure the mission. Firstly, they had to consider the emotional and psychological aspects of being entombed, then the physical aspects, everything like food, drugs, exercise, sanitation and clothing.'

'Incredible,' Sebastian murmured. 'How did they generate power, for light and for the transmissions?'

'Believe it or not, with a battery powered by a stationary bicycle. It was equipped with a leather belt to avoid the noise a chain would make, and gave the chaps their exercise at the same time. They were told to always talk in muted voices, and the floors were laid with cork tiles to absorb sound.'

They were now walking along a narrower tunnel, clearly meant for pedestrians or troops. It had intermittent downward steps. As they descended, Carlo went on with his account of Operation Tracer, now in his stride to show that Jose Molina would have been a lightweight in comparison. Sebastian was totally absorbed by the story, but he made a point of noticing where they were going. He wondered why they were going downwards and not up, but decided not to ask. Surely an observation post would be quite high up, but then, being inside a mountain felt like what he imagined was the weightlessness of space, where up and down could become confused.

Carlo continued to talk as they walked, torches bobbing; throwing light around the rough walls of the tunnels. 'Extensive trials of the equipment began in January 1942 under the eye of an MI6 radio expert and the full team was in place by the end of summer, their cavern fully equipped and ready for occupation.'

'How far down are we going?' Mohammed asked. 'I have to be at the—'

'Just listen up, Mohammed! This information is vital for a guide to know,' Carlo interrupted. 'The operation had become a bit of a myth until the discovery of papers at the Public Records Office in Kew, and in 2006, they actually traced one of the volunteer doctors, living in the UK, who by this time was ninety-two years old. What was interesting was that this man's description of the chambers differed considerably from the ones which had been discovered, and pointed to the existence of a second hideout, deeper inside.'

'A second chamber?' Sebastian asked. 'Somewhere else in the Rock?

'Well, yes,' Carlo said.

'Has this been verified?'

Carlo seemed not to have heard his question. 'In the end, Operation Tracer was never put into operation as Hitler turned his attention towards the Eastern Front.'

'But this other hideout,' Sebastian insisted. 'Have they found it?'

Carlo hesitated for a moment. 'No, but there were quite a few such tandem operations in other locations during the war.'

'Is anybody looking for it? I mean have they any idea where...'

'No,' said Carlo curtly.

'Well, that *is* truly fascinating. Perhaps you can point me to someone who knows more about it.'

Carlo stopped abruptly and turned around. 'I know more about this subject than anyone in Gibraltar or elsewhere for that matter, so you can direct all your questions to me.'

Sebastian was taken aback by the force in his voice. 'Okay, Carlo. I will.'

'I told you I was going to show you something that will fascinate you.'

'But surely a lookout post would be higher up the Rock?' Sebastian said reasonably.

'I didn't say we were going there. When I said I was going to show you something interesting, I didn't mean the chambers of Operation Tracer. Only authorised MOD personnel have leave to enter those.'

Sebastian and Mohammed glanced at each other.

'What I'm going to show you is much further down. Until I discovered it, not one living soul has been there since 1773.

He turned his back on them and began to walk quickly downwards.

Sebastian tapped Mohammed on the shoulder and whispered, 'How do you feel about this?'

Mohammed frowned but looked resigned. 'We must follow Mr. Montegriffo. I would not like to offend him.'

'Well, if things go wrong I can find the way out of here,' Sebastian reassured him. 'I've got an internal compass.'

Mohammed nodded, then bounded down the steps to catch up with their leader. The young man was right; better not offend a man who knew his way inside a mountain. He quickened his step to join the two men in the dim light ahead.

Mimi

She walked towards Landport Gate – the gateway to medieval Gibraltar – where the sea once sloshed against colossal stone walls. Crossing the wooden drawbridge, she entered the tunnel that passed through the wall itself. Coming from the harsh July sunlight it was pitch black, as there was a kink in the middle of the tunnel. The cool of the interior felt exquisite on her sunburned arms and she slowed her pace to enjoy it. A hauntingly beautiful sound came from further down the passage. People pushed past her, walking in both directions, to and from Casemates Square. Some were obvious tourists; the rest were Yanitos leaving work to go for a drink, or Spanish workers hurrying home to their families across the frontier. The locals were always the most confident, jabbering proudly in their quirky language. She'd begun to pick up some of the strange words, Spanish and God knows what else, randomly intermixed with English.

She pushed up her sunglasses to see better in the dim passage and followed the sound of the music. Right in the middle of the tunnel, a young man sat leaning against the tunnel wall, playing softly on what looked like a flying saucer. It was an angelic sound, spiritual…what was the word? *Transcendent*! She dug in her bag for some coins so that she could justify standing there a while.

He smiled at her and nodded, happy to have an audience – a paying one at that – and his music took on even more loops and circles. He was good looking, she decided, though skinny as a rake. His shorn head sported a couple of lone dreadlocks sticking out from his neck.

A gang of local teenagers walked past. They ignored the musician but looked at *her*. She'd noticed how the gradual ditching of her bad-ass gear had softened the faces of strangers; cashiers, waiters, even walkers-by sometimes smiled at her for no reason. Guys looked her over with an interested gleam in their eyes, rather than the blank or even hostile looks she used to attract.

After a while she noticed that the kid with the heavenly music was playing just for her. Finally, he stopped playing and started to gather up his stuff. A skinny dog sleeping in some blankets got up with ill grace. She crossed the path of pedestrians.

'I really enjoyed that.'

He gave her a humble smile.

'What on earth is that weird instrument?'

'It's a sound sculpture,' he said. 'You can touch it if you want.'

She tapped it with her fingers and it rang for several seconds. 'Wow, I'd like one. Where can you get one?'

'Ah,' he said, tapping the side of his nose. 'Have you got a rich daddy?'

He started making a rollup. The dog stretched and farted loudly. She looked into the little bowl on the ground. Apart from her two pound coin, it just had some paltry coppers in it.

'I couldn't score a joint off you, could I? I've just quit the fags,' she said, thinking it would be nice to get high for a change.

'I have a stash, so if you want more…'

'How about ten quid's worth?'

'Let's go,' he said.'

He picked up his stuff and they walked out of the tunnel with the dog lumbering at their heels. Standing in a corner by the vaulted entrance into Casemates Square they did the exchange.

'Have you got any food, by any chance?' He sized her bag up, and she felt ashamed. Some people actually went hungry, even in the western world.

'No, sorry,' she said. 'Why don't you go and buy yourself some grub?' she said pointing to the pocket into which her tenner had disappeared. 'Or you could come to my place and I'll fix you a sandwich or something. I live with my brother.'

He hesitated. 'Is he going to be cool about it?'

'Why not?'

'With my dog and all.'

'He's on a tour of the tunnels today.'

'Okay then. Yeah, alright.'

She led the way up Main Street, then dipped up Horse Barrack Lane, followed Cornwall Lane and City Mill Lane, panted up Hospital Steps, Fraser's Ramp and Shakery's Passage. He carried a backpack with the rolled-up blankets, his sound sculpture in a scuffed case and the dog following listlessly behind.

'How do you find your way around here? I've never seen a place like this.'

'It's right out of Dickens,' Mimi agreed. 'You should see the inside of some of these places.

The sun was still hot and the climb onerous. The dog wheezed as though it were breathing its last while the musician seemed used to physical hardship. Mimi herself was getting fitter from all this city mountaineering, and quitting the fags had helped.

'Have you got a name?' he said after a while.

'Imogen. What's yours?'

'Horst,' he said.

'I think my bro would like seeing me with someone my own age.' Having said it, she very much doubted that Sebastian would like the look of the travelling musician. But he'd made such a fuss about her relationship with Carlo, having her drag this young guy home ought to bloody well reassure him.

Sebastian

They'd been walking through ever narrower and lower tunnels for the best part of three hours, taking countless turns. He knew there were over fifty kilometres of manmade tunnels within the Rock, but apparently there were more that had not been recorded or explored.

It felt like being deep in water – in fact they were probably well below the level of the sea – but he was used to diving, so he didn't mind it in the least. The further down they went, the better he felt physically. It made him realise how his mind and body lacked substance on the surface of the world. He was forever floating off, coming unstuck. Here, in the depths of the earth, he felt solid and supported. *Anchored* was the word for it. Also, his superb sense of direction had always been three-dimensional – four-dimensional actually – telling him their approximate location

Psychologically, however, he felt vulnerable. He could see that Mohammed felt the same. The young man was sweating copiously. Carlo occasionally stopped to consult some kind of map, but he seemed to be quite confident where he was taking them. Sebastian asked no more questions, his curiosity now seemed inappropriate.

Something told him not to voice his ability to find his way around in any space. He didn't want to unsettle Carlo Montegriffo in any way. If the man thought that either of his charges could find their way back to his treasured find, he might decide he would not let them come back up... especially after what Sebastian had done to him in the apartment. The mystery of what had really happened there kept coming back to him as they walked. How could Montegriffo have risen from his death bed? Or how could he himself have been so mistaken? Dead was dead, no pulse, no breath.

'Watch your head,' Carlo said, interrupting his thoughts.

They were turning into a tiny sliver of an opening, and began to scramble downwards through what seemed more like a crevice than a manmade opening. The rock walls were jagged and uncut. There was little to hold on to and alongside the footholds were black plunging voids. Twenty minutes of this was hard work, and dangerous. Twice he had to steady the Moroccan boy, who was clearly getting distressed though trying his best to hide it.

When they finally reached the bottom of this downward climbing feat, they were standing on the flat surface of a large natural cave. The torches had been growing dimmer, and Carlo groped in his rucksack for batteries.

'Let's rest for a moment,' said Carlo. 'We need to keep up our strength.'

They sat on the smooth rock floor and he offered them a handful of nuts and raisins from a bag and gave them each a bottle of water.

'Are you ready for this?' he said, cryptically.

He directed them towards the far end of the cave. Down at floor level was a half-metre-wide horizontal slit.

'The only way to get in through there, is to lie down and push yourself through,' said Montegriffo. He turned to Mohammed, 'You go first.'

'What's on the other side?' asked the boy.

'That which I want to show you,' said Montegriffo impatiently. 'When you get there, just turn your light off and stay put.'

'Why must I turn off the light?' Mohammed asked.

'Don't argue with me.'

The kid looked unhappy, but did what he was told. He lay down on the floor and inched himself through the slit, disappearing from sight.

All was silent for a couple of minutes. Sebastian knelt down, trying to look through the slit. He could still see a flicker of light, but it seemed to be quite far off. How could they be sure that there wasn't a plunging void on the other side?

'Are you through?' Sebastian shouted after a long moment, fearful that the boy could fall to his death.

'No,' came the strangled reply. 'I can't see anything.'

'Just keep pushing yourself through,' shouted Carlo through the slit. 'Don't panic. Just keep going.'

Another few minutes passed. Sebastian tried to shine his torch in but the crevice seemed empty, jagged and ominous; it was hard to imagine a body getting through it. He felt a growing sense of outrage. Why send the poor kid in first?

Mohammed was shouting something. It sounded as though he were far away. The echo of his voice was muted by the narrow passage, but they couldn't hear what he'd said. 'Come quickly, please,' he shouted again, now with obvious panic.

Sebastian hurriedly lay himself down on his back and began pushing himself through the cavity, using his heels as propulsion. It was further than he'd imagined. He was squashed by the rock all around him and grazing his head and his hip as he went. A sense of dread assailed him when his chest became wedged and he found he could not move either forward or back. Sweat poured into his eyes as he tugged back and forth to get free. Finally, he was loose and he slithered the rest of the way, thankful that he had not given way to terror. When he got on his feet he found himself in yet another cave.

Mohammed stood trembling with the torch pointed at the wall. There, in the light of the torch beam, sat two corpses, their grinning faces intact. They appeared to be soldiers, still in their uniform. Sebastian stared at the men, half expecting them to open their eyes. His heart thumped and he felt cold despite sweating profusely. After a minute, when he'd recovered a little from this gruesome encounter, he took a step closer to examine the remains. Apart from the flesh having shrunk back a little over their bones and features, there seemed to be not a speck of dust on their clothes, as though they'd died there just weeks ago, although their uniforms were clearly from some other era. No insects, bacteria or mould seemed to have affected them, and rodents surely didn't live this far down.

'We're well over two hundred years too late in rescuing these gentlemen,' said Carlo, who had joined them. 'The records show them to have been missing in 1773. They went in to explore the interior cave system and never re-emerged.'

'How are they so well preserved?' asked Mohammed, staring at the corpses.

'This is a dead cave,' said Montegriffo. 'Completely dry. Most of the caves in here are live, with water dripping constantly through the millennia.'

'But why did they lie down and die?' asked the boy. 'Or were they killed?'

Montegriffo regarded the corpses at length. 'I imagine they got lost, then ended up here, disorientated, exhausted and dehydrated, and probably with their source of light extinguished. They obviously didn't find the opening so low along the floor.' He paused. 'They thought they'd come to the end of the line.'

All three were silent, looking at the men sitting there, shoulder to shoulder.

'So...is this the end of the line?' Sebastian spoke into the closed silence.

'As far as you're concerned, it is,' Carlo said.

'What do you mean?'

'I mean...that's all you get.'

'There is more?'

'No,' said Carlo. Something about his voice gave him away. He obviously had more up his sleeve than he let on and was wavering between secrecy and his vanity. 'That's it. And just remember, this find is not known to the public. We're waiting for the 'experts' to come from London to decide what to do. Probably the MOD would want to give them a proper burial. I think someone is looking into possible descendants.'

Mohammed seemed to find his voice. 'You shouldn't have sent me in here without warning me.'

Sebastian was glad to hear the boy speak up for himself. Making him enter the cave unprepared for what he might find had been a downright sadistic move on Montegriffo's part. But he already knew that the man had a wicked streak. That fact that Carlo was alive gave him no comfort. More than ever he realised how much Mimi needed his protection.

Mimi

Approaching DiMoretti's Ramp with her new friend, she saw a familiar-looking man coming towards them on the Castle Steps. It was Carlo Montegriffo. The sight of him startled her as she had not set eyes on him for ten days.

Carlo looked dishevelled and weary; far from the immaculate figure he usually cut. He was wearing lace-up boots and some kind of flannell trousers that were wet and covered in mud stains, certainly not the sort of clothes you'd wear in summer. He slowed his steps and looked at her.

'Hello, Imogen.' He looked Horst over. 'Who is your friend?'

'This is Horst,' she said, flustered. 'He's a musician.'

'That's debatable, but I've seen him hanging around the passages, trying to get money off people.' He addressed the young man. 'I'm amazed you got across the border!'

'I don't beg, I *busk*,' said Horst defiantly. 'Anyway, it's none of your business.'

'It *is* my business, as it happens. Where do you live?'

Horst turned to Mimi. 'This isn't your brother, is it?'

'God no, he's—'

Carlo cut her off. 'You're not planning to bring that animal into our building, are you?'

Mimi thought for a moment he was referring to Horst and felt her hackles rise, but belatedly he pointed to the dusty dog. She battled with her feelings about Carlo, being both cowed and angry. All this time she'd been agonising about what she'd done wrong and what had become of their budding friendship, but she couldn't let him get away with being so rude to Horst and treating them like naughty schoolchildren up to no good.

'Actually, Horst and his dog are coming into the building. I've invited them for dinner.'

'Absolutely not,' said Carlo. 'The only pet allowed in this building is Raven, and Raven would not tolerate that scabby mutt.'

Mimi glared at him. 'You have no rights over our apartment. It's got nothing to do with you.'

Horst tapped her on the shoulder. 'I don't need this shit, but nice to have met you, Imogen. Have a good life.' He turned and began walking back from where they'd come. The dog turned lethargically and followed. She was about to call him back, but the whole scene had become too humiliating.

Carlo's eyes followed the young man and his dog as they ambled away. 'You shouldn't have shown him where you live. That sort of element is...'

'What's it to you?' she cried, her voice choked up. 'I know *I* can be fucking rude, but you sure as hell won the prize. How dare you? I really liked that guy.'

She turned and started walking quickly up the ramp. Something was welling up in her – tears probably – but to cry would be totally ridiculous.

Carlo was right behind her but said nothing, just followed quietly in her steps. She ran up the stairs and he ran too. When she passed his door he reached out and grabbed her by the arm. 'Imogen, stop! Stop! Don't pull away. You're angry. I understand that.'

'Let go of me!' She struggled to get out of his grasp, but he held on.

'Don't you understand that I got concerned, well frankly...jealous when I saw you with that waster.'

239

She stopped trying to tug herself free and stared at him. 'You and I are not...you have no reason to be jealous, no right...

'Dear girl... you must know how I feel about you.'

'No, I don't.'

He looked into her eyes. 'Don't you *really*?'

She wanted to halt this crazy conversation. 'So where the hell were you?'

'In both worlds.'

He was talking gibberish. 'Both worlds? What does that mean?'

He laughed a little. 'Both Worlds is a *place*, Imogen, a little community on the east side of Gibraltar. I have a place there. It's my spiritual retreat.'

'You could have just told me you were going away? If you like me that much, you could at least have sent me a text.'

He held her by the shoulders. He looked intently into her eyes. 'I thought you were quite worldly, more worldly than me, in fact. But I see now you don't understand what's going on here.'

'What don't I understand?'

'I'm only human, Imogen, and you're only seventeen.'

Her mouth was open. She didn't want to fathom what he was getting at.

'I should have known the minute I laid eyes on you, Imogen. Look at us! We've been drawn together against all odds. Don't *you* find our attraction a bit bizarre?'

'Well, yes,' she admitted. He had a point.

'Apart from the age gap and cultural disparity, there is another important factor that will keep us apart...*must* keep us apart.'

'What are you talking about?'

'Your brother.'

'What's *he* got to do with it?'

'Exactly! I agree with you absolutely that his opinion is of no consequence in regard to our relationship, but I've told you this already: the problem is the Frontiers Development Project. I firmly believe your brother has no place here, and I'm doing everything in my power to stop his development from being built.'

'Oh, my God! Please don't. You can't do anything anyway, can you?'

Carlo clenched his teeth. 'Oh, no? Watch me!'

He looked down at her, his face hard, but seeing her expression softened him instantly. With one firm movement he drew her into his arms.

After a moment, he spoke, his mouth in her hair. 'I need to be totally honest with you, so you know where we stand. What your brother is doing will bring ultimate ruin to this unique corner of the world. It's nothing personal, but I want to dispatch Sebastian Luna and his concrete monstrosity as far away from the Rock as it is possible to send them.' He stroked her neck with his long fingers. 'So, my little flower, you see how even just a friendship between us would be fraught with conflict.'

Her anger and confusion had ebbed away and – pressing her face against his shirt – she mumbled, 'We don't have to feel the same way about Sebastian's project. Whatever you might think, I'm pretty sure you've lost your cause anyway.'

'Nothing is ever set in stone,' Carlo murmured, holding her firmly in his arms. 'But then there is still the problem of us. I've been deep in prayer to receive the strength to subdue the feelings I have for you.'

'But, Carlo! Let's not mix things up. We can be friends, right?'

She knew she had been giving him jumbled messages,

241

being flirtatious, getting pie-eyed on vodka and probing him about his love life. And right now, she ought to pull away but was enjoying his embrace. She was lonely and besides, their relationship might even be for the good. With some cunning female persuasion, she might make Carlo see what a wonderful contribution Sebastian's project was to Gibraltar.

'Just don't ever say anything bad about my brother to me. He's an amazing guy and he's been through a lot in his life.' She hoped that she'd scanned her writings carefully enough and not given Carlo further ammunition against Sebastian. The way he was talking, he might stoop to use any damaging information to support his cause.

A sound made them turn towards the stairs. They stepped away from each other while Sebastian, standing on the top step, peered at them through the gloom. He was wringing his hands. She felt a familiar dread, seeing his impending rage and knowing he might pounce on Carlo and punch his lights out. He'd done a bit of boxing when he was younger and was still good at it. That would be an end to her friendship with Carlo for certain. He would've had enough of her and her whole damned family.

'What are you doing?' said Sebastian.

'What's the problem?' Carlo said.

Mimi coughed up a shrill little laugh that echoed around the stairwell. 'Hey, bro. Where have you been in that gear? Come to think of it, you're both dressed as if you'd been hiking in the arctic or something.'

'We've been on a hike, alright,' said Carlo. 'I was showing your brother the tunnel system. It's not something I do for just anybody.'

'What? You two have been down the tunnels *together*?'

Sebastian was no longer wringing his hands, but gripping them in restraint. His brow was shining with moisture. 'I

242

appreciate the time you've taken and it's been a fascinating day, but it doesn't entitle you to grope my little sister.'

'Carlo wasn't "groping" me,' she protested, 'and don't call me little.'

'I saw him with my own eyes.'

Sebastian bounded up to her and put a protective arm around her shoulder. 'We're going home, Mimi. This instant!'

She should have objected to his command, but she couldn't bear to see Sebastian humiliated by her refusal. He mattered more than Carlo, he mattered more than her pride.

'See you around,' she said to Carlo.

'Good night, Imogen. You know where I am.'

Eva

She smacked her hand down on the living-room sofa and a cloud puffed into the air. Waiting for the dust to settle she sat down, realising that none of them had ever used the room. It was large and elegant but suffused in perpetual twilight. In some bygone century, bishops had sat here looking at the view of the Moorish castle and the pinnacles of the Rock, while waited on hand and foot by Irish nuns.

She had the phone in her hand, and was trying to forget that battered and broken woman whose name was Chantelle. How hard it was to shed that persona and assume the shiny casing named Eva. Adrian had hated the Hebrew origins of the name, even though she'd tried to prove to him that Eva was universal. He insisted she rename herself Chantelle, properly, by court petition. She never knew exactly why 'Chantelle'. It wasn't as if he had a relative by such a name.

When he told her to apply for a passport in her new name, some instinct of self-preservation made her hide her Eva Eriksson's passport above a ceiling tile and claim that it was lost. Into the same space had gone her diving certificates and her paramedics diploma, before he thought to confiscate them. Had she seen into the future, a future where her identity had been eradicated and she no longer owned a credit card, a driver's licence or money, a future where she was totally flattened beneath the boot of Adrian's escalating tyranny?

She tapped in the numbers. It rang for a long time before Linda picked it up.

'Yeah?'

'Hello, Linda. It's Eva.'

'Hey, is that you Chantelle?'

Eva realised her mistake and cursed silently. It was Lucinda, Linda's fifteen-year-old daughter.

'No,' she blurted. 'Is Linda there?'

'Sure,' said the girl and shouted for her mother. 'Mum, I think it's Chantelle on the phone.'

A moment passed.

'Eva?' Linda whispered.

'Yes, it's me.'

'Look, I've got a family breakfast happening. It's difficult to talk...you know what I mean?'

'Sure, I won't keep you,' said Eva. 'Just...have you heard anything, seen anything?'

'No, nothing, sweetie. But like I said, I don't keep in touch with anyone. Because of you, I literally have a whole new set of friends.' It was said without so much as a twinge of resentment. How could Eva ever thank her enough for the sacrifice she'd made?

'You know...it occurred to me that he's got all the means at his disposal to tap your phone, or put a bug in your house. I mean, that's the sort of stuff he does for a living.'

Linda was quiet for a moment. 'You're kidding me?' Another pause. 'Of course he can.'

'I can't think of any other way he's got hold of my number.'

'So you're sure it's him.'

'Yes, I'm sure.'

'Oh God! I'd better have my phone checked out.'

'It's too late. He knows my number, he knows I'm in Spain. He'll want revenge, if nothing else.'

'I'm so sorry, Eva. I don't know what to say. Look,

perhaps you should just grab the bull by the horns, literally, and call him up. Talk to him.'

'He's not much of a talker, is he?' Eva exclaimed. 'He just wants to torment me. You know what he's like. The beating comes first, then the talking…if you're lucky.'

'Look, sweetie, I can't really advise you on this one, I've got to go. My scrambled eggs are burning. Call me soon, okay?'

'I will,' Eva said, knowing she wouldn't. With tears running down her cheeks, she said goodbye to Linda.

It was not that Adrian would go to the ends of the earth to pursue a woman out of love. He was, and always had been, driven by his power-fuelled chauvinist pride. No woman, ever, could be allowed to give him the boot, and he was a man who held a grudge for however long it took. He'd reminded her often enough: 'Don't try and leave me, baby. If you're tempted, remember Remus.'

With only a Spanish number to go on, it would be difficult to track her down to Gibraltar, but as a U.S. Federal agent, he had a number of cards to his hand. While following her scent, the silent phone calls were meant to unnerve her, break her down. She'd thought to cancel the mobile contract and simply get another one, but she'd ruled it out. It was better to have some contact with the devil – however frightening – than to have him approach her stealthily and pounce on her unawares.

*

'I found out what you're doing down there,' said Jonny Risso, his face deadpan as he steered the boat nearer to the rock-face. He turned to Sebastian. 'I saw your picture in the *Chronicle*.

You're the guy who's spearheading the Frontiers Development Project. You had me for a right fool, didn't you, believing you were Neanderthal hunters?'

He'd been bound to find out that they'd misled him on purpose, and now he felt humiliated.

'Look, I'm paying you to take me out on your boat,' Sebastian said. 'I've never denied my guiding hand in the Frontiers Project, but I don't always feel like offering it as a point of discussion or debate. I get enough of that wherever I go.' He peered at the boatman. 'But now that you know, why don't you tell me where you stand on it?'

'Me?' said Risso, still looking put out. 'Catalan Bay is a very special place for us Genoese descendants. Of course we're worried about what this development is going to do to our culture and community. We've been there almost four centuries, speaking Genoese until a few generations ago. Where do you find a place like that? It's a sociological museum.'

'The project is well away from Catalan Bay,' Sebastian said with calculated patience. 'It won't even affect Both Worlds.'

'What about Gorham's Cave?' said Jonny Risso, pointing south. 'They're still excavating there, you know. They're finding more and more Neanderthal stuff in there. I know you don't give a damn about all that, but how are you going to get your development around it?'

Eva looked across the water at the enormous black mouth that was Gorham's cave. If it wasn't one thing, it was another. Since they got wind of the Frontiers Project, a prominent London archaeological society in conjunction with the British Museum was campaigning to postpone any development – yet again – until more excavation in the caves had taken place. The Princeton archaeologists had established beyond reasonable doubt that Gibraltar was the very last place inhabited by man's Neanderthal forefathers as they clung to life, having died out in the frozen wastelands of Europe some seven thousand years previously.

Much as she was firmly in Sebastian's camp, it seemed inconceivable that a big development should be allowed in a place where such an important archaeological treasure was unfolding. At the same time, history marched on. Thousands of years in the future, Sebastian's work would be studied and treasured in turn.

'They've just carbon dated a cooking hearth to twenty-eight thousand years,' said Jonny. He paused and shrugged. 'You can't blame them for wanting to investigate, even at the expense of "progress"!'

Eva saw Sebastian draw too deep a breath and pre-empted him. 'Look, we've got to get on. The tides don't wait.'

They got busy gearing up, helping each other get into the heavy scuba units and adjusting all the straps and valves. When they were fifty metres from the works barge, they slipped on their fins and slid into the water. Sebastian swam hastily towards the cliffside. She had to accept that this was work; he wasn't interested in the flora and fauna.

The barge was supposed to be attached to the cliff by an articulated steel arm, but a couple of mishaps during the anchoring of the arm had dislodged a large chunk of rock the size of a camper van. Until this fiasco was reassessed, the barge remained unusable, bobbing merrily on the waves, anchored to the seabed and attached to the cliff by some cables. She had heard from Sebastian that the team's lead geologist, Lars Bengtson, had been down to assess it and admitted that this particular section of Early Jurassic Shale Formation contained atypical streaks of soft shaly sandstone interbedded with the harder bluish-black limestone. This wasn't a catastrophic discovery, but the barge had to be secured to the cliff, come what may.

Sebastian began his inspection and when they found the place where the chunk of cliff had fallen away, he spent a long time examining the freshly sheared rock. Meanwhile, Eva saw a deep hollow at the rear of the collapsed section. She swam towards it. Far into the concave depression there was a small aperture, about half a metre in diameter. She approached it and shone her torch beam into the blackness within. A cave opened up beyond the entrance. The collapse had created a tiny window into a cavity inside rock. It was no particular surprise. The whole of the Rock was a veritable Swiss cheese, with over a hundred-and-sixty caves discovered to date.

The hole was very small, but at a glance Eva was certain a diver could get through. It would be a bit of a squeeze, but she was dying to have a nose about in its interior. Brian had asked her more than once – should he obtain clearance from the Ministry of Defence – if she'd join him diving in the Ragged Staff Cavern, one of the most spectacular and unusual underwater caves so far discovered in the world. Perhaps here was something she could show him in return.

As she studied the hole, Sebastian approached and touched her arm, signalling that it was almost time to ascend. She pointed to the opening, and he shone his torch in then shook his head. This was his work after all. There was no way she could argue with him underwater, but for once she felt she ought to be allowed to take the initiative. There was plenty of time left. She was by far the more experienced diver, with many accreditations to her name, so he should follow her lead. She hesitated, then signalled forcefully to him to follow her. She squeezed through the hole and swam into the submerged interior of the cavern.

Mimi

Two days had passed since the uncomfortable confrontation between Carlo and Sebastian. Seeing her brother so disturbed by it had worried her, so she thought it prudent to appease him by staying home like a good girl, and immerse herself in her writing.

Yet, she was torn. Carlo's emotional declaration had made her hyper-aware of his proximity. She wanted to go and see him, at least to talk about her work, but she couldn't quite come to terms with his unequivocal disapproval of Sebastian's project. Thinking back on his words, they even contained a kind of threat. Hadn't he said he'd do anything to send Sebastian and his monstrous development packing to the ends of the earth? At the same time, it was a free country and he had a right to his opinion. She could hardly blame him for his feelings. Gibraltar was his home and he felt strongly about it.

She sat on her bed with her iPad on her lap and struggled to concentrate on the fifth chapter. Useless: it was all over the place, nobody would make sense of it. Occasionally, getting mildly stoned would give the creative process a kick up the backside. She got up and looked around for the package of weed she'd scored off Horst and found it in her Omani bell-bag. The ziplock sandwich bag was partly filled with a powdery low-grade cannabis. She'd not examined it properly at the time, but now, just by looking at it she could tell it was shit.

She held the bag in her hand and wondered what to do

with the damned stuff. She could make cookies with it, perhaps, though not just now. Baking was not her strong point.

She wandered around the room, studying the furniture, looking for somewhere to stash it. She couldn't discount the possibility that her guardians snooped around to see what she had in her room when she was out. Sebastian had caught her with drugs once before, and she hadn't forgotten that Eva had found her birth control pills (much bloody use they were!). Then she remembered the loose floorboard that creaked loudly when she stepped on it.

Archetypal, she said with a chuckle. The plank was a mere foot in length and warped by age, easy to prise up with her penknife. She peered into the space below. It was filled with dust and cobwebs and smelled of old history books. She leaned in closer. A corner of something pink and silky poked out from the hollow space under the next board.

A strange excitement came over her and she pushed her hand through the cobwebs to retrieve it, then looked at it in consternation. It was an old-fashioned washbag. It had a snap lock instead of a zip. Weighing it in her hand for a few seconds, she popped it open.

Holy Jesus!

She stared into the bag, mouth agape.

This could only be one thing. Something to do with Mrs. Cohen's lottery win. What else could it be? She stared at the bundle in her hand. They were all five-hundred euro notes. She threw the toiletry bag onto the bed and, one by one, she counted the notes. There were forty-four in all. With sudden dread she tossed the money aside, the notes fluttering like startled birds all over her sheets and pillows.

Sebastian

Eva had wedged herself through the opening and disappeared into the dark interior. He shone his torch into the cavern to see the graceful dancing movements of her fins, the bubbles from her breath rising in bursts towards some unknown place above. He smiled behind his mask. Leading the way was the woman he adored, the fearless rider of waves, a conqueror of the deep and – even though he was wary – he had no choice but to follow. He would swim to the bottom of oceans to follow her willowy shadow, but she would always be disappearing in the distance. He could never quite reach her, much as he yearned for the closeness she offered.

His tanks bumped against the edges of the aperture; it felt like a pinhole but was clearly big enough to get through. Once inside, he looked around and found himself inside a tube-shaped cavern. As he made his way inward through the passage, stalagmites began to appear along the floor. Directly overhead hung their icicle-like counterparts, the work of thousands of years of dripping water during some dry period of the cave. In some places the two had met, forming pillars, some thin and fragile as a finger, others the size of an arm.

Eva was swimming ever further inwards and he followed, dodging the slender pillars as he went. As they left the entrance cavern behind, they entered a huge chamber. The floor dropped away, the walls retreated and the ceiling rose to ever greater heights. Most striking was the astonishing clarity of the water. His torch beam illuminated no suspended particles whatsoever, but instead lanced cleanly through the water to pick out impossibly distant objects. The water was so transparent that to swim through it was like flying; but for the familiar burst of bubbles there was no sensation of being underwater at all. Their beams revealed distant rock faces, giving the impression of great spaciousness. Far below, on the floor, piles of sharply splintered rock were strewn about as though from some prehistoric calamity. For a time they just floated around in the absolute stillness of the giant cavern, until Eva pointed upwards and he made a reluctant gesture to indicate she was in control.

As they rose, everything in his torch beam suddenly became blurred and unfocused. Sebastian looked at his pressure gage, but it was impossible to read. His hand signals passed through a bizarre wobbly haze and Eva looked strangely distorted in the distance. After a moment, he emerged from this twilight and, adjusting his buoyancy, he continued the ascent.

As he swam towards the roof of the cavern he suddenly broke through and was floating on the water's surface. Eva had already pulled out her mouthpiece and was obviously breathing real air. Perhaps it wasn't surprising: air had to filter through fissures, and fissures there were many.

He regarded Eva's excitement with a mixture of worry and indulgence. He was himself a seeker of thrills, but this was different. The implications of their find were coming to him, one by one. He was almost certain this space was directly in the way of a bracket site.

They lifted up their masks.

'Unbelievable,' Eva said.

He looked around at the space, which had the dimensions of a cathedral. 'Awesome.'

'Are we lucky or what?' she said with childlike enthusiasm.

'A very strange thing happened to me down there,' he said.

She laughed. 'Yeah, that's a rare phenomenon. We swam through a halo-cline, the division between fresh and salt water. Fresh water must be seeping in. If no man or beast has ever set foot in this space there is nothing to stir the water. It probably hasn't been stirred for millennia.'

Using their torch beams they illuminated the cave. It was more extensive than it had looked at first glance. They swam up to a ledge, beyond which was a dry receding floor, big enough to house an orchestra. It tapered towards the back, becoming narrower and lower, then disappearing from view.

'Let's explore a little?' Eva suggested, pointing to a step in the ledge. 'Look, it's easy to get up on dry rock over there.'

'Oh no, come on, we'd better not leave Jonny to wonder where we've disappeared to. He's pissed off enough as it is. We can do a proper cave dive here sometime and anyway, look at your oxygen gauge.'

'Well, okay,' she said, looking disappointed. 'Let's do it another day. If we're allowed.'

'What do you mean…*if we're allowed?*'

'When we report it, they might want to close access to it, pending research.'

'Report it?' he said. 'Are you kidding?'

Eva looked at him. 'Have you any idea what this might mean? Thirty thousand years ago the water level was a hundred meters lower than it is now. If Gorham's cave is a jewel, God only knows what this cave might house.' She pointed her torch into the receding back of the cave. 'That opening there might even join up with a larger cave system.

Do you realise we're probably the first ones to set foot in here for thousands of years, perhaps *ever*?'

She was right of course, but his first priority was his project, and the further delays this discovery might cause. He also acknowledged a fierce need to own the cave. Eva was prodding his arm. 'We can go to see someone at the Gib museum. They'll know what to do about this. They're the ones who—'

'Listen, Eva. Let's keep this place to ourselves for the moment, OK? I mean it. A few weeks here or there don't matter. And don't let on a single thing to the tobacco smuggler. His eyes and ears are too keen for my liking.'

'I don't agree, Sebastian.'

'Don't do this!' he implored. 'You *know* what'll happen. Think of my project, for Christ's sake!'

'Sebastian…this has to be reported. We can't just keep quiet about it. It would be iniquitous, verging on criminal.'

'Yes, we *can* keep quiet about it, and we *will*.'

She stared at him. 'You can't be serious?'

'I *am* serious. I can't bear having further delays to my project. To hell with the Neanderthals and whatever else might be lurking here. They've been left alone for thirty thousand years, another few hundred won't make a difference.'

He didn't like what he saw in her eyes the moment before she put her mask on. And she hadn't given him a promise.

Mimi

Every time she was alone in the apartment she carried out a systematic search, room by room. She tried to *be* Esther Cohen, think, worry, walk, reason and be confused like Esther Cohen. She found all sorts of interesting things, like a gold ring behind the bath tub, and some ancient love letters from her young husband.

She speculated relentlessly about the money under the floorboards. To withdraw a chunk like that from the bank confirmed her serious gambling problem. Or perhaps she was worried that the bank might go bellyup or that the world was coming to an end. Poor old lady, she'd lost track of how much, where and how the money got spent, and forgot about the stash she'd hidden. Perhaps things would have turned out differently if she'd remembered, or would she just have gone on, gambling until her pockets were well and truly empty?

Should she tell Carlo? Mrs. Cohen had confided in *him* about the money, she'd trusted him. He probably was the most deserving of it, but with his moral righteousness he might decide that Mrs. Cohen's rich and neglectful nephew should have it, or that 'found' money belonged to the Gibraltar taxman.

No, neither the taxman or the nephew was going to get their paws on it. For now!

Mimi continued her search, but as the days went by its aim started to change. She realised she was searching not for more money, but for the woman. She began to make notes about Esther Cohen, tried to let her spirit tell her story, her hopes as a young woman, her marriage, her faith, losing the husband she loved, her loneliness, the desperate message scratched on the violin. Then the thrill of the lottery win and how it fed her addiction to gambling, the humiliation of it being known around Gib. Her subsequent poverty, followed by forgetfulness, terror of losing her mind, the decision to hang herself.

One morning she found a pink half-knitted baby's jacket, abandoned with the needles still in it. It was wrapped in a green cloth and hidden on the top shelf of the hall cupboard. The little jacket spoke to her – there was something significant about it – even if it just meant she'd got fed up with knitting.

She located a music shop on Main Street and bought new strings for Esther's violin. It was both scary and thrilling to play the first notes. Her sadness about Dad and the loss of music first suffused her, then gradually vanished as she felt the instrument warm in her hands and the young Esther Cohen inhabit her.

Her new preoccupation awakened and energised her, taking her mind off the man in the apartment below. There was a story in this, a poignant story, both touching, brave and tragic. She could write Esther's story. She knew she could. Esther was dead now and the money could be used to honour her life. Absolutely no-one knew about its existence except Imogen Sofia Luna.

Sebastian

He was sitting at the kitchen table eating a baguette stuffed with olive oil and grated tomato like Papito used to make it. He refrained from sprinkling on the essential raw chopped garlic, knowing he had to talk to people...and kiss Eva, although they'd not done a lot of kissing lately.

'Honey,' said Eva, coming up behind him and messing up his hair. 'You ought to get a haircut.'

'Hmmm,' he said noncommittally.

She was quiet for a moment, her fingers combing through his hair. 'What to do about our mysterious cave? We ought to make a decision.'

'I thought we'd decided already.'

'No, *you* decided,' she said, her hands withdrawing from his head. She came around the table and sat down opposite. Her lovely mermaid face looked tense. 'Do you mind if I consult Brian on the matter? I think we need a third opinion.'

'Brian, Brian, Brian... What the hell makes *him* the expert?'

'Oh come on, Sebastian. He's a sensible, intelligent, long-term resident. He knows about caves.'

Sebastian looked her in the eye. 'He'll be on your side, of course.'

She smiled a little. 'I do declare, you're a teensy bit jealous.' She leaned across the expanse of the table over his heaps of papers, to take hold of his hand. 'I think he'll be impartial on this issue. Don't forget he is one of the supporters of Frontiers.'

He was tired, there was too much on his mind. 'Whatever,' he said with feigned indifference. 'Do what you want.'

She looked at him through an unconvinced frown. 'You really mean that?'

The issue of the cavern put a subtle frostiness between them in the coming days, though both tried to make light of it. That damned cave had gotten under his skin, for some reason. He wanted it for himself, and more importantly, going public with it would almost certainly create further delays to the project. He longed to go and spend time there alone, but Jonny Risso was unavailable, and, clearly, another man might beat him to it.

As the hassles with the authorities went on, Sebastian felt increasingly removed from his project. He'd begun to realise he was fed up with it all. As far as he was concerned, his part in it was done and dusted. He'd created the concept, done the drawing and calculations, built the model. From that point he should be allowed to let it go, release it to be assembled – like a simple painting-by-numbers artwork – by teams of lesser engineers, surveyors and contractors.

Like many mornings of late, he decided to forgo his taxi and walk to the site, having discovered all manner of different roads and paths over the last couple of weeks. Who would have guessed there was so much nature on this rock?

He passed the morning prowling around the nature reserve of the Upper Rock; enjoying the idea that a person could get lost on it. On the way he sniffed out every hole and opening. There were quite a few unmanned entrances to the interior where anyone with motivation could access the tunnels. He was not dependent on people like Montegriffo to guide him.

He reached the highest point of the Rock, and stopped

in wonder at the sight of the sea beyond, and then the faint outline of Luna's Crossing. If he could already see the bridge, it must mean something. He thought of the word 'foreshadow' and smiled. Now he understood the deeper meaning of it.

The Levante flicked the air up over the crests. He balanced himself on the ledge of a cliff and allowed the turbulence of gusts and eddies to sway him. Yesterday he'd felt confused and fearful, wondering how it was possible to kill a man and then find him alive, but today he felt beyond danger. Today he felt powerful. He realised the universe he inhabited was so much larger than this Rock, so for today his own universe protected him. It was important to hold on to both feelings, both truths; being here, owning this place, but at the same time being in touch with these powerful universal forces. He could see that being around people brought him down. It had always done so, actually. He loved Eva and Mimi fiercely, but it was still a relief to be alone. Only he could understand the transformation taking place within him.

In the days that followed, his expeditions began to take longer and he often arrived dishevelled and muddy to the works site. Not that it mattered in the least. It was a place where men worked, and there was no standing on ceremony where clothes were concerned.

Some days he never made it to work at all.

*

There was no-one left in the yard and the sun was about an hour from setting. He walked towards Azzopardi's hut and saw the man already dialling, with Pavlovian predictability, for his taxi. Sebastian waved and shook his head.

'I need a leg-stretch,' Sebastian said as he joined the security guard on his doorstep. 'I think I'll walk back into town.'

'You shouldn't really walk through the tunnel, Mr. Luna. They've not made provisions for pedestrians. A huge mistake in my view. Look at all the joggers going through there, they're really risking their necks.'

The tunnel had been closed for near enough a decade – due to a fatality caused by rock-fall – and since it re-opened it had brought ever more cars and pedestrians to his side of the Rock. 'You're so right. I'll take some other route.'

Azzopardi peered at him. 'You've got a long way to walk though, the other way around.'

'A man needs his exercise, and while I walk,' Sebastian tapped his forehead, 'I work.'

Azzopardi laughed. 'They say you're a genius, Mr. Luna. I'd walk to Sotogrande and beyond, if I could *averiguar* a way to build a sundeck *detras de la casa* for my wife.'

'If I have a moment, I could take a look at it,' Sebastian said. He had grown quite fond of the man, and he hardly ever did anything personal for anybody.

Azzopardi looked pleased. 'I'll bring some photos tomorrow and you could give me some advice.'

'I don't mind popping by your house if it's of any help.' Sebastian patted him on the back. 'I'd better get started or I'll be walking the whole way around the Rock in the dark.'

Azzopardi was clearly touched by the offer. 'I think I could help in turn,' he said. 'I have a friend with a car he doesn't need and a parking space, very near where you live. He broke his leg at the weekend and can't drive for at least six months. If you'd like to rent the car and the space, I'm sure he'd be glad for a bit of money to help with his own taxis while he's recovering.'

Sebastian looked at him, grateful that this ordinary man

wanted to help make his life simpler. In fact he seemed the only friend he had in Gib, bar his family. 'Listen, Jorge, that's a very nice offer, but I don't drive. I haven't for nearly two decades.'

'Really? How come, Mr. Luna?'

Sebastian bit his lip. For once, it would actually feel good to confide in someone. 'I'll tell you why, so long as you keep it to yourself.'

Azzopardi looked puzzled, but placed his right hand on his chest. 'You have my word.'

'Good… Well, when I was eighteen I got my licence and my first car. So one morning I took it for a drive in the country. It's relevant to the story that I had an enemy in my year at college. This guy tormented me constantly over some personal trouble I'd had. He went around and spread rumours. He really victimised me and made my life hell. Also, he nicked my girlfriend who I was besotted with. So early this rainy Sunday, I take the car out to practise my driving. As unbelievable misfortune would have it, my tormentor was himself out on a bicycle; he was a member of the university cycling club and was out for his morning training. He had one of those fancy road bikes with ridiculously skinny tyres. Because of his distinguishing cycling jacket and the fact that he never wore a helmet, I recognised him as I came up behind him, and he looked back and saw me coming. Well, the impossible happened. It was very wet and slippery, and just before I passed he turned to give me the finger and the action made him slip and lose his balance. When I saw him going down, I slammed on the brakes and swerved away from him. But he'd slid under my front wheels. The bump I drove over was his head. It was crushed and he died instantly.'

Sebastian stopped for a moment to take a deep breath.

The telling brought the impact back to him, the feel and the sound of it, as though it had happened yesterday. 'It was a very difficult time for me. In fact, I had a nervous breakdown and had a spell in hospital.'

Azzopardi face was grave and he was shaking his head in sympathy. He put a hand on Sebastian's shoulder. 'How terrible. I can only imagine the guilt and horror of causing this…to someone you know…and I wouldn't be surprised if it isn't in fact worse with someone you dislike.'

'You're absolutely right. So now you know why I don't drive. I was too traumatised by the accident to take up driving again, and I still can't imagine doing it.'

The temperature had cooled and he half walked, half jogged towards Europa Point. At the roundabout, he turned up Europa Road for the long trek back into town. Cornering the roundabout was the Ibrahim-al-Ibrahim Mosque, an impressive place of worship donated by the King of Saudi Arabia. Sebastian stopped to peer through the iron railings. The beautifully inlaid marble forecourt was empty, and he wondered what King Fahad had been thinking when he chose the location. The mainly Moroccan worshippers would have a hard time getting out here to the very southernmost point of Gibraltar at the end of a day's labour.

Just as he turned his eyes towards his destination, a haunting chant issued from the mosque's tower, calling believers to Salah, the evening prayer. He noted someone walking quickly across the forecourt towards the doors. The brown *djellaba* looked familiar, especially with its distinctive hood.

'Mohammed!' Sebastian called down. Of course there were many *djellabas* and many Mohammeds in the Moroccan community, but he felt sure this was the one he knew.

The man looked up, removing his hood to see better. It was indeed the young trainee tunnel guide. 'Mr. Luna,' he called back.

'Can I come and have a word?'

It was hard to see his expression, but with obvious hesitation Mohammed waved in assent. Sebastian ran back, following the railings full circle and entered the mosque's courtyard.

Mohammed waited for him. As Sebastian walked up the stairs, the man standing there looked a striking sight against the beautiful façade of the mosque. He was a fine-looking young Arab, of Berber blood, probably, short but erect, with a long neck and delicate features. A sudden gust of wind made his *djellaba* flap dramatically, but at the same time revealed the yellow trainers.

'The Levante,' said Sebastian. 'It looks to be a windy night.'

The sun was setting and the translucent marble floor of the forecourt shone as though it were lit from within.

'What can I do for you Mr. Luna? I'm going to prayer. I can't talk for long.' From having been such a deferential presence in the tunnels, here the young man looked very much on home ground.

'I won't keep you long,' said Sebastian jovially, not sure what to say next.

He was about to make some comment about their extraordinary day in the depths of the tunnel system and what they'd had the dubious privilege of seeing, but somehow it didn't seem appropriate.

'Can non-Muslims visit the mosque?' Sebastian asked, stalling for time. 'I've walked past here so many times, I'd love to see the inside.'

'Yes, of course. But it's always best if you make an appointment to be shown it.'

'Right, I will.'

'I can arrange it for you, if you like. Then I can let you know via Mr. Montegriffo, since you are neighbours.'

'Wonderful. In fact, I wanted to ask you about Carlo Montegriffo...your association with him.'

'What would you want to know, Mr. Luna?'

What to ask? Really he wanted ask him outright what the hell the man was about. Here was someone who very obviously under Carlo Montegriffo's authority, the only person he knew who had close contact with the man.

'I heard he was in Both Worlds for a couple of weeks recently. I was worried that he was ill or something.'

Mohammed looked at him, waiting to hear where this was leading. Sebastian battled with an urge to grab the kid by the shoulders and fire questions at him. Did he know if Montegriffo had some weird syndrome that mimicked death, some transient loss of consciousness or blackouts? He couldn't get this out of his mind, much as he tried; it just didn't make sense. He'd killed the guy with his own hands, yet he'd risen from the dead as if he was in some cheap horror movie. And worse...now he was blatantly trying to seduce Mimi, if he hadn't already.

'Mr. Montegriffo looks very well,' said Mohammed said at last. 'You saw for yourself how fit he was the other day, in the tunnels.'

'Yes...yes, he was. Of course! How *is* the training going? You obviously know a lot about the tunnel system by now, Mohammed. When do you think you'll be let loose on the French-speaking tourists?'

'Soon, I hope.'

'I thought it was incredibly generous and trusting of Carlo to show us his find. Don't you?'

Mohammed nodded but could not hold back a boyish

grin. 'When Mr. Montegriffo goes underground, his pride in his knowledge takes over.'

'You reckon? I still can't quite understand why he showed us those two corpses. I know about his pride, but wasn't this find supposed to be shrouded in secrecy?'

'It's a macho Latin thing, you see?' said Mohammed. 'If I know him, he's regretting it now, but he just couldn't help himself.'

'Perhaps he just tried to scare the shit out of us,' said Sebastian, laughing too loudly.

Mohammed did not look amused. 'Perhaps.'

'Or maybe he was going to show us the Operation Tracer bunker but changed his mind and didn't want to lose face.'

Sebastian nodded conspiratorially, but Mohammed was drawing back, clearly not sure where this conversation was heading.

He wondered how to retain the boy for further questioning without sounding creepy and intrusive. 'Does Carlo have many young trainees and friends? I mean, like you?'

'We are not friends, exactly,' Mohammed said cautiously. 'But I owe him very much.'

Sebastian smiled. 'Perhaps Mr. Montegriffo sees himself in the role of protector of young people, like a benefactor, right?'

Mohammed looked at him quizzically.

'I don't suppose you've met Imogen, my sister?' Mohammed flinched. A long moment went by without an answer forthcoming, and this pause made Sebastian all the more uneasy. He felt the skin on his neck prickle. 'So you've met my sister?'

'Yes.'

'Carlo Montegriffo has begun to take great interest in her

266

welfare…now Imogen is only seventeen years old, and she does misunderstand…'

'I know…nothing about this,' Mohammed stammered. 'About what?'

'What you were asking me.'

'Yes, you do,' Sebastian retorted on a hunch.

'Look, it's Mr. Montegriffo's kindness,' Mohammed said hurriedly. 'He is worried that she might come to harm.'

Bloody nerve! If Mimi needed that sort of safeguarding (she certainly did now) Montegriffo had no business taking on the job. Anyway, it wasn't Mimi's safety that the man was interested in, of that he was sure. Sebastian was about to protest but then looked at the boy's expression and paused to think. Why did he look so anxious? Carlo must have discussed Mimi with him. Perhaps Carlo was exerting his nefarious power over him as well. If he wanted to know what was going on, he'd better ask the right questions.

'What about you, Mohammed…where are *your* parents?'

Mohammed looked wistfully towards his homeland across the strait where the proud summit of Jebel Musa rose. 'I don't know right now. They're itinerant workers in the south of my country, very poor. Mr. Montegriffo has helped them… I am indebted to him very much.'

Sebastian tried not to frown. Indebted or *indentured*? 'How good of him. Is he a personal friend of your family then, or…?'

'I trust him,' said Mohammed, clearly beginning to sense the darker implications behind Sebastian's questions. 'He's a very respected person in Gibraltar.'

'Yes, of course.' He paused again, studying the boy. He'd recently seen an article in the *Gibraltar Chronicle* concerning a truly sinister type of slave trade; young workers from Morocco, some underaged, were being 'bought' from their poverty-stricken parents. A large number were shipped to work illegally in Spain, but a few of them ended up in Gibraltar.

'Mr. Montegriffo is right. I do worry about Mimi. She's very vulnerable. Perhaps *you* could keep an eye out. I mean...' He hadn't really meant to try and engage Mohammed in anything like that, but maybe this kid could report back, tell him things he needed to know.

'But, I am,' Mohammed exclaimed. 'I'm doing my best.'

'Your best...with what?'

'Looking out for Imogen.'

'You are?' Sebastian looked at him, perplexed. 'How do you mean?'

'I must go now. Excuse me, Mr. Luna. It is time for Magrib Salah.'

The call to prayer had stopped while they were talking, and a few worshippers had slipped past. Mohammed turned and walked rapidly towards the imposing doors of the temple, his *djellaba* flapping wildly in the gusts of the Levante.

*

When he got home, the apartment seemed deserted. It had an eerie empty feel. He went straight to Mimi's room and knocked on her door. There was no answer so he peeked inside. No Mimi, and the place was in chaos. He could not recall Mimi being so messy. In her childhood years she'd been highly organised, as if realising she was the only female in the household and thus had a particular role to play. Perhaps Dad and he, both, had subconsciously put this burden on her.

He'd not spoken to her for a couple days – their paths hadn't crossed – and he felt terrible about his neglect of her.

If anything, her vulnerability was his fault. According to Eva, she'd been holed up inside her room getting down to some serious writing. *So where was she now?* It was no good carping about Montegriffo when he himself was not there for her, supporting her and making sure she was safe.

He would change. They would eat meals together, like a family, and go for outings. He would take her shopping, go to the beach, play scrabble. Her birthday was approaching and he would make a huge fuss of her then, get her some amazing presents.

Just as he was closing the door to her room, he heard the front door open. Thank God, there she was. No need to panic.

'Hey Mimi! You're home!' he called out. 'How about a game of scrabble?' He felt foolish, knowing how contrived it sounded. It had probably been four years since they'd sat down to one of their ferocious games. She'd been a mean opponent, even at thirteen.

But it was Eva who appeared in the hallway, carrying her wetsuit in a bag. She looked at him in consternation. 'Scrabble? Do we even have a set?'

His shoulders slumped. 'I don't know. We always used to.'

She looked him up and down. 'You've really lost weight, honey,' she said. 'Let me make us something to eat?'

'Why don't we wait for Mimi?'

'We could get very hungry indeed, waiting for Mimi. I've just had a full day's wreck diving and I'm ravenous.'

He went up to her and, taking her face in his hands, kissed her tenderly. 'Listen, Eva. I know I've been a neglectful partner and brother, and I've made a resolution to try and be more present. I want us to be more like a family. I think it would be a nice idea if we could sit down in the evenings and have a meal together, all three of us.'

She smiled back at him, her expression unconvinced. 'Yes, Sebastian. In principle it's a wonderful idea. If you and Mimi both commit to showing up at a given hour, I'll take it upon myself to have food on the table.'

She made her way to the kitchen to rinse out her wetsuit in the Belfast sink. Sebastian followed.

'We need more continuity around here,' he went on, 'for Mimi's sake. And in the last couple of weeks even you and I have been like ships passing in the night. I miss you.'

She spoke over her shoulder. 'Yeah, I've missed you too. But don't forget, that's what you warned me life with you would be like. You cannot have restraints put upon you, be expected to settle to routines. Your work is always going to be a priority. Those were your very words, and I abide by them.'

'Christ, Eva, I didn't mean *you* aren't a priority. Anyway…can't a man change his mind?'

'Of course he can. And I suppose I should abide by your change of mind?'

He was taken aback by the bitterness in her voice. Then he got angry about the way she'd made him sound.

'Oh, Christ, no,' he said. 'I forget you don't want that for *yourself*. You're a free spirit. No shackles or ties for you either. You certainly let me know where I stood when you refused to marry me.'

'Because you flung it on me in the middle of a public place – the embassy, for Pete's sake, wanting me to sign up on the spot.'

'Oh, well,' he said in a falsetto voice. 'There I was, thinking the gesture was quite romantic.'

She had her hands in the tub, furiously squeezing her wetsuit. 'I felt tricked, Sebastian, like I wasn't given a choice, or time to think about it.'

'Water under the bridge,' he growled. 'We agreed to forget the damned incident.'

She turned abruptly and looked him in the eye. 'You know I love you. I admire you and respect you. I *adore* you... isn't that good enough? A marriage ceremony means nothing really, it's what's behind—'

'It means something to *me*, Eva,' he exclaimed. He grabbed her wet hands out of the sink. 'Marry me, please. Let's be a family. A real family. Marry me tomorrow.'

'Stop it, Sebastian. I can't.' Her expression had changed into one of agony, and she tried to pull her hands away. He held them fast and fell to his knees before her.

'Of course you can. I want you to be my wife forever and ever. Don't you understand? Marry me, Eva! Make me the happiest man on earth.'

She began crying. 'I can't.'

'Why not, damn it?'

'I'm already married,' she wailed. 'That's why!'

Eva

There had been times when she'd planned to leave him, but Adrian always seemed to be a step ahead of her, almost as though he could read her mind or sniff out the anxious buildup of an escape. He always said that if she ever left him, he'd find her, put her in a dog collar and only give her water to drink.

As a federal special agent, and older than her by ten years, he'd been a glamorous boyfriend to begin with. She liked his air of authority: it made her feel secure. When he proposed, in grand style, she didn't have the wherewithal to say no. Besides, she thought she loved him, and he quite clearly was fixated on her. He was interested in everything she did, her diving, her work, the people she met. He always knew where she was and what she was doing. It felt oppressive at times – hard work – but she thought his vigilance was a symptom of his love. Because of his profession, she assumed an upright decency in him that, month by month, proved false. Right after their wedding, he deliberately swerved his car to run over a cat. Not long after, he slashed a neighbour's car tyres in the dead of night because of a parking dispute. It was not a good idea to protest; less so when he raged about the filth – African-Americans, Jews and homosexuals – that should be cleansed from America. He had a staunch belief in the order of things. Women occupied a low rung on his particular ladder and she soon learned to choose her words carefully.

A couple of months after the wedding, he declared there

was no need for her to work, and it did not take long before he said that diving was too dangerous for a woman. He discouraged her from seeing friends, and later, forbade it.

When she witnessed him strike his own mother across the face, she began to fear what her own future with him would hold. He had her firmly in mind as the mother of his children, but he knew nothing of her stealthy trips to the clinic every three months for contraceptive injections. She was terrified of getting pregnant because studies on adopted children had proved conclusively that nature was stronger than nurture where evil was concerned. An aberrant gene could and did pass from generation to generation. A murderer could breed a murderer, and there was nothing a loving mother could do to change it. Adrian had killed men in the line of duty and he thought nothing of taking a human life. He was proud of it. And then there was Remus. Starving a dog to death, in order to punish your wife, said enough about a man. It was all you really needed to know.

When Kurt, Adrian's colleague and best friend suggested a camping holiday in France together with their wives, she knew why she had hidden Eva Eriksson's passport. In preparation for the trip, she'd mailed it, and all her diplomas and certificates to Poste Restante in Marseille.

They got a fly-drive deal, renting two camper vans from Paris. The girls had no say in where they went in France, but Eva kept reminding Adrian how much she'd like to see the Riviera. As they headed towards the south-east she found her appetite vanished and her knees were shaking all the time. She went running in the early mornings and tried to stay away from alcohol. Being a fitness-fanatic himself, and liking the fact that she took care of her figure, Adrian didn't object to her early morning sprints.

At dawn, on an overcast day in a wooded campsite near Avignon, she'd lain awake listening to Adrian's rumbling snores. Adrian and Kurt had stayed up till the early hours around the campfire, polishing off a crate of beer and half a bottle of cognac between them. She'd been in bed, wide awake listening to the men getting increasingly drunk, and when they finally staggered back to their respective beds, she knew the moment had come; It was the right time, perhaps the only time.

With her heart racing wildly, she got up and slipped on her tracksuit and trainers, then pulled out the little bag she'd hidden under the passenger seat. She found Adrian's folder on a shelf and from it grabbed Chantelle's passport and a stash of euros, then slid the door open and got out of the van.

Kurt and Mona's van was in darkness. It was a cool morning and everything was still. As the door clicked shut Adrian's snores ceased abruptly. 'Chantelle?' his voice was low and raspy.

'I'm just going for my run,' she said through the half open window.

'Get your ass back in here,' he said. She knew what he wanted. A blowjob was always on the cards when he was hungover.

Panic stricken she called out, 'Just going to the toilet. I'll be right back.'

She hoped he would go back to sleep, but if he didn't, she would only have a five- to ten-minute start. It was too late to change her mind. Her courage was only good for one attempt. She forced herself to walk towards the toilet block, bag clamped to her chest, then – fuelled by terror and pure adrenaline – she glanced behind her and began to run. There were many paths through the woods, and she chose blindly at each intersection, looking behind her at every turn.

She got away, but the act of fleeing is a pitiful solution, riddled with terror and forever leaving one open to capture. And how to shed the woman she had become?

So she ran and ran until she thought Chantelle Hepping was no more.

*

Two days had passed since Sebastian stormed out of the apartment, having asked no question about Eva's marriage. He stayed at the site all day, or so she assumed. Late in the evening he would come in and ensconce himself in the living room. She heard him in the kitchen during the night, working. In the mornings he was gone, drafts strewn all over the table, balled-up papers littering the floor. His phone was either turned off or out of range.

His reaction to her duplicity made it seem not only morally outrageous, but criminally negligent, and he was probably right. She felt a coward and a fraud through and through. Yet she'd never actually lied to him about anything. At any time, had he asked outright why she wouldn't or couldn't marry him, she would have told him the reason, but he had never posed the question that called for an honest answer. It was a pathetic excuse, nevertheless, motivated by her yearning to be loved, to belong, to feel safe. She should have bared the whole of her past before agreeing to come to Gibraltar.

Contacting Adrian for a divorce had seemed out of the question. If she could only make Sebastian understand that, in all the ways that mattered, her marriage was well and truly dead. At least from her perspective. But she knew that few men wanted to tie themselves to a woman still married to another man, a man who refused to let go.

'The sun is shining, Mimi,' she said through the door. 'Come out and sit with me on the terrace. I've made some cheese and lime-pickle sandwiches. And I've downloaded some new music I think you'll like.'

After a few seconds, the door opened a little and Mimi peered through the crack. She looked tired.

'My God, kid. I insist you eat something.'

'Okay, yes all right,' Mimi said. She was wearing black knickers and a little black tee shirt. Almost everything Mimi owned was black. 'You go ahead. I'll just throw some clothes on.'

Mimi was an odd girl at the best of times, but her behaviour over the last few days had been peculiar. She hid in her room, saying she was making good progress with her novel. The three of them seemed like lonely islands in a small lake, so close yet unable to reach out to each other.

Mimi appeared on the terrace ten minutes later, in cutoffs and a baggy top. She sat down and wolfed her sandwich. When she'd finished she inhaled a big glass of milk. Wiping her mouth on the back of her hand she burped, then looked at Eva for a long while, as if researching a character in a novel.

'What are those phone calls you're getting?'

Eva stopped chewing. 'What are you talking about?'

'You got a secret lover or something?'

'Yeah, like, *really!*'

'Are things going tits-up between you and Sebastian?'

Was it that obvious? 'If you must know…things aren't great at the moment.'

Mimi was quiet for a few moments staring into the

distance. 'You're not going to fuck off or anything like that, are you?'

Despite the accusatory delivery, it sounded like a plea. Eva thought about the question, not having really considered what it might mean if Sebastian, or she herself, felt there was little to salvage. They'd been so besotted with each other and it had been easy while reality was held at bay. Ultimately, the past had a way of sneaking in through the back door, unravelling the illusion of happiness.

'No,' said Eva resolutely. 'I'm hanging on. It's my fault and I'm going to put it right.'

Mimi shook her head. 'Hey, it takes two to tango. I'm sure it's not all your fault.' After a pause she said, 'Has Sebastian said anything to you about the medication he's on?'

'Do you mean for his migraines?'

'No, the other stuff.'

'What other stuff?'

Mimi's eyes fixed on a spot on the back of her hand. 'Why don't you ask him about it? It'll probably make you see him more clearly.'

'Why don't *you* tell me about it?' Eva asked. 'He's not talking to me right now.'

'It's better if you hear it from him. I've been on at him to tell you. It's not my business to do it.'

A police siren screeched in the alleys below, a dog barked, and Raven, the cat, flew up on the balustrade from thin air. His appearance startled them and both gave a little shriek. Instinctively, as though to join forces against peril, Eva reached out and grabbed Mimi's hand. To her surprise, she met neither rejection nor resistance.

*

It was well after midnight when she heard the click of a door closing. After a while there was the telltale squeak of the living-room floorboards. Despite the heat of the summer night, Eva pulled a dressing gown around her and tiptoed down the hall. Without knocking, she opened the living-room door and slipped in.

He was standing at the window looking up at the summit of the Rock. The moon had risen and threw a pale glow on the craggy ridges above. He must have heard her come in but he stood mesmerised by the unearthly panorama, his hands deep in the pockets of his shorts. He looked a forlorn figure, desolate even. Approaching him from behind, she put her arms around his torso and held him. He did not react, neither for nor against her.

'I know I should say sorry,' she said, 'but neither of us have been honest with each other, have we? We could change that.'

He said nothing for a while, but then turned around and wrapped his arms around her. 'I've missed you,' he murmured. 'I missed you terribly, my love.'

'Can we talk?' she said. 'I want to tell you everything.'

He took his time answering. 'It's okay, Eva, there's no need. I accept what you sprung on me. I've thought about it and logic tells me you are with me because you want to be. You're with me, not with him. I don't need to know anything else.'

'Yes, but there are things...'

'No. Please. Don't talk. Just be with me, darling Eva.'

His warm hands raised her face to his. They kissed tentatively and she felt herself go limp with wanting him. After a while he lifted her into his arms and carried her to the sofa.

Mimi

August the second. Finally, after all those tedious years of adolescence, she entered the domain of the real people. Her eighteenth birthday dawned. She opened her eyes, turned and looked at the floorboard. Wakefulness flooded her instantly. Not only was she eighteen, she could drink in bars, go travelling, self-publish, buy a car. Age plus money equalled freedom.

She pulled the sheet up to her chin. A church bell began clanging and she counted ten clangs. She heard a soft swishing sound and lifted her head from the pillow. A pink envelope was being pushed under the door. She ignored it until, a minute later, she heard the front door close. Disentangling her legs from the sheet she got up. She knew what kind of envelope it was. But *pink*, for heaven's sakes! Did she look like a pink person?

She opened the flap and took out the card. A Barbie-doll caricature of a flirty girl in a pink dress and mile-long eyelashes (that just had to be Sebastian's purchase, surely Eva wouldn't sink that low) topped with a glittery *Happy Eighteenth Birthday*. And a message from her bro: *So sorry, love. Neither of us could wait for the birthday-girl to wake up. But we'll be home early to celebrate and take you out for a slapup dinner. Get your gladrags out, girl. Let's whoop it up! Tons of Love, Sebastian and Eva.*

Gladrags? What the hell were those? She didn't do glad clothes. Furthermore, she didn't do slapup or whoop-it-up. The whole affair, with the cheery camaraderie and the singing would be exceedingly trying, especially if the lovebirds weren't talking to each other (though she'd heard some promising noises last night). Perhaps she could fake illness and get a rain-check, or better still, insist they go to a seedy bar in Irish Town and get rat-arsed. It ought to be her choice, right? It was *her* birthday.

Even while these thoughts circulated, she was touched. The pink smily girl almost made her choke with sadness.

She tossed the card onto her bed and ventured out into the kitchen. The aroma of freshly made coffee filled the air. At the counter she saw the cup placed ready beside the coffee maker. No milk, no sugar; she liked it black. There was a plate of fresh croissants and a wedge of cake with a little candle stuck on it. Beside the wedge was a lighter. The corners of her mouth pulled upwards a little. Well, hell, it was kind of sweet. She poured the coffee, lit the candle and sat at the table.

She'd just wolfed the last of the delicious cake when there was an insistent knocking on the door. She flinched, then wondered if this could have anything to do with her Big Day. Would mother have bothered, perchance? Hardly! Not after receiving her terminal texted message. There was aunt Beth and gay cousin Raymond, they sometimes sent cards, and there was a relative in Seville, her Spanish grandfather's cousin's son. He had no children of his own and had a soft spot for Sebastian in particular, and for her too, though he didn't understand the feminine species at all, being a bachelor. At any rate, it was rare that someone came knocking. So the postman, possibly, with something that didn't fit through the letterbox.

She glanced down at her knickers and T-shirt. Well, it was still summer, wasn't it? She'd seen women crossing the street in bikinis.

Opening the door, all she could see was roses. Very dark red roses, so dark they were verging on black. There seemed to be dozens of them and she bent sideways to see who was the bearer of these, though knew that it could be none other than Carlo.

'My respect and compliments on a very significant day,' he said.

She was overwhelmed but caught the fine nuance of what he'd said. Not 'Happy Birthday' but 'respect and compliments'. She felt instantly valued. And 'significant' was the most appropriate word for the day. It was highly significant…its meaning seeped through her and lengthened her spine.

The roses, the first ones ever given to her, were divine. Nothing pretty or romantic about them, they were almost sinister. On the verge of opening, the petals were firm and moist with tiny droplets, as if they'd been dipped in blood. Carlo watched her while she stared at them with glazed eyes.

'*Wow!*' She found her voice. 'Well, thank you. I've never seen roses like that. How the hell did you know it was my birthday?'

'When you care about someone, you just know these things.'

They were still standing on the threshold, and Carlo rested the roses in the crook of his arm. 'My God, come in,' she said. 'Come into the kitchen and I'll see what sort of thing we have to put these in. They need a bucket, I think.'

He followed her and in the kitchen laid the bouquet on the table, on top of Sebastian's many drawings. Carefully she unwrapped the beautiful paper enfolding the roses. They had long stems with vicious thorns.

'They represent you,' Carlo said, reaching out to stroke her cheek. 'Their dark moist beauty combined with the danger of their barbs, an intriguing and challenging mix.'

She looked at him, wide eyed. Oh God…this man cut right through everything and saw the raw essence of her, or else he just had a bloody good way with words.

'You think you know me so well?' she said with a little laugh. 'Let me go and put something decent on.'

When she came back he took her gently by the shoulders and pulled her to him. He smelled of some musky aftershave. She allowed herself to be hugged. He was slim but solid, and it felt good. When her arms went around his waist she could feel him hardening against her, and her own body responded with a sudden rush.

He pulled away too soon. 'Let's put these roses in some water,' he said, flustered. 'Where did Esther keep her buckets?'

She smiled as she went into the larder to get the pewter wine-cooler. All that holier-than-thou talk of chastity and prayer; when it came down to physical contact, the body did all the talking.

They did it together, pulling the roses apart one by one carefully, so as not to damage their perfection. Carlo showed her how the stems should have a fresh cut, diagonally, with very sharp scissors under a stream of water from the tap. Preferably the wound of the stem should not come into contact with air at all. They worked in silence for a while, arranging the roses.

'I've been thinking about you a lot,' he said quietly. 'I respect the fact that you've not come to see me. It shows wisdom and self-restraint. Myself, I've been praying, waging battle with my feelings. I wonder if you've been sent to test me.'

'Aren't there some guidelines?' Mimi said with a chuckle. 'There's got to be a manual or something?'

He did see the funny side. Laughing, he took her hand in both of his, then pressed it to his lips. 'You're very pragmatic.'

'*Pragmatic*,' she repeated, memorising it. 'What does it mean?'

He thought for a moment. 'Practical, no nonsense and down-to-earth. I do admire that about you, Imogen. Young as you are, you can certainly teach an old dog some new tricks.'

She could think of a brazen riposte but thought better of it. They finished the floral arrangement and stood looking at it for a moment. 'So what are your plans for the big day?' he asked.

'Sebastian and Eva are taking me out for dinner,' she said.

'That sounds nice.' He hesitated for a moment. 'Listen, Imogen. Remember me telling you about my little place in Both Worlds. Why don't you and I celebrate your birthday tomorrow? I'll put champagne on ice and bring some nice food, and we can eat to the sound of waves. I'll set it all up and you can come over midmorning. I'll order a taxi for you and prepay it. Would you like that?'

'Well,' she said, uncertain. 'It sounds…nice.'

He flushed a little. 'Don't worry. I'd just like you to see my retreat and give you a special birthday lunch.'

She scrutinised his face for ulterior motives, but he looked so sincere – nervous, almost – like a young lad arranging his first date. She felt reassured. Carlo thought champagne and the sounds of waves rolling up on the beach would make her feel special. It seemed like good old-fashioned romanticism.

'So will you come?' he said, holding out a slip of paper with an address.

'Yes, okay, I'll come.'

'I'll tell the taxi to be here at 10.30 sharp.'

Alone in the kitchen, she studied the roses for a moment. She touched her thumb to one of the thorns. The sharp sting left a budding pearl of blood.

For old times' sake, they had a drink on the Wisteria Terrace of the Rock Hotel. She had to concede that it was quite special: 'iconic' was the word the brochures used, shaded by vines and large palm trees through which you glimpse the busy harbour. Winston Churchill had sat there, and a whole bunch of other famous people, such as Hemingway, Sean Connery, Alec Guinness and the Prince of Wales.

The gladrags she'd managed comprised a short black dress with a silver collar. Her only semi-elegant shoes were a pair of flipflops dotted with tiny black skulls (a find from Carnaby Street). After some deliberation, she removed the safety pin from her eyebrow and three of the rings in each ear. Yes, that did make her look more sophisticated, more like a grown up.

The old waiter recognised them instantly and kissed her and Eva on both cheeks. Sebastian had to blabber about her birthday and the waiter brought her a pink (not again!) concoction with little umbrellas and flowers and other junk, very obviously alcohol free. And there she was, about to order a double Bombay Gin with three droplets of tonic. Eva ordered it on her behalf and – ooops! – the pink drink accidentally got tipped into the flowerbed.

She couldn't deny to herself how relieved she was that Eva and Sebastian were back to being lovebirds. They were holding hands, looking relaxed and starry eyed, and she didn't begrudge them it, even if it was her birthday. Sebastian had clearly made up his mind to have a break from his sobriety. She just hoped he was going to remember that booze interfered with his medication. Anyway, he was in fine form, telling tall stories about Papito in Seville. He was a great mimic and could sound just like *un Sevillano* with very bad English. Mimi and Eva giggled helplessly.

When they'd had three rounds of drinks, they staggered, arm in arm, down through the enchanted Alameda Gardens. They aimed seaward through the tunnels of lush vegetation and those fairytale Dragon trees with their fat upside-down dragon legs reaching for the sky. Mimi tilted her head to look upward and saw the cable car zooming past. A flash caught the corner of her eye and she turned her head. She just caught a glimpse of a yellow Nike trainer. She'd seen those before.

Was the kid still at it, doing Carlo's bidding? Surely not? Well, let him report back that Imogen hung out in the Wisteria bar in her finery, that she'd put away oodles of Bombay Gin and could drink Churchill and Hemingway under the table.

They exited the park and wandered down to Rosia road, where apparently there was a local dive which served the best seafood in town. It was hardly marked as a restaurant, but the rickety tables outside gave it away. They were the first customers on the scene but as they sat down in the 'yard' and ordered, the place began to fill up as if on cue. Soon every table was taken – the whole place buzzing – and it became almost impossible to hail a waiter.

When they'd finished their plates of every fish in the seas, Eva slipped her a package from her handbag. She tore open the silver paper. Inside was an amazing silver necklace, a large star-shaped pendant studded by black onyx stones. It was just the sort of thing that Mimi would have chosen herself: not pretty – not even chic – but unique and distinctive.

'Thank you,' she mumbled. 'It's…just *me*.'

'I thought so,' said Eva with a smile.

'OK, here goes,' said Sebastian. 'To use one of your own poignant expressions, *I've fucked up*.' He pulled out a folded piece of glossy paper, torn out of a magazine or catalogue.

He handed it to Mimi. 'This is on order. They tell me you'll have it in a couple of weeks.'

She unfolded the paper and looked at the picture. It was a scooter, a very futuristic kind of scooter in black and silver. She was speechless. 'Gee, bro,' she said.

'I thought about a car,' he said, 'but who wants a car in Gibraltar? Everybody's on a scooter. There's a matching helmet to go with it. The damned helmet almost broke the bank. But it's *your* head, and your head is precious.' He reached over and tried to muss up the top of her hair. She leaned over to kiss him on his cheek. 'Thank you, Sebastian. It's a great present. Freedom of the road and all that.'

They drank a toast and – just as she was about to remind Sebastian that there would be absolutely no singing Happy Birthday in the restaurant – he stood up and bellowed it anyway, without a trace of embarrassment. 'This amazing and beautiful eighteen-year-old girl is my precious sister,' he boomed at the end. A few people were clapping. Oh, for fuck's sakes! Mimi cringed, almost disappearing under the table.

'I'm going to the loo,' she hissed. 'I might be a while.'

The Ladies was in an outside block, and there were several Yanito women queueing outside it. She took her place, then got impatient and wondered if she couldn't just as well squat in the shrubbery at the back of the building. It was almost dark by now and there were no lights at the back. But just as she came around the corner to the carpark, someone took her lightly by the elbow. She'd had enough to drink not to be startled but she yanked her arm away and glared at her assailant.

'Mohammed, honestly! What are you doing here?'

'I'm sorry.'

'I can't believe Carlo wants you to spy on my birthday party. Are you counting my drinks, or what?'

'Carlo doesn't know I'm here,' he said.

'Well, if you're freelancing, there's nothing to report. This is just a family dinner. It'd be more fascinating to watch paint dry.' She saw his shame and felt a sudden empathy. 'Forget it, Mohammed. Come and join us for a drink?'

'Oh, no. I don't want to intrude…but listen,' he took her elbow again and drew her further into the shadows. 'You must not go to Both Worlds tomorrow. For your own sake, don't go.'

She tried to see his expression in the darkness. 'Why not?'

'Just don't go,' he said. 'Just trust me when I say this.'

She thought about his words for a moment. 'Don't worry so much about me, Mohammed. I appreciate it, but you know, I'm quite wily.'

'What does that mean, *wily?*' Mohammed asked impatiently.

'What I mean is, I'm quite shrewd, quite street-smart. Do you know what I mean? I can look after myself, and I don't do things I don't want to do. Not as of today, for sure.'

Mohammed was like a dog with a bone. 'Don't go. Don't go,' he insisted.

'But why?' she said. 'Just tell me why I shouldn't.'

'It's not right…this interest he has in you.'

She peered at him through the shadows. 'So why do you care?'

'He made me go and buy things for tomorrow…'

'So?'

'Things he was too embarrassed to buy himself.'

'Things?' She was astonished. 'You mean—?'

'Yes, things,' Mohammed insisted.

Did Carlo really hope for something? More likely, he just wanted to make absolutely sure that if there was a chastity breakdown he had a moral obligation to be prepared.

She reached out to touch Mohammed's cheek. No hair grew on it; it was smooth as a baby's. 'How old are you Mohammed?'

'Eighteen.'

'Same as me, then. I know you are trying to be protective – and I really appreciate it – but I'll be fine. Carlo is not a mad rapist; he just likes me.' Her hand went to his hair. It was much finer and softer than it looked. Mohammed reached out to touch her face in turn. She took a step forward and enveloped him in her arms. The boy stood motionless for a long moment, his arms around her shoulders. Then, to her horror, he started to cry. She kept smoothing his hair, and whispered, 'There, there. Everything's cool.'

'You don't understand,' he said between sniffles. 'I want to keep you safe, and now I have helped to put you in danger.'

She could see his dilemma. The very employer on whose goodwill he depended was plotting to corrupt the girl he fancied. How to explain that if any corruption was going to happen, she was the more likely corruptor? 'You don't have to keep me safe. It's not your responsibility.'

'I'm sorry, Imogen. I'm a fool.'

They stood there a while longer, in that quiet embrace, Mohammed's tears gradually drying up. She didn't mind, suspecting it was himself he needed to save from the clutches of Carlo Montegriffo, but it was easier to project this need onto her, a defenceless girl. In any event, she'd enjoyed being party to a cuddle like this, with no expectations or gains or need for guilt or gratitude. She twirled the curls that grew on his neck around her fingers.

'I really do need a pee,' she said at last and released him. 'Wait for me and then come and have a drink. My brother will love you, trust me. He so wants me to have friends my own age.'

Looking over at the toilets she saw the queue had gone. When she turned back to Mohammed, he'd scarpered. All she could see in the dark was a flash of yellow trainer, disappearing into the stunted olive trees behind the carpark.

When she got back to the table she could see that Sebastian was drunk. He'd obviously not bothered to keep count of his drinks and – being on this high of reconciliation – he seemed not to give a damn. His loud voice went on uninterrupted about this Azzopardi fellow that he liked so much, and how he was going to go to the guy's house and advise him on a deck he wanted to build.

Mimi tried to ignore him, thinking of Mohammed and his concern for her. All at once she felt alarmed by tomorrow's visit to Both Worlds. Maybe Mohammed was right about putting herself in danger. Of what…she wasn't sure.

'– And I told him why I don't drive, too. I felt I could confide in the guy,' rambled Sebastian drunkenly.

'You did?' said Eva, her eyes alert. 'Why don't you tell *me* why you don't drive. I'm your best friend. You can confide in me, can't you?'

Mimi quickly sat up and put her hand on Sebastian's arm. 'You're drunk, bro. Why don't you wait till tomorrow? Tell her in private.'

'No,' said Eva. 'Tell me now.'

'What the hell!' Sebastian said and took a large slurp from his wine glass. 'Well, you see, I killed a guy when I was eighteen. I ran him over with my car. I squashed his head like a pumpkin.'

Eva looked shocked. 'Oh, my God, Sebastian.'

'It was an accident, of course, but I knew the guy. I've got to live with what I did, but after what happened I can never drive again. You can understand that, can't you?'

Eva pulled her chair up close to his and put her arms around him, and he leaned his head on her shoulder. 'Yes, of course I understand,' she said lovingly. 'Poor darling…and you've kept this horror to yourself.'

'Oh, for fuck's sake!' Mimi blurted furiously, taking even herself unawares. Sebastian stayed where he was, pretending not to have heard, while Eva stared at her with an indignant, questioning expression. 'Let's get this guy home,' Mimi decreed.

Eva began to try to get the attention of their waiter so they could pay their bill and go. It was hopeless. 'I'll go inside and pay,' she said.

As soon as she'd disappeared into the interior of the restaurant, Mimi slapped Sebastian on the arm and hissed. 'What the hell's going on with you?'

'What do you mean?' he slurred.

'That accident never happened, and you know it. You never killed that guy, you never even got near him.'

He glared at her. 'Yes, I did. Telling me I didn't was a coverup.'

'No bloody way. There was no coverup.'

'You were just a foetus in your mother's womb. What do *you* know?'

'I know *everything* about it. Dad told me. He had to explain many a thing to me, even though I was too young to be burdened with it.'

'Let me tell you the *real* story,' Sebastian said, jabbing his forefinger at her. 'Everybody tried to get me to believe I hadn't done it, just so I could get better and come out of hospital. Back then they thought *denial* was the best therapy.'

'I cannot believe I'm hearing you say this,' she said through clenched teeth. 'I'm going to fucking find the guy and get him to Skype you, so you can see his living face for yourself.

You never hurt a hair on his head. You weren't even near him. How much time and energy has gone into getting you to realise it?' She sat back and shook her head. 'You yourself admitted it'd been a fantasy... Something's not right with you. It's about time you told Eva, you know? Lay all your cards on the table. If *you* don't, *I* will.'

Sebastian seemed to sober up in an instant. 'Don't even think of it,' he said aggressively. 'She'll leave me. That's what you're aiming for, isn't it? You've been doing your best to get rid of her since the day you arrived.'

Mimi shook her head vigorously. 'That's not fair. Eva and I are getting on just fine now. She's cool. *Really*. I like her. But I don't know why you don't just tell her. She'll understand. She *needs* to know.'

'*Jesus Christ!* Can I please have one single person in my life who doesn't have preconceived ideas about me, who's not judging me by my past?'

'She wouldn't judge you. She's not that kind of person.'

'She wouldn't judge me, perhaps, but her whole view of me would alter.' He put his head in his hands and hissed though his fingers, 'Can you *please* allow me to be the person I am to her? Don't you see, it's the model I live up to. It keeps me sane.'

She backed down. Perhaps he was right, and anyway, who understood the feeling better? She herself loathed to be judged by who she was yesterday. She suspected Eva too was running from something. So, when Eva came towards them, she tried to smile. It had been a pretty good birthday, after all.

Eva

They sat down on Jonny Risso's shabby seat-cushions, made even grubbier by a group of Norwegian fishermen that had commandeered his boat for over a week. Squashed beer cans spilled over the edges of a bucket, and Jonny himself looked rough.

Eva leaned towards Brian and whispered. 'Be careful what you say. He's quite capable of organising an expedition so that he can cash in on it himself.'

'Got ya,' Brian said, nodding.

'Sebastian is not happy about this, so if you meet him, don't speak of it, please.'

Brian seemed to consider her statement. 'Okay, but I think I'll be going with your view on it. In fact, we'll have no choice but to report it, sooner rather than later.'

Eva glanced at Jonny, but he was busy starting his boat up.

'So the uber-worker didn't want to join us?' Brian asked.

'Don't be cheeky,' she said with a frown.

'The only time I've met him – when we ran into each other in town – he scowled at me as though I was plotting to abscond with his woman.'

'I didn't notice. He's often got that face on him these days, but he doesn't mean to be rude.'

'You're going to have to tell him we've been here,' Brian said, then indicated Jonny with a tilt of his head. 'Or he will.'

Jonny finally got his engine started up, and the sudden

motion made her gag a little, a reminder of Mimi's birthday dinner. It had been a good evening. Everyone had been on form, perhaps due to the sheer amount of alcohol they'd consumed. Mimi seemed to have grown an inch in just one day, and she herself had recaptured her loving relationship with Sebastian. His easy laugh had made her conscious of how he'd not really been himself for weeks. He'd been troubled about the project, going off on tunnel expeditions on his own, at times rambling about his damned bridge, and obsessing about Mimi's relationship with Montegriffo. Finding out that his 'fiancée' was a married woman had been yet another blow.

Hopefully, now that Mimi was eighteen, he could let go of her a little. By now she had realised that Mimi and Sebastian shared all kinds of secrets. One of them seemed to have something to do with the medication Mimi had hinted at. It would come as no surprise if Sebastian was on antidepressants. He was so intense and obsessional, it was probably just what he needed. Why hide it? She'd been on them herself, more than once. It was nothing to be ashamed of.

Jonny steered them past Catalan Bay, its sandy beach obscured by hundreds of parasols in vivid colour. Caleta Hotel sat on its southern end, perched on a cliff overhanging the water. A stretch of rocky shore followed and then the strange little community called Both Worlds. It was a long, narrow strip of housing above its own little beach. Between Catalan Bay and Both Worlds, the coastline was topped by a curious natural phenomenon, a massive slope, smooth and even, as if God had poured a fistful of sand down the precipice. Above it arose the soaring cliffs of the Rock.

Her eyes searched up and down the shoreline, trying to

visually superimpose the Frontiers Development Project on its southern end. For the first time, she couldn't do it. The place was too beautiful, it's natural ruggedness and dramatic backdrop too spectacular, somehow. Instantly she felt disloyal. She never doubted Sebastian's creative brilliance. He *was* an uber-genius…but so was God!

'Look at it,' she exclaimed, nudging Brian's arm. 'What an amazingly beautiful place this is.'

'I was just thinking exactly the same thing,' he said. 'You know, I was mostly in favour of Sebastian's concept, but I think we're destroying Gibraltar with this endless development.'

Jonny swerved sharply and turned his engine off. They drifted shoreward for a while, slowly coming to a stop. Jonny plopped his anchor in.

They left an ill-humoured Jonny Risso to his radio and his rollup cigarettes. Eva swam ahead, leading the way. If it wasn't for the markers that Sebastian's team had left on the cliffside, the little window to the cave would be practically impossible to detect. She checked with Brian before entering, and he nodded vigorously. She could tell; he too was excited. They swam through the opening, through the forest of stalagmites, stalactites and columns, into the gigantic cavern where the water was clear as air and they were flying over a landscape of colossal shards and slivers. They lingered there for a time. After swimming up through the halo-cline they finally broke surface.

'What an extraordinary place,' Brian exclaimed. 'Clever girl! What a find!' He looked up and lit up the roof with his torch beam.

'What did I tell you?'

'Let's not waste any time. Where do we get up on this ledge?'

She pointed to a corner where the ledge was lower, almost at the waterline.

He swam towards it. 'Let me get up first and I'll pull you out.'

It was a bit more tricky than it had appeared but nothing was going to stop them now. All the while, Eva was aware of what a special experience this could turn out to be and she was sorry that she'd kept it from Sebastian. Perhaps this whole expedition was unwise, not least because Sebastian would be extremely unhappy about it. Their fragile reconciliation needed no further knocks.

They took off their gear and took several deep breaths. The air was good, alpine fresh. Where did it come from?

'Right,' she said, bracing herself for what they might encounter. 'Let's see where the back of this cave ends.' She laughed nervously. 'What if we find a Neanderthal? I'll faint.'

'Relax, petal, I'm good at mouth to mouth.'

'I bet.'

'What's that?' Brian took a step forward and knelt down to illuminate something with his torch.

She barely dared to approach and waited for him to say more.

He didn't take his eyes off whatever it was, but motioned to her with his arm. 'Come and look at this.'

Excited, she went up to him and bent low, shining her own light on the object where it nestled in a crevice. Yes, there was no doubt about what it was.

A half-smoked cigarette butt.

Mimi

She'd been messing around with her hair all morning, selfishly occupying the bathroom. No matter what she tried, nothing looked right. In the end she opted for curly. It made her look more feminine, something a mature man would probably most appreciate. She used some heated rollers that she found at the back of the bathroom cabinet that probably had belonged to Mrs. Cohen. She checked the result in the mirror. It still looked funny, with the sides so short. Perhaps it was time for a change. Her kinky hair had been gawped at enough to last her a while.

On her way back from the bathroom she ran into Sebastian. He looked her over with a puzzled expression.

'You look different,' he said. 'Sort of feminine.'

'Yuck, no way,' she said. 'I'm a bad-ass.'

'Yeah,' he said, ruffling the curls. 'Go sort yourself out. Someone might take you for a *nice* girl.'

'Aren't you late for work?'

He kissed her on the cheek and headed for the door, his briefcase under his arm. Mimi went back to her room to tackle the problem of what to wear. Thankfully she had rinsed out the dress she'd worn last night; it was the best she had. Her makeup took ages. She debated for some time whether to squeeze a spot or not – didn't in the end – and she nicked her leg shaving.

It was time to catch the taxi so she left the apartment and headed down the stairs, then flinched in surprise when Sebastian stepped out of the shadows in the ground-floor hallway. He must have been waiting there since leaving the apartment, or returned, acting on a hunch.

He looked her up and down, noting the dress, shoes and makeup.

'Where are you going?' he said.

'Why are you lurking here?'

'What are you up to, Mimi? Why are you dressed up?'

'Listen, I can't stop,' she said. 'I've got a taxi waiting. You know how it is, they just move on if you're not there to jump straight in.'

He took her by the arm to restrain her. 'Where is this taxi taking you?'

'Oh, for God's sake. I'm in a hurry. Don't hassle me.'

'I'm not letting you go. I ran into Montegriffo on my way out. He looked suspiciously smug. When I asked him, he said he was going to his retreat in Both Worlds.'

'What's that got to do with me?' She shrugged with feigned irritation.

'Because that's where you're going too, isn't it?'

She whipped her arm out of his grasp. 'What if I am? I'm eighteen years old, Sebastian. Carlo has invited me for lunch, and I'm going.'

He tried to block her way and they grappled for a moment. She couldn't believe they'd come to this. He held her firmly by the arms and stared her in the face. 'You live under my roof, you eat and shower and occupy the biggest bedroom. You'll bloody-well abide by my rules. You're not going to Both Worlds to have sexual congress with that Bible-thumping pervert.'

'Who's the pervert?' she hissed. 'You have no business even speculating about what I might do or not do. If you want me to, I'll move out.'

He dropped her arms. 'No, Mimi, you can't do that.'

'Oh, Sebastian. Come on…let's not fight.' She lowered her voice. 'You gave me a very special birthday and I appreciate it massively, and I love you to bits, but you've got to stop controlling my life and begin to deal with your own stuff. You've got some huge problem going on, that's becoming obvious. I sure as hell hope you're taking your pills. We've been here all summer and I bet you've not signed up with any doctor or attended any clinic. If you don't want to tell Eva, at least go back to London and see Dr. Matthews. Just take care of it, or you're in danger of fucking up your relationship and your work and *everything*.' He stared at her. 'You hear me, bro?'

When he didn't answer, she put a hand on his cheek and looked him in the eye. 'Come on, now. Why don't you come with me? Both Worlds is on the way to your site. You can drop me off.'

'And deliver you to that creep myself. Never!'

'Suit yourself.'

She ran out of the hall, past an astonished-looking Moroccan woman who'd been sweeping the ramp and had probably heard the whole interaction.

Traffic in town was murder. Too many planes were landing, so cars and pedestrians were stopped from crossing the runway. The backup caused a tension-filled congestion in town. The temperatures were soaring. Finally, her taxi hit Devil's Tower Road, leading out of the town centre along the east side.

The road was narrow between the sea and the slope of the old water catchment, so the driver had to drop her off in a layby. She walked self-consciously towards her destination. The row of tiny white chalets looked careworn up close, yet their setting was spectacular. She finally found the right entrance and chose amongst the doorbells. The door buzzed open and Carlo instructed her through the intercom which way to go.

The door was ajar and she walked in without knocking. In a small living room, on a leather sofa, Carlo sat waiting for her. She noted that his retreat-wear was different from his town look: he was actually wearing shorts and a vest from which thin, long legs and arms protruded. He jumped up and came to her, kissing her on both cheeks.

'You look exceptionally beautiful,' he said, holding her hands in his and settling his large liquid eyes on hers for a long moment. 'Let me get you a drink. I've got gin, vodka, rum, wine and beer plus an array of mixers. And champagne, of course. But I thought we might leave that to have with lunch.'

Mimi had a snoop around the apartment while Carlo mixed the drinks in a tiny kitchen. There was a fabulous little terrace, right over the beach, a nice marble bathroom and a closed door which had to be a bedroom.

'Let's sit outside,' said Carlos, bearing a tray.

They sat down in the two cane chairs. The drinks and a bowl of mixed nuts were on a little table. The usually relaxed air between them had morphed into awkwardness. She took a big gulp of her drink. It was vodka all right, or nine-tenths of it was. Within seconds it had gone to her head and she realised she'd not eaten a thing all morning.

'Do you own this place?' she asked.

'Yes. I have my writing to thank for it. The down-payment was the advance for a poetry collection.'

'Really? So writing sometimes actually pays.'

'Yours will,' he said. 'You have a future there.'

She laughed. 'Flattery will get you nowhere. But give me your worst. How do you think I'm getting on with it?'

An hour later, they were still talking about writing and

she had another drink in her hand. It felt good, and any tension had evaporated in a haze of vodka, helped by the dappled sunlight and the sounds of the sea. Groups of gulls swooped in and out over the building and she watched an ape having a nap on a terrace further down while its baby bounced around like a rubber ball, playing with thin air, as kittens do.

'Let me ask you something about Mrs. Cohen,' she said.

'Nothing gruesome, please,' he warned.

She bit her lip: best to begin with something neutral. 'She played the violin, didn't she?'

'Yes, how did you know? Is that *her* violin I'm hearing sometimes?'

'Maybe,' she said, trying an enigmatic smile.

'No end to your talents, Imogen. Well, Esther was a real virtuoso. When her husband went to work in the mornings, she would begin to play and sometimes she played all day. But the music she played was so haunting it used to really affect me. She made it up.'

'What do you mean?'

'The music, it was all improvisation. But she didn't write anything down. A big loss to the world of music, I am sure of it.'

Mimi braced herself for her next question.

'And…did she have a daughter?'

Carlo looked away. After a moment, he said, 'Yes, a long time ago she had a little girl. She died tragically at three months. She had a bout of diarrhoea, and Esther – who was only nineteen at the time – didn't know about dehydration. After a couple of days, the baby seemed better. She slept peacefully but never woke up. All moisture had left her body and she was light as an eggshell.'

'Oh, please,' said Mimi, covering her face.

'Esther never got over it,' he said, 'and she never stopped blaming herself for not taking the little girl to a doctor. And what's worse, after the death she had a stillborn baby and a long series of miscarriages. She told me all this after her husband died. The two of them were bound by the tragedy and rarely interacted with others. Sol's death was perhaps the last straw. That's when she stopped making music and her addiction really took hold.'

Shocked by the story, Mimi stood up and looked over the railing. The half-knitted cardigan... Esther didn't just get bored with knitting.

'Did she tell you the girl's name?'

'Sofia,' said Carlo.

'How strange,' Mimi said. 'That's my middle name.'

After a few moments of silence, Carlo got up too and together they stood watching the waves rolling up on the beach. A little girl threw a Frisbee right into the sea and her mother gave her a loud telling off. Nearby, two lovers were snogging heedlessly on a bright orange towel. They watched the lovers for a while.

'Let's go inside, shall we?' Carlo said at last. 'I need to feed you some real food.'

'Let's eat out here,' she said.

'Please,' he insisted. 'It's too hot.'

In the living room he put his arms around her. They kissed for the first time, and she thought the kiss was – if anything – quite childish. He clearly was not practised at snogging and seemed to be trying to avoid their tongues coming into contact.

'I better see to that lunch,' he said, drawing back.

'It can wait,' she said, holding on to him.

After a moment, his long fingers worked their way over the surface of her dress to her breast. She found herself

301

enjoying being touched. He fondled her ever so gently, teasing her nipple to a hard point. Her breath came faster and she felt herself weaken at the knees. She was getting turned on, *hallelujah,* she was actually wanting it for herself. Perhaps this was the man who could give her the first orgasm... That would make her coming of age truly memorable.

For a long time, they stood there. His eyes were closed, seemingly in a trance just over her pathetic little nipple. She felt a bubble of mirth rise in her throat and impatiently moved his hand down over her belly.

'Was that not okay?' he asked anxiously, peering down at her.

'Yeah, it was okay,' she said. 'How would you feel about going to bed?'

He searched her eyes. 'How do *you* feel about it?'

'I'm more concerned about you, the chastity and all that.' She tried not to smile. 'We don't have to do anything.'

'Of course,' he said, looking relieved. 'You're in charge.'

The bedroom was small and ascetic, like a monk's cell. Heavy black curtains were drawn over the window, and in the gloom she saw that Jesus was there too. He hung bleeding on a cross above the headboard. That's going to be helpful, she thought as she kicked off her sandals and flung herself onto the narrow bed. Her head was spinning pleasantly, and she could feel the awakening inside her. Her whole body felt jittery and alive.

He stood by the bed looking down on her for a moment, as though still trying to resist the ultimate and fatal temptation. Then he took off the chain with the silver cross and laid it carefully on the bedside table.

They lay facing each other, fully clothed. 'I won't do anything to hurt you,' he said.

'Okay,' she said. 'But just so you know, I'm not a virgin.'

She saw his frown in the gloom. 'I meant, I couldn't penetrate you.'

'Why not?' she asked, flustered, remembering the condoms.

'It's too soon. We need to be sure.'

'If you say so, but we can touch, right?'

When he didn't seem to know what she meant, she took his hand and guided it over her body, her hip and belly and down under the waistband of her knickers. He clearly had no idea what was down there or what to do with it. She was wet and ready and arched her back in frustration. She put her hand under his vest and explored his cool skin, smooth and hairless, but he tensed when she began fiddling with the button of his shorts.

'Hold on,' she exclaimed, pulling away from him. 'This is no good. It's just too formal. Open the curtains and let's get some light and air in here.'

'Won't it be too bright? It'll get very hot,' he protested feebly.

She chuckled. 'You just don't want to see what you're doing.'

He hopped up and did as he was told, then lay back again and sighed deeply, as if preparing for round two.

She burst out laughing. 'This is supposed to be fun, you know. It's not some kind of march to the gallows.'

'It's a historic occasion,' he said with a wry smile.

'What would you like me to do?' she said huskily, feeling brave and mature.

'Let's practise kissing,' he ventured.

Kissing got better, but at the same time she felt exasperated. For once she actually felt a physical urge, the real deal: sexual arousal. It was rare, it happened mainly in her head, the thought of power over a guy and *him* helpless with lust. This was the other way around, Carlo was holding out on her.

A couple of times she opened her eyes and saw a man with greying hair and lines around his eyes, a man old enough to be her father. It was best to keep her eyes closed and just remember she was kissing a poet.

Their kissing petered out after a long while, and they lay on their sides trying to read each other. While she debated whether to give up on the endeavour and go get a drink of water, he reached over, pushing her dress up a little more, baring her to the waist. He hooked a finger into the elastic of her knickers and pulled it gently downwards off her hip. She could feel his eyes hot on her skin and his scrutiny paralysed her.

'That is a very sinister tattoo,' he said. 'A human skull! How could you do that to yourself?'

'I bet you like it, really,' she said hoarsely. 'Pull down my knickers and you can inspect it more closely.'

He didn't move, just kept looking. Suddenly he leaned down and touched her tattoo with his tongue. A long raw groan escaped his throat and his body twitched. A stunned silence followed where only a gull shrieked in laughter outside the window. He flopped onto his back and covered his face with his hands.

'So, what's for lunch?' she said. 'I could eat a horse after all that.'

After a quiet lunch he wanted to call her a taxi, but she insisted she preferred to take the bus back to town, and Carlo did not protest for too long. He didn't look her in the eye when they said goodbye at the door.

'I'll get better at this,' he murmured, lifting her hand to his lips. 'Like you said, there must be a manual.'

'Thanks for my birthday party, and for the roses,' she said.

'Don't sound so formal,' he said. 'My hope is to give you roses and champagne on every birthday.'

She walked away without looking back. Roses and champagne, my God, he's planning ahead, she thought. At once the expression 'sugar daddy' popped uninvited into her head. She cringed in mortification. With her back turned to it, the whole event had an unhealthy feel. Though you could say he'd been plying her with alcohol, it was in fact she who had made the first move, merrily portraying her own idea of the mature, sophisticated seductress. She hoped she'd not awakened something in him she couldn't deal with. What the hell was she doing, treading on such thoroughly dodgy ground? For all her sexual experimentation, she was still a kid, a virgin where orgasms were concerned. As for her feelings for the man, he was nice enough, but her yearning for a substitute father was just a fucking cliché! Dad had loved her, her older brother loved her, she did *not* need a sugar daddy.

It was a short walk to the bus stop between Both Worlds and Caleta Hotel. Mohammed was standing in the shade of the bus shelter, waiting for her.

'What are *you* doing here?' she said with a sigh, but in fact she was ridiculously happy to find him there. If ever she needed someone normal to keep her company!

The number four came almost straight away from town. It was the end stop and it turned in a layby to go back. They waited, alone in the bus, while the driver stood outside and ate a cheese sandwich. They watched a blonde woman, whose car had been towed away, fire questions at him.

Her head was buzzing now and her mouth dry, the

alcohol spent and paving the way for a hangover. She was desperate to brush her teeth, get out of her clothes and makeup and have a long hot soak in Mrs. Cohen's giant tub. Mohammed must have sensed her discomfort.

'Was it bad?'

She shook her head. 'No. It was a very nice lunch. Lobster salad and champagne.'

Mohammed's dark eyes were trying to read the truth in her face. She wanted to hug him, thank him for waiting for her, but suspicion crept into her gratitude. 'Did Carlo tell you to wait for me and take me home, or what?'

'Of course not. I told you. I do everything for him, but I'm not spying on you any more or buying condoms.'

'No worries, he's got no need for them.'

The driver had finished his sandwich but he took out a comb and began to rake it through his greasy hair. Finally, he boarded and started up the bus. There were no other passengers.

'I looked it up on the net the other day,' she said as they watched the scenery go past along Devil's Tower Road. 'Moroccans can apply for a resident's permit as long as they've got a legitimate job in Gib. Didn't you say you got a job in the mosque?'

'Yeah, but…'

'And you won't need Carlo Montegriffo,' she insisted, 'or his permission.'

'I owe him, you see, or I should say my parents are in his debt.'

'Really? How come?'

'Mr. Montegriffo is a director of a charity that helps destitute Moroccan people. He gave my parents a personal loan to pay off a debt, as long as I stay under him.' He turned to her. 'You are not to speak about it, Imogen. He would be very angry. This is a confidential arrangement between him and my parents.'

She felt terrible for him, and slightly outraged. Behind his pious front, was Carlo exploiting a vulnerable foreign kid? He did treat Mohammed as his personal dogsbody.

'Can he really hold you to a loan made to your parents?'

'Mr. Montegriffo is very powerful. He usually gets what he wants. The loan was nothing.' Mohammed tapped his forehead. 'It's here where he has the power.'

'Don't worry. It's my turn now. I'll protect *you*.'

The young man smiled through that grim expression he wore. She noticed that his hand was holding hers. They studied each other for a moment. A glimpse of joy began to lighten his features. God, he was sweet. She leaned towards him. He was the second man she'd kissed in year eighteen.

Eva

She ran into Sebastian on DiMoretti's Ramp. He was on his way out, apparently in a hurry. Brian had dropped her off on Engineer's Lane, the closest point to which he could bring her in his car. She was carrying her wetsuit in a big plastic bag and all her other paraphernalia in another.

'Hi honey,' she said, running up to give him a hug.

He put his arms around her. 'My beautiful mermaid. Thank God you're back. Where have you been?'

Her heart sank. Normally he didn't ask her many questions, and this was one that she could have done without, but she was too aware of – and fed up with – all the subterfuge between them.

'Remember, I told you I let Brian in on our secret cave! Well, our French group cancelled this morning, so I thought it was an opportunity to show him the place. And Jonny was free, though terribly hung over. He'd been partying with—'

'You showed Brian our find?'

'Yes, well, I told you I might.'

'I thought we'd talk it through, not jump into some action we'd regret.'

'Well, *you* said that, Sebastian. Then you said you didn't care. This was an opportunity to—'

He put a hand up to stop her. 'Sorry, Eva. I've got to go.'

She frowned at him, then sighed in frustration. She could have expected this. 'Are you mad at me again?'

'I'm disappointed, but right now all I care about is Mimi.

She went off to Montegriffo's lair in Both Worlds this morning and she's not back yet. I'm going to go looking for her.'

She put a hand on his arm. 'Do you know where his place is? There must be nearly a hundred apartments there. Have you tried her phone?'

'It's switched off.'

She shook her head. 'Come on, honey! Carlo is a known person in town and works for the Ministry of Defence. I don't think for a moment that he's any kind of rapist.'

'You wouldn't! You obviously don't know what men are capable of.'

At once, an image appeared in her mind and she looked away to prevent him seeing the shadow of pain cross her face. She knew better than anyone what men were capable of. *Some men.*

'Have you thrown away any of my drawings?' Sebastian asked out of the blue.

'Of course not,' she said. 'But if they're scrunched-up and on the floor, I assume they're for throwing away. We'd be drowning in paper balls if I didn't.'

He nodded, looking at her. Then he cocked his head. 'How was it?' he enquired flippantly. 'Did you find a Neanderthal hotspot in your cave: bones, drinking vessels, spears?'

She responded to his mocking tone in turn. 'Oh yes, we certainly did. You'll be amazed to hear that our stone-age ancestors smoked tobacco. It'll make headline news, I'm telling you.'

He frowned. 'Tobacco? What did you find to figure that?'

'A cigarette butt. There was no mistaking it.'

Despite his mood, he burst out laughing. 'You found a cigarette butt.'

'I thought you'd find that amusing.'

'So what you're saying is, someone swam in through the hole we made the other day, and smoked a fag? Who'd carry cigarettes on a dive? Come now! You're taking the piss.'

Seeing that he was moving away from her, she said, 'Is it really sensible to go looking for Mimi? She could be anywhere right now, probably on her way home. Look, it's not even five o'clock.'

'I'm fucking worried about her! It's all very well for you, off diving with some guy, with not a care in the world.'

She almost smiled. 'You're being childish now, Sebastian. All right, I'll tell you all about the cigarette butt when you come home.'

Droplets sprinkled her bare arms. She looked up. Mrs. Amirah, the Moroccan woman who'd moved in next door, was hanging out wet sheets on a wheeled line between the buildings.

'Tell me now, but quickly. I'm in a hurry.'

'Here? Must we stand here and talk?'

She'd been looking forward to sitting down with him and telling him what they'd found. After last night's fun, she was determined to deepen their restored intimacy. But he stood there, expecting her to just blurt out her story.

'All right then,' she said, exasperated. 'After finding the butt, we also found an empty metal tin. It had Duke of Durham Cigarettes stamped on it, have you heard of it?'

He shook his head.

'We thought the only way it could have got there was if the cave were connected to the outside world in some other way, so we decided to explore. The passage at the back was about fifty metres deep and narrowed to a point. We had to crawl on our bellies for the last five metres, and we were right. The end of the passage connected with the roof of a manmade tunnel. I've no idea what tunnel it was; for sure it was an older one, not a World War Two job. We didn't jump down into the passage because we might not have been able to haul ourselves back up again. So there you have it. The cigarette butt was pristine, but the tin looked very dated; not a current brand. We thought we'd best leave it exactly where we found it. To think someone in some distant past took a ladder up to the hole in the roof of the tunnel, crawled along and found the enclosed cave.'

She prodded him lightly in the shoulder. 'Don't run off on me, honey.'

He softened a little. 'Maybe I just don't like you spending so much time with Brian.'

'Well, if you're jealous, spend more time with me – not just in bed. Come for a walk with me...for coffee in the *piazza*. You rarely even take the time out to have a drink with me on the terrace, or make good your own suggestion to join me and Mimi for dinner.'

'You're not in cahoots with Brian, are you?'

She stared at him, open mouthed. 'In cahoots...what does that mean? Are you asking if I'm having an affair?'

He looked at her pensively for several seconds. 'I don't know. Are you?' Before she could answer he shrugged, turned on his heel and walked quickly down the ramp.

'Wait, Sebastian!' she called after him. 'Don't you dare walk away.'

She power-walked up the stairs two at a time, the adrenalin of her fury as good as rocket fuel. How dare he make a suggestion like that? *And then walk away.* Mrs. Amirah had heard every word. When Eva glanced up she'd shaken her head in commiseration, as if to say: *Men! Immature, jealous, unreasonable.*

Inside her front door, she flung down her gear and headed for the kitchen. She opened the fridge and took out a bottle of beer. '*Mimi!*' she shouted. 'Do you want to hear a funny story? About a one-hundred-thousand year old cigarette butt!'

But of course, Mimi wasn't home, she was in the clutches of the nefarious Montegriffo. Mad though she was at Sebastian, she still felt for him. He'd become almost obsessed with worry, convinced that Carlo was a danger to Mimi. She had to remind herself that Sebastian had effectively been Mimi's father during her childhood, so it wasn't surprising that his protectiveness was so deeprooted. On top of that was the burden of guilt that he carried, having been forced to hand over thirteen-year-old Mimi to their ice maiden of a mother, a woman he loathed with all his heart.

She headed for the living room, bottle in hand, and on an impulse opened the door to Mimi's room. Messy and unremarkable but for a huge bouquet of dark red roses sitting in the wine cooler on her dresser. She stared at the roses. Never had she seen such an extravagant bouquet. Who the hell had given her those; surely not Sebastian: she would have known about it. It had to be Montegriffo. The sheer size of the bouquet was excessive, the colour of the roses provocative somehow, darkly suggestive! With a shiver she wondered if Sebastian's instinct about the man could be right. Should she have offered to go with him?

In the kitchen she opened her laptop and tried to google 'Duke of Durham' cigarettes. Her mood lightened when she discovered that the cigarettes hailed from 1890, well over a century old. There was the tin, with an Art Nouveau painting of a woman with a fan leaning over a rose covered balcony, offering the packet to an invisible lover below.

How charming was that? The find was almost as amazing as the Neanderthal cooking hearth.

Her phone rang. Should she answer? She was still annoyed about Sebastian's ridiculous insinuation but he was probably calling to apologise. He was usually quick to put things right if they'd had words, and she, in turn, was grateful for his initiative.

She ran back to the kitchen to grab her phone. 'Yes, hello.'

It wasn't Sebastian.

The breather did his usual thing. She listened for a few seconds, that feeling of dread spreading through her belly. Just as she was about to hang up, he spoke for the first time. A strange voice said something she could not catch.

'What!' she whispered.

'Come back to me,' came the reply, his voice distorted and far away.

'I am never going back, Adrian.' She tried to keep the tremor out of her voice, but she was shaking so much she could not. 'Wh…where are you?'

'Near you. Very near you. Come away with me, Chantelle.'

Panic flooded her. She was about to throw down the phone and just run. The clichéd scene she'd enacted in her mind so often flashed before her: the suitcase on the bed, flinging things into it; an overwhelming feeling of hopelessness.

Suddenly she couldn't bear for all this to begin again. She didn't have the strength to go on running. And something else rose within her: *anger*. How dare he go on torturing her with his malice? She'd handed over her power to him, and he toyed with her as though she were a mouse. She'd had enough of it. *Enough!*

'So come and get me, you bastard,' she hissed.

'I will,' he promised.

'No, don't bother,' she said icily, determined not to let him torment her another moment of her life. 'I'll make it easy for both of us. Let's meet face to face. I want a divorce or you can kill me. I don't care which way we go. You never loved me, it's just your ugly pride, your fucking chauvinistic conceit. You're not a man. A real man doesn't abuse his own mother or torture defenceless animals. I have no feelings for you, no respect. I'm not even scared of you anymore.'

He didn't answer, no doubt wanting to see how long she could maintain her bravado, waiting to hear her crumble… so she waited too, wondering how far away from here could she get in a day.

'All right, Adrian,' she said after a long moment. 'There is a small town, quite near Malaga airport, called Benalmadena Pueblo. I'll be there by tonight and I'll check into the most central hotel I can find. There shouldn't be many to choose from. I'll be waiting for you.' She listened for a response, but when none came she repeated, 'Did you hear me, Adrian? I'll be in Benalmadena Pueblo, alone, ready and waiting for you.' She pressed the off button and slipped the phone into her pocket.

'What's going on?'

She swung around and there stood Mimi with her hands on her hips. She was wearing the same dress she'd had on the night before. Her topknot was curly instead of gelled up and she looked strangely grown up, as if *she* were the adult catching a teenager hatching a plot to run away.

'Nothing.'

'Who was that on the phone, this Adrian?'

Eva stood still, looking at her. Enough of lies and pretences: Mimi had a right to know what was going on. It had been a wonderful few months, a whirlwind of love, excitement and romance, but now the whole pie-in-the-sky charade was over. There probably wasn't even time to sit down and explain her decision to Sebastian, and anyway, it would be a drama which might end conclusively. Conversely, he might want to come with her and take on his rival. Sebastian was both strong and formidable in his own way, but he'd be no match for Adrian who lived his life and his work by violence.

'Eva, answer me,' Mimi insisted. 'Who is Adrian and why were you shouting at him?'

'Just so you know, Mimi, your brother is running around the length and breadth of Gibraltar looking for you. He's probably in Both Worlds right now, kicking doors in.'

'Oh, for fuck's sake,' Mimi groaned. 'Well, that'll keep him busy for a while. Who the hell is Adrian?'

'Adrian is my husband.'

'Adrian is your husband? So, you're married?' She didn't sound angry, not even particularly surprised. Perhaps she'd taken some of those phone calls herself. 'Does Sebastian know?'

'He does now.'

'And what's going on? Judging by your shouting, you're not going back with this Adrian real soon.'

'Never,' Eva said. 'Adrian is a vicious and dangerous guy. He would never let me go and I was too scared to ask for a divorce. So I ran. He's catching up to me fast, but I can't keep running. I don't want to put you and Sebastian in jeopardy, so I'm going on a trip… I'm going to meet him.'

'You just said you're not going back to him.'

'Oh, no, of course I'm not. I'm going to ask him for a divorce.'

'So you'll be back with us, right?' said Mimi anxiously. 'He won't hurt you, will he?'

'Can you call Brian – here is his number – and ask him if he can drive me across the border? Tell him to meet me where he dropped me just now. In fifteen minutes.'

Mimi followed her into the bedroom and stood looking at her as she flung some clothes into her case. 'What about Sebastian? Does he know you're off to meet this vicious Adrian?'

'I've been trying to tell him everything, but he doesn't want to hear it or take it seriously. Of course he was pissed off to find out that I was married and he thinks I'm still hanging on for some reason. Just phone Brian for me, please, Mimi. And why don't you phone your brother too and put him out of his misery.'

Mimi nodded, went out to the kitchen with the address book she'd given her and returned within a couple of minutes. 'There's no answer. I didn't leave a message. I wasn't sure... And Sebastian's phone is out of range. If he's in Both Worlds, there's a lump of fucking rock between us.'

'Okay, Mimi. Would you do me a huge favour? Cut my hair, please.'

Mimi stared at her, wide eyed. '*No*! What do you want to do that for?'

'I want Adrian to see a different me, someone he no longer knows. Everybody associates me with my goddamned hair,' she said bitterly. 'Even your brother!'

Eva sat down on the chair in front of the little dressing table and took the trimming scissors and a comb from the drawer. 'Do it! Cut it straight, page-boy type of thing, right at the jaw.'

'Oh, fuck,' Mimi groaned. 'Your gorgeous hair! Are you sure?'

'Yes, I'm sure. Please hurry.'

Mimi took the scissors from her hand and, combing with

her left hand, she began a straight cut from the side of her face. Her hand was steady enough. 'So, go on,' she said without looking up. 'Tell me everything.'

'Look, Mimi, I love your brother. I'm totally in awe of him...or I was. In those first few weeks together I was caught up in a kind of fairy tale, and Sebastian never asked me any questions. I think a lot of people working in Dubai come there because they're leaving something behind, so I didn't feel like I was obliged to own up to the complex circumstances of my past. It was my own business. Besides, if I'd told him I had a husband – a spiteful U.S. Federal Agent who'd be casting the net far and wide to find me – he might have felt differently about me. I'd have had to explain a whole bunch of stuff and, to be honest, that was exactly what I was wanting to get away from. Moving here with Sebastian was different, of course, and it was cowardly of me not to tell him then. I should have given him the choice. I should have owned up to everything before we even left Dubai.'

Eva looked up into the mirror and met Mimi's eye.

'Yeah, perhaps, but Sebastian is not a man who asks questions. He might be brilliant, but where relationships are concerned he doesn't see further than his nose,' Mimi said, matter-of-factly. 'He'll be gutted, though. He's not as emotionally strong as you think. This might just tip him over the edge.'

'In what way? What edge?'

She could see Mimi hesitating. 'There is no point explaining Sebastian to you now,' she said, 'but there's plenty of stuff he ought to have shared with you.'

'I'll give him a call once I'm on my way, but if for some reason I can't get him or he doesn't want to talk to me, can you please explain on my behalf? Right now I'm getting out to keep you guys safe. You understand, don't you, Mimi?'

317

Mimi nodded, her eyes on the cutting. Long tresses of hair fell slowly, like feathers, to the floor. Mimi looked at her through the mirror. 'Could you phone me every few hours?'

Eva smiled. 'I'll let you know exactly what's going on.'

'And if you don't call. What do we do?

'I guess call the Spanish police.'

'Oh God. Why don't you just call them now and have *them* confront the guy?'

'He's not done anything against the law. Anyway, they'd be in awe of him, a six-foot-four senior FBI agent: they'd be eating out of his hand. Probably hand me over in chains.'

They stayed silent for a few minutes while Mimi finished cutting. She'd done a remarkably good job. It would hardly need touching up. Instead of making her look older, as she had hoped, the short hairstyle did the opposite. Damn! Well, at least she looked different.

'Mimi…please could you sweep all this hair up after I go? It wouldn't be very nice for Sebastian to see it.'

'Yeah, of course.'

Eva got up from the chair and brushed the wisps of hair off her clothes. She looked through her handbag, checked that her passport was there and counted the notes in her wallet. 'Thank God I've had a job. Brian knows I'm an illegal alien so he pays me cash. Will you try calling him again for me, please? Otherwise, I think I'll just walk to the bus station across the border.'

She searched through the drawers for something she might have missed, then sat down for a moment, put her head in her hands and tried to think straight. Mimi came back and patted her on the shoulder. 'It's okay, I got hold of Brian. He said he'll pick you up at the end of Galetta's Passage in ten minutes.'

Eva stood up and gave her a quick hug. 'Take good care of yourself, Mimi. I know you've got your head screwed on right. Just be careful with Carlo. He's not the right kind of guy for you, surely you must see it.'

Mimi nodded. 'Yeah, I know he isn't.' She hesitated a moment, then said, 'I think I've met someone else. He's young, like me.'

'That sounds more like it. You need to be young and have fun. You're far too serious, too alone. Enjoy being a teenager. You haven't got long and you never get it back.'

'Fuck!' Mimi exclaimed. 'You're talking as if we're never going to see each other again.'

'Be good, Mimi. I'll come back. I hope I'll be welcome.'

Mimi nodded. 'Hey, let me make you a sandwich for the journey.'

Eva smiled, then looked at her watch. She'd not eaten and her stomach felt hollow. 'Okay, but make it quick, though. Just cut me some bread and a slab of cheese.'

Mimi went to the kitchen and Eva pressed down the lid on her little case, regretting that her new wetsuit would have to stay behind. She wondered if she'd be coming back for it. She looked around one last time. The floor was strewn with her long blonde hair. Hopefully Mimi would remember to sweep it up and put it at the bottom of the trash can.

'I've got to go, Mimi,' she called from the hall.

Mimi came to the door, pressing into her hands a grey sandwich bag with two rubber bands around it.

'Thanks, Mimi.' The sandwich made her tearful but she didn't want to show it.

'It's a book, actually,' said Mimi with a shrug. 'We didn't have any bread. Don't throw it away, whatever you do. You're going to need to read it, you hear me.'

319

'Okay, if you say so. I'll read it.' She tossed it into her handbag and put the bag over her shoulder.

'Do the zip up,' said Mimi anxiously, like a mother sending her little girl off to her first day at school.

'All right. Look after yourself.'

'Look who's talking,' said Mimi wretchedly and threw her arms around her.

Sebastian

In Both Worlds, he walked up and down the coastal road and looked at the many entrances and the huge number of apartments. He rang several intercoms but few of them answered. The ones that did were suspicious or indifferent, and all claimed to be ignorant as to who Montegriffo was and what number he lived at. Someone buzzed him in and he went around rapping on doors. After half a dozen tries, none other than Montegriffo himself opened the door, again in his bathrobe.

He sighed deeply on seeing Sebastian. 'Now what?'

Sebastian felt his pulse beginning to race as the scene of a few weeks ago came back to him. 'Is Imogen here?'

Montegriffo just opened the door wide and stood aside, waving him in with a curt gesture. Sebastian didn't bother with courtesies but ran around the tiny, sparsely furnished apartment. Two plates, champagne flutes and other glasses stood on the kitchen counter, a testimony to their encounter. The single bed was made up, but the counterpane was rumpled as if two lovers had wrestled on it. Fearful of his own impulses, Sebastian made for the door.

'Clearly you've *entertained* her,' he said giving the man a cold stare. 'When did she leave?'

'Just after lunch.'

'Do you always hang out in a bathrobe when inviting young girls in?'

'Enough!' said Montegriffo. 'Get out!'

Once out on the road he made his way towards Dudley Ward

Tunnel, a short ten minutes along the coast. When he saw the No Pedestrians sign, he remembered Jorge Azzopardi's admonitions, but the mouth of the tunnel loomed cold and dark, and he welcomed the feeling of entering the Rock, being embraced by it.

It was not the peaceful silence he yearned for, but rather the noise of the traffic was amplified to a thunderous roar. With his hands clamped over his ears he sprinted like a hunted rat along the tunnel wall, cars hooting their horns and swerving to avoid him.

When he staggered into daylight at the other end, his work-site was right ahead of him. The search for Mimi had drained him and it was a welcome refuge.

Everyone except the security team had gone. He shuffled papers around his desk for an hour, trying to get through to Mimi at regular intervals to check that she'd arrived home. When the sky began to darken, he went out to look at the lights being lit on the tankers anchored in the waters off the coast. His eyes settled on the foaming turbulence where the rock-face plunged into the sea, and he tried to imagine the dramatic sight of his development lighting up the cliff against the night sky. The reality of that image seemed such a long way away. There had been further delays in shipments of materials, and some of his team had walked off since they had nothing to do. The planners had been to the site earlier in the week, checking and re-checking the boundaries of the development. They'd left without saying a word to him, effectively left him standing.

Never in his career – relatively short as it had been – had he suffered such disruptions and setbacks. This farcical state of affairs, involving so many factions and agencies, was simply not what his vision was about. He'd become a kind of minion of his own project. Daily he had to justify his actions and plead his case; he was weighted down by minor irritations. Neither was it good for the men in his teams to see the creative mastermind behind the project paralysed by what they might perceive as misgivings or doubts, to see him having to humble himself and be plain ignored by the visiting inspectors.

He jumped when his phone vibrated in his pocket. Taking it out, he saw it was Mimi herself.

'Mimi, for fuck's sake. Where are you?' he bellowed.

'At the place we call home.'

'Are you okay?'

'Why shouldn't I be?'

'I've tried calling you about a hundred times today.'

'What for?'

'I've had the most awful feeling about you today. I'm sure you know why.' He refrained from telling her he'd been running around Both Worlds, ringing door bells and then searching through Montegriffo's apartment to save her.

'Come home, bro. We need to talk.'

'I'd like that,' he said, his bad humour fizzling out. 'Mimi, sweetheart, I'm sorry about this morning,' he said, 'I know I should have been more…'

'Forget that,' Mimi interrupted. 'Just get your arse back home.'

Somehow, knowing Mimi was safe, he was reluctant to hurry home to have to deal with his appalling behaviour towards Eva. He felt ashamed of the way he'd acted when she got back from the dive with Brian, but when it came right down to it, he'd begun to seriously question how much of herself she'd been hiding from him. He didn't want to mistrust her, but after the bombshell of the other day, finding out that he was living with a married woman, quite a number of things had begun to fall into place. She'd cheated on her husband, for a start, even if it was with him. And she was still married to the guy, whoever he was, with no apparent plan to get divorced.

He slipped the phone back into his pocket, dragging his feet as he headed towards Azzopardi's hut to ask his man to call him a taxi. Jorge looked a bit more serious than usual when he took his leave.

'I'm sorry about the news,' he said as he accompanied Sebastian up the ramp. 'It couldn't have cheered you up much. I was in two minds about it myself. It's good for Gibraltar on the one hand, but what it'll mean for the project, God only knows.'

Sebastian looked at him, perplexed. 'Sorry. What exactly are you talking about?'

Azzopardi pointed to Gorham's cave below the parapet. 'Look, they're in there poking around as we speak. Even in the dark, with torches.'

'I know,' said Sebastian. 'It's ongoing research, isn't it? I don't think it'll affect us much. The last thing the planners said about it, was that we can wrap around it or have the outside bracket just to the north of the cave. I'm trying to sell it as a feature, an attractive boardwalk connecting the cave to the southern end of the development.'

Now it was Azzopardi who looked puzzled. 'But it said in the papers that it would mean all the caves along the cliff would be protected.'

'Protected from what?'

'Well, once they've proclaimed Gorham's cave a UNESCO World Heritage Site, absolutely no development can be undertaken along here, as I understand it.'

Sebastian felt a sinking feeling in the very pit of his being. *World Heritage Site*! Why the hell had he not heard anything about this? Did Saunders know? Dear God, that could well be the kiss of death to the entire project, at least in this part of the world. It could even affect his credibility and reputation, never mind that this unforeseen kick in the teeth was none of *his own* doing. Damned Gibraltar! Nothing, absolutely nothing had gone right since they came here. To be the last to know...it was fucking humiliating.

He tried his best not to show his distress. 'You know, I just go along and do my work. If I don't do the shelf project here, I'll do it in Norway, or in Japan, or some other deserving country. The politics of this whole thing has been a damned nuisance, and I've tried to stay out of it as much as I can.'

'Of course, of course,' said Azzopardi. He shifted his feet and looked out to sea. 'You know, it hurts me to tell you this, but I've been offered another job. It's a good one, and I think I ought to take it. I don't mean to be disloyal or anything, you mustn't think that. You'll get another head security man easy enough. There are many good guys here in Gib, with all the construction that's gone on.'

Sebastian closed his eyes for a moment and sighed. He realised, with painful clarity, that – apart from Mimi and Eva – Azzopardi was his only friend in Gibraltar. He would sorely miss their little interactions at the end of each day.

He reached out to shake Azzopardi's hand. 'Well, congratulations. I don't blame you in the least. If this is a sinking ship, we must all do the best for our respective careers. I might well have to do the same.'

It was with a sense of devastation that he got into the taxi. To add to his grief, his head was throbbing and small red dots flew like shooting stars crossed his vision. As soon as he got home and inside the door, he'd get down on his knees to beg Eva's forgiveness. He needed her and wanted her. Making love to his mermaid would make him forget everything. Only she could make him feel better when he felt as low as this.

Eva

Brian insisted on driving her to Benalmadena Pueblo, though she begged him to drop her at the bus station in La Linea, or better still, in Algeciras where the buses ran continuously along the coastal highway. There was time enough, but he was adamant. They got across the frontier without the border guards of either country so much as glancing at their passports. Brian drove through La Linea towards the motorway.

She took her phone out of her bag and tried to call Sebastian for the third time. He still did not pick up the call. Surely he was ignoring her on purpose, punishing her for her 'affair' with Brian. How would he feel about what she was doing right now, in a car with the man himself, on their way east along the Spanish coast? She would let Mimi tell him.

Finally, Brian broke the silence between them. 'Now for heaven's sake, Eva, tell me what's going on. Why that drastic amputation of your lovely hair?'

'I'm having a break for a while,' she said quietly. That's why she didn't want to have him drive her. She didn't want to explain her predicament to him. Not because he wouldn't be understanding, but he would take a stand, offering to go with her, protect her. Or just plain refuse to let her go. He was just that kind of man.

He reached over and patted her hand. 'Are you sure you're not overreacting about something? Maybe you ought to give Sebastian more of a chance; you haven't known him all that long. Running away is often a knee-jerk reaction.'

She grimaced. 'Yeah, I'm a jerk all right!'

'I know he doesn't drive, so when you've sulked long enough I'll come and bring you back.'

She turned to smile at him. He was a gem of a man, and in a different life she might even have loved him. He was down-to-earth, rational, sensible and, above all, humble. All the things that Sebastian was not. But she'd fallen for Sebastian because of his passion, his originality and his charisma. He had a fanatical belief in what he was doing, he was dynamic and enthusiastic and grasped life's opportunities like no-one she'd ever known. He made her feel alive, inspired, but she acknowledged the other feelings he brought out in her. Often she felt low on the scale of his priorities and his energy sometimes drained her, as if in some strange way his own vitality were topped up by sucking it out of his surroundings, from the people close at hand. His increasingly domineering attitude towards Mimi was another concern, reminding her all too often of the tyranny in her own past. At least, with Sebastian, it had never been directed towards her.

'I appreciate it, Brian. But for now I've got to get away.'

He turned to scrutinise her face for a second. 'Are you perhaps going to meet someone?'

She paused. Why not tell the truth? It was the lack of truth that was the root cause of all her problems.

'Yes, my husband.'

'Your *husband?*'

'I'm hoping the bastard will agree to a divorce.'

Brian turned to her then shook his head. 'Do you want to tell me about it?'

'Not really. The talking cure never worked for me, and for you it's better not to know.'

They passed Sotogrande and stayed on the toll road

where the traffic was sparse. At the brow of a hill, just at the last moment before leaving Cadiz province, she turned around to look behind her. There, in the far distance, was the Rock of Gibraltar. It stood like some other-worldly megalith, rising straight up from the sea and piercing the sky. She looked at it in wonder. Shrouded in mist, it was like nothing she'd ever seen. Would she ever go back there?

They passed over the hill and it disappeared from view.

She had sometimes wondered if she could turn back and face Adrian? Now, finally, her fury and indignation had awakened her courage. If she was ever to have a life, she would have to face him first. She *wanted* to face him. She was never going to run again. Ever! Wherever he'd called from, wherever he lurked, she'd wait for him until he showed up. Perhaps bruises would be all the penalty she'd have to pay. He'd given her bruises enough, and often. Three tooth implants, concussion a few times, a broken arm and plenty of stitches.

'When will I see you again?' said Brian.

'I don't know.'

'I expect you to show up for work if I need you.'

She smiled wanly. 'Look. There is the sign for Benalmadena.'

They stopped at a service station right off the motorway. While Brian went to the counter to order some coffee, she rifled through her capacious handbag. She took out her compact mirror and stared at herself. She looked so different, and she was glad. That angelic quality that her waist-length hair had lent her was gone. This new short style made her look gutsy and rebellious, much more in keeping with the person she'd become in the last few hours. She took out her comb and felt her hair bounce back when she combed it. The lightness of it felt wonderful, actually, like a burden shed.

She dropped the comb back and took out the package that Mimi had pressed on her. Was it a favourite book of wisdom, perhaps? However, handling it, she noticed that the contents moved in a strange way. Popping off the rubber bands she unwrapped the plastic.

All she could do was gape at the open package on her lap. Money! A huge sum, by the looks of it. With a trembling hand, she picked up one of the two bundles and searched through the bills. Every single one was a five hundred euro note. She shook her head in shock. Where the hell did all this come from? How had Mimi laid her hands on such a vast amount of money? Was it stolen? A drug deal? She must have held up a bank or something! What sort of secret life did this young woman have? She'd always been dark and unfathomable. But this?

She glanced up to see if she was alone. No-one was sitting nearby. Quickly she counted the notes. There were ten to each bundle. Twenty times five-hundred. That meant there was ten thousand euros on her lap. *Ten thousand!*

She sat there, stunned, until she saw Brian approaching with a tray. She wrapped up the bundle, popped on the rubber bands and quickly shoved it in her bag. No wonder Mimi had wanted her to zip it up.

'As soon as we've had our coffee I'm going to say goodbye to you, Brian. I want you to turn around and go straight back.'

He quietly took the coffee cups and some packets of sandwiches off the tray. He pushed one of the cups towards her.

'Milk?' he said, though he knew she didn't. 'Sugar?'

'Did you hear me, Brian?'

He put down the spoon with a clunk on the table and looked up at her with his deep blue eyes. 'Do you honestly think I'm going to leave you here...with your scruffy suitcase to carry? There's nothing around here.'

'I'll call for a taxi. I'm going to lie low and wait, and I just don't want anyone to know where I'm staying; anyone, Brian. When you're in as much trouble as I am...you just don't want anyone you care about involved. Can you understand that?' She reached over and cupped his cheek in her hand. 'You're a lovely and decent man and I care about you.'

'There is obviously more to this than just asking nicely for a divorce. I don't like the sound of it, but I'll have to trust you know what you're doing.' He knew her well enough by now, but a moment later he said, 'I have a surplus of money in the bank, Eva. If you need some I can...'

'Stop it. Really, I'll be okay.'

They sat for a while looking out of the window. The Spanish *costas* spread below them, a far-reaching urban sprawl inhabited mainly by sun-starved expats. How very different it felt from Gibraltar which – admittedly – had its tourist façade of tacky Britishness, but was layered with history, peculiarities and mystique.

She drank down the last of her coffee. She'd not been able to touch her sandwich, but out of consideration for Brian she put it into her bag for later consumption. They got up and went outside. The sun had begun to set and a mild wind cooled her. They stood by a railing and watched lights going on along the coast.

'There is nothing stopping you from giving me a call. You've got my number.'

'All right, Brian. I'll keep you posted.'

'I'll be waiting.'

She turned to say good bye and, on impulse, threw her arms

330

around his neck. He hugged her so close, with such genuine concern, she almost wished she could have stayed there.

The woman at the counter told her that Benalmadena Pueblo was only fifteen minutes' walk from there. She set off in the sunset along the slip road, passing a huge Tibetan style stupa sitting incongruously on the Spanish hillside. She peered at the driver of every car that came up from behind, and every so often she turned to survey the road behind her. There was no-one there. She knew it was sheer paranoia. It was hardly possible that Adrian had been so close he'd been behind them, following them here. Was it?

Sebastian

'Hello, I'm home,' he shouted.

Mimi came out from her room to meet him. Her meek appearance startled him a bit. Her hair was wet, combed back like a boy's and she looked smaller, dressed in a pair of jeans rolled up several turns as they were way too long for her. Normally she only wore tight, black clothes...and wore them with attitude.

'Aren't those Eva's jeans?'

'So?'

He laughed. 'They don't look quite right on you.'

'I guess it's comforting or something.'

'Comforting?' He smiled quizzically. 'You're not the sort. Is she home?'

'No, she's gone, Sebastian.'

He stopped dead and looked her in the eyes. 'Gone? Where?'

'I don't know, but she wanted me to tell you she's gone to meet her husband.'

'I knew it,' he groaned, covering his face with both hands.

'Don't panic, Sebastian,' Mimi said and came up to him, taking him firmly by a forearm. 'Let's have a cup of tea or something and I'll tell you what she told me.'

He had a sudden terrible hunch and rushed into the kitchen. The piles of papers and notebooks looked more or less as he had left them, but he began to rifle through them in a panic.

'What the hell are you doing?' said Mimi, following behind him.

'Nothing, nothing. What else did she say?'

To stop his frantic search, Mimi wormed herself in between him and the table. 'Sit down now and take it easy, bro,' she mumbled and led him to Eva's armchair. 'Just cool it. She has to deal with it in her own way.'

He grabbed her hand. 'Did she take anything? Did she take anything from this table?'

'Of course not.' She gave him a strange look. 'I'll just put the kettle on. Try to chill a bit. You know you'll get a migraine if you get worked up.'

'Just tell me straight. Has she left me?'

'No, that's not the deal at all.' She paused and sat down opposite him. 'You probably haven't noticed, but Eva has been getting some weird phone calls for a while, a couple of months I think.'

'Yes, she told me: from her husband.'

'They sounded like threatening phone calls, but I don't know what was said.'

'What makes you think they were threatening?'

Mimi shrugged. 'I could hear it in her voice. We didn't have much time to talk about it before she took off. I know she was going to confront him and ask him for a divorce... but I have the feeling she wasn't sure if she'd come back. I guess it depends on how you feel about her.'

'Well, I *knew* it was coming to this,' he murmured to himself. 'She's gone looking for him.'

'Exactly!' Mimi said. 'To ask him for a divorce. It's bad, but it's not what you make it out to be.'

Sebastian punched the table with his fist. 'It's bad enough, Mimi! I don't think you understand.'

She glared at him. 'I'm not stupid, Sebastian. You two are

crap at communicating, that's what I understand. She's been trying to tell you about it, but you never want to look beyond the end of your own fucking nose. This Adrian guy wants her back. He's pissed off, apparently. Big-time pissed off.'

He was silenced by her outburst, but the truth was: she *didn't* understand. He'd known all along that Eva was hiding things, and it wasn't just her 'personal' secrets. Of course he'd known something was going on. It was his own fault. All along he'd been balancing intimacy with familiarity, yearning for one while avoiding the other. If he'd begun asking probing questions, she'd have done the same.

Mimi stood before him with a cup of tea, that all-embracing elixir of life. He harnessed himself back into his senses and took the cup from her hands.

'It's only you I care about,' he said.

'Bullshit!'

'How little you know me, sis.'

'Have you taken your pills?' she asked with narrowed eyes.

'Of course I have,' he said. 'You can leave me alone now. I need to think.'

Sebastian leaned back in Eva's armchair. So she had left. But was the man she'd gone back to really her husband? What proof did he have that she was married? That passport she had in the name of Chantelle Hepping could mean something else, something totally different.

Moment by moment he began to understand everything. The truth dawned on him as clear and flawless as crystal. It was as if he'd lived the last few months with a film over his eyes. Now he crossed straight through all the lies, evasions and subterfuge, beyond the boundaries of their pathetic intrigues, onto the universal truths. It was such a surge of power and insight, it literally flooded him with energy.

Mimi

Sebastian's mood had been odd all evening, and now at 10.30 in the morning he still had not left his room. She sat in the kitchen debating whether to go and check on him, but if he'd given in to some much-needed sleep, she'd probably disturb him. Perhaps he'd left in the night, gone in search of Eva, prowling around the empty ramps and lanes and passages of Upper Town, stopping at times to howl into the darkness. Judging by how he'd been behaving lately, it wasn't hard to imagine.

She crept to his door and opened it a little. He was there, still dressed, on the bed. His eyes were open and she wondered if he was dead. He blinked. Closing the door, she went back into her room. She put on a pair of black satin pants and grabbed a powder-blue long-sleeved T-shirt of Eva's. It still had that faint smell of Angel, Eva's favourite scent. Mimi had given in to an urge to nick some items of Eva's clothes, even if they weren't her style at all. It was pathetic, like a toddler missing her mother.

The landline rang in the kitchen and she dashed to answer it, assuming it to be Eva.

No sooner had she blurted 'Eva?' than she realised it could well be this Adrian. Eva had given her no instructions about how to handle a call if it came.

'Hello, Eva?' A man's voice.

'No, she's long gone,' Mimi said emphatically. 'And she's not coming back.'

A brief silence. 'Are we talking about Eva Eriksson?'

'She's got a job in New Zealand. Leave her alone.'

'I'd like a word with her. Have you got a number for her, please?'

Mimi was quiet, trying to think clearly. This did not sound like a vicious stalker, more like someone phoning on some business purpose. 'Who is this?'

'Oh, I'm sorry,' there was a hesitation in his voice, 'this is Henry Saunders.'

'Who is Henry Saunders? What do you want with Eva?'

'Henry Saunders of SeaChange International. I'd like a quick word with her, as I said.'

'SeaChange? Isn't it Sebastian you want to talk to?'

Again, a pause. 'No, actually, this concerns his fiancée. Who am I speaking to if you don't mind?'

'I'm Imogen, Sebastian's sister.'

'Ah, right, well, hello… I'll try and reach Eva some other time.'

Mimi thought about this. Perhaps it was better not to let on that there was trouble in paradise. It was none of their business anyway. 'Yeah, good idea. Sorry I was stroppy. She's gone shopping across the border. Call her another day.'

She went back to her room and tried to write. Claustrophobia was making her skin twitchy, and her concentration was nil. Eva's departure had left a yawning void in the apartment, and she couldn't bear to look at the walls another minute.

She looked for her bottle of Baileys and poured the last tiny squirt down her gullet. Would a joint settle that scuttling feeling? Prising up the plank to her hiding place, she reached into the spider nests for her stash of camel shit, but only succeeded in pushing it further under the boards. With her sleeve pulled up and her eyes closed, she was hauling out her hidden treasures, one by one, when the tips of her fingers grazed an unfamiliar object.

With trepidation she pulled it out and wiped dust off it with her sleeve. It was a book, bound in leather and covered in grime. The pages stuck together and were crinkled with age. Rubbing at the cover, her finger traced the Ten Year Diary embossed on its surface.

Soon she'd forgotten her terrible restlessness and – sprawled on Esther's bed – became immersed in the life of its owner. The hours passed while Esther told Mimi her story. She told of her parents, Yanitos of old, who were the backbone of Jewish Gibraltar. She cried over her older sister who married a Pole and was murdered in the postwar pogroms with her husband. She begged God's forgiveness for losing the first child she'd borne, Sofia, who died because of her mother's ignorance, and the second who died fully formed in her womb. She laid bare her terrible grief, her wrenching guilt, her efforts, year after year, to carry a baby to term. She told of the husband who tried his best, but was of feeble temperament and frail health. She confessed her obsession with all forms of gambling, so unbecoming in a devout Jewish housewife. She berated her eating disorder, the constant weight gains and losses that drained her energies and made her ill. Then her frequent attempts at some final respite – mixing pills with alcohol – that never resulted in anything but a hideous hangover…and shame, an ever-present shame.

When she could read no more, Mimi pulled out the green cloth with the tiny half-knitted cardigan, and cradled it to her chest. She looked at the pink toiletry bag where Esther had stashed that money and forgotten about it. She looked up and saw the beam with that awful hook in it, and understood why Esther's final act had to be foolproof. There could be no redemption, nothing could be undone, and all the future held was a failing memory and loss of the last vestiges of dignity.

Esther's sorrow was too much to bear, on top of the fear she felt for Eva, and for Sebastian's state of mind. Mimi drew her knees to her chest, and all the grief and fear she felt for the people she loved poured out of her in a tidal wave of tears.

*

She left a note on the floor in front of Sebastian's door: *Gone out for some groceries. There is hot decaf in the thermos. If you go to work, or* anywhere, *leave me a note.*

She zigzagged down through the upper town following ramps and steps, avoiding the streets that allowed traffic. The season was still at its height, but she thought the tourists had thinned out a little in Casemates Square and on Main Street.

In the square in front of the cathedral she slowed her step. Where the hell was she going? She had little money on her, and she had no friends to go and visit. She'd seen Horst around and had listened to his sound sculpture from a distance, but was too embarrassed to talk to him. Mohammed was working at the mosque. He had her phone number and they'd made a vague arrangement to meet later, depending on his duties, but she sensed he too was at some crisis point. The thought that he might have packed up his meagre belongings and hopped on a ferry to Morocco brought another rush of misery. It was bad enough that Eva had left.

She came to a stop and just stood there in the square. People passed on every side, oblivious to her paralysis. Above her, the Levante cloud trailed like smoke from the summit, and the air was clammy. It felt as though a summer rainstorm were on its way.

She turned to go back and jostled with groups of people going into the cathedral. In the crowd she saw Carlo's head above the throng. Looking at him, she chuckled quietly to herself. Only yesterday he had his hands and mouth under the dress of a teenager. Now here he was, looking pious in a sombre suit, with a large crucifix around his neck, about to attend Mass.

His gaze passed over her but it took him a couple of seconds to register that it was her – Mimi – devoid of makeup and in a too-large blue T-shirt. They were at opposite ends of the crowd and he waved briskly for her to join him in the queue. She didn't really want to see him so soon after yesterday, but she could hardly ignore him.

'Imogen,' he said and kissed her on both cheeks, seemingly delighted to see her. 'I was going to call you after Mass to see how you are.'

'I'm okay,' she said with a shrug. She could have used a friend to confide in, but he was the last person she trusted about any problem relating to Sebastian.

Carlo bent down and peered closely at her face. 'Have you been crying?'

'No,' she lied. 'It's hay fever or something.'

'Come on,' he said, putting a paternal arm around her shoulders. 'Come with me to Mass. It will help.'

'No,' she said, pulling away from him. 'It wouldn't help.'

'Then let me buy you a cup of coffee somewhere.'

'No, really. You go ahead.'

'You're more important,' he said resolutely.

They went to a tea shop up Canon Lane. It seemed to cater mainly to Moroccan men, wearing fez hats and long robes. The wonderful smell of honeyed mint tea wafted around the interior. The men looked sideways at the odd couple sitting down; him to a coffee and her, a mint tea.

'Listen,' he began earnestly. 'I've been extremely unhappy about the way things concluded yesterday.'

'What do you mean?' She knew what he meant. 'We had a lovely lunch.'

'Look. I wasn't referring to the food. I mean what we...'

She interrupted him. 'There's no need to talk about it, Carlo.'

He clearly needed to talk about it. 'You must be patient with me. We've merely begun to explore the possibilities.' His eyes had taken on a disconcerting intensity. 'Last night I realised we can break down the boundaries. Life is too short to worry about conventions.'

She put her hand on top of his across the table. 'I've done a lot of thinking, too. I don't really want to pursue the... carnal aspect of our relationship.'

'Oh, Imogen,' he said, his eyes shiny with emotion. 'I know I disappointed you, but give this bumbling beginner another chance, please. You won't regret it. We need more time to explore each other and I've got a lot to learn. I want to make you feel very special. Please trust me.'

She would usually give anybody a second chance –the first time was always tricky – but the certainty had dawned on her after yesterday's lunch that she was never going to be romantically involved with Carlo.

'I trust you,' she said, 'but I'm not in love with you, Carlo. For that reason alone, it's not right. And add to that all the other reasons you yourself brought up the other day. It just wasn't meant to be.'

He withdrew his hand from hers and looked at her. 'But Imogen, have I totally misunderstood you? You're a true Renaissance woman, an explorer of life, a person searching and experimenting, taking risks and learning from those risks. That's why I am so attracted to you, so fascinated by you.'

She tried hard not to feel flattered.

He leaned forward again, grabbing her hands and looking deeply into her eyes. 'You wanted me,' he whispered. 'I know you did. That much I could tell.'

She recoiled slightly. 'Perhaps I did. But what does that mean? It's not something that makes a relationship.'

Carlo didn't accept what she was trying to tell him. He held on to her and spoke vehemently. 'I really let you down yesterday, didn't I?' he said. 'I *will* put it right.'

She glanced at the other tables, trying not to show the crawling unease she felt. She realised how she'd led Carlo down the garden path. Why had she not understood the sort of man he was and the expectations he might have? He was an ex-priest with just one unconsummated love affair behind him. Breaking his chastity vow had been a momentous step, especially for a man his age. He had not done it lightly. Oh God, she should have been more cautious! Even poor Mohammed had seen it coming and tried to warn her.

'I mean it,' she said. 'I'm sorry if I've given you the wrong impression.'

'Wrong impression!' he said heatedly. 'We went to bed together. We were intimate. What impression am I supposed to take away from that?'

'I don't mean to trivialise it, but in my book, we didn't actually do anything, Carlo. Anyway, I guess my generation sees things differently. It's not a big deal to…you know… have a one-time fling with someone.'

She immediately regretted her words. She could see on Carlo's face that he detested the very concept and anyway, she herself had never enjoyed one-night stands.

'You contradict yourself, Imogen. You just said it's no big deal to have a loveless 'fling', yet you say our relationship is untenable because you're not in love with me.'

'Maybe it is a contradiction, but I am sure you understand what I'm telling you.'

'If you find it that easy to have a fling with someone, does it mean you pick men up and dump them at will? Was that what you were planning for that Horst?'

'That's well out of order!' she protested.

Heads turned in their direction. Reaching for her bag, she hooked it onto her shoulder and pushed her chair back but Carlo leaned over and grabbed her wrist, forcing her down into her seat.

The hairs on her arms rose and a shadow of fear fluttered through her chest. She glanced around, trying to reassure herself. The place was full of men. Nothing could happen in this public place, surely.

'Let go of my arm, Carlo,' she murmured.

His grip on her wrist instantly relaxed, but he didn't let go. He looked pale and almost in shock at her rejection.

'Look,' she said, her voice too pleading. 'Why don't we clock yesterday up as a mistake and just go back to being fellow writers and friends. These little blunders can happen between friends.'

'I don't deal in superficialities, flings and blunders,' he answered coolly. 'I've fallen in love – deeply – even if you haven't. It's early days, Imogen. You owe me another chance.'

'No, Carlo, I owe you nothing.' She got to her feet and just as quickly, so did he. They looked at each other across the table. 'I'm leaving now. I am going by myself.'

'Okay Imogen,' Carlo said at last. His voice was calm but his eyes said it all: He was angry and distraught by the rejection. 'If that's how you feel. But I'm not giving up on you.'

Eva

Benalmadena Pueblo turned out to be just that, a small traditional pueblo perched between the motorway and the conglomeration of the coast. She wandered through pedestrian alleys lined with whitewashed houses, old wooden doors and geraniums spilling out of window boxes. Several restaurants surrounded a quaint little plaza. Just off it was a nice-looking hotel.

'Oh, yes, we have vacancies,' said the proprietor. 'Two days ago we were booked up, but now there are lots of rooms! The high season has gone on holiday.'

'I don't know how long I want to stay, but can I pay by day?'

'No problem.'

Three days went by and she paced the streets, glancing behind her, sometimes trying to concentrate on a book, rolling restlessly on the bed at night, unable to eat more than bites of food. Come nightfall, she would go straight for a double of anything in one of the bars. Adrian could be anywhere. He could be watching her every move, taking pleasure from her squirming like a worm on a hook, waiting for her bluster to deflate and fear to set in – or he could have lied about being near her. He could be on his way, he could be laughing back home in Half Moon Bay, California, or at work in L.A. And she would be here waiting. The wait was intolerable, but even so, she tried to settle into it and began to like Benalmadena Pueblo. The people were friendly, the streets clean, the hotel impeccable.

The thought of Sebastian caused a hollow pain in her chest. She'd tried calling him a few times but he was clearly avoiding her calls, and she felt a deep sense of shame for what she must be putting him through. Sebastian was a proud man, and perhaps he thought she and Adrian had reconciled and were having a second honeymoon in some nice hotel. She wrote him an email, trying to explain her feelings and actions, but got no reply. And Mimi… she dropped her a line every day, but didn't mention the money lest committing it to paper would compromise the girl in some way. She wanted Mimi to forgive her for letting her come close and then abandoning her like this (being no better than her mother). Her only excuse was her thoughts for their safety, and her determination to put an end to her past by coming face-to-face with her pursuer.

Enjoying a beer in a cosy bar with mainly English-speaking customers, she picked up a local English-language rag. In the Wanted ads she saw a car with UK licence plates for sale. Having wheels would make the future (whatever it held) so much easier. The ad said it was a 'desperation sale', so she dialled the number and agreed to meet with Mr. Eccles and his car.

It was with some trepidation that she took three of Mimi's notes out of the safe in her room. She would give it back, every euro, because she now had an inkling where the money had come from. In her nightly ruminations it had suddenly come to her. Sebastian had mentioned it once: Mimi's and Sebastian's father had been well off in his day. The mother had engaged a shark of a divorce lawyer and managed to pocket most of his wealth, and the rest had gone on living expenses and on Sebastian's education. Left was a paltry trust fund in Mimi's name, some two or three thousand pounds. It wasn't totally inconceivable that it had been invested astutely and had grown. A bit unlikely, but the only logical explanation. The trust fund had probably matured on Mimi's eighteenth birthday, and she'd simply gone and cashed it in. It was an overwhelmingly generous gesture, handing her inheritance over without so much as a need for a thank you.

She took a taxi to the house of Bill Eccles, the desperate car owner. The thoroughly dented thirteen-year-old grey Citroen was perfect for her needs and, after a bit of haggling, they agreed on fifteen-hundred euros. She dug into her bag for the three five-hundred Euro notes and handed them to Mr. Eccles.

'Oh, no,' said he, holding his hands up. 'I can't take those. Nobody takes those big notes any more, they're considered suspect; money laundering, and all that. I'll give you a lift to the bank down the road and they'll give you change for them.'

'Can't you take them to the bank yourself?' she asked, perplexed.

'No… I've lost my passport, and they ask for it. You've got yours on you, I hope.'

She didn't feel altogether confident about Bill Eccles and this whole transaction, but the car was a bargain and she needed it.

Bill Eccles had been right. With a pinched expression the cashier asked to see Eva's passport before she even touched the cash. Eva Eriksson's passport changed hands. Claiming to need a photocopy, the cashier disappeared with it. Little by little Eva began to realise her mistake. She'd spent so many months in the lull of Sebastian's shadow, she'd lost her edge. Suddenly her theory about Mimi's multiplying trust fund seemed ever so implausible if not downright naïve. If this money had been stolen or otherwise used in some illegal transaction, the serial numbers would ring bells in some crime-fighting database within seconds, which would lead the law right back to Benalmadena. She realised it was an unlikely scenario; it wasn't as if Mimi were a big-time outlaw, but even the remote possibility of being caught with dirty money or being the agent of further damage to Mimi's life made her want to kick herself, and it was too late to change her mind.

After getting her change and giving it to Mr. Eccles, she dropped him off at his house and drove back to the hotel. In her room she began to gather up her things, pack her bag and make sure there was nothing left behind. She was about to grab the key card and go, but then hesitated. Was she being ridiculously over-cautious and in her haste hadn't thought things through? Firstly, she must try and get hold of Adrian and suggest another meeting place, but how? She didn't have the number of Jean – his mother – and the idea of talking to her made her recoil in any case. However, Martin, his half-brother, was someone who would pass the message on. He was very different from Adrian and she'd always got on well with him.

Retrieving her laptop from her suitcase, she sat down on the bed and turned it on, then went into Yellow Pages, Big Sur, California. She could have done this weeks ago; Linda wasn't the only source of information.

Hepping's Scaffolding Services came up immediately and – one by one – she pressed the numbers into her little mobile.

'Martin Hepping!' Her bygone life rushed back to slam into her chest. She tried to steady her breath and her voice.

'Martin, this is Chantelle… Adrian's Chantelle.'

There was a pause. 'Holy shit, Chantelle,' he yelled. 'Where might you be?'

'I'm in Spain, Martin. How are you? How are the kids and Gina?'

'They're good, they're good. And you, girl? How're *you* doing?'

'Listen, Martin. I don't really have time to chat. I need to ask you about Adrian.'

Again a silence. 'What about Adrian?'

'I think he's in Spain, that's what he told me over the phone. So I gave him a meeting place and I've been waiting for days now. I want to get this over with, Martin, I want a divorce. I know he's livid. He's been tormenting me with phone calls for weeks, and it's got to stop. Listen Martin, you know the reason I left was—'

'Chantelle... Chantelle...*stop*! What on earth are you talking about?'

She paused and took a breath. 'I'm talking about meeting up with Adrian. I'm waiting here in—'

'Chantelle... Adrian is dead.'

Mimi

It was early morning and Gibraltar had been washed clean by a sudden downpour. She walked quickly through the empty lanes and passages. The pavements were still glistening and she breathed deeply of the cleansed air. The pubs in Irish Town were closed, though last night's dirty pint glasses still littered the tables behind the windows.

She slowed and took a right up Tuckey's Lane. There was the barber shop and the betting office and the dark entrance between the two. First she peered into the dilapidated corridor and, as her eyes adjusted to the dark, she entered. She had to turn sideways to get past several flimsy clothes horses covered in discoloured laundry obviously belonging to the male species. A smell of exotic spices permeated the corridor; at least they knew how to feed themselves. She climbed the darkened staircase and knocked on door number 6. His footsteps were light and quick and he opened the door. He was fully dressed and looked surprised, as if he had been expecting someone other than her.

'Hello, Mohammed,' she said and kissed him on both cheeks.

'Imogen!' He looked troubled but gestured for her to enter. 'I can't see you for long. I'm meeting Mr. Montegriffo in ten minutes.'

'This early? *Now* what does he want with you? Haven't you done enough for him?'

'We're going down into the tunnels. He wouldn't like to know you'd been here,' he said.

'So don't tell him.'

'He wants to be in control of things. You understand, don't you?'

She ignored his alarm and smiled at him. 'I keep looking out for your yellow trainers, but I don't see them anywhere.'

'I'd protect you with my very life,' he exclaimed. 'But I don't—'

'Aha,' she interrupted, 'only if Mr. Montegriffo tells you to.'

'No. Absolutely not.'

She stepped forward and hugged him and he responded with feeling, kicking the door shut with his foot. There was nothing sexual about their contact and she was glad. They could be close and look after each other. That's what they both needed right now.

'I'm so sorry I've not called you. I've been so busy working at the mosque,' he said, his mouth to her ear. 'I think I might be able to get a permanent job there.'

'Will it not scupper your job as a guide?'

'I hope not, but I need money to eat and pay rent, Imogen. I can't be an unpaid trainee forever.'

'No, of course. How much do your parents owe Carlo?'

He pushed back the flop of hair over her eye to look at her. 'I think about six thousand euros, but the interest is high so it's probably more. Why do you ask?'

She disentangled herself from him and dug in her bag for the envelope. 'Look, Mohammed. I won't accept any protests.' She held out the envelope to him. 'With this you can free yourself. It's ten thousand euros. If there is anything left over, give it to your parents or better still, use it to live on.'

Mohammed frowned, peering at the envelope. 'What?'

'Listen now! Ask Carlo to meet you at the Moroccan café

on Canon Lane, on some pretext or other, and give the money your parents owe him in front of all the men there, so you have witnesses. Not that I think Carlo is dishonest, but don't take any chances. Tell him your parents sent the money to you, and they want a receipt.'

He stared at her in disbelief. 'Imogen...where did you get this money?'

'You probably won't believe me, but I found it. It belonged to someone who died. Just take it. I have more, and I don't need it as much as you do.'

He held up his hands, clearly fearful of the thing she held out to him. 'You can't give me all that money. It's not right.'

She went up to his food table and put it there. 'I'll leave it here. Accept it and do as I tell you.'

He came to her and took her gently by the shoulders. 'You crazy girl. Why are you doing this for me?'

She looked into his dark eyes. They were so innocent yet she saw something old and tired there too. 'I know what it's like to be beholden.'

Mohammed nodded.

'And Mr. Montegriffo?' he asked after a moment. 'What do you feel for him?'

'Nothing romantic, if that's what you're wondering.' She was happy to be able to tell him the truth. 'He's been good to me and I hope we stay friends, but that's all.'

He shook his head. 'Who says? You or Mr. Montegriffo?

'It's my choice, and he has to accept it.'

'He won't like that. He won't accept it.'

His declaration made her uneasy. 'Never mind. I'm on top of it,' she said. 'Let's worry about you now. You just give him the money, get a receipt, and then ask him to keep training you to be a guide. With all this holy talk, I'd like to see how sincere the guy really is.'

'Imogen… I have an idea. You could come with me to visit my parents. I'd like to show you my country. You'll be totally safe with me.'

'I'd love to, but maybe some other time. For the near future I have to be here for my brother.'

'In that case I'll be here for you,' he said.

Sebastian

He'd not gone to work and his mind had been churning for four days and nights. The clarity that he'd experienced on the night of Eva's departure had been the most amazing experience of his life apart from his vision as a teenager when he'd seen his brilliant future bared, as though curtains had been drawn aside. It was a gift he possessed, and it had been right both times.

He'd written scores of emails to people to explain what he'd discovered, about truth, about the universe, about his mission. But the clarity had begun to fade into fuzzy confusion. In order to recall the transparency that let him understand everything, he'd stopped taking his medication altogether. It was a case of waiting for the drugs to leave his body so that he could be whole again and transcend any residual limitations.

In the meantime, he continued fretting about Mimi's safety. He knew he should remove her from Gibraltar. In one of his emails he'd even asked Jane to take her back and keep her safe in the Featherington-Haugh mansion until he found somewhere else where he could take her. Despite the acrimonious mother-daughter relations, surely it should be a safe haven for the vulnerable Mimi, at least until she got over Montegriffo and was out of his degenerate influence.

When not worrying about his sister, he speculated about Eva. What woman would treat her beloved like that? It was one thing to pull a stunt such as not telling him she was already married; it was quite another to abandon him without a good bye nor any explanation. She'd tried to call him a few times, but he had not picked up her calls and she'd soon stopped. A long email followed, trying to explain her actions but he'd already figured out what she was doing. Happier times kept coming back to him, and despite realising he'd misjudged who she was completely, he missed her terribly. She was the stranger he'd always known her to be, but never had courage to question. 'Love is blind': a ridiculous saying, but how true!

Mimi was always about, but he couldn't force her to stay in the apartment. Sometimes he'd lie down on the floor in her bedroom and put his ear to the floorboards. He was sure he could hear her voice in Montegriffo's apartment. There were sounds of them laughing, and strange moments of silence, Montegriffo grunting and snuffling, wet noises, like a hog foraging in a swamp. He knew better than to run down and kick the door in. He would lose Mimi, and that he could not bear. He could still count on her; she always returned to the apartment. His tearaway little sister had shown herself to be quite caring when he needed her. She saw to it that he ate some food and drank water, tea and juice. She'd even washed and ironed his clothes.

On the fifth morning, he woke from a deep sleep into a surge of renewed vigour. He decided to go back to work and discharge this energy in the way he knew best. Jumping out of bed, he stretched, trying to loosen the stiffness of having lain motionless for hours. His clothes were creased and sweaty. He tore them off and wrapped himself in a towel to go and have a shower. He washed his hair, brushed his teeth and had a thorough shave. Then he got dressed in his usual summer work clothes: dark blue knee-length shorts, a long-sleeved white shirt and sandals.

In the kitchen, he found a note on the table from Mimi: *Gone to do some research in the library. Don't know when I'll be back. I've got my mobile on me so you can call me.* He smiled. Research! What a sensible girl she pretended to be. He poured himself a cup of decaf she'd made for him and heated up a pot of porridge she'd left on the cooker.

Getting ready to leave the apartment, he began thinking of the state of the project and another catastrophe came back to him: the Unesco threat. He had completely put it out of his mind. Again, he felt that anger and distress gather in his body, fuelled by the unexpected energy that had befallen him. It was so unfair! While he was being made whole, everything around him was falling apart.

He found his phone and called up Henry Saunders on his private line.

'Luna here.'

'Oh yes, Sebastian. How're you doing?'

'Not great. What do you know of Gorham's Cave being designated a UNESCO World Heritage Site?'

There was a brief silence. 'I've tried to call you for four days, and talking to the boys at the site I was told you've been lying low. Are you ill or something?'

'No, I'm not ill. I'm pissed off. So what about it? Is it just a rumour, or is it *fait accompli?*'

Saunders coughed up a wry laugh. 'You sure took your time in asking. It's a very good contender for a heritage site, and the submission is under consideration so it looks as though we might have to down tools for a while. If the project is laid down long term, I think we will recoup most of the moneys paid to the Gibraltar government. But of course, they have other suggestions about how it could be spent, like for example a housing estate on MOD property. It has severe ground stability issues and will need your—'

Sebastian cut him off. 'So this is under discussion already without me being informed of it? A simple switch to a housing

354

estate with ground stability issues, and you think I'm the man for the job?'

'Take it easy,' Saunders said. 'There is possibly Japan. But you know, with the global economy as it is, it looks like people are biding their time. Big projects are few and far between. Right now I think we should be happy with anything that's coming our way.'

'Happy?' Sebastian exclaimed. 'I can't believe you expect me to—'

'There is no point in getting riled about it,' Saunders cut in. 'We're all in the same boat.'

Sebastian bit his lip hard to stop himself from blurting out something he'd regret. The fucking arrogance of it! The principal engineer being left in the dark, and then told his own project is off and he should be grateful for 'ground stability issues' on a housing estate! He'd never been treated this disrespectfully since he was a junior at his first job.

'While I've got you on the phone, there is something else I'd like to talk to you about,' Saunders said. 'Are you having stress-related problems, Sebastian?'

'Of course I am,' he responded with gritted teeth. 'We're fucking talking about them.'

'I'm referring to behavioural indiscretions,' Saunders said, then paused for a second. 'I've had a call from a Gibraltar resident who claims you have harassed and been abusive towards neighbours, including vandalising their property. Apparently the police were involved in one incident.'

'Don't even go there, Henry! This guy has had it in for me since day one. Yes, I kicked in his door, but if you know what this guy...'

'Listen,' Saunders interrupted. 'Spare me the details. Take a holiday if you have to. Go away somewhere for a few weeks.'

He grabbed his keys and his wallet and stormed out of the apartment. On the middle floor landing he came upon the very man he'd come to hate with an unbridled passion. Carlo Montegriffo stood there, talking to Mimi in his oily voice. He had his hand on her shoulder in a downright insolent attitude, and Mimi was looking up at him with an uneasy smile.

'What's going on here?' Sebastian said sharply.

'Nothing,' said Mimi. 'We're talking.'

'Mimi. Go upstairs, please. I want to talk to Carlo alone for a moment.'

'Okay, bro,' she said and ran up the stairs. If he wasn't mistaken, she seemed positively relieved by the request. When they'd heard her close the door to the apartment, Montegriffo pre-empted him.

'Stay out of it, Luna. Imogen is eighteen years old and an adult in law. If she wants to be with me, there is nothing you can do about it.'

'I've had enough. Keep away from her, you fucking pervert.'

Carlo regarded him coldly. 'I've said it before: you're the one with the problem. You're in love with your own sister, and you can't cope with the idea of her having another man in her life.'

He could easily have attacked Carlo, but despite his anger, Sebastian knew this was a trap. The taunts were a way to get him to do something unacceptable. The sensible thing was to just go, walk away before he lost his temper and did what Montegriffo obviously was goading him to do.

He turned and continued down the stairs, biting his lip hard, his hands wringing each other so tightly they were numb.

'Stop interfering,' Montegriffo shouted down after him. 'Your sister is a free woman.'

Mimi

She stopped inside the door to try and listen to the muffled conversation below, but only heard Carlo shout 'Your sister is a free woman'. She covered her ears with both hands. Bloody men! Both Carlo and Sebastian were control freaks – each in different ways – and she'd had enough of being controlled. All the same, she knew she was to blame for all this male aggression. She was a monumental idiot to have allowed things to go this far.

She wasn't the only fucked-up member of the household. She could tell Sebastian was heading towards some dark place, but he was good at covering it up. It was not just about losing Eva and the trouble he'd been having with his project. He kept telling her he was perfectly all right and warned her not to meddle where she wasn't needed. What should she do? What *could* she do?

She stood at the door a little while longer but could hear no more angry exchanges from the downstairs landing. She went back into her room and almost went flying over her holdall. The place was in complete chaos. Looking around, she felt a sudden overwhelming need to put order into her life. She gathered up her clothes and ripped the sheets off the bed, stuffing it all into the washing machine. With a large garden-sized rubbish bag she gathered up all the shit she'd accumulated over the last few weeks; all the paper balls, cartons of sour milk, empty packets of this and that, some leftover cigarettes and the foul cannabis. Lastly, she grabbed the blossoming roses from the wine cooling bucket and scrunched them head-down into the bag.

*

Carlo intercepted her on the landing when she was on her way out.

'We didn't finish our conversation,' he said.

'Well, Sebastian finished it for us,' she said with a weak smile.

'You don't have to obey him, you know.'

'I know,' she said to cut the conversation short. 'I do it out of habit.'

He reached for her hand. 'Look, I have a proposition for you.'

'Carlo, please—'

'No, hear me out. This has nothing to do with you and me. I can see that you're having a stressful time at home. I've deduced that Eva has left, and you're struggling to keep some semblance of normality with your brother. I can offer you a place where you have peace and quiet to write. I would like to give you the keys to Both World, rent free. You can move in there and make yourself at home. I could bring you groceries, but otherwise I would stay clear of the place…unless invited.' He put his hand over his crucifix. 'That's a promise.'

She was both touched and wary. 'It's a very generous offer, Carlo. But Sebastian needs me.'

'You need to think of yourself.'

She pulled her hand away. 'Thanks, but no,' she said. 'I don't have that same need for isolation as you do. I like it here.'

He looked disappointed. 'The other thing – we've not got around to finishing our tour.'

'Give me a few days, Carlo. I've got a lot on at the moment.'

*

'Wait!' he called out, catching up with her on Fish Market Road. 'I wondered where you went to.'

'Were you following me?' she said with a frown.

'Of course not,' he said with a laugh. 'But you're always prowling around town. Where are you off to now?'

'I've just got out for a bit of air,' she said in irritation.

'I know what you mean. The Levante makes the atmosphere so oppressive. I haven't asked you lately...how is the writing going?'

She hesitated. 'I've started something new. The story of Mrs. Cohen. Of course it's fiction, but living with her presence has affected me. It's as if she were asking something of me.'

'The story of Mrs. Cohen!' He smiled and nodded. 'Interesting idea.'

They came out by the bus station and went through the arches into Casemates Square. He pointed towards the thick wooded area high above the square. 'Have you ever been to the Jungle?'

'What is it?'

'That wooded slope above the cliff. I was just heading up there. I've been dying to show someone this secret way into the tunnel system.' He pointed to his rucksack. 'I've even got two torches, as it happens. The writer in you would find this fascinating.'

'Not today.'

'Why not?'

'It's too hot,' she said.

359

'It's ever so cool in the tunnels.'

She liked to think of herself as adventurous and up for a challenge, but was that self-image in fact a fake, a construct of wishful thinking? In some ways she was actually quite chicken. A chicken hidden under puffed-up words and clothes with attitude.

'All right. What the hell! Let's do it,' she said.

They walked a few steps up Main street and turned left up Crutchett's Ramp. Further up the hill, they took a hairpin turn up Demara's Ramp which was in fact a long staircase up to the weirdly named Road-to-the-Lines.

Further up the steps and passage, they wedged themselves through a narrow gap in a fence. The fence was made of thick vertical iron bars — obviously meant to keep out trespassers — but one bar had been cut by some heavy-duty tool and bent sideways. Once on the wrong side, she stopped and took a deep breath. They were high above Casemates Square, but she could still see and hear the crowds down there. She could even see the ants' trail of people walking, cycling and driving across the airport runway. The landing strip, beginning and ending in the sea, stretched like a taut ribbon between the two countries. On the other side was the whole expanse of southern Spain. All those people seemed so nearby. Yet up here, squeezing through a vandalised barrier, one entered forgotten territory.

Eva

'*Dead*? Adrian is dead?'

'Jesus H. Christ! Don't tell me you didn't know?' said Martin.

Eva threw herself back onto the bed, her hand pressed over her mouth.

A moment passed.

'Are you there, Chantelle? *Hello*?'

'I'm here,' Eva murmured. 'Adrian dead? Are you serious?'

'Come on now, would I lie to you about something like that?'

'Of course not,' she said, still reeling in confusion. 'But I've had these silent phone calls, and when I asked, well, he didn't deny being Adrian.'

Martin was quiet for a moment. 'I don't think he can call you from beyond the grave, Chantelle. Adrian is not your man.'

'Martin, I'm so sorry. I feel awful now, making that assumption, but you know it was not unlike Adrian to –' she stopped herself. It was unacceptable to speak ill of the dead. For a mere moment she wondered if Martin was lying, if Adrian had put him up to this, but no. Martin was so totally unlike his brother: a decent man, honest to a fault.

'What happened...was he ill?'

'Ah...well, I guess you have no idea. It was just a few days after you scarpered. He had a traffic accident in a camper van. He was driving on the Lyon-Paris péage, lost control

361

and hit the central barrier at hundred-and-twenty miles per hour. It was instant, apparently!'

'I'm sorry,' she murmured. 'Please give your mother my condolences.'

'You need to contact a lawyer, Chantelle, so we can finally put his affairs in order.'

'Of course. I'll be in touch soon.'

She sat stock-still on the hotel bed and stared at her phone.

Adrian dead! It wasn't possible! Dead…he was dead! The relief of it, the ecstasy of it. She was free.

Another part of her was strangely frustrated. The news of Adrian's death was an anti-climax. She'd come into her own power and was ready, willing and able to get him out of her life by fighting back. Now she didn't have to.

She fell back, rolling around on the bed, not sure whether to hoot with joy or smash the pillows with her fists, so she did both. After a couple of seconds she stopped and lay still, staring at the ceiling.

So who had been making the phone calls? She bit her knuckles in bewilderment. If it wasn't Adrian, it had to be Carlo Montegriffo, after all. Hadn't she suspected him at the start? She'd found him weird from the very first time she'd met him, and his unhealthy interest in a teenage girl should have been proof enough of some character flaw.

She sat up abruptly. What a stupid lack of strategy not to call Martin in the first instance! The possible consequences made her insides turn unpleasantly. Why hadn't she taken Sebastian's gut feeling about Montegriffo seriously? She'd dismissed his concern for Mimi as neurotic over-protectiveness.

She grabbed the phone and dialled Sebastian's number. She had to let Sebastian and Mimi know what a – possibly

– dangerous and deviant character they had as a neighbour. He answered instantly.

Before she had time to speak he cried out, 'Have you found her?'

Her heart skipped a beat. 'I'm here,' she said quietly. 'You're talking to me.'

'Not *you*,' he barked. 'I can't speak right now, Eva. I've got the keep the line free.'

'Wait!' she shouted. 'Don't cut me off. What did you mean, "have you found her"?'

'It's Mimi. She's gone missing.'

Mimi

The chemical smell burned in her nostrils and she was in a fog, as if she'd been blinded. Some light-source made grey liquid streaks appear along curved walls. She felt herself being dragged, then carried, then dragged again. Her arm hurt, her head too. Her stomach churned and she vomited suddenly. Then the fog closed over her. All she knew was that soothing voice, making promises. But she hurt too much to listen and her body wanted to sleep.

Eons later, the fog began to lift. She was lying on a soft surface, but the smell of it was wrong. There were many sounds – hollow and echoing – as though someone were throwing rocks against a metal sheet. The clanging made her head pound unbearably and she covered her ears with her hands.

Eventually she began to wonder what these noises were. She opened her eyes. There was a faint glow somewhere. Gradually she realised it wasn't her eyes that were faulty, it was the place. She sat up and everything spun around. She heaved, but there was nothing but bile in her stomach.

The sounds ceased suddenly and everything was quiet. Patting the surface on which she was sitting, she recognised it as a mattress on a hard floor. Gingerly, she explored the space, and her hand encountered a tubular object. She picked it up and – turning it in her hand – the faint glow suddenly turned into harsh light. It was a large torch. Her eyes took a while to adjust to the brightness. She looked up and realised what this was, then remembered everything.

She began to scream.

Eva

The queue to get across the frontier into Gibraltar was snaking far back along the La Linea seafront. Her nerves were getting more and more frayed as maverick drivers in the parallel lane kept jumping the slow-moving line, taking advantage of every little gap. Road rage clearly got its name from this lineup, with its crazed drivers constantly beeping their horns. She tried to be calm, but it felt as if every moment counted.

Finally, she passed the border but was thwarted again, as a plane was approaching and the road across the runway closed for fifteen minutes. Once into the city she drove as fast as the traffic allowed and found parking in one of the free carparks near Ragged Staff Gate. Trying to hail a taxi was a non-starter so she had no choice but to walk all the way up to Upper Town carrying her suitcase.

She still had the key in her bag and she opened the door. The apartment was quiet and already had a scruffy air about it. She found Sebastian sitting in the kitchen looking awful. His hair was greasy and unkempt, and he had dark circles under his eyes. His clothes were rumpled as though he'd slept in them for days. The floor was littered with hundreds of screwed-up papers.

In trepidation, Eva went up and put a hand on his shoulder. 'Has Mimi come back?'

He looked away from her and didn't answer.

'Listen. I just want to tell you. Adrian, the man I was married to, is dead. He died days after I left him, over a year

ago now. He is dead, do you hear me? I'm a widow…
Sebastian…are you listening to me?'

He still refused to acknowledge her. She could see that
he had been crying. With a rush of pity, she put her arms
around him. 'Please, talk to me, Sebastian. I do love you.
I've never done anything to make you doubt it.'

Slowly he turned his head and looked at her. The
expression on his face as he studied her made her heart race.
It was as if he didn't know her, as though the Eva that he'd
loved had ceased to exist. She let go of him and stood back.

'I loved you too, Eva,' he said in a detached voice, 'but
none of that matters now. All I care about is Mimi.'

'Since when has she been missing?'

'Since yesterday morning.'

'What's happened? Did you have an argument or
something?'

'No,' he said, his voice anguished. 'She just disappeared.'

'Are you sure? I mean, perhaps she…' She put her hand
out and stroked his hair. 'You know, she did tell me, last
thing before I left, that she'd met someone. Someone her
own age. Surely she must be with him. And there's Carlo
too, remember. We know she's attracted to him.'

He snarled at her like a dog. 'Oh, you think it's that easy
to explain, do you? Just off for a fuck with some guy or other.'

'I'm sorry,' she whispered. 'I didn't mean it like that.'

Again he buried his face in his hands. 'I just have a bad
feeling about it!'

'She's always come back, hasn't she? I mean, you told me
she used to run away when she was younger, but she always
came back. Even in Dubai, she…'

'Shit, Eva!' he cried. 'Do I really need reminding of that?'

She couldn't blame him for being sharp with her. 'Do
you want me to go down and ask Montegriffo?' she offered.

'I've already asked both him and the lad, but they claim they've no idea where she is.'

'You know the boy?' she said, surprised.

'Yes, of course I know him. It's that Moroccan I told you about, the trainee tunnel guide. He was there, at Montegriffo's. Neither of them have seen her since yesterday. Or so they say.'

'Do you want to call the police? Perhaps they should be informed.'

'I called them this morning, but since Mimi's eighteen they're reluctant to do anything this early on. She could be anywhere and she doesn't need permission – in their words – to go walkabout.'

'I think the police have a point,' she said. 'Let's just sit tight for a day, Sebastian.'

'*Oh*,' he said with feeling. 'You wouldn't be saying that if it was *your* child.'

'Mimi isn't your child, Sebastian. She's your sister and she's a grown woman.'

He buried his face in his hands again and began to sob. She couldn't bear to see him so distressed. She tried to calm him, stroking his shoulder.

'Listen, Sebastian,' she said gently. 'Have you given Mimi a large amount of money for some reason?'

He looked up, his face blotchy and tearstained. 'No.'

'What about that trust fund she had?'

'She can cash it in when she's twenty-one. What's that got to do with anything?'

Eva paused for a moment. Did he need this now? But perhaps it was relevant. 'She gave me a whole wad of cash before I left. Where could she have gotten it?'

'Did she? How much are we talking about?'

'Ten thousand.'

'*What*? Pounds?'

'Euros.'

'*Jesus*!' He got up and walked around the table. 'What has that girl been up to?' He grabbed hold of the edge of the table, swaying slightly. His face had gone deathly pale. 'Could it be drugs?'

'I doubt it, but to be honest, I have no idea.' She went to him and made him sit back down on the chair. 'I'm going to make you something to eat, honey. You look like you've not seen food for days.' He did look terribly gaunt. He was unravelling. It was all too much for him. Mimi was right, he was not so strong, emotionally.

As she cracked some eggs into a pan, she thought about Mimi and her disappearance. Would she really have been so insensitive as to go off on some venture of her own, after Sebastian had been left high and dry by his woman? Somehow she didn't believe it. Mimi could be bloodyminded, but she was sensitive, and her heart was in the right place. No – Sebastian was absolutely right – she would not be off for a fuck somewhere, not with her brother in this fragile state.

What could they do? She hoped that their mutual love and concern for Mimi could restore something of their tattered relationship. Perhaps, when Mimi came back, they could become some semblance of a family again.

That night, Sebastian slept in Mrs. Cohen's bedroom and Eva laid down on the rumpled sheets on which her lover had tossed and turned. She would have loved to be in his arms and comfort him in any way she could, but he claimed he needed to be alone and would just keep her awake. They had barely talked. He'd asked no questions about her escape from Gibraltar, nor about her motives for what she'd done, nor about the dead husband. He was lost in his own thoughts.

In the morning, she woke to hear him talking to someone. Quietly, she got dressed and opened the bedroom door. She gathered that he was on the phone to the police.

'But I'm telling you...this is highly irregular... No, she never...of course she doesn't... Now, come off it...she's a missing person and I expect you to do something about it!' His voice had risen an octave. She'd seen him agitated – even frantic with worry over Mimi – but his voice had a note of desperation she'd not heard before.

When he'd rung off, she joined him in the kitchen. They looked at each other in silence and she went to him. At last he let her hug him, and they clung desperately to each other, each for a different reason.

'What did they say?' she asked, releasing him.

'The usual. But someone is coming over to take some particulars. I think they're just doing it to humour me.'

'Let's be straight with them, Sebastian.'

He seemed to think about this for a moment, then said, 'Just leave out the money. Just in case she's been involved in something...illegal. All right?' He frowned at her to force her approval. 'It would just be too much to bear.'

'But, Sebastian...what if she's in trouble because of a drug deal gone wrong or something?'

'Oh God, Eva. Let's explore the most likely avenues first.'

She reluctantly agreed. 'Yes, well. All right.'

Mimi

She had screamed for some time...hours, maybe. Perhaps it had just been minutes, but in fact it felt more like days and days. She hadn't moved from the mattress, not knowing what was beyond its boundaries. It felt like a raft, surrounded by nameless horrors. Pits of snakes and rats or bottomless crevices. Centipedes, scorpions, bats. She came to feel that, as long as she stayed put, she wasn't going to suffer some monstrous fate. Occasionally, she harnessed her panic and tried to think rationally. Bit by bit, she made sense of her predicament. She was a prisoner, entombed in some underground cave. When this fact became totally clear in her mind, she began screaming for help again.

After a while, the sound of her own screaming scared her more than silence, so she stopped. Her throat was raw. The chemical she'd inhaled and the vomiting had scorched it, and it felt swollen, almost closed. Her breathing was ragged, and panic tore at her again. What if she could no longer draw breath? She'd had a touch of asthma as a child, and she remembered that horrible feeling of not being able to empty her lungs. Whilst trying to control her breathing, she soon found that panic could take other forms. It was a welling up from the very core of herself, like a surge or an explosion. This was followed immediately by an implosion, a shrinking or caving-in.

It was best to lie completely still with her eyes closed, and force pictures of life as she'd known it into her mind's eye. She found it was the only thing that kept her from dying, though at the same time she thought sensibly about death. She understood that she might soon welcome it.

Her thoughts took her back to a counsellor she had seen a couple of times who had tried to teach her a simple form of meditation. She remembered the stillness it brought to her body and mind. Trying it now, she just focused on her breath. After a while it slowed her gasps and unknotted her belly, and in this calm she began to hear something, a faint, rhythmic sound. It was the dripping of water. Hadn't he said that there was food and water? At once her tongue felt like a wad of cotton wool, stuck fast within a cavity of parched flesh. The sound of the drips began to torment her, until the yearning for water became greater than her fear.

Finally, she turned on the torch and pointed it around the chamber. It was big, like Mrs. Cohen's bedroom. The floor seemed to have no pits or crevices, nor did any snakes or rats scuttle across it. Slowly, she rolled herself onto her hands and knees, and began to explore her prison.

Sebastian

When he heard the knock on the door, he dashed to open it. There were two police officers, and unfortunately one of them was PC Malcolm Garcia. His heart sank. Why did it have to be him? The guy was already thoroughly prejudiced against him, and with good reason. To give him credit, no adverse feelings showed in his expression. He introduced his colleague.

'This is PC Marianne Peralta. She deals with most of the missing persons cases in Gib.'

Sebastian invited them into the kitchen and they sat down around the table. Eva put the kettle on to boil and started making a pot of tea.

PC Peralta began to ask the obvious questions. Did Imogen have a boyfriend?

Sebastian saw Eva look at him. He had to be totally honest. 'She's been seeing quite a bit of Mr. Carlo Montegriffo who lives in the apartment below us.' He glanced at Malcolm Garcia. 'I suppose you remember the visit we had there a couple of months ago?' Garcia nodded but said nothing. 'She's apparently also been seeing a young Moroccan fellow, who is in the employ – directly or indirectly – of Mr. Montegriffo. His first name is Mohammed. That's all I know.'

The two police officers exchanged glances. 'Has there been any kind of argument or conflict in the family that might have made her want to leave home?'

'No,' said Sebastian. 'Not really.'

'That's not true, exactly,' said Eva. He looked up at her sharply. 'Sebastian and I were temporarily separated. That's to say, I left home and went to stay in Spain for a few days.'

'Could that have made Imogen want to – say – get out of the home situation?' asked Peralta.

'Not any more than normally,' said Sebastian, then wondered whether this had come out right.

'So normally the home situation is quite volatile, perhaps?' said Garcia in a friendly tone.

'No, that's not what I meant.'

Eva intervened. 'Imogen is quite a sensitive girl and she'd be very unlikely to take off, considering Sebastian had been left here on his own after I'd gone.' Sebastian looked at her with appreciation. At least she saw the best in Mimi.

Peralta sipped the cup of tea that Eva had just put before her, then asked, 'Has Imogen run away before, I mean when she was a minor?'

Sebastian shook his head. 'No.'

'Yes,' said Eva. 'She ran away several times before she came to live with us.'

'So, it's not unusual behaviour for her, then?'

Sebastian threw Eva a warning glance. Why contradict him? Why reveal things that might make them take Mimi's disappearance less seriously? He turned to Peralta. 'Not exactly. She's never run off since she came to live with us here. Since Dad died, she lived with her mother, *our* so-called mother, and it was a very unhappy situation, not at all Imogen's fault. But the company she keeps now – and I'm referring to Carlo Montegriffo specifically – is quite worrying. The age difference, for a start. She's eighteen, and he must be at least forty, perhaps more.'

Malcolm Garcia looked at him intently. 'From your phone calls to the station, I understand that you've already spoken to Mr. Montegriffo about Imogen's whereabouts, and he has no knowledge of it.'

'Yes, but he could be lying.'

'Is it true to say that your relationship with Mr. Montegriffo is quite tense? You don't like him much, correct?'

Sebastian shifted impatiently in his chair. 'Yes... for the very reasons I just said. The man has designs on my teenage sister. What have my feelings about him got to do with her disappearance?'

Eva joined them at the table with her cup of tea. 'Look, there is something I'd better tell you which I hope is unrelated to Mimi going missing.' She paused. 'I've been getting some strange phone calls over the last few months. The person making them never said much; mainly just breathed down the phone, but the other day he said he was about to get me and he wasn't far away.'

Sebastian noted that Garcia looked more interested. *Typical!* Suddenly this was about Eva. She always drew men's attention; she just had that vulnerable look about her, plus her beauty, of course. He noticed for the first time that her hair had been cut off. He stared at her in disbelief. He'd been so wrapped up in his fears for Mimi, he'd not even noticed how different she looked. He'd loved her hair – it was part of her; the mermaid he had so loved but now she was gone too.

'Did you report these calls?' Garcia asked her.

'No, I didn't.'

'Why not? We can often trace calls even if they are "number withheld" ones.'

'Because I thought the person was far too shrewd to get himself caught. He was a U.S. Federal Agent.'

Peralta frowned. 'So you know the caller?'

Eva looked down at her hands and said quietly. 'All along

I thought I knew who it was. The man I'm…I *was* married to. But yesterday I discovered that he's been dead for over a year.'

The officers looked at each other.

'Is there anyone else you suspect making the calls?' Garcia asked.

'I did think…in the beginning…that it might have been Mr. Montegriffo. There was just something about him, and the way he felt about Sebastian's work here, and then his interest in Mimi…well, but…I can't say I have any proof whatsoever.'

Malcolm Garcia got up from the table. 'Shall we go and have a word with him?' He hadn't touched his tea.

'He won't change his story,' said Sebastian.

Sebastian followed closely behind the two officers as they started down the stairs, but Garcia turned and laid a large hand on his arm. 'There is no need for you to come, Mr. Luna. In fact, it's better if you don't.'

'I absolutely insist,' said Sebastian. 'I have a right to be witness to this.'

Garcia closed his eyes for a moment, reigning in his irritation. 'Mr. Luna, we need a calm assessment of this situation, so if you insist on being present just don't…just let *us* do the talking.'

Sebastian nodded reluctantly and the three of them continued on down to knock on Montegriffo's door. Almost immediately, the man himself appeared before them in the doorway, looking the picture of health and respectability, clean shaven and well dressed.

He obviously knew PC Malcolm Garcia quite well, as he reached out to shake his hand warmly. '*Buenos dias*, Malcolm. *Como ha ido el* golf tournament?'

'Brilliant, *gracias*. You know why we're here, Carlo. Imogen Luna has been missing for two days.'

'I'm aware of it,' said Montegriffo. '*Me lo dijo* Sebastian here. I'm very worried about her, too.'

'You're friendly with her, aren't you?' Marianne Peralta said. 'Was there anything about her – her state of mind or whatever – that you felt was different in the last few days? Did she seem upset? Did she say anything at all about wanting to get away?'

'No, no more than usual. Obviously her brother here is overbearing and over-protective, and she undoubtedly feels smothered. It's easy to see why she'd want to have a break from him. I offered her my place in Both Worlds if she wanted to get away, but she's been really worried about his state of mind, so she declined the offer for the time being. She doesn't have a key, and I've been there to check.'

Worried about his state of mind! What a shamefaced liar! The urge to inflict damage on that smug face rose in him, but it was important not to let his feelings show. At least the police officers would take note of how insolent Montegriffo could be.

He approached the door and peered in. Montegriffo must have painted the walls. The dusky green was gone and they were now a sunny yellow. From inside came the sound of the news on radio or TV. Mimi could very well be in there, drugged to the eyeballs, even restrained. He turned to the officers. 'I think you should have a look around inside. Imogen could be here by her own choice but told Mr. Montegriffo not to disclose it. If she is in there, we'll know she's alive and well, and we can all go away.'

Malcolm Garcia looked very uncomfortable with the idea, but Officer Peralta turned to Montegriffo and said,

'Mr. Luna has a point. If you wouldn't mind? It doesn't prejudice you in any way.'

Montegriffo stood aside and, with a gesture of hospitality, motioned the officers inside. When Sebastian was about to enter, he put out his arm to bar his way. 'Not you.'

There was a horrible déjà vu about this whole visit, especially when Garcia came out and said, 'There is no sign of Imogen in here, Mr. Luna.'

He could see that he'd lost them. He'd proven himself to be a neurotic and sociophobic squanderer of police time – the head of a hopelessly dysfunctional family.

Grasping at straws, he turned to Peralta, 'Why don't you ask the man about the phone calls?'

'What phone calls?' said Montegriffo.

He turned to his antagonist. 'The ones you've been making to my fiancée, breathing down the phone to intimidate her, probably to make us move from here. Most likely with the intention of keeping Imogen with you, but without me around to protect her.'

Montegriffo looked to Malcolm Garcia with a deep frown. '*Pero, hombre!* What on earth is he talking about now?'

'Look, there's your answer, Mr. Luna.' Garcia said pointedly. 'I'll tell you what we'll do. We'll put Imogen on the 'missing persons' list the minute you come to the station with a recent photo of her and a description of her 'last seen' clothing. But I expect you to inform us the moment she shows up. Which no doubt she will. *Buenos dias!*'

'Wait a minute. Hold on,' Sebastian pleaded. 'I still think this man has everything to do with Imogen's disappearance. He actually claimed that she *belonged* to him.'

Garcia ignored his accusation, but Peralta said, 'Is this true, Mr. Montegriffo?'

377

'Of course it isn't!' Montegriffo said, shaking his head in mock disbelief.

Marianne Peralta turned to Sebastian and made a 'there-you-go' gesture, then said, 'Tell your fiancée that she can contact the Nuisance Call Bureau and they can trace the offending calls she's getting. You can find them in any directory.'

Garcia had already gone ahead, and Peralta threw Sebastian a last concerned look as she followed. Sebastian leaned over the railing and saw them talking in hushed tones as they walked out of the arched entrance.

Montegriffo tapped him on the shoulder. 'What the hell do you think you're doing, accusing me of kidnapping Imogen and making nuisance calls to your girlfriend? You need help.'

The cursed man was already on his way inside and he slammed the door before Sebastian had time to reply. The slamming door... Suddenly it came to him. Of course. He knew where Mimi was. He knew it absolutely. How could he be so complacent and leave it all this late? He stood there for a moment – stunned by the certainty – then ran up the stairs, all the while thinking what he would need now. His diving gear, torch, rope...a claw-hammer.

Eva

She heard Sebastian come back from the encounter with the police and Montegriffo, and went to meet him in the hall.

'What happened, honey?'

'No luck with that bastard.' Absently, he patted her shoulder. 'I'm sure it's not as bad as it looks. You know me, Eva. I'm just neurotic when it comes to Mimi.'

He'd been so distressed and agitated during the interview, she was pleased to see he'd calmed down a bit. It didn't help her own anxiety, however. Mimi's disappearance was inexplicable, and not something to take lightly, but then again, how well did she really know the girl?

'I wouldn't call it neurotic, Sebastian. You're a wonderful, caring brother.'

At last he met her eye. He reached out and touched her cheek. 'I love you, Eva,' he said. 'Whatever happens, don't forget that.'

She wondered what he meant but didn't want to ask. The moment seemed precious so she put her arms around him, holding him close. They stood there for a while in a tight embrace. Finally, he spoke into her hair. 'I can't sit around; the wait is killing me. I'm going to look around town, asking people.'

'Do you want me to come with you?'

He released her from his arms. 'It would be better if you stayed here and manned the phone; be here if she comes back. And could you look on my laptop for a recent photo of her?'

'Of course, but take your phone, all right? Don't you disappear on me too.'

She left him rooting around in the hall cupboard while she went to find a photo of Mimi to print out. She remembered they'd taken several nice ones on her birthday, and quickly found an excellent closeup of Mimi smiling happily on the Wisteria Terrace of the Rock Hotel. She was just printing it off when she thought she heard the front door close. The sound produced a jolt of relief. Thank God! It had to be Mimi, coming back.

She ran out. 'Mimi? Is that you?'

Her heart sank finding the hallway empty. 'Sebastian?'

She dashed through all the rooms, but she was alone in the apartment. In his distress, Sebastian had run off without the photo.

What would she do now? Just sit there and wait, not able to help anyone with anything? Oh, God! Where was that girl?

As she paced the cavernous rooms of the apartment, the last couple of days with all its troubles and confusion were bearing down on her. Mimi missing, the dodgy money she'd acquired, Sebastian unrecognisable in his distress, his loss of trust in her, Adrian dead, and the silent caller still out there. Montegriffo did seem the most likely culprit, but what about Jonny Risso; he was a dark horse, to say the least. It hadn't occurred to her until now that he could be the breather, even though she'd seen in him a covert hostility, a chip on his shoulder about this good-looking diving couple with their – probably – glamorous lifestyle and stacks of money. He'd known her before the calls started. Of course, there were other possible culprits. Plenty of people had negative feelings about the Frontiers Project, or it could be someone at the site who'd caught Sebastian on a bad day. Her number was on his mobile after all, and he often left it lying around. But why her, why not him? The calls had ended when she rushed off to Benalmadena, but she'd assumed that was because she'd proposed to meet Adrian in person. She shuddered. The offender could be anybody, he had his eye on her – his target.

Or maybe Mimi had been the target?

Poor Sebastian, he was the one with the biggest burden to carry. He tried to deal with it the best he could, but besides the stress of Mimi being missing, it had become obvious that something within him had changed. Had her departure been the last straw for him? Perhaps it was all about Brian...

Oh damn...Brian! If anyone deserved to know what was going on...

'Brian, it's me; Eva. I'm back.'

'Thank God!' he exclaimed. 'I've not been able to forgive myself for abandoning you at a motorway services.'

'Listen. I'm not a heinous adulterer after all. My husband is dead.'

Brian was silent for a long moment. 'Eva...you didn't kill him, did you?'

She coughed up a cheerless guffaw. 'I was ready to, because I assumed he wanted to kill *me*. No, he died a year ago in a traffic accident.'

'Well, Eva. You never cease to amaze me. So much for a boring life. But...now what? How does the uber-genius feel about you running off like that, and who the hell made those threatening phone calls?'

For a second, only a brief second, she wondered about Brian. He seemed so utterly solid and stable, but he could be hiding his true nature. Just as quickly, she remembered that the phone calls had begun well before they'd met. She felt terrible. How could she even have thought such a thing about him? He was a rock – no – a mountain.

'Are you still there?' Brian asked, gently.

'Yes, yes, I'm here! But... Mimi – Sebastian's sister – has gone missing.'

Mimi

She found the door. She banged on it and screamed. She
bashed it with rocks and clawed at its edges. It was made of
thick metal, and something else was piled against it on the
other side. She could tell by the muted sound it made when
she smashed it. After a while she gave up; her knuckles were
torn and it was a pointless waste of breath. She shone the
torch all over the place trying to find some metal bar or any
implement to try and wedge it open. There were metal trunks
– locked with padlocks – but nothing with which to open
them.

She wasn't wearing a watch and no longer had a phone
so she didn't know where the time went. Or how it came.
It could have been hours or days. She measured time in
units of hunger and thirst or by how many times she had
to crawl to the gravelly corner where she'd found a whole
in the floor, a large package of toilet paper beside a bucket
of white stuff that was probably lime. Those visits had been
quite often but her stomach had settled down a little by
now. There was nothing in it to process. She discovered the
food store, a large recess where there were boxes. She ripped
one of them open and found sealed packages containing
some kind of biscuit. She was sure he'd said there was food
for seven years. Seven years was an eternity. It didn't matter
what other edibles she might find in there, because after a
time she could no longer eat. Perhaps her body was shutting
down and had no need of food.

Another recess had a huge store of batteries sealed in

cellophane. There was a water tank into which water dripped continuously, the only sound in the place. At times she liked the gentle dripping and splashing, it made her know that there was something outside of herself; at other moments it was like Chinese water torture, because it wouldn't stop. The taste of the water was sweet, though, and she sipped at it from time to time, using a plastic bottle with a spout.

Up there on the surface they'd be actively looking for her by now. She hoped Eva was safe, that she'd found out about her being missing, and hurried back to Sebastian. The police and the border guards would have been alerted. Everyone in her life would be searching and asking, all of them blaming themselves or each other, for her disappearance. She had a history of disappearing; running when she was too bored, angry, sad, rejected… or when she could no longer bear herself. When she was nowhere to be found, they'd be hoping she'd come back of her own free will. Time would pass. No-one would think to go down into the bowels of the earth to search for her.

Her panic erupted again like a volcano, overflowed, but gradually dwindled, burning itself out. Fear was a different matter: it was always there like a slow but all-consuming fire. She chose to stay with it because it would alert her to danger. In some strange way, it even calmed her in her darkest moments.

Sebastian

He stood on the landing, laden with gear. Knocking on the door seemed to have little effect, but he refrained from banging on it. Finally it opened and there stood Montegriffo in his black bathrobe.

Carlo's face furrowed in contempt when he saw who it was. 'Well? Have you found her?'

'No,' he hesitated, trying to look sincere, 'but I've come in peace.'

'Well, I can't help you any further,' Montegriffo said, and made to close the door in his face.

'Please wait a moment,' Sebastian said and gestured to his gear. 'Eva has encouraged me to go off for a little dive, as you can see. I've been under a lot of stress and I confess you are absolutely right about Imogen's disappearance.' He paused and looked earnestly at his enemy. 'This has always been the way she's responded to my excessive brotherly love. She goes off on a jaunt.'

'Truth will out,' said Montegriffo. 'So no need to involve me.'

'The thing is, I've talked it over with Eva, and I realise now that I've been acting like a lunatic. I think I've come to see sense regarding your friendship with Mimi.'

Montegriffo regarded him with suspicion.

'I'd like to settle this as gentlemen.' Sebastian gestured towards the interior of the apartment. 'Can I come in for a moment?'

When Montegriffo put his hands up in protest, he said,

'No, don't worry. I'm not here to harass you. Eva has just convinced me I'm totally wrong about you. You've not taken advantage of my sister, I believe that now. You see, I've been like a father and guardian to her ever since she was born, a role that has worn me down many a time. In fact, in many ways I wish some other adult male could take over.' He looked up at Montegriffo and chuckled companionably. 'A hundred years ago, I would have sold her into a suitable marriage by now. But today...I have to accept that Mimi is eighteen and she is free to do as she wants.'

'This is perhaps something you should tell Imogen in the first instance,' said Montegriffo with a tight smile. 'When she comes back.'

'Before she comes back I would just like to be sure of your sincerity.' He shrugged and pointed to the interior of the apartment. 'Can't we do this in there, rather than stand here on the landing?'

Montegriffo looked at him guardedly for a moment, then relented and motioned him in, leading the way into the living room. Sebastian followed, dragging his gear along. Montegriffo gestured for him to sit down on a blue sofa – which Raven was already occupying a good half of – and sat down in an armchair opposite.

Montegriffo preempted the questions he had prepared. 'You should know I talked to your boss the other day and told him you were making a nuisance of yourself here in Gibraltar, harassing and threatening your neighbours, vandalising their property and wasting police time.'

'I gathered, and I wish you hadn't.'

'You've been an intrusive and quarrelsome neighbour, and it's my misfortune to have fallen in love with your sister,' said Carlo Montegriffo. 'However, I realise our age difference is a concern to you. It's a concern to both me and Imogen as well.'

Fallen in love. Sebastian had not been prepared for this confession, but it confirmed what he already knew. 'Yes, you're old enough to be her father.'

'In fact, so are you,' said Montegriffo, 'which you claim explains your over-protectiveness. I suspect that jealousy is a problem for both of us as regards Imogen. I'm trying to keep my feelings in check. So should you, Sebastian. It's unseemly for a brother to be so…possessive.'

'Like I said, I've been her guardian until now, which has placed a number of responsibilities on me,' Sebastian corrected. His hands, pressed between his knees, were burning. 'So, where do you think your liaison might lead?'

'I have faith in our…affections, and from there, I can only hope.'

'Have you seduced her?'

Montegriffo raised his eyebrows a little, then smiled. 'Something tells me you don't know Imogen all that well.'

'I can only interpret that comment one way,' Sebastian said evenly. 'And it answers my question. So that's how you justify it, you make *her* responsible for her corruption.'

'I thought you came here to have a friendly and reasonable discussion.'

He should have realised that there was no point in trying to clarify or discuss anything with Montegriffo, and he wasn't about to give Mimi's location away. It was a miracle that he himself knew where she was. With some regret, he knew what he had to do. There was only one way.

'So where do you think she's gone?' Montegriffo asked, his voice tense. 'Not with some *other* man, I trust.'

Sebastian almost smiled at the pathetic attempt to mislead him. 'Look, I didn't want to have to do this,' he said, rooting in his bag. 'I was hoping you'd confess what you'd done and reassure me in some way, but I knew I was hoping in vain. You will always pose a threat to my sister, and I can't have that.'

Montegriffo sprung to his feet when he saw the claw-hammer. 'What do you think you're doing?' he gasped.

Sebastian was faster and caught up with him half way to the door. With a wild downward swipe, he caught the man on the shoulder. Something snapped, perhaps his collarbone. He half sank to his knees, but regained his balance. His arm went up to shield his face.

For a second they stood there.

'Calm down, man. Don't do this,' Montegriffo said, his eyes wild. 'You needn't worry. Imogen doesn't want me. She's adamant there is no future in it.'

'Where is she?' Sebastian said, panting. 'I am guessing, but do tell me.'

'How should I know? Honestly, I don't where she is.'

Montegriffo's open hands patted the air in a calming, reconciling gesture while his gaze shifted from the hammer, then left and right, looking for an escape route or some weapon with which to counterattack. With sudden speed and agility, he was sprinting for the door. Sebastian sprang forward and, as the man ran for the hallway, Sebastian lunged. The two-pronged claw went in cleanly as if his skull was a melon. With a choked gasp, Montegriffo began to fall forward, but the claw was well embedded and Sebastian did not react swiftly enough to let go. He was yanked forward and crashed headlong on top of Montegriffo on the floor.

It took a moment for him to realise what had happened. Scrambling up into a kneeling position, he still had the hammer in an iron grip, knowing that to release it would jeopardise his advantage. He tugged to get his weapon free and on the third pull, it came away with a squelch, bringing with it a palm-sized wedge of skull from behind Montegriffo's ear. He stared at the man's bared brains in horror. He'd put the hammer in the bag for a good reason, but never did he imagine it would be used quite like this.

It seemed an eternity before the hole in Montegriffo's head began to fill with blood. Once it began, it was soon gushing in rivers to the floor. Dark stains spread on the knees of Sebastian's jeans and he stood up.

God almighty, it had all been so quick, so easy. Too easy. Wide eyed, he ran his forefinger along the edge of the claws. With one stroke the danger had been eliminated and just lay there, while the pool of blood spread outwards over the floor. This time it was no wishful impulse played out in his imagination. He smelled the blood, and when he looked down, he saw that it was all over his clothes, soaking his hands and forearms.

Leaving the prone body where it had fallen, he walked to Montegriffo's bathroom, carrying his weapon. He turned on the tap in the walk-in shower and waited for the warm water to come through. Stepping in, he turned his face up to the spiky assault of the shower, letting the water rinse his entire body, his clothes, sandals and the hammer. The whole incident seemed to run off him in streams and rivers of red, and was sluiced down the drain into the sewers beyond.

Eva

She had heard nothing from Sebastian, and it was late afternoon when she called his mobile. Within seconds she heard a faint ringing somewhere within the apartment. She walked towards the sound, and found his mobile tossed onto the bed. She smiled faintly. It was rash of him to have left it at home, but clearly he wasn't in his right mind, half-crazed with worry as he was. She wondered when – and if – he might return. She had no way to contact him with any news of Mimi.

The wait was starting to tear at her nerves. She took both her own phone and his, and went to the front door, flinging it open. She put the wooden wedge under it and walked out onto the terrace. Out in the open, the world looked normal. She breathed in deeply, and felt the air on the back of her neck which her abundant hair had once protected. The sun was low in the sky and no Levante cloud darkened the sky. The views were clear except for the industrial smoke rising from Algeciras across the bay. The ships, tankers and ferries continued to plough their way across the waters as though nothing in the world were wrong.

She turned around and looked up at the Rock as it rose sharply behind the upper town, covered with wild olive trees and an array of old military bunkers, lookouts and other signs of centuries gone by. The Moorish castle – latterly a prison but now a tourist attraction – looked severe, rising over the edge of the buildings with its massive wall descending right down through the town. The drama of the backdrop never failed to stir her. Would she stay in this place if Sebastian left her? Perhaps. It had gotten under her skin, after all.

'Miss Eva?' A voice came from the hallway.

She turned around and saw a young man standing there. He was obviously of Arab origin, with a slender physique and delicate face. Instinctively, she knew it had to be Mohammed, Mimi's new love-interest.

'Are you Mohammed?'

'Yes. I am.'

'Come out here,' she said, motioning him to approach.

He came and for a moment they just stood there looking out over the city.

'All right. Where is Mimi?' she said quietly, turning to him. 'I truly hope you're here because you know where she is.'

'I *don't* know where she is,' he said and suddenly sunk to his knees in front of her. 'I'm so sorry. I didn't do what I'd pledged to do. I didn't keep her safe. I could have been more watchful.'

'What pledge? What are you talking about?'

'I've looked everywhere, all over the Rock. I've asked Mr. Montegriffo a hundred times, but I'm almost sure she's not with him. I've been to his place in Both Worlds, I even broke the lock, but she's not there. I've been to all the pubs and bars.'

She felt cold rush across her back. If Mimi wasn't with Mohammed, then where? She didn't believe him yet, even though his angst seemed sincere.

'Get up, Mohammed, get off the floor,' she said. 'What about all that money she had? Do you know anything about that?'

He stood up and looked at her, his eyes filling with tears. 'It's too late. I've done it already.'

'Done what?'

'I've given the money to Mr. Montegriffo.'

She shook her head in perplexity. 'What are you talking about?'

'She told me to do it. She insisted. It worked. Mr. Montegriffo signed the receipt and I am free. He had no choice. Everyone saw him take the money. But there is lots left. I'll give it back to her. I wasn't going to keep it. She knows that. I told her absolutely. I was waiting—'

'Stop, stop. Calm down,' she said putting her hands up. 'Come and sit down and tell me what the hell you're talking about.'

She led him to the rattan sofa, in the shade of the sail. 'Talk me through this slowly, one step at a time, please. And then tell me how we can find Mimi.'

He burst into tears. 'I have no idea where Mimi is. Allah forgive me.'

Eva put her arm around his heaving shoulders. For every moment that went by, she felt colder.

*

Once Mohammed had left, she began to try and locate Sebastian. She scanned the contacts on his mobile and found Azzopardi's number.

No, said the man at the other end of the line. He no longer worked at the site, so he had no idea of Mr. Luna's whereabouts. He gave her several phone numbers for other team members, but subsequently saw that the numbers were already on his contact list. She wondered about all these people he interacted with on a daily basis. She'd known from the start that he was a loner, but she hadn't realised that none of them were his friends.

She went through his list and called the numbers one by one. Nobody had seen Sebastian or knew where he might be. She poured herself a glass of neat gin and sat down at the kitchen table. It probably wasn't a good idea to drink, but she did it anyway. A warm glow spread around her limbs, relaxing her body if not her mind.

Finally the phone rang, and she grabbed it.

'Mimi!' she called out, and when no-one responded, 'Sebastian?'

'Eva?' a man said.

'Is this the police?' she blurted.

'No…this is Henry Saunders from SeaChange. Do you remember me? We have met.'

'Yes, of course. Hello, Henry. Sorry, Sebastian is not here right now.'

'I expected as much,' he said in a exasperated tone. 'I'd better talk to *you*, actually.'

'It's not a good time,' she said impatiently. 'I'm expecting a call.'

'This is important, Eva.'

She frowned. What could he possibly need to speak to *her* about? 'What is it?'

There was a short silence while Henry Saunders cleared his voice. 'How is Sebastian?'

'Worried right now,' she said. 'His sister, Imogen… Listen, can we talk some other time?'

'Give me two minutes of your time, please,' he said forcefully. 'Yesterday morning I received a hand-written letter from Sebastian. I won't bother you with the contents, but I found it quite disturbing. I've been trying to call him ever since, but he's clearly not wanting to pick up my calls.'

'There is a good reason for that, Henry. His sister has been missing for the last couple of days.'

Saunders was silent for a moment. 'I'm sorry to hear that. But I do need to tell you this. Whilst trying to speak to him I did some heavy-duty detective work and spoke to a Dr. Liam Matthews who signed the medical report we request from all our employees. He admitted that there were inconsistencies in Sebastian's report.'

'What are you talking about?'

'In case you were unaware, he's not attended his routine medical appointments for many months; since leaving London, in fact, and he's not renewed his prescriptions, nor does it appear that his treatment has been transferred to any doctor in Gibraltar.'

'What treatment?' Eva felt goosebumps rise on her arms. 'Are you talking about his migraines?'

There was another pause. 'I don't know exactly what we're dealing with here because medical records are strictly confidential, but I'm drawing some conclusions based on Sebastian's letter and my subsequent chat with Dr. Matthews.'

'Sebastian has not mismanaged his work in any way, has he?' she said. 'He's been thwarted by so many issues that have nothing to do with him. He's put a super-human effort into everything that—'

'Yes, I know, but that's a different matter. I would like you to tell him he's suspended from his duties until we have a legitimate medical report on him. Preferably carried out by a medical team of our choice with Sebastian's full authorisation. I was going to send him an email to that effect, but perhaps it would be less…upsetting, coming from you.'

Eva could not find her voice.

'Hello, Eva? Are you with me?'

She took a big gulp of gin. 'Yes.'

'What's your own assessment of Sebastian's state of mind?'

'As I said, he's frantic with worry. Finding Imogen is the only thing we can deal with at the moment. I'm sorry.'

She pressed the little red button and hoped that she could erase from her mind the conversation she'd just had. At least for now.

Sebastian

He stepped out of the shower and dried off a little by patting his clothes with a towel, leaving a trail of pink puddles on the floorboards as he went into the living room to get his gear.

He stopped short and stared at the crumpled heap on the floor. If it hadn't been for the lake of blood, it would have looked like a booze-addled vagrant sleeping off a binge. There was nothing menacing about it. The blood was real, however; the blood was everywhere.

He thought back to his altercations with the man, and accepted that perhaps the first killing had been a fantasy after all. It had been so convincing, down to the last detail. When he was a child, he would sometimes wreak revenge on some deserving person, and then find to his relief that he'd not actually caused any harm. At other times, of course, he had caused harm.

Approaching the body, he nudged it with his foot. Fantasy or not, dead or alive, the state of Montegriffo had no bearing on his plan. His plan had been conceived in that spell of all-encompassing clarity, and he knew it was flawless. When confusion set in, he brought himself back to this plan. It was clear and must go ahead, each step ticked off in turn. He'd got hold of Jonny Risso before leaving home. Risso had hesitated but as soon as Sebastian had suggested a fee of three-hundred pounds, it was a done deal. He'd remembered to grab the cash from his drawer. He'd ticked Eva off the plan, left her with words of his love. Now it would all be just steps, each one implemented in turn.

Glancing at his watch, he realised he still had an hour or so left before calling for a taxi. He was glad to have spotted a landline in the hall; had he not, he'd have to have risked a meeting with Eva in the hall as he made his way to the taxi ramp. There was nothing to do but wait, so he sank down into the sofa with a sigh. His eyes closed and, after just a few minutes, he dropped into a twilight state not unlike sleep. Eva's footsteps could be heard pacing around the rooms above. He even perceived the faint sound of her voice talking on the phone, no doubt arranging her own evacuation.

He'd had an inkling of some ulterior purpose the moment she arrived in Gibraltar. Then finding the hidden passport with her alias, Chantelle Hepping, should have alerted him, but he was so hopelessly in love and blinded by a need to be loved in return. Eva Eriksson was no doubt another fictitious identity, just another assignment. It was only since she disappeared to the meeting in Spain that the mist had cleared from his eyes and he'd come to realise the full extent of her involvement. Her target had been the blueprint for Luna's Crossing; he'd known it really since the drawings began to disappear. She'd waited patiently, lovingly even, for him to complete the first set of plans, then she and Brian had driven to some meeting point on the Costa del Sol to pass them over to his rivals and sell him out. She'd even had the gall to show him the money they'd paid her for the job, pretending Mimi had given it to her. As if! She was sharp and skillful, and it had been almost impossible to catch her out, though he'd tried in a variety of ways. The phone calls had confused her – made her nervous, de-stabilised her – but not enough to let slip who she was working for…except those couple of times she'd given the code-name away: *Adrian*.

Though it seemed far-fetched, it was even possible that she'd engaged Montegriffo to do her bidding, especially when she'd discovered how Montegriffo's seduction of Mimi would send him into a frenzy of anxiety and make him drop his guard. She'd always condoned the bizarre relationship, almost goaded him with it. Having Montegriffo get Mimi out of the way had perhaps been part of their plan, and Montegriffo would no doubt take personal pleasure in putting Mimi where he could have unlimited private access to her. But they had no idea just how badly this would backfire, how far he was prepared to go to protect his sister.

Eva had fulfilled her mission, and Luna's Crossing was irrevocably gone. Despite what she was, he still loved her. Human beings were faulty, greedy and easily corrupted – he himself was a bundle of defects – and his beautiful Eva was no exception. But all of that was water under the bridge.

He smiled at his own pun, he smiled as he thought of the future. From now on, his focus would be on Mimi alone. It was on her he should have concentrated his care and his watchfulness. He'd got his priorities all wrong.

Mimi

She was beginning to feel that she was in the centre of everything: the Rock, the world, the solar system, the universe. It was not a bad place to be, if she could just hold on to that feeling. Sometimes minutes – even hours – went by, and she spun slowly in that centre. She knew she wasn't God (in the way that Sebastian often believed he was) but nothing and everything mattered when you were at the centre. You were part of everything, and everything was part of you. She easily conjured up a vision of the world, the seas and the skies, the stars and suns and beyond: the ever-expanding universe of which she was the centre.

Sometimes she woke up with a start, clear-headed and realising that this heightened state was some sort of delirium, probably caused by fear, and by lack of food and water. She'd read somewhere that severe mental and emotional stress can lead to hallucinations. The next phase of sustained trauma was catatonia, a state of mute numbness, a kind of living death. It was a horrifying possibility, but at the same time, she knew that if there were no hope of leaving this hellish cave, it was the most bearable way to end. In a place like this, the idea of death lost its sinister meaning. It was just another state, another phase of non-existence. In some ways, it was a logical choice.

She crawled over to the recess where the 'food' was stored and, from one of the boxes, tore open another packet of biscuits. She filled the water bottle from the cistern and scuttled to the toilet pit and back to the safety of her raft.

She would leave the choice till later. Perhaps someone would come for her, after all.

Sometimes she was spoken to. 'Yes, ok, you're adopted,' said Jane. 'We just lied to you both; your dad insisted.' Esther Cohen soothed her brow with her cool hand. 'Don't worry, little one; at least now, I have a daughter.' 'Silly,' said Eva. 'Why didn't you tell me everything?' Carlo looked at her lustfully, 'we will learn together, Imogen. We have a lifetime...' Dad was on the other side. He reached out his hand to her, beckoning. 'No,' she pleaded, 'not yet. I need time.'

Again she retreated into that centre. She lay still, knees touching her chin, her mind focused on her breath, sometimes on the loud pulse in her body. Her heart beat louder and her blood thumped through her veins. And so it came that she began to hear the clash of sound, at odds with the rhythms of her heart, her blood or her breath.

First, a scratching, rasping, clawing. It was the nameless horror – the phantoms of the Rock – scrabbling to get to her. She felt the damp walls of the cavern begin to move in towards her. She tossed hysterically on her mattress, wanting to wake and fight back, before stone slowly enveloped her and crushed her bones.

'Imogen, Mimi. Are you in there?'

Her eyes snapped open and she yanked herself into a sitting position. It was the voice of a human being. A man. Frantically she patted the space around her and found the torch.

'I'm here,' she shouted weakly. Her voice had lost its strength from not talking for a long time, or perhaps it was permanently damaged by her screaming and the dry-cleaning fluid she'd inhaled. Her words seemed to thud to a stop against the cavern walls. She scrambled up and shone the torch towards the narrow metal door. On trembling legs, she ran forward and beat on it with her fists, then with the torch itself.

He heard her.

'I'm coming. I'm almost in. Imogen! You'll be okay. I'm here.' His voice sounded as though it came from the bottom of a well.

There was the sound of rocks being moved. They clonked and clanged as though they were being shaken inside an enormous metal drum. When he finally came through the door, she stumbled forward and fell into his arms.

Sebastian

The two men watched in silence as the evening light faded.
The crests of the waves glowed red and the soaring limestone
ridges of the Rock looked magnificent. Why everyone was so
enamoured with the Atlantic side, Sebastian could never
understand. This was beautiful beyond belief. He could see
his development hovering on the sea, the slender buildings,
the domes and towers, the lights reflecting on the water. It
made him sad that it would never come to pass. Or if it did,
he would not be there to build it.

He scanned the whole of the world around him. It would
be the last time – perhaps ever – that he saw the sky and
the sea. It was beautiful, all right, but he knew he preferred
the depths, the darkness. He wanted to be anchored. He
wanted safety. He yearned for that womb to which he
would return.

'What is it you're looking for down there? Be honest now,
Mr. Luna,' said Jonny Risso.

'Call me Sebastian, for heaven's sake, man.' Sebastian was
starting to gear up. 'This is the site of my development and
there are problems that need to be solved.'

'But I read in the paper that your development will
probably be scrapped.'

'By God! People take everything they read in the papers
as given.'

The boat rocked on the rollers. 'The tide'll turn in half
an hour. You have forty minutes, all right? Don't make me
nervous, now.'

'What do you think? I'm not mad!'

'Set your watch,' Jonny admonished. 'Your missus would have my guts for garters if the tide carried you out through the strait.'

'Yes, yes. I'm setting my watch. Anyway, she worries too much.'

'They do, don't they?' Risso said with a knowing smirk. '*Women!*'

By the time Jonny steered the boat in towards the barge, it was almost dark and he was lighting up the black waters with his headlights. He threw his anchor in. Sebastian slipped into the water and turned on his torch. The sooner he found the little window to the cavern, the sooner he could be down in the bowels of the Rock and reunited with Mimi. He hoped that she wasn't suffering alone, in the dark. She would know that he was coming. She trusted him, she always had. They shared the same genes; were one and the same entity.

As he prepared to ditch his tank onto the seabed, to leave the necessary evidence of his drowning, he felt a sudden rush of terror. What if Eva had lied to him, and the alleged passage from the dry cavern did not lead to a manmade tunnel, *but to a dead end?* He would never be able to swim out again without the tank. But perhaps that was his fate. And Mimi's. To die alone, in their separate caverns. His death would be swift, with no food, just water. Hers could take years.

He was within metres of the hole in the rock-face when he began to unclasp and unstrap himself from his gear. He struggled with one of the clasps that had become wedged sideways, but couldn't dislodge it. He tried to shrug the harness off but it sat too firmly around his body. The seconds passed and he felt the prickle of panic. He groped for his diving knife, and began to saw at the strap. It was made out of tightly woven nylon, but at least the knife was sharp. A hazy memory floated by, of cutting the tresses of a mermaid, far under the sea.

The knife made inroads into the nylon until suddenly it snapped free. He took twenty deep inhalations of air from his mouth piece, then shrugged his gear off and saw it sink, disappearing towards the seabed. There was not a second to lose. He pushed himself through the hole, using his hands to propel himself between the pinnacles and columns of the outer passage. Once inside the vast spaciousness of the inner cavern, he blindly swam upwards, upwards…for an eternity. He hit the surface with a long gasp, his blood begging for oxygen, his lungs aching from the strain.

He climbed up onto the ledge, disorientated and nauseous. The strain of the day finally caught up with him and he collapsed onto the smooth rock, shivering with cold despite his wetsuit. Half an hour passed before he could move. His limbs had stiffened, so he crawled on all fours, the beam of his torch searching the narrowing channel at the end of the cave. As long as this cursed passage ended at the roof of a tunnel, he could find his way to Mimi. If it didn't, he would slip back into the water and draw it deeply into his lungs. It was quick, he'd heard, and he still felt some compassion for the tormented man that he was.

Mimi

It seemed to take forever to move just a few metres. She could hardly walk, and she'd become aware of the terrible smell of her body. Mohammed alternated in supporting and carrying her. Despite his slight physique, he was strong. He stumbled along in silence, but that surge of strength was soon spent, and finally he had to stop for a rest.

They flopped down on the tunnel floor. She failed to repress a moan; he took her into his arms and cradled her.

'I'm so foul, I can't bear myself,' she whispered, trying to push him away. 'Don't touch me.'

He held her closer. 'You're like a rose,' he said.

'I don't like roses,' she cried. 'I hate them.'

'Okay. How about a wet dog, then,' he suggested, 'or a wart hog?'

But he didn't let go of her. They both must have slept for a few minutes, then her body jerked her awake. 'Is someone after us?'

'Be brave, Imogen. We mustn't lose our cool. As long as we stay calm, I'll get us out of here.'

She began to realise what a hair-raising mission her rescue had been for him. He'd brought a rucksack, and from it pulled a chocolate bar. Despite her sense of urgency and menace, she savoured the little pieces he put into her mouth. It was the most delicious thing she'd tasted in all her life. She felt the sugar rush right through her body. He passed her a bottle of water, and she took one sip, then another.

Mimi rolled in to face him and covered his face with feeble kisses. 'Oh my God, Mohammed. How did you find me? You've rescued me. You've saved my life.'

He chuckled and returned her kisses. 'One rescue deserves another! You saved *me*, remember?'

They walked and stumbled. He carried her piggyback for a while. He dragged her by the arms, and sometimes they both ran hand-in-hand, panic-stricken by some real or perceived noise. Hours must have passed before she became aware of a soft draught on her face, and she knew they were getting close. They came around a corner and air hit her like a blow. She gasped like a baby just out of the womb.

She had no idea where they'd come out, but it wasn't in the Jungle. They were on a tarmacked road littered with stones and debris, obviously barred to cars and people. It was evening or night; on the west side of the Rock because the lights of Algeciras twinkled across the bay. There was little sound of traffic.

She took all this in, then sank down on her haunches. 'What time is it? How long have I been gone?'

'You've been gone three days, almost four.' He looked at his watch. 'It's three in the morning.'

She lay down on the tarmac and was glad of the darkness. Only the lights across the waters pierced her eyes.

He pulled at her arm. 'Imogen, please. We can't stay here.'

She allowed him to raise her up and help her straighten her knees. Looking ahead up the road, she was sure she saw the place called Devil's Gap Battery, where she'd once walked and seen kids hanging out smoking weed.

'Come on, Imogen. We've got to keep moving. We don't want anyone to catch up with us.'

He led her around a locked gate and down a footpath which looked as though it might take them to Upper Town. The path was disused and overgrown, but it wasn't too long. He was holding her by the waist and they half stumbled, half slipped down it, her legs loose like spaghetti. They reached a set of crumbling moss-covered steps, then saw a proper street sign: Bacca's Passage.

'Can we sit for a moment?' she cried. 'I'm shattered.'

'You've lost weight,' he said and sat her down on a step. 'You're light as a feather. I can carry you home. Just think how happy your brother is going to be.'

She scowled at him. It seemed a bad joke but she let it pass, too tired to protest. 'How on earth did you find me?'

'Mr Montegriffo showed me the place once,' said Mohammed.

'He *did*?' She turned to look at his face. 'Sebastian told *me* the chamber was undiscovered. No-one had been there for fifty years.'

Mohammed chuckled. 'He thought he could keep his cave secret, but he was too vain. I sort-of knew he'd found the tandem chamber. It's on the other side of Operation Tracer, and much further down. He had no-one else to show it to, so in a weak moment he took me there. We were nearby and he offered to lead me to it if I wore a blindfold. I know he led me round and about in order to confuse me.'

'You're talking about Carlo, but how the hell did Sebastian find the chamber?'

They stared at each other.

'*Hold on!*' He grabbed her arm. 'It *was* Mr. Montegriffo who kidnapped you, wasn't it?'

She shook her head in silence.

'You mean…?' Mohammed stared at her.

'Yes…I do mean! It was Sebastian. My own brother.'

Eva

She recognised that she was in shock. Another glass of gin had not really helped at all. Everything around her seemed to be disintegrating. The disconcerting joy and relief she'd felt at Adrian's death had been offset by Mimi's disappearance and the disturbing phone call from Henry Saunders. And now Sebastian had abandoned her here in this gloomy apartment to wait it out alone.

The days had grown shorter: dusk had long ago spread its shadows around the rooms. She'd lit the lamp over the kitchen table but the rest of the apartment lay in darkness.

Sitting down in her armchair in the kitchen she saw all the drawings spread helter-skelter over the table. It looked as if a gang of apes had got in and ransacked Sebastian's files and drawing pads, looking for scraps of food. He sometimes lost his temper when he couldn't find something but never had she seen him make such a mess of his precious work.

She still had his mobile in her hand and was jolted into soberness when it rang.

'Sebastian...' she shouted. 'Mimi?'

There was a long silence at the end of the line. 'Not you again,' she howled at the breather. 'Who the hell are you?'

'This is Jane Featherington-Haugh calling,' declared a haughty female voice.

'Yes. What? Who are *you*?'

'With whom am I speaking, please?'

'It's Eva Eriksson answering Sebastian Luna's phone,' she said impatiently.

'Well, I am Sebastian's mother,' said the woman icily. 'I assume you're my son's girlfriend.'

Eva cringed. A bit of a bungle not reacting to the name, but Sebastian only ever called her 'that woman', usually with some offensive expletive in between.

'Yes, well. Hello. Sebastian is not at home right now.'

'Listen,' said the woman, her voice softening slightly. 'Just as well I'm speaking to you. I hadn't checked my emails for a couple of days, and I have just now seen one from Sebastian.'

A silence followed, and after a moment Eva said, 'Hello, are you there?'

'Is Sebastian on his way here, or has he booked a flight for Imogen to come here?'

Eva closed her eyes, trying to make sense of the questions. 'Why would he have done that?'

'If you have any influence over Sebastian, I ask of you, please, do not, under any circumstances allow him come to the UK and drop in on us. I don't think my husband could tolerate another—'

'Hold on,' Eva interrupted. 'Has Sebastian said he's coming to England?'

'No, not exactly, but in the past, when he's had a…a relapse, his first agenda is to come and harangue me about what he imagines are my failings as a mother. And he threatened to send Imogen to us. But just in case that occurs to him, this would be the worst possible time. My husband's children and grandchildren are coming to stay and—'

'I can assure you, Sebastian is not in a position to leave Gibraltar at the moment, Mrs. Featheringheight… Mimi has gone missing.'

'Featherington-Haugh,' the woman corrected. There was a pause. 'Well, what exactly is going on?'

'What did you mean by *relapse*?' said Eva.

'I'm referring to Sebastian's episodes, of course.'

'What episodes?' Eva whispered, shivering with dread.

'For heaven's sake,' said the woman impatiently. 'His illness, his episodes of paranoid psychosis. You live with him. You must have noticed a deterioration. I could tell by his email that he's unravelling. I imagine he's come off his medication, has had it changed or he's meddled with it in some way.'

Paranoid psychosis! Her head swam with images and fragments of conversations. It felt as though a series of keys were slowly being turned – one by one – and the corresponding windows clicking open. She'd been looking at them all along, not thinking (or daring) to explore or try to name what she was seeing. Eva sank back into her chair and closed her eyes. 'Tell me more about his episodes. To be honest, I don't know about his condition.'

'You don't?' the woman said, clearly taken aback. 'Well, frankly, Sebastian himself has always kept quiet about his illness. It shouldn't come as a surprise; he has to be ever so careful to safeguard his career and international reputation.'

'His medication?' Eva said. 'What is it? What must he take?'

'My goodness, I don't know. Our wonderful Dr. Matthews here in the UK has kept him stable for many years now on a combination of drugs and he knows very well that as long as he takes them religiously he stays balanced and rational. I mean, just look at what my son has achieved!'

'What exactly does paranoid psychosis mean, in his case? Please tell me all you can,' Eva implored. 'I need to know what I am dealing with.'

'Oh dear, I'm not the right person to explain it to you, but his first psychiatric diagnosis, aged about twelve, was severe manic-depressive disorder: now they call it bi-polar of course, but his condition is at the more serious end of the spectrum and more complex and debilitating than the label suggests.'

'The episodes –' Eva whispered, 'what exactly happens?'

'It usually starts with Sebastian getting increasingly obsessive and self-absorbed, followed by bizarre, elaborate fantasies and selective loss of memory. Surely you must have been aware of a decline. Especially the delusions of grandeur and the paranoia, thinking that the world is out to steal his ideas, do harm to his sister, and whatever else.'

'Oh, God.' Eva sank deeper into her chair. She couldn't believe her own blindness, her ignorance, her sheer stupidity.

'Of course, he's highly intelligent and as such very skilled at hiding his condition,' Mrs. Featherington-Haugh paused, then continued in a firm voice. 'There is one thing I must make clear. Regardless of Sebastian's mental state, it is not convenient for him to come here, and there is absolutely no way I can take Imogen onboard again. Having her in residence – after her father died – proved a veritable nightmare. Imogen is eighteen now, and she should be able to stand on her own two feet. If it's a matter of money, my husband and I are willing to…'

'Listen, lady; Mimi, your daughter, is missing.'

'Well, please make this clear to Sebastian and to Imogen herself when she comes back.'

'She is missing!' Eva shouted. 'Are you hearing me?'

There was a pause. 'When Imogen was living with us she ran away countless times, so I'm afraid I can't get excited about her disappearances.'

'There is a difference. Here she's loved and wanted. She has nothing to run away from.'

'Perhaps she does if Sebastian is in the throes of one of his episodes,' said Jane Featherington-Haugh indignantly.

Eva considered this. No, Mimi cared too much for her brother to abandon him, especially knowing he was ill. That was *not* the reason she had disappeared.

'I dare say it must be comforting for Sebastian to have a woman to lean on,' continued the mother in an appeasing tone. 'He is such a brilliant man, such a talent. Mr. Featherington-Haugh and I read up on his achievements on the engineering web sites. We follow his career closely, and we are so, so proud.'

'You are so, so proud,' Eva repeated coldly. 'But you wouldn't welcome either of your children to your home.'

'As I explained, right now it would be most inconvenient to...'

'Or help them when they need you, or care if they were missing.'

'Over the years, my husband and I have been put at an inconvenience plenty of—'

'Go to hell, Mrs. Featherstone,' Eva snapped. 'You and your husband, both.'

She rang off and dropped the phone into her lap then smiled sadly, realising how little she had known about her heavy-breathing stalker.

*

She'd fallen asleep in the chair waiting for Sebastian to come home, and woke up with a start at a knock on the door. Daunted by whatever incident, development or person would present itself, she sprang up like a coil. Glancing at her watch, she saw it was nearly five o'clock in the morning. It just had to be Mimi or Sebastian, preferably both. Barefoot she ran to open the door.

Before she had time to make any exclamation or ask any

questions, Mohammed put a finger to his lips in a hushing gesture.

'Imogen is safe,' he whispered. 'I've found her.'

'Thank God!' she exclaimed. 'Where is she?'

'Is her brother here?' he mouthed soundlessly.

She shook her head, but then whispered, 'Unless he's returned and I've not heard him come in.' She ushered him into the hall. 'Wait here.'

Mohammed detained her with a hand on her arm and murmured, 'If he's here, don't tell him about me finding Imogen. She just wants *you* to know.'

She stared at him, uncomprehending. 'Why ever not? He's been frantic with worry.'

'Please, Miss Eva. Check first and then I'll explain.'

She ran around the apartment but there was no sign of Sebastian.

'He's not here, Mohammed. Tell me what's going on?'

'You need to know it was him. *He* kidnapped Imogen,' he told her at once. 'He locked her in a chamber inside the Rock.'

Eva stood by the hall table and reached out to steady herself. She'd finally come to know that Sebastian was sick, but this was much worse than she could ever have envisioned. She sank onto a chair. 'Good God! Poor Mimi! *Where is she now?*'

'In my room at the hostel. She's safe there, for now.'

Eva jumped up. 'I want to see her. Let's go there.'

'Just a moment,' said Mohammed. 'Imogen is very worried about Mr. Montegriffo's safety. He's the only person in the world, other than Mr. Luna, who knows about the chamber where she was held. She thinks Mr. Luna would have made sure of stopping him going down into the Rock and finding her.'

'Stopping him… How?'

Mohammed stared at her, his eyes wide with dread. 'Imogen says her brother is ill. She wanted me to get you, to accompany her to the police station. She doesn't want to cause her brother any trouble but she thinks he is dangerous…to Mr. Montegriffo.' Mohammed looked suddenly tearful. 'She is a very strong person. No-one could endure such terror, Miss Eva. Alone there in the dark, locked in a hole deep underground, not knowing if anyone would ever come for her or if she would die there.'

'Oh, God, that's unbelievable, *atrocious*! Let's go to her, please.'

She ran to get her shoes and bag. They tiptoed down the stairs, as if this would somehow prevent Sebastian noticing them if he were to meet them there. Mohammed paused on the first-floor landing.

'Should we perhaps warn Mr. Montegriffo?' he whispered.

'No,' Eva said, taking him by the arm. 'He'd be furious if we woke him up at five in the morning. If we're going to the police, *they* can warn him. What's Sebastian going to do to him, anyway? He's suffering from…he's in a deluded state, but surely he's not going to cause him any physical harm.'

She pulled on the young man's arm, but at the last moment stopped to cock her ear. From somewhere deep in Montegriffo's apartment, she heard an eerie sound which she could not identify.

'Shhh,' she whispered to Mohammed. 'Listen.'

They stood there motionless for a moment. The sound came louder now, an insistent howling.

'It's Raven,' Mohammed said. 'Why is he wailing like that?'

'Let's go,' Eva insisted. 'Mimi first. I can't cope with anything else.'

Mimi

Her hair was still wet from a shower in some awful men's cubicle, and she was wearing Mohammed's best cotton trousers and T-shirt. He'd left her lying on his bed after covering her with a woolly blanket. It was way too hot for a blanket, but the gesture was so very tender, she'd waited until he'd gone before she kicked it off.

She slept fitfully for a little while, waking regularly to ascertain she was above ground, on the surface. He'd left a little light on, and she focused her eyes intently on the Moroccan posters. What a wonderful, exciting place Morocco must be. She studied the terracotta pots and the vibrant market stalls with red and orange rugs, big baskets filled with colourful spices and women in exotic clothes and beautiful silver jewellery. Looking deeply at the beauty helped keep her body from shaking. When she'd studied the posters, she turned to the bronze platter Mohammed had put beside her on a chair. On it he'd arranged some oranges, figs and dates, nuts, bananas, a mango and pear, making the whole thing look like a work of art. He'd assumed she must be hungry for fresh food, but she couldn't bear to destroy the beautiful display he'd made. To think that on earth, trees grew these fantastic things just from the dusty soil and water. And the sun, of course. Everything needed sun to grow and live and thrive.

She rubbed her cheek on the velvety surface on which she lay. It smelled of some musky spice, like sandalwood. She wanted that smell forever against her cheek. After a while, she rolled over and looked down under the bed. Perhaps there'd be another living being – perhaps a mouse – she could look at. Lined up ever so neatly under the bed were a pair of sandals, a pair of Moroccan leather slippers and the dear yellow trainers. She reached down and touched them. Still, she stayed on the bed. It was all she needed for the moment. It was safe. Another raft in an unpredictable sea.

She was in a deep sleep in which a simple word, *deliverance,* hovered over her forehead. Then another word: her name. Eva's gentle voice woke her and she gave a wail of joy. Eva leaned over her and they held on to one another for a few seconds. Eva looked so different, and now she remembered that she herself had cut off her hair. It seemed that years had passed since that day.

'I thought you were on some mission to confront your husband.'

'I found out I don't have a husband anymore, so I came straight back.'

'Thank God,' Mimi said and hugged her again. 'Thank God you're here.'

Dawn was lighting up the empty streets when the three of them walked to the police station in Irish Town, a quirky old building which looked as though it belonged in *Dr. Who*. Mimi stopped outside the long row of arches and turned to Mohammed. 'What am I like! This is *not* a good idea for you.'

He frowned and looked at his shoes for a moment. 'They will need a statement from me, no doubt.'

'Not!' said Mimi decisively. 'I am not going to risk them dumping you at the frontier as an illegal alien.'

Mohammed glanced at the entrance and said bitterly, 'I

was in there yesterday morning and told them I thought the missing girl was in a chamber inside the Rock, but they seemed to think I was a crazy man. They wouldn't listen. And when I mentioned that Mr. Montegriffo might be the kidnapper, they practically threw me out.'

'I'll tell them I broke out of the chamber and found my way back on my own.'

'It's a bit unlikely. If you knew how complex—'

'I don't care. They'll have to believe me,' said Mimi. 'Go home and sleep, Mohammed. 'You've saved my life, and I refuse to have them deport you.'

Eva put a hand on his arm. 'She's right. Go on. We can handle it.'

Mimi kissed him on both cheeks, as did Eva, and they watched his slight figure striding down Irish Town towards the safety of Tuckey's Lane.

Mimi turned to Eva. 'Must we tell them it was Sebastian?' Can't I just say I went walkabout for a couple of days?' As she was saying the words, she knew it was impossible. She couldn't go on protecting Sebastian. There was no telling what he might do if he found her missing from the chamber.

'Mimi honey,' said Eva, reaching out to smooth her flopping fringe off her face. 'I think it's best not to lie. I'm sure the police will be more inclined to be sympathetic if we tell them about Sebastian's...condition. Besides, we need their help to find him.'

At reception, they explained who they were and why they'd come, and as it happened, PC Marianne Peralta was on the early-morning shift. She came into the lobby to see them. After taking one look at the pair of them, she had the sense to lead them to a private interview room.

'So this is the missing Imogen Luna,' she said kindly when they'd sat down at a table.

'I was kidnapped,' Mimi said. 'My brother Sebastian is ill, you see. He's been all right for years, but for some reason he must have stopped taking his medication, and I guess all the stress of his work here has...got to him.'

PC Peralta nodded as if she weren't very surprised. 'So it *was* him, then. Where did he take you?'

Mimi felt her face twitch slightly. 'Down very deep into the tunnel system...to a chamber... He wasn't trying to harm me or anything; just the opposite. He only wanted me to be safe from Carlo Montegriffo. He imagined we were having an affair.'

Mimi knew that Sebastian's motivations were deeper, but she preferred not to think about that right now, even less talk about it. If she let herself really remember what he'd proposed – his true plans for her future – she feared she would break down and have some kind of screaming fit from which she might never recover.

'A chamber inside the Rock?' said PC Peralta, her eyes widening slightly. 'And how did you get out of there? Did he come to his senses and let you out?'

'No. I broke out; it took me hours and hours to find my way. In fact, I think it was just sheer luck that I did. It was very deep down the tunnel system, that's all I can say.'

'*Ay, cariño!*' Marianne Peralta murmured, looking at her with genuine concern. 'You look ever so worn-down. I think you should be seen by a doctor.'

'No, I'm all right, really. I don't want a doctor.'

'We'll talk about that in a minute. So, your brother accused Carlo Montegriffo of harbouring you, when he himself had done the kidnapping. Have I got that right?'

'That's because he's ill, like I explained,' Mimi said sharply. 'It's called *projection* or something like that. He was breaking down and probably got his part in it muddled. Lost the plot, if you know what I mean?'

Peralta nodded again, then looked at Eva. 'Would you say he's a danger to himself or others?'

'I wouldn't take any chances after what he put Imogen through,' Eva said emphatically. 'When he finds her gone from the chamber, he'll no doubt assume it's Montegriffo's doing...and go after him. For all we know the man might be in jeopardy.'

'He's been antagonistic to Sebastian since we arrived and I've not been much help,' said Mimi. 'Basically, all this is my fault. We should try to find Sebastian a.s.a.p. He needs to be sectioned.'

Eva turned to her with a frown. 'Sectioned?'

'It means being hospitalised under Section Three of the Mental Health Act, against his will if necessary,' Mimi said.

'You've done this before, then?'

'Dad did, a number of times when Sebastian was in his teens. Since then, Sebastian has volunteered to be hospitalised, once or twice. He's been good for ages, especially since the last combination of drugs. They really suited him.'

Eva looked as though she were close to tears. 'Why did you never tell me all this? Why didn't *he*? I think I deserved to know.'

Mimi tried not to look annoyed. 'You know the answer to that. He was desperate to leave his past behind, to hide it from everyone, and he was scared you'd leave him. Can you blame him? I tried to force him to tell you, but it wasn't my business to blabber. I kept hoping you two would start talking to each other.'

'Look!' Peralta said to get their attention. 'Where do you think Sebastian might be?'

'Neither of us has any idea where he is,' said Eva. 'He disappeared yesterday, late afternoon, and he didn't come back all night.'

Peralta looked troubled. 'Well, we'll do our best to find him.'

'Someone should be in the apartment to wait for him,' said Mimi. 'He might be there right now for all we know. But I kind of doubt it.'

'All right,' said PC Peralta briskly. 'We'll go up there now. I just need to take some details to close your missing persons file. Can you describe the place where your brother took you?'

'Absolutely no way. And I refuse to set foot in a tunnel as long as I live.'

'How did your brother know about this chamber? Did you get a feeling your abduction was pre-planned?'

'The chamber was there already, if that's what you mean, and stocked with food to last seven years. Dried and canned stuff. There was water, batteries, and toilet...facilities.'

PC Peralta shook her head, her professionalism finally slipping. 'Unbelievable!'

'He did it for my own protection,' said Mimi defensively. 'He's a very good and caring person. He's just...you know, mentally ill.'

'Of course,' Peralta said, chastened. She turned to Eva. 'We'll send an officer or two to wait for him in your apartment. Would one of you – or both – like to be there as well, or do you have somewhere to go in the meantime?'

Eva

They sat in the back of the police car and were driven up as far into Upper Town as it was possible to go. Having parked up on the curb of the narrow street, Eva and Mimi, plus PC Steven Gonzalez and PC Nigel Goldsworthy, walked briskly up the steps.

DiMoretti's Ramp was deserted, not even a pair of Y-fronts hanging from Mrs. Amirah's window. When they entered the darkened hallway and were about to climb the stairs, again Eva thought she could hear that awful howling.

'Stop,' she said. 'You hear that?'

They all stopped at once. Yes, there it still was.

'What is it?' said PC Gonzalez. The young man – probably a recent recruit – looked spooked.

'Oh, no,' said Mimi. 'That's got to be Raven. It sounds as if he's trapped somewhere.'

In single file, they hurried up the steps. Outside Montegriffo's door, they stopped and listened to the haunting cries of the cat. Mimi's face had paled, looking as though she could not endure any further trauma.

'Mimi, honey. Shall you and I just go?' said Eva. 'You don't have to come back here, you know. We can let the officers deal with all this.'

Mimi ignored her and rapped her knuckles hard on the door. 'Carlo,' she shouted. 'Open the door.' She bent down on one knee and shouted again through the letter flap. 'Carlo, for fuck's sake! Open this door.'

The two officers looked at each other.

'I take it this isn't your own apartment,' said PC Goldsworthy. 'Shouldn't we be checking if Mr. Luna has returned home?'

Eva took her keys out of her bag and handed them to PC Gonzalez. 'Our place is upstairs,' she said hurriedly. 'Why don't you go and check if he's back?'

Mimi was still banging on Montegriffo's door and shouting for Raven though the letter flap. The cat had gone quiet. Mimi turned to PC Goldsworthy and said, 'I've got a terrible feeling about this. Something's wrong in there. You've got to open this door, somehow.'

The officer nodded. Peralta had given him a brief outline of the situation and he clearly saw the need to act. 'I'll call for a locksmith,' he said and took out his mobile.

'Fuck that,' Mimi cried. 'Kick the door in.'

PC Goldworthy said nothing but began to look around. He passed his hand along the top of the door frame. He checked under a pot with a dead plant. He felt under the treads, at the side of the stairs. Eva and Mimi watched this strange routine until they heard him say, 'Ah,' and prised a key from a lump of Blu Tack under the wooden bannister. He put the key to Montegriffo's keyhole and it turned and clicked open.

'I'll have a look inside,' he said. 'You ladies wait here.'

As soon as he opened the door, Raven shot out as though his tail were on fire. Mimi was just as quick and grabbed him. A moment later they heard Goldsworthy talking on his intercom. His voice was quiet but urgent. 'Yes, Carlo Montegriffo...no...looks like homicide...send the team up.'

Eva shivered. *Sebastian, my love...what have you done?*

She put an arm around Mimi. The girl stared through the door as if hoping for a miracle. The cat had gone quiet in her arms.

She put Mimi in the police car with the cat and PC Gonzalez, while she ran up to the apartment, gathering some clothes and personal items from her own and Mimi's rooms, and packing them into her suitcase. There was a violin on Mimi's bed, and she realised at once it was not Carlo or Mrs. Amirah she'd heard playing late at night. She put the violin and the bow into a carrier bag. Hearing the wail of a police siren, she quickened her step. In the kitchen, she stopped briefly to look at the disorder on the table and the floor beneath it. There lay all Sebastian's papers and drawings in a jumble. His cup of decaffeinated coffee stood half-full beside his stand of pens and pencils. One of his sandals lay on the floor by his chair. The very air vibrated with his presence. But that was the sort of man he was. His aura was so strong, so dominant, he'd left an imprint on every space he'd occupied. He'd left an imprint on *her*, his lover of a mere eight months.

Where was he? It was hard to imagine him escaping without taking Luna's Crossing with him. All those drawings. He'd spent months creating his fantasy-masterpiece.

She thought to write a note and leave it for him in case he came home, just to say she loved him despite what he'd done. But it was best not to. The police would be here, waiting for him.

She passed Montegriffo's door on the way down. It was open and people were arriving. A homicide! She hoped with all her heart that Sebastian wasn't the man responsible for the killing, but the hope was a feeble one. She didn't want to see anything and hurried past, down the stairs, down the ramp, through the lanes and into the waiting police car.

Mimi was sitting in the back, sobbing.

'Mimi...?' Eva murmured. 'Come on, sweetie. It has been awful...'

PC Gonzalez turned to her. 'I would have waited until you got here, but Miss Luna overheard my call from the station.'

Eva felt the blood drain from her face. 'What about? What's happened?'

'They've just heard from the Police Marine Unit, Miss Eriksson. I'm sorry to tell you that Mr. Luna has disappeared at sea.'

Mimi covered her face with her hands and let escape a terrible howl. Eva put her arm around her shoulder and held her fast.

'How do you mean, disappeared at sea?' she asked in a shaky voice. 'What was he doing at sea? He's a very good swimmer and diver. Surely—' her voice closed up in a sob.

'Last night a man called Jonny Risso took him out on the east side for some night diving. Risso wasn't happy about it, but Mr. Luna was very insistent, and Risso knew he'd been diving there on many occasions.'

'What happened?' Eva whispered.

'He never emerged. The tide turned and it seems he got pulled under. The tides are treacherous, but I needn't tell *you*, Miss Eriksson. Miss Luna just told me you're a professional diver yourself.'

Tears blurred her vision, her throat tight. 'Did Sebastian say anything to Risso? Did Risso wait long enough? I mean, perhaps—' Her voice broke again.

'Mr. Risso didn't find anything unusual about him or his state of mind, and yes, he stayed out there for several hours, searching up and down the coast, but there was no sign of Mr. Luna whatsoever. Then he called the Unit. Mr. Risso provided them with your home number and they tried to reach you during the early hours, but there was no answer.' He paused for a moment, clearly quite traumatised himself. 'I'm so sorry to have to give you such distressing news.'

Mimi reached out and grabbed her hand, and they looked at each other in silence.

*

She woke at dawn and looked out of a set of huge glass doors. The peak of Jebel Musa on the coast of Morocco rose out of a low-lying sea mist. The ever-present gulls shrieked hauntingly above the Rock. Eva sat up with a start. She jumped out of bed and into a walk-in shower, then rummaged in her suitcase for clean clothes.

It was their third morning in a Moroccan style house in the South District, owned by a friend of Brian. Gerard, based in Zurich, was more than happy to loan his pad to two civilised ladies (the cat was not mentioned), liking the security of having it occupied.

After the noisy and over-crowded Upper Town, the South District was a haven. The house was at the end of a cul-de-sac, had a pool, and was surrounded by towering Washingtonia palm trees.

Flinging open the patio doors, Eva walked out on the balcony and looked at Jebel Musa; it was so beautiful, so dramatic. She tried in vain to stem the tears. As always when the sun rose, the mountain began to fade in sharpness, an illusion that would soon dissolve. Sebastian's strong definitions had begun to fade and crumble too, and she struggled to hold on to them...she couldn't bear to lose the man she'd believed him to be. Her brilliant, passionate and captivating lover...had she not read it somewhere? Genius and madness were two sides of the same coin.

She'd not noticed, never mind paid attention to cracks as they'd appeared, then begun to widen: his egomania and grandiose beliefs, his obsessiveness and paranoia, his migraines and sleeplessness. The silent phone calls… The breather had been impatient – exasperated even – wanting something from her; reassurance, perhaps. If only she'd told her phantom caller she loved Sebastian, but she'd never even mentioned him by name. Would the outcome have been different if she had? In the end, the belief that Adrian was on her heels had transformed her. His persecution of her from beyond the grave had made her uncover the seat of her fear and conquer it. Alive or dead, Adrian would have continued to wield power over her, but threatened by what she perceived as his wrath, she'd at last found the strength to fight back.

In the end your phone calls empowered me, Sebastian, she whispered with a wry smile, then began to cry again.

She felt a hand on her shoulder and turned. Mimi had come to join her, and in silence, they looked over the Atlantic towards the fading Moroccan coast. Neither wanted to comment on the obvious – in that huge body of water, on one side or the other of the strait, Sebastian's body floated, nibbled by sea life while waiting to be found.

Instead, Eva said to her, 'You know, last night, digging in my bag I found the package with the money you gave me. It was a very generous gesture, but you still haven't told me where it came from.'

'I found it under a floorboard in the bedroom. Mrs. Cohen had a windfall in the Spanish National Lottery and, because she was getting senile, she must have forgotten she'd put it there. She gambled the rest away and was really scraping the barrel, even for food.'

'*Holy Jesus!*' Eva stared at her. 'How do you know all this?'

'Carlo told me…in confidence.'

'Did he know you'd found the money?'

'No, I kept it to myself.' Mimi turned to her. 'I gave some

of it to you and some of it to Mohammed, to release him from his bondage to Carlo. The rest, well, I'm writing Esther's story, and I am planning to use it to support me while I'm writing, and hopefully part of it to self-publish... that is, if no bona fide publisher wants to take it on.'

'Esther's story?' Eva shook her head in amazement. 'Do you know enough about her?'

'I do know a lot. Apart from what Carlo told me, I found a diary, the violin and some other objects, plus a big pile of letters. More things come to me every day. In fact, Esther tells me she wants me to write her story, so she and her children, born and unborn, should not be forgotten.'

Eva stared at her, wondering if she was suffering from post-traumatic stress disorder.

'No, I'm not loopy,' said Mimi, reading her thoughts and laughing a little. 'I'm not going the way of Sebastian. Of course, I want to do a lot more research, about her life, about the history of Gibraltar. Esther was a very private person so I need to think about whether to name her. Perhaps she will give me a sign.' She winked at Eva and laughed again. 'Either way, her life and her death deserve to be told.'

'You do amaze me, Mimi. What about your semi-autobiographical novel?'

Mimi looked down, a shadow passing over her face. 'It can wait. I'll tackle it when I'm older.' She glanced up at Eva. 'But you keep the money I gave you. You're going to need some yourself.'

'We'll see about that!'

They heard a car pull up into the driveway and looked down over the railing. Brian's brown mop of hair emerging out of a blue Renault was a welcome sight. He got out several Morrisons shopping bags and looking up, saw them waving to him.

'Meals on wheels,' he called.

'We'll come down and open the door,' Eva called back.

Half an hour later, while Eva was trying to operate a complex coffee machine, the doorbell rang. Both she and Mimi froze and looked anxiously at each other. Much as they had thought and talked about nothing other than Sebastian, neither of them was ready to cope with news of him... or his remains.

Brian saw it on their faces. 'Would you like me to get that?'

'Yeah, you go!' said Mimi anxiously. 'But there is no reason it should be about Sebastian, right?'

'Perhaps a neighbour, or the postman,' said Eva.

Brian went to the door, and a moment later returned to the kitchen with PC Goldsworthy and detective inspector Carmen Ledbury, a sturdy dark-haired woman in her mid-fifties.

The officers looked intimidatingly serious when they all shook hands. 'Would you like a cup of coffee?' Mimi asked.

'No, thank you,' they said in unison.

They sat down in the living room, a luxurious expanse of big sofas and abstract art.

'Miss Eriksson, Miss Luna,' began Carmen Ledbury. 'The Marine Unit has been searching for three days now.' She paused to compose her words. 'I'm very sorry to have to tell you that Sebastian's body has not been found, but we have found what we now know is his scuba gear, the tanks and the harness. It seems he must have taken them off deliberately very near where Mr. Risso anchored his boat. It's a pretty clear sign that—'

Mimi interrupted, 'That he saw no way out of what he'd done.'

Carmen Ledbury nodded. 'I'm afraid they are now

calling off the search. That doesn't mean much in the case of Gibraltar because, as you're probably aware, the Marine Unit has vessels continuously patrolling the waters, both the Mediterranean side as well as the Atlantic. The Spanish authorities have also been alerted and are on the lookout.'

'He must have been desperate, knowing that everything was lost,' Eva said.

'Have there been other attempts...?'

Eva looked at Mimi and took her hand. She was the only one who could answer the question.

'Well...yes,' said Mimi. 'When he was in his teens he took an overdose a couple of times. But then he had this vision – his 'calling' – about building stuff, and got a place at university. Of course, I was just a baby at that time, but Dad has told me how much he changed. Between his calling and the right medication, he was on his way to fame and fortune. He never tried to harm himself again.'

They lapsed into silence for a moment. Eva fought an image of a body floating in water, bobbing on the waves, swollen, surrounded by fish.

'I know this is terribly painful to take on board right now,' said the detective inspector finally, 'but I have to tell you that our forensic team has ascertained that Sebastian was in Carlo Montegriffo's apartment on the day of his death, and was the bearer of the crowbar or claw-hammer which caused his fatal head injury. I'm afraid that – were he alive – Sebastian would be charged with his murder.'

'He's my brother and I love him, but there's hardly any doubt, is there?' Mimi blurted angrily. 'He took me down into that damned grotto for my own safety, and probably felt he had no choice but to bump Carlo off, because Carlo was the devil incarnate in his eyes. He probably felt it was his duty to do it. To save me... save the world, even. Sebastian tended to think he was in charge of the world. And why do you call it murder, anyway? Isn't it manslaughter when a man is out of his mind?'

They all looked at her, her bravery and honesty, but no-one could think of anything else to say.

When they stood up to leave, Carmen Ledbury put out her hand to detain Eva in the living room. 'Can I just have a private word?'

Eva nodded and they waited for the others to go out into the hall. 'Yes, tell me!'

'Sebastian was a good swimmer and an experienced diver, correct?'

Eva frowned. 'Correct.'

'We've not discounted the possibility that he swam over the frontier line to the Spanish shore. The tides would have made it difficult, but a strong swimmer might just manage it.'

Eva looked out of the window for a long moment. 'You're inferring that he escaped after killing Montegriffo?'

Carmen Ledbury shook her head. 'No...but he *could* have.'

Eva sank back into her chair. This had never even occurred to her. 'Yes, I suppose he could have.'

'So...if he did contact you...if you heard from him, what would you do?'

She burst into tears. It was too much to think that Sebastian could still be alive, after she'd endured the start of such a confounded grieving process. 'Oh, damn it all... what do I know? I guess I would try and talk him into giving himself up.'

Carmen Ledbury touched her lightly on the shoulder. 'Okay, all right. It was a question I felt I had to put to you.

You wouldn't be in possession of his passport or know where it is? And what about money? Would you know if he had recently withdrawn some from the bank or had some in his possession?'

She hid her face in her hands. 'No to both.'

'Do we have your permission to have a little look around your apartment?'

Eva flung her arm out. 'Be my guest.'

'I'm sorry to cause you further grief.'

'I'll get the key. Then just go, please,' said Eva. 'I'm about to have my daily screaming fit.'

Mimi

Jane and Gordon Featherington-Haugh had taken a room in the Caleta hotel, next to Both Worlds, as it was out of town and a good distance from the scene of Sebastian's crime.

Mimi had asked Eva to come along for moral support, and the four of them sat stiffly around a table in a suite on the top floor. A coffee pot stood cooling on the table, untouched.

'Let me say again, I am very sorry for your loss,' said Gordon to Mimi and Eva.

'Fine,' said Mimi and turned to give Jane a cold stare. 'What about *your* loss, Mother? Have you cried buckets?'

'Don't bother getting sarcastic, Imogen,' said Jane. 'This has been an ordeal for all of us.'

Eva moved her chair closer to Mimi's and put an arm around her shoulder. 'What's the main purpose for you being here?'

Gordon coughed and turned to Jane, 'Shall I?'

Jane gave a small nod and looked away.

'Sebastian inherited a bit of money from his grandfather Luna in Seville. Not a fortune, but a nice tidy sum. Of course the old man died before Imogen was born, so,' he turned to Mimi, 'naturally you're not in the will.'

'This meeting is about money?' Mimi asked, incredulous. 'Have you never heard of a phone? No worries, I don't need any money,' She stood up to go, but Eva held on to her.

Jane got up and stepped out onto the balcony.

Gordon coughed and tried again. 'Sebastian left this money in the UK, for Diana Cousins to administer. Diana is retired now but the accountancy firm she founded is still managing the funds. Normally, if no will is made, this money would have been divided between the nearest and dearest, such as are left, namely Sebastian's mother and sister… but –' he turned and looked towards the balcony, as if appealing for his wife's support.

'Just come out with it,' said Mimi. 'Don't waste our time.'

Gordon seemed lost for words and turned to Jane. She stood in the balcony doorway, her immaculate hair style blown asunder by the wind. 'That money is coming to you, because…you are Sebastian's sole heir, Imogen.'

Mimi snorted. 'Are you surprised?'

'Not because of Sebastian's will – he left none – but because *you are his daughter.*'

After an eternity, Jane broke the silence with her shrill voice. 'I regret we didn't tell you before, but you're eighteen, now, and the situation has come to a head.'

'It can't be true,' Mimi whispered. The world she'd known was tumbling crazily in every direction, trying to find purchase in some index of sanity. 'It simply can't.'

'I'm afraid it is,' said Jane. 'The good news for you is of course that you'll inherit all the money, with none of it coming to me.'

Mimi was unable to speak. She turned and stared at Eva. Eva, too, seemed shocked into silence.

'This bombshell could have waited,' said Eva finally. 'Mimi has been to hell and back and—'

'Of course, we understand,' Gordon broke in. 'We heard about the kidnapping. The whole saga is lamentable, highly

433

upsetting. I've gone to some lengths to keep it out of the press in the UK.'

Again, everyone went quiet; only the sea and the wind had returned.

'Shall I send for something strong?' Gordon asked, his hand hovering over the telephone, but no-one reacted.

Mimi got up and wandered about the room. She stopped by the window and spoke to the sea. 'I always knew I was a changeling of some sort. I thought I was adopted, but I look too much like Sebastian.' She turned abruptly to Jane and shouted, 'I don't believe this crazy story. Sebastian and I were sister and brother, we always were. You've got to be lying. There's got to be some scheme in this.'

Eva got up, taking her hand and guiding her to a sofa.

'You'd better tell us how and why,' Eva said to Jane, her voice sharp. 'If what you say is true, you owe Mimi a damned good explanation.'

Jane came back inside and sank down on a chair. She looked pale, and with an anxious gesture, flicked the tousled hair from her face.

'Sebastian was going through a very difficult period when he was eighteen. He had a girlfriend named Tanya,' Jane grimaced at the name. 'Tanya was not a very nice kind of girl and she messed Sebastian around, cheated on him, dropped him and picked him up at will. Despite her cat-and-mouse games, he was quite besotted with her. Finally, she ditched him for a boy who was at college with Sebastian, and it was the final straw. Sebastian had fantasies of harming the boy in question, and in fact believed he'd run him over with his car. Subsequently, he suffered a severe breakdown and was hospitalised. He had innumerable shock treatments, and they tried a variety of drugs but it took over a year for him to be released from hospital.'

'I know, I know,' Mimi wailed. 'Don't tell me what I know. What's that got to do with me?'

'After his hospitalisation, that brain-dead little tart discovered that she was four-months' pregnant. First, she thought there was money to be had and named Sebastian as the father, but after you were born she met some man and decided to give you up for adoption.'

Mimi flinched. 'Me? I was the baby?'

'Of course, Sebastian was in no shape to find out, so your dad, that is to say your grandfather, offered to foster you pending a DNA test.' Jane brushed some invisible crumbs off her skirt with her bejewelled hand. 'He was adamant that no offspring of his loins should be brought up by unknown entities.'

Mimi felt faint and flopped against Eva. The shock of the revelation had sucked all the strength from her. Only a tiny part of her was not surprised. So many things were starting to align themselves in her mind.

'I presume Sebastian knew,' said Eva.

'We never told him. My ex-husband refused to,' said Jane, then hesitated. 'Perhaps he did know, though...'

'He was over-the-top protective of Mimi,' said Eva. 'He did call her his child, once.'

'Did he really?' said Mimi. There was a dangerous lump in her throat, threatening tears. She would not let that fucking woman see her pain, even if it crippled her insides.

Mimi straightened up. 'So you're not my mother, then, Jane.'

Jane looked her straight in the eye. 'No, by God, I am not.'

'That explains why you couldn't stand me,' Mimi growled. 'So why the hell didn't you tell us? This is not the dark ages, for fuck's sake! Isn't there a law against keeping children ignorant about their real parents?'

'Don't blame *me*,' Jane shot back. 'That was your grandfather's idea. He felt we shouldn't rock the boat when Sebastian was on his trajectory towards the stars. Much as I didn't want to raise another child, I knew your dad… grandfather…was right on that score. That same son in hospital, devastated by mental illness, came out to make a big name for himself. We knew this was going to save him, and we did everything not to risk his delicate emotional balance. Rightly or wrongly, we just did the very best we could…'

'"The very best you could"!' aped Mimi. 'Don't make me laugh. You ran out on Dad. You ran out on Sebastian. Then you dumped me with them when neither were in any position to look after me.'

'Imogen, enough! Don't be rude,' interjected Gordon. 'Jane is your grandmother.'

'And that's supposed to redeem her?'

'You ungrateful little witch,' Jane snarled. 'We could easily have allowed Tanya to give you up for adoption. We didn't need Sebastian's signature for that. You seem to forget I looked after you until you were six. And then again when you were an impossible thirteen, God help me.'

Gordon Featherington-Haugh put his hands out as though to calm a storm. 'Now, now,' he admonished. 'We're all upset, but let's try and keep this civil. If there is anything else you want to know, Imogen, ask now, and we can conclude this meeting.'

'Yes,' said Mimi. 'A fuck of a lot. For a start, what do you know of my real mother, this Tanya? Who is she?'

*

She'd had a choice between attending the Vigil or the Mass

436

for Carlo, and had chosen the Vigil, mainly because it was in the evening, when she'd be less conspicuous.

Carlo's murder had been all over the papers, but she trusted that no-one knew who she was, especially with her transformed appearance. She'd bought a dress from Monsoon in muted pink. Her hair was short all over – a boy's cut – and it suited her, at least for now. She'd ditched the makeup and the metal, well...she'd kept the stud in her nose and the expanding loop in her ear.

Not that she was grieving over Carlo. Even if she had been a bit infatuated, she didn't have a speck of grief left over to cover him as well as Sebastian. However, as her father was the cause of Carlo's death, it was right that at least one Luna ought to be there to pay their respects.

'Won't you come with me?' she said to Mohammed as they stood in front of the cathedral. 'You're getting the guide job, after all, and it was Carlo who put in a good word.'

'My face doesn't fit in there,' he said, sitting down on a bench where the Jewish mothers always sat. 'I'll wait for you here. I'll think about Mr. Montegriffo and wish him Godspeed.'

She sat at the back and listened to all the eulogies, the tributes and the praises. Carlo's brother read several of his poems. Mimi recognised one that she'd edited. A curator from the Gibraltar Museum came forward to say a few words about Carlo's contribution to Historical Gibraltar, and how his books, explorations and research into the tunnel system had enriched their knowledge of past military installations. He was followed by a whole queue of people wanting to say something about Carlo Montegriffo. Most of it was formal and impersonal yet he had clearly commanded people's respect.

Mimi was certain she'd known him more intimately than most. She'd touched him, and he'd questioned his entire belief system because of her. She'd opened a few of his doors, just as he'd opened some of hers. But despite all this praise and accolades…he was not as pious or as perfect as they made him out to be. He was just a man, as self-serving and inadequate as any other.

'How was it?' asked Mohammed.

'Stiff and formal. No wailing or tears shed,' she said. She leaned her head against his shoulder and cried a little. She'd cried buckets during the last weeks, all the tears for Sebastian and then all the ones she'd been storing up from before. And there were more to come, the tears for her sorrow because she'd unknowingly denied the father in Sebastian, for losing 'Dad'– her grandfather – and for hating the mother who wasn't her mother, as well as tears for Esther Cohen whose grief for her daughter felt like her own. And then the tears she should have cried each time she'd given herself away without so much as a scrap of love in return.

*

The three of them were standing beside the grey Citroen in the airport carpark. It had rained all morning and there were puddles everywhere. The air was autumnal and most of the tourists were gone.

'You're not going anywhere, are you?' she said to Eva. She felt stupid asking, like a kid worrying about her mum disappearing with a travelling circus.

'I'll be here. You and I are family. Just make sure you email me every day.'

'Of course I will. I'll call you, too. But I've got to get into this *emancipation* lark.'

'You're doing just fine with that,' Eva said. 'I'm the one needing to catch up.'

'We can compare notes on our progress, can't we?'

Eva held on to her arm for what seemed ages, hesitating, then led her a few paces away from Mohammed. 'Listen, Mimi. I was going to wait till you came back to tell you, but...I will really need you, you know... Don't make long term plans, please.'

Mimi peered at her, intently. 'What's wrong? You're not ill, are you?'

'No, not ill,' she said with a weak smile. 'Mimi, you're going to be a sister in six months' time, so don't get any ideas about staying in the UK, all right?'

Mimi jumped back, her eyes wide. Her mouth hung open and for a moment she was speechless. 'Fucking hell! Are you serious?'

'I never actually intended it. Sebastian didn't want children, but my injections must have been running low or something. It happened, and I'm hurtling towards forty. Last chance, and all that.'

'Oh, but Eva...do you want his baby?'

Eva's chin quivered and her eyes looked blurred. 'Of course I do. Some genes you got there.' She tried to laugh and poked Mimi's nose with her forefinger. 'Besides, I loved your father. I don't have to remind you of that, do I?'

Mimi rolled her eyes. 'God, no! But what about his *crazy* genes? Aren't you worried?'

'Nah,' said Eva with a shrug. 'Look at *you*! You're totally whacky, but you're perfectly sane.'

Mimi studied the puddles at her feet. 'I guess I still don't know enough about mental illness but I wouldn't be surprised if Sebastian's problems were partly caused by childhood trauma or emotional neglect. Jane had a psychopathic gene herself; a sadistic one. She never touched children except to punish.'

Eva closed her eyes for a moment. 'Why couldn't he just have talked about it?'

'For Sebastian, all that mattered was what he was going to become, not what he was before. You know what he was like.'

Eva nodded, wiping something from her eye.

'Do you want me to stay? I don't have to go.'

'Don't be ridiculous!' Eva snorted. 'You've got to meet this Tanya woman, no matter how she turns out to be. And with Linda coming over, I'll be well looked after. She's awesome. I hope you're back in time to meet her.'

'And then? Will we stay in Gibraltar…the three of us? Mimi looked at Eva's tummy. It seemed perfectly flat like it always had been, but it was early days.

'Let's talk about it when you come back,' said Eva. 'Who knows how we'll feel when the dust has settled?'

They clung to each other for a moment. Mimi was filled with some unfamiliar emotion, a sort of vicarious maternal tenderness for that speck inside Eva. She'd never herself had a mother who'd loved her and cared about her, but now she was to be a big sister, an aunt and best friend rolled into one. That would make up for it. And the speck. It was like a miracle. They'd lost Sebastian, but the universe had seen to it that they got something of him back.

Mohammed kissed her on both cheeks and held her briefly in his arms. 'I'll check on Eva and make sure she's okay. And you be careful. I heard there are lots of pickpockets in London.'

Mimi put her hand over his mouth. 'Mohammed, for

Christ's sake, you can stop that now, the protective thing. I've had enough protection to last me till Doomsday.'

'When you come back, perhaps we'll go to Morocco for a little visit.'

'We will, but one thing at a time, sweetie. Get stuck into that new job now, and put those yellow trainers in the nearest bin. That's enough!'

Mimi turned around and waved twice as she joined the queue. Grief still clung to her like a heavy blanket, but knowing the mystery of her birth had made her feel more whole. Despite losing the brother/father she loved, she felt lighter than she had in years. Not only was she sane, she'd grown up, and through the terror she'd experienced in the bowels of the Rock, she'd found a strength she could call forth whenever she needed it. Something important had happened to her underground. She'd experienced the illusion of being at the centre of the universe, at its very core. Any time she felt like it, she could close her eyes and summon up that powerful state.

Epilogue

He came out on the cliff ledge above the Jungle. It had been a long time – he couldn't tell how long – since he stood on the surface. The sun glared without pity and he used his hands to shield his night-adapted eyes.

The air was humid, so different from the dryness below, and breathing it felt a bit like drowning. He panted and coughed as he inhaled it. After a moment, he calmed and peeked between his fingers. There was the expanse of land that was Spain spreading far into the distance. There was the sea dissolving into grey mist.

He wasn't sure what had brought him up; nothing in particular, just some strange longing, some misplaced nostalgia. He sometimes missed his beloved child, but surely she would not have stayed on this craggy Rock, and anyway, it would be unsafe to venture into the city to look for her. Not that anyone would recognise his face – as it was now. He thought there had been a woman too, some creature of the sea with fins and hair of seaweed. He smiled to himself; in the days of his sickness he'd been prone to wild fantasies.

He'd forgotten the peculiar nature of time: that the earth turned and revolved around the sun. It had turned as he stood there and was now entering its shadow phase. As the light faded, he felt more comfortable, and with unpractised gait he made his way towards the very summit of the Rock. Again he panted like a sick man. It tired him to walk.

Once there he sat down on a patch of grass, shivering in

the chill of the night, and watched the lights of the tankers for a while. Searching the horizon and the glittering city below, he found to his satisfaction that the surface held nothing for him. The life and work he had now constituted a different dimension, outside of time and space.

Morning came and he had not moved. His naked skin had frozen; from time to time, his body was seized by violent shudders. He watched the roll of the earth, how it tipped forward, making it look as though the sun rose from the sea. His mouth was dry but there was nothing to wet it with.

Sometime later in the phase of the sun, he saw them approach. He tried to get up but his body was rigid and refused to obey him. Something was draped around him that made a barrier against the cool wind. They wanted to straighten his legs and had to hold him under the armpits. As they helped him down the slope towards a road and a red light that flashed, he turned one last time to catch a glimpse of the open sea. Rising majestically out of the mist, he saw the arch of a giant bridge.

'See that,' he croaked, turning his head towards the man on his left. 'That's my brainchild.'

'What is?' asked the man, peering out over the water.

'The bridge.'

'What bridge, where?'

'Right there, in the mist. The one that joins what Hercules split asunder.'

'Ah, yes, I see it now,' said the man and smiled. 'Impressive!'

Sebastian smiled too, finding he was no longer interested in praise. The austerity of life below had detached him from the vagaries of the ego and made him humble. As long as Luna's Crossing was to link the continents as he'd intended, it didn't matter who basked in the glory of its conception. The author's name would fade and be forgotten with the passing millennia. It was enough to see this miracle and know that it was his own – that he was the creator.